RED SEASON RISING

D.M. MURRAY

D.M. MURRAY

THE RED SEASON

D.M. MURRAY

THE RED SEASON

For Polly

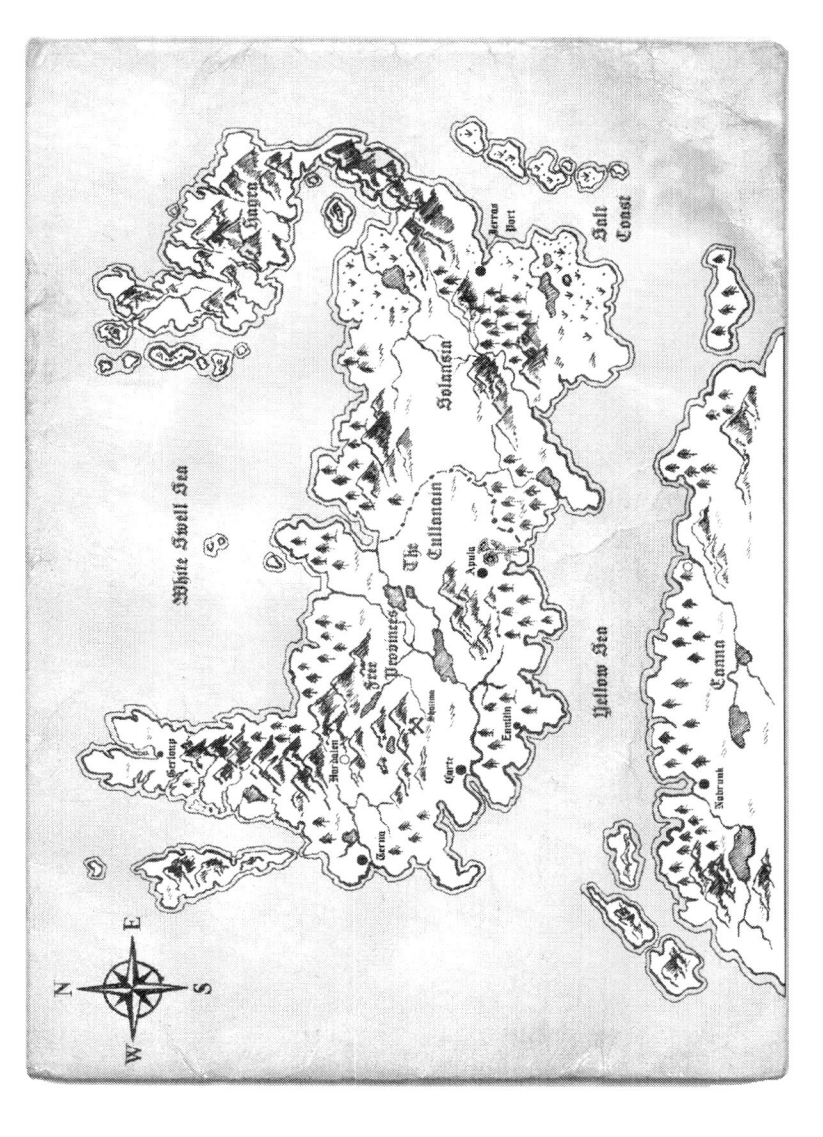

Chapter One

HE DREW a breath through his nostrils, and smelled the storm on the chill, earthy air. Kalfinar opened his eyes and peered beyond the torch-lit rampart of the battlements, and into the twilight-draped shadow of the woods.

"Think we're getting some wild weather tonight. What do you think, Captain?" a young soldier asked.

Kalfinar didn't need to look at the man to know he felt cold more keenly than those seasoned to the Hardalen peaks. "First of the North Storms will hit tonight. We'll miss it. Night Command will relieve us shortly." Kalfinar's gaze remained fixed at the dark fringe of the forest that slid down the side of the mountain towards the garrison. "Something watches from the tree line."

"Sir?"

"I can feel eyes on me." Kalfinar turned and looked at the soldier.

The man tried to hide the shiver that convulsed up his body, despite wearing a coat of oiled leather and fleece on top of his chainmail.

"Can't you feel it?" A humourless grin stretched crookedly between the stubble of Kalfinar's beard. He grunted and turned back to the woods. "Don't fret it, boy. You'll get the sense of it like the rest of us sorry old bastards."

Eighteen years and a day since I took my commission. Longer than this lad's been off the tit.

Kalfinar could smell the pungent oil from Sergeant Subath's chain-mail before he heard the veteran's footsteps. He turned to greet his former mentor and his platoon of Night Command troops as they began the nightly ritual of relieving the watch.

"Major Kalfinar, sir. In welcoming the moon, let me relieve you of your duty. Anything to report?"

"It's captain, Sergeant. Must we do this every night?"

"But, Major, these words have been our tradition for centuries."

"Not the words, Sergeant. My rank."

"Still a major to me, sir." Subath winked in distracting fashion. His battle-damaged eyelid twitched lazily.

"Thought I was still a cadet to you."

"Aye, you're still that, too. You can be both."

"I'm gratified, Sergeant." Kalfinar leaned in closer to Subath and lowered his voice. "But in front of the lads, let's just stick to captain. You know as well as anyone it was deserved."

"Perhaps so, sir."

Kalfinar sighed. "There is the correct order of things, Sergeant. Let's not corrupt the judgement of our young officers too much, too soon."

"As you say, Captain," said Subath, wearing an ill-suited mask of reverential innocence.

"Better." Kalfinar turned to face the woods as the first of the snowflakes began to float downwards. The small snowflakes sizzled as they drifted into the oil torches. "Quiet so far. Nothing to report. The first storm will hit tonight."

"Aye. Could feel that in my knees these last few days," Subath grumbled.

"One other thing. Probably nothing. I think there's something in the tree line. A wolf, perhaps. I could feel eyes on me."

"We'll keep a watch. If we see it, we'll drop it. The lads could do with some target practice."

"Good." Kalfinar fidgeted with the pommel of his sword.

"I've got it from here," Subath said in hushed tones. "Get back in there and get yourself some sleep. You look like shit."

Kalfinar smiled and clasped hands with Subath. "Thanks for your kind words. Good watch to you, Sergeant." He strode off along the battlement and towards the stairs that led to the courtyard. Kalfinar ignored the huddled troops. He knew they watched and whispered as he made his way across and the mud-clogged courtyard towards the large stone keep. He had learned to stop caring what words were issued in dark corners.

He made his way towards the accommodation wing and lit an oil lamp before he entered his chamber. He shivered as he entered.

Window's open again.

He strode to the window and shut it as best he could, in spite of the faulty latch. The room was the standard accommodation for officers. It comprised a square with unadorned stone walls, and a floor of age-smoothed wooden boards. A thin bed lined the wall nearest the door. Across from the bed were a writing desk and chair. Beside this stood a wardrobe and a large wooden chest, upon which sat a single worn book. He unbuckled his sword belt and hung it beside the bedside table. Kalfinar kicked off his boots and rubbed his hands to get the blood moving, not that it did any good. He walked the short distance across the room and hunkered down by the stone fireplace. He built a small pyre of birch bark and kindling, then picked up the alloy spark-rod and scraped his knife down its length. The shower of sparks caused a timid flame to grow upon the curling edges of bark. Kalfinar carefully placed a trio of logs atop the flame, and gradually brought the fire to life.

Bloody winter again, and so soon.

He heaved a sigh and removed his belt and chainmail shirt. He hung the mail and the rust-splotched under-jacket over the back of the chair, and pulled on a simple shirt. Kalfinar walked to the chest and picked up the book. His nightly ritual.

"The word of Dajda," he read aloud from the cover, and then opened to where a page had been earmarked.

The printed ink had been stained and distorted by liquid at some point in the past, but that didn't matter. Kalfinar knew every word within. He smiled bitterly at the marks of his tears. "For Dajda will welcome her children to her bosom, when their souls do rejoin. Rejoice, and let thy sorrow fly, for all are reborn in the mighty hall of Dajda." Kalfinar hawked phlegm and spat into the tear-streaked text. "Fucking shit on you. No more." He tossed the book into the fire.

The little girl running towards Kalfinar could not have been more than three years old. Her hair, curly and brown, was like her mother's, but her eyes were deep green like those of her father. Kalfinar knelt and embraced his small, smiling daughter. As he held her, she laughed, and what a rich little sound it was. It was so familiar to him, as though he had heard it a thousand times before. But he knew he had never heard his daughter's laugh, nor felt the warmth of her embrace. The image began to run and wash away like ink in the rain. She was gone again, as always.

Kalfinar woke slowly. The craving gnawed at him, as it always did when he awoke. He shivered and hot tears welled in his eyes. His hands fumbled as they searched the small bedside table for his jalsinum pipe, or anything that could relieve the hurt. There was nothing but the pommel of his sword. There hadn't been any relief for over two years now. He offered a curse to the night and pulled his wool blanket tight about him. It was hopeless. The blanket provided little comfort against the gale that howled through the tall trees outside, or the chill within. It was a cruel night, and the weak fire that smouldered in the small fireplace put up little fight. He rested his head once more upon his bed and closed his eyes.

When sleep came, it was fitful and nervous. It was the sleep of one afraid to dream.

But Kalfinar did dream.

An oily blackness welled around him. A pervasive sense of malice stalked him as though he were quarry. Out of the uneasy darkness burst flame, broken by guttural and alien whispers. As the flames grew more violent and hot, the dread in his mind swelled, and flooded with panic.

Wake up!

He opened his eyes and saw a figure in the corner of his room. A blacker form in the shadows. It moved quickly in the murky dark. The gusts outside rose to a scream and lightning crashed as the being shot towards him. Kalfinar lurched from his bed and grabbed his attacker's wrists. He held firm, struggling against his assailant's strength, before directing a short punch to its throat. The attacker gurgled, strength wavering for just an instant.

It was all the time Kalfinar needed.

He pushed out and sent a kick into the figure's midriff. It grunted and crumpled into the fireplace, raising a cloud of sparks and embers. Kalfinar turned and pulled his sword from its scabbard. As he spun back to face his risen foe, he brought the blade down with an overhead blow. With a wet thump, the sword cleaved into the body between neck and shoulder. Kalfinar tried to free his weapon, but it had become fixed in bone. From his assailant, there was no cry of pain. It took no notice of the wound, and slid the point of its knife into Kalfinar's body beneath the shoulder.

Unable to free his sword, Kalfinar cried out and released his grip. He pushed at the attacker with one hand and grabbed at the knife in his shoulder. The blade made a faint sucking noise as he pulled it free. He then thrust the knife into the black figure's chest. As Kalfinar released his grip, the would-be killer fell to the floor. Kalfinar's head swam.

He fell into darkness.

———

Broden burst into the room, a bloodstained knife in hand. He moved cautiously towards where Kalfinar lay motionless upon the bed. He knelt beside him. "Kal! Come on, wake up!" He turned towards the door and roared for the physician. "Olmat!"

"What's happening?" a young soldier asked upon entering the room. The young man brought a lantern with him, revealing the blood-shed within. "In Dajda's name! Is he alright?"

"Get me the physician!" Broden stayed focused on Kalfinar as he searched for further wounds.

"Who's that?" the young soldier nodded towards the lifeless form on the floor.

Broden turned and locked eyes with the young soldier. "Boy," he said, his voice low and steady, "get me the physician. And tell Sergeant Subath to alert the Night Command. We're under attack."

———

The sound of trees moaning stalked around the mountain garrison like a restless spirit, haunting the Night Command's every step as they searched halls and manned battlements. Broden knocked on the door and entered Commander Lucius's private study. The commander stood by his roaring log fire with his chest pushed out. He turned with a sneer.

"You sent for me, sir?" Broden asked.

"Captain, would you be so kind as to tell me why in Dajda's name my troops are manning the battlements and thundering around my garrison? I know I didn't issue any such orders."

"Sir, I beg your pardon but I felt there was no time to seek permission. I was only acting in the interests of the garrison's security." He gritted his teeth on his words. *Self-important prick.*

"Oh, you were only acting in the interests of my safety. I do beg your pardon. The next time you decide to leap to—"

"I had reason to believe we were under attack." He left just enough time to show his contempt before adding, "Sir."

"Under attack! What, here?" The commander's expression oozed disbelief. "Captain, have you lost your mind entirely? Need I remind you where we are? What are you suggesting? That we are being assaulted by a handful of hungry brigands and some bears? Please, spare me your fantasies."

Broden drew his knife from his belt and unwrapped the leather cloth from around the blade. He lifted it to the face of the commander, and revealed the sticky blood along its length. "I thought it would be easier to bring a bloodied blade than a bloodied corpse."

Lucius's expression loosened, the outrage being replaced with uncertainty.

"I killed a man in my chambers. An assassin, I'll wager. Kalfinar killed one too, though he's been hurt." His teeth again clenched, his thick red beard flexing as jaw muscles tightened.

"How badly?" Lucius looked away as he spoke, inspecting his fingernails. His lack of respect for Kalfinar was no secret.

When the strong fall, it's always the weak that maul them first and most viciously. Curse you, Lucius. "I don't know, sir. Your aide demanded I present myself here before I could find out." Broden felt his face begin to flush with anger. He took a slow and calming breath. "Sir, we've two dead assassins that we know of. The Night Command is manning the battlements and making ready our auxiliary archers."

"I can hear that, Captain," The commander snapped. "The whole bloody garrison can hear that! What did this assassin look like?"

"I couldn't tell. It was dark and he was masked. I was just about to check on Kal when the attacker slipped in my window. I pretended to be asleep until he was above me, and then I introduced him to my knife. I imagine he wasn't expecting that."

The commander cast an edgy glance towards the blade in Broden's heavy-knuckled fist, and moved to place his armchair between himself and the captain.

That's it, gulp down your fear, you little crow. "I went straight to Kalfinar's room afterwards. In the midst of the excitement, I heard him cry out. That's where I was when your man ordered me to present myself." He displayed little further outward emotion as he recounted the goings on.

"Very well, Captain, I've always preached readiness. You at least appear to have been listening." The commander's voice cracked as he spoke. "Let's go look at these corpses, and see if they can tell us anything." Commander Lucius slipped on his sword belt and pulled his light rapier from its scabbard, swinging it in a transparent act of bravado.

"Sir, with all due respect, there could be any number of assassins out there. We can't afford to have your life at risk. This is the safest part of the keep. You should wait until we've secured the entire garrison grounds. After all, a ship without a captain will only be dashed upon rocks." Broden feigned flattery and concern, his blue eyes acting out every persuasive emotion with aplomb. The less Lucius was around, the better, he thought.

"That much is true, Captain," the commander made a show of his thought on the matter. "In the interests of all of our wellbeing, I suppose it would indeed be best if I remained here." The commander relaxed and turned his back to Broden.

The big man's fists balled. *You're a fool. If it wasn't for your blue blood you'd be just another wretch on the streets, but with half their heart.* "A most wise decision, sir." He felt a surge of relief and loosened his primed fists. "Sir," Broden added, "perhaps it is best if you keep your door locked."

"I shall. You can take the key and lock it on your way out. I have a spare. You are dismissed, Captain." The commander settled into his leather armchair in front of his roaring fire. He called over his shoulder, "And, Captain, do inform me the instant this racket is over with."

As he left the commander's study, Broden rolled his eyes and, with feigned reverence, replied, "The very moment, Commander Lucius, sir." As he left the room, Broden withdrew the key and closed the large oak door behind him. He locked the door and turned to the two young soldiers on guard. "No one is to approach unless they present a direct order from me or Sergeant Subath. And men, make sure and swear oaths every now and then. Maybe run up and down the stairs a bit. If we make him think there's a bit of action, he'll stay cowered down in that wormhole of his."

Together, the two young soldiers grinned at their captain and agreed, "Yes, sir!"

"That's my boys." With that, Broden dashed down the stairs towards the physician's room.

Thaskil watched as Captain Broden rushed into the chambers of Olmat, the garrison's physician.

"Where in the outer hells is he?" Broden shouted in frustration as he entered the hallway. Seeing Thaskil, he called out, "You! Where's Captain Kalfinar and Olmat?" Broden's voice was thick with worry. "Does he live? Does my cousin live?" His eyes pleaded with the young man.

"Sir, as I know it, they're both still in the captain's chambers. The captain was too weak to move. I've not been back since you sent me to Sergeant Subath, sir." The young soldier felt his palms sweating, despite the chill in the hallway.

"Right, come with me." He turned and marched towards Kalfinar's room.

The young soldier walked behind the large captain, a man close to twice his mass and a head taller. Thaskil's mind then flashed back to what the captain had just said. "I wasn't aware you were kin, sir."

"He's my cousin." Broden's voice was quiet as they walked briskly along the stone hallway. "Spent much of our lives together, one way or another." They approached Kalfinar's room. "Boy, what's your name?"

"Officer Cadet Thaskil, sir."

"Well, Cadet Thaskil, don't just stand there. Open the door." Broden offered the lad a half-hearted smile and entered.

———————

Kalfinar watched groggily as Olmat tied off a sling and reviewed his handiwork. The old physician had stemmed the bleeding and stitched Kalfinar's wound. The arm was hung in a sling across his stomach and then bound mid-arm around his chest.

"You'll not have much use of that arm for some time yet, but you'll live," Olmat said. "Lucky that the blade cut through flesh alone, and there's no poison immediately obvious. Nevertheless, there could be a problem with the wound turning bad. We'll need to be careful with it."

"How do you feel, Captain?" asked Thaskil.

"Tremendous, lad," croaked Kalfinar. With a grimace, he spluttered and tried to raise himself onto his elbow. "I'll need something for this pain." Kalfinar noticed Olmat and Broden exchange a worried look. Nothing new in that regard. "Is the garrison secure?"

"The Night Command has been alerted. It doesn't appear this was an assault on the whole garrison. I'm awaiting Sergeant Subath's report," said Broden. "Good to see you!"

Kalfinar nodded and tried to sit up. His eyes screwed up in a tight wince and his teeth clenched as stabs of pain shot through him. "Got to get something for this pain."

"It's best you stay lying down for now," Olmat urged. "I can give you a tonic for the pain, if you wish it, though it will probably lay you out for most of the night and morning."

"Ah, thank you, but in that case I'll hold off for the meantime." *Tonic, what use is a damn tonic. That's not what I want, not what I need.* "I think we may have a lot to talk about tonight." *Give me some of my poison. Yes, my old smoke and blood, good old whores and mud.* He shook his head and looked at the grimly damaged body on the floor surrounded by the pool of dark, sticky blood.

"That we do, but wait one moment," said Broden. "Cadet Thaskil, it's time to put you to use again. Go into my chambers and bring in that mess on my floor."

"At once, Captain." The young soldier hurried out of the chamber.

"Helpful young man," Olmat said.

"That he is," Broden replied. "He's quite handy on the practice field, too. Maybe a good one there."

"Captain Broden, sir." Sergeant Subath, a bald and scarred veteran, walked into Kalfinar's chambers. The sergeant saluted crisply. "I've carried out your orders. We found nothing. No breach, no tracks. Not even as much as a mouse shit out of place." He glanced at Kalfinar as he lay on the bed. "Captain, glad to see you made it." His thatch of a grey beard split and revealed a wild smile. The loss of several teeth adding to the animal-like grin. "Another scar to add to your collection? If you're not careful, you'll end up as pretty as me."

"If the hells will it." Kalfinar rubbed the crescent-shaped scar that split his right brow and rounded his eye socket. It almost mirrored the scar on Subath's face, though the old sergeant's was received in battle. The origin of Kalfinar's was not quite as honourable, if he even remembered correctly, which itself was not entirely guaranteed. *Smoke and blood, whores and mud.* Kalfinar coughed out some humourless laughter. "Thanks, Sergeant. I think I'd endure a thousand of your sword drills rather than feel like this right now." His wound burned as it continued to swell.

"Well, my good captain, my drills made you the swordsman you are today." Subath glanced at the body on the floor and noticed the knife and sword embedded in the assassin. "Although, judging by the state of this." He reached over and stood on the chest of the corpse and, with great effort, freed the sword with a grunt. "You could be doing with a few hours of drill." The sergeant shook his head at the wounded captain. "Don't ever overcommit! I'm guessing that hole in you wouldn't be there if you'd listened to me."

Kalfinar rolled his eyes. He felt like he was a cadet again, learning from the old dog of war. "Anyway, moving on from my failings with the blade, you were saying there are no further signs o—"

As he spoke, Thaskil came huffing backwards into the chambers. He dragged behind him a masked body clothed from head to toe in black. He dropped the lifeless form next to its very dead comrade. He turned and stared at the floor, his face sheet white.

"Ah, make that two." Olmat looked at Broden and poked his heavy shoulder. "Any holes in you?"

"Of course not. You know I never overcommit." Broden grinned.

Kalfinar looked at the young soldier who remained staring at the floor, his pale gaze unflinching. "Thaskil, what's wrong?" The young soldier was distant. "What's the matter?"

"It's the body, sir. I wanted to take a look at his face so I lifted the mask and it grabbed my wrist. I manged to knife it a couple of times." At that moment, the young soldier raised his hand. It was slick with blood.

Kalfinar remembered the first time he had taken a life. "You did what you've been trained to do. I'm sorry to say it does get easier."

"It's not the killing, sir." The colour was returning to his face. "It's the face. It's not like yours or mine." The young man knelt and pulled off the mask that concealed one of the dead assassins.

The three seasoned warriors stared at the corpse before them. Olmat knelt and inspected the body. The skin of the assassin had a blue-grey, almost clay-like hue. The lifeless pupils were surrounded with irises of red and yellow flame. It appeared that the eyes blazed, even in death. Through the open mouth, Kalfinar could see a top row of triangular teeth, seemingly filed to savage points. Behind the creature's teeth lay the shrivelled remains of a tongue, its function long since burned out. Upon the head was plated white hair. Coarse and oiled, it appeared to grow from beyond the nape of the skull and down the back of the neck.

Looking around at his colleagues, Kalfinar muttered, "We may have a problem here." He coughed through his words, wincing with pain. "I think I'm going to need a tonic, but make sure it doesn't dull my wits. We're in for a long night."

Kalfinar swept away the strands of brown and grey-streaked hair stuck down the side of his face and tangled with his beard. He watched Olmat as the garrison's officers filed into the infirmary and passed the covered bodies of the assassins. The old man appeared troubled.

What are you thinking, old friend?

"Sergeant, as chief constable of the Night Command, you have the floor." Broden's voice tore Kalfinar from his thoughts, and he regarded the old warrior, Subath, as he stepped forward from the side of the room. Experience and knowledge like his was rare among many of the officers and, as such, his rather lowly rank was largely irrelevant. Kalfinar knew the rest of the officers would defer to the grizzled veteran, for he had beaten and moulded many of them as cadets. With history on his side, he commanded their respect, and, in this moment, their silence.

Broden took his seat around the examining table, and leaned in close to Kalfinar. "Kal, you look terrible."

"I'm fine." *I'm awful. I'm wretched.* "If I look terrible, it's because I have just had a hole ripped in me." *There's been a hole in me for so long now.* He glared at Broden. The moment was bitten off by the booming voice of the sergeant.

"Sirs, it appears we have a slight problem here. I've served in army of the Free Provinces since I left my old Mam's tit, but in all of my long days—"

Two of the younger officers laughed.

"I am not joking, sirs!" Subath roared, slamming his large fist into the table. The humour evaporated from the young officers and their faces flushed red at the rebuke. Subath continued. "In all of my long days, I have never seen anything like this." He pulled off the linen sheet covering the two bodies.

Thunder growled angrily in the night sky. Wind-driven rain lashed against the windows like the tapping of claws. The officers within the infirmary had been inspecting the corpses for several minutes. A look of shock and confusion remained upon many faces. Kalfinar watched as Subath tired of the murmuring. The crescent scar on the old sergeant's face, a legacy from one of his many past conflicts, caused his eyelid to twitch. The nerve had been damaged, and famously betrayed his irritation.

"Enough goggling!" Subath barked. "You'd bring a monk to murder!" His temper cracked, and he thumped his fist into the table. "You, sirs, are the commanding outfit of this garrison, and, as such, must act like it. As chief of the Night Command, and with the blessed moon still in the sky, I have jurisdiction here. So stop saying nothing, and start acting like officers. I want to know what in the sweet, suffering hells we're supposed to do about these things." Eyelid flickering, the old warrior puffed his cheeks and heaved out his breath as he finished his rebuke.

The slightest of grins crept onto Kalfinar's face. *You would have been general by now, old Subath. If you hadn't been so damned stubborn.*

He was pulled from his thoughts as Broden leaned in and whispered, "Think he gets more frightening with age. Did you see his eye?"

"Aye. He's no book of secrets, that's for sure," Kalfinar sighed. "Well, I suppose I'd better back him up." Kalfinar shakily raised himself to stand by the table. Looking his colleagues in the eyes, he spoke, his voice strong despite his body's weakness, "Thank you, Sergeant. I couldn't have put that better myself. Brothers, we have before us two corpses. They appear somewhat fearsome to us, and of their nature, we do not truly know. But their features are of no moment. It is their presence and motive that offers concern. They came here to kill, of that there is no doubt. With two alone, and the Night Command's reports of nothing further, should we rule out an attack on the garrison as a whole? Could this be a scouting party or is this, perhaps, simply what it appears to be: an assassination attempt on Captain Broden and myself?" He looked questioningly at his fellow officers, prompting them to rise above their silence. He sat down and waited for the hush to break.

It was one of the laughing officers who spoke first, "This garrison has not seen bloodshed for over two hundred years. We lie at the heart of the Free Provinces. We offer virtually nothing in terms of strategic value here. Why would we be the target of an attack?"

Broden stood, and as he did so his massive frame blocked the oil lamps and cast a large shadow over the bodies on the examining table. "Brothers, see this for what it is. There appear only to have been two. With that number surely this does not constitute an attack on the garrison. We appear to have been targeted by no more than assassins. It is clear that these two things were sent here for one purpose, to kill Kalfinar and myself."

The officers paused and discussed amongst themselves before finally voicing their agreement with the big man's summary. Broden eased his large frame into his seat as Captain Merkham rose to address those gathered.

Kalfinar regarded Merkham for a moment as the thin officer waited for silence. Merkham was a studious officer, better suited for the libraries and classrooms than the blood and shit of war. However, he was patient and well respected.

"The question now remaining, brothers, is twofold. What are these beings, and why have they tried to kill our own?" Merkham paused a moment, his slender fingers woven together on his stomach. "Olmat, you have examined them. Few would profess to know more of the people and creatures of our world than you do. What do you say of this?"

The old physician's face appeared lost in deep thought. His bushy white brows hung over his brooding, somewhat rheumy blue eyes.

Kalfinar reached out and rested his hand on the old man's shoulder. "Olmat." He inclined his head towards the thin figure of Captain Merkham as he stood awaiting an answer.

Broken from thought, the old physician acknowledged the question. "My friends, I believe these assassins to be men. Although certainly not men we have seen before. I fear not an attack on our garrison here, but I suggest we keep our wits keen. I'm sorry I cannot give you an answer as to what we have here in any greater detail, but I do believe they are men." He remained seated as he spoke. It was obvious to Kalfinar that the passing night was tiring him.

Discussions carried on for a short while longer. It was agreed that the garrison would remain on alert and that a dispatch party would be sent to the Noehmian capital, Terna, before travelling onwards to the Ilsinian capital Carte to inform the High Command. Reluctantly, the officers also agreed that it might be about time to inform the imperious commander of the night's developments.

Kalfinar sat in Olmat's chambers as the old physician cleaned his wound and replaced his dressing. The sun would have been on the rise, though the depth of the early winter storm would not permit its light to shine. The wind passed through the smallest of gaps between the stonework of the building. The fire in the chambers was weak, and so the wind chilled him to his core.

"The tonic is working." He looked up at Olmat as he busied himself with the wound. "How's it looking?" He shivered and goose bumps prickled over him. *Damn it's cold.*

"You heal quickly, Kal. You always have done."

Some wounds never heal, do they, old friend?

Olmat touched Kalfinar's nose. Once straight, it was now slightly crooked after having met with a Solansian buckler. "This took just days to heal." The old man turned Kalfinar's chin into the light, inspecting another scar. This time it was a ragged mark from the side of his chin to the dimple. Partially obscured by his grey-shot beard, partially peeking out, bald and pink. It was all that remained of where a deflected arrow had caught him, breaking his jaw. "That was a lucky one. An inch lower and you'd have been beyond my skill to heal."

Kalfinar grunted, "Fortunate, indeed."

Olmat shook away the comment. "You're not going to die from this wound. I don't think so anyway." Kalfinar glanced up as the old man and forced a troubled grin. "But it would be best for you to head to Terna. You can receive some more advanced treatment there. I'm afraid my supplies are limited."

He tensed and frowned. "You've tended my ills all my life. You brought me into this world, and you've kept me in it more than once. I trust you, old friend, but you know I've no wish to return." He gripped the old man's arm.

"I understand you have fears, lad." Olmat's voice sounded weary. "But you must seek treatment in Terna. Trust me now. Go with the dispatches, and onwards to Carte. It may be that it is time for you to return home."

Kalfinar knew Olmat was looking at him, but he avoided the old physician's gaze and focused his on the stone wall. *Carte. I can't. There's nothing there but memories for me. Memories and pain.* "You know I can't go back. My home is in these mountains now." *All there is in Carte is pain and the cold fog of a life I used to know. And shame, so much shame. And smoke.* Kalfinar's tone was low, his voice heavy with burden. Although it had been over two years since he had lost his wife and daughter, Kalfinar had found a kind of peace, if he could even call it that, high within the mountains and their damp, earthy woods.

"You must go. Please heed me this morning, you must." Olmat released Kalfinar's grip from his arm, old hands trembling. Olmat looked at him with wet eyes. "Someone came here to kill you. And your wound needs aid that I cannot give you here. Heed me. You must go."

Kalfinar looked into his old friend's eyes, and knew he was right. *Maybe it would be best for all if the monster had finished me, or even if I had died back in Carte. Should've finished myself. Didn't have the stones.* "Aye." He sighed under his decision. His mouth was dry and his heart thundered. "I'll go. Someone has to make sure the message gets back to the High Command. I suppose it may as well be me." *Back into the fires for me, into the smoke and back to my own empty nightmare. Smoke and blood, whores and mud.* Kalfinar stood, and with the help of Olmat, pulled on his shirts and fastened his leather vest. He began to leave the chambers.

"Kalfinar, come and see me before you leave. I'll need to give you some correspondences."

"Of course." He shivered as the cold touched him yet again.

The old man sat himself at his desk and removed his parchment and quill. "And do take Broden with you. He'd be lost on his own, and he'd just get under my feet." He smiled at the injured captain as he left his chambers.

When the latch fell upon the door the old physician's smile evaporated and his head fell into his hands. "And so it finds us at last," he mumbled through dry lips. "Now comes our sorrow." Tears crept between his fingers, and fell heavy upon his desk.

Chapter Two

THE STORM CLOUDS had not lifted by midmorning, and the garrison remained in darkness still. Although the violent wind had eased, a thick and chilling mist took its place. The torches lining the battlements appeared as glowing nimbuses, and offered scant light. The soldiers of the Night Command peered at shadows amidst the fog and muttered curses under their breath.

Kalfinar and Broden hurried across the central courtyard towards the quartermaster's store. As they strode through the muddied court, Commander Lucius's aide scurried towards them. His long black robe was smeared along the bottom with mud.

"This'll be trouble," Broden muttered under his breath as they approached the man. The two captains continued their steady pace and bypassed the clerk. Broden smiled to himself and glanced to Kalfinar, but his face showed no such pleasure.

The aide cleared his throat and spluttered from behind them, "Ah, excuse me, Captains. Commander Lucius has ordered you both present yourselves in his study at once, sirs." His hands were clutched together nervously below his chin.

Turning around at the same time, they looked the clerk in the eyes. Kalfinar's glare was even less friendly than his companion's. Closing the distance, they stopped before the aide. Broden rested a hand on the aide's shoulder, drawing a wince.

"Would you suggest we comply with the commander's wishes?" Kalfinar's words were barely more than a whisper as he stepped in close. The breath of his words in the chill air wrapped around the man's neck like a pair of spectral hands.

The aide turned, and emitting a whimper like a kicked hound, went speeding back in the direction he came from.

Broden threw back his head, and laughed. "You, Kal, are a very bad man."

Kalfinar's stern look cracked under a slight smile. "I suppose we'd better pay the commander a visit before that poor man gets a beating into the bargain."

Broden followed behind, chuckling to himself. "A very bad man indeed."

———

Olmat knelt on the floor surrounded by dozens of scrolls and loose leafs of papers. He was alone in his chambers, save for the two corpses lying on his examining table. He glanced over his shoulder.

Dead or no, can't say I like having you two back there. He chased away his unease and turned back to the large chest. His hands searched busily. He opened one scroll, then another. More and more bindings were undone and still he could not find the one he sought.

"Curse this memory of mine." He snapped off his words with frustration and slammed the chest closed. He groaned as he stood. It had been the best part of an hour and his knees had stiffened from the cold and fixed position. *Too old for kneeling on cold stone floors. Should've known better, silly fool.*

Too complacent, too damn complacent. Where in Dajda's name could I have put it? His eyes surveyed his chambers. After coming to Hardalen with Kalfinar and Broden over two years previously, his room had gradually grown more cluttered. Disorder reigned around him. The shelves that lined almost every wall sagged under the weight of books and journals, elements and chems. There were assorted herbs and dry mosses in pots, and an array of brightly coloured powders leapt from the dull greys of the walls.

A prayer ran through his head. He had to find those documents before Kalfinar left. His heart hammered in his chest as the words of the prayer fell silently from his lips. The prayer stopped. His eyes flashed open and he shuffled through the chambers. His old knees and hips popped and creaked as he moved. He entered his bedroom and dropped to his knees, regretting his rashness as the stone floor met his joints painfully. Spurred on by memory, he opened the chest by his bed with a ragged groan. He dug between the scrolls and jars, feeling for the bottom. He stopped and glanced over his shoulder once more at the bodies, heart still pounding with fear.

Don't be foolish.

He pulled up the false bottom and permitted himself a small smile. "There you are." He lifted up a small tube bound in blood-red leather, cracked and peeling with age. He forced himself to his feet and sat on his bed. The cord binding the roll proved difficult to undo. With ageing fingers, he struggled to loosen the knot. "Curse it!"

Growing more frustrated by his efforts, he lost his patience and held the cord above the candle by his bed. The roll snapped open as the cord burned through, sending a small plume of dust into his face. He coughed and wiped his nose, then sneezed. He held the candle to the scroll. The parchment was stained with time, but Olmat's rheumy eyes were able to infer the meaning within. "An eight-pointed star, wreathed in fire."

He let the parchment fall from his hands and then walked through to his examining room. Olmat approached the two bodies on his table, stopping by the side of the nearest. He turned it onto its front with some effort. His hands trembled as he cautiously reached to the back of the body's head. He pulled aside the oiled and plaited white hair on the back of its neck and searched, his eyes squinting to focus. He moved the candle closer to the neck, and there it was.

The grey skin was tattooed, the flesh marked with an eight-pointed star, wreathed in fire. Olmat moved to his desk, and began scratching text onto parchment. He finished and sealed it with wax, then placed it into an oiled leather tube. Olmat offered a prayer before placing the tube into a drawer in his desk. The old physician opened another drawer and looked inside. Reaching within, he looked at the two bodies and drew out a knife.

"You can't be serious?" Kalfinar seethed. "We're to carry these dispatches to Terna and Carte on our own? Without even a platoon?"

Lucius had returned just over an hour before, after having seen the dead assassins. The gaunt commander's face appeared drained of all courage by what he had seen stretched out wretched and cold on the examining table. Kalfinar stared past the man, his anger quivering under his skin. *Coward, I should rip your fucking throat out here where you stand.*

"Captains," the commander's voice shook. He did not look the two men in the eyes. "I believe the safety of this garrison is crucial to the continued well-being of the Free Provinces. We house a full battalion of Pathfinders, and one twelfth of our officer cadets. What's more, in Hardalen, we control an area of critical strategic importance. As such, this garrison cannot fall to our enemies, whoever they may be. We must remain fully equipped and manned, so as to protect the mountain passes."

Kalfinar felt his scorn simmering. *Strategic importance. We are in the least strategically valued garrison in the whole of the Free Provinces. Your fear fills the air with a stench.*

Lucius glanced up at the two captains and briefly held their gaze. "Anyway, you'll move quicker without a body of men. Officers of your experience ought to know that already."

"Kalfinar has only the use of one arm, Commander. He'll struggle to ride at any decent pace," Broden snapped. "Even if he had the use of both arms, we'd still have to move cautiously. The storm is upon the passes."

"I've made my decision, Captain. I am the commander of this garrison, and, as such, it is my duty, and mine alone, to ensure the continued wellbeing of both this garrison and its men."

Kalfinar's lip twitched. *Watching your own arse, Commander. You'd better get used to it, because I'm about to shove your head up it.*

Lucius continued, voice quivering. "I believe men of your reputation," he paused long enough to smirk at Kalfinar, "are more than capable of completing this mission unscathed. Captain Kalfinar will have to overcome and adapt, like the good soldier he is. Or at least the good soldier he was."

Prick. What would you prefer, Lucius, my fist in your nose, or my knee in your stones?

"Here, take these." The commander handed Broden two scrolls bound in leather envelopes. "Make sure these are delivered directly to the chief marshals. They're not for any other eyes. I'm sure you'll understand." The commander was trying hard to appear calm, but his hands trembled as he handed the scrolls across.

Broden tried again to reason with the commander. "Sir, I must insist that you give us some men. It would be folly to send us out there alone."

"You insist?" Lucius's eyes bulged as he hid his fear behind rage. He stood toe-to-toe with Broden and stared red-faced up at the bigger man. His fear finding voice in fury as he screamed in Broden's face, "You insist upon me? Who do you think you are? You forget your station, Captain. Dare not question my judgement again. I'll make you walk to Terna in your bare feet, if it pleases me. Or if you prefer, I could throw you in the fucking brig for insubordination and let your pipe-smoking husk of a cousin walk to Terna on his own!"

Kalfinar stared at the commander, and felt his anger grow cold within him. *Someday your antics will see your precious little throat slit. Perhaps that's too good. Maybe a bag and then the harbour would be better. I could toss you in the waters down by the dock and then go fill my lungs with the pipe after the bubbles stop. Smoke and blood, whores and mud.*

The commander had ceased huffing and the colour had drained away from his face. He fussed with the collar of his jacket and moved back behind his desk. "Captain, I will not put this garrison at risk. You are up to the task, so I suggest you get on with it. You are dismissed." With that, he raised his hand and shooed them off as though they were bothersome flies. They saluted and turned to leave the study when Lucius called out, "Captain Broden, when you get to Carte, please do ensure you keep Captain Kalfinar on a short leash. We wouldn't want him visiting those whore houses and the jalsinum warrens down by the docks again, would we? They say once a man takes a taste for the smoke he never stops craving it." Lucius looked across to Kalfinar. "Tell me, Captain, do you still hunger after it?"

Every day, and every night. And every moment between the seconds within each.

The commander sniggered as he sank into his tall-backed leather chair.

Broden bundled Kalfinar out of the room and closed the door. "Don't let the shit get to you, Kal." As they walked away from the commander's study Broden scratched at his beard and asked, "So what are we going to do about this?"

Kalfinar's voice was quiet and steady, his throat thickened with anger. "I intend to do the same thing I always do when it comes to Lucius. I'm going to ignore him." *Or kill him, slowly, methodically.*

———

"We need some good men, Subath." Kalfinar had gone straight to the veteran sergeant after leaving the commander's study. He had dispatched Broden to the quartermaster to fetch supplies for their journey.

"Major, you look a bit better now. You don't look so much like a corpse."

"It's Capt—" Kalfinar shook his head in exasperation. "Never mind. Good men. They'll have to be ready for hardship, Subath."

"I'm guessing our beloved commander has issued you an order contrary to your request."

Kalfinar said nothing, and held Subath's eyes.

"I'm also guessing you're disregarding this order, correct?" Subath asked. A thin smirk crept on his face.

"You're a shrewd man, Sergeant. Perhaps too shrewd." Kalfinar returned the slightest of grins.

"Ach, come on, lad. I may have a face like an arsehole, but my head isn't full of shit. Anyway, whilst I would doubtless agree with your razor-sharp assessment of Lucius' character, he appears to have been goading you. He's issued me an order to provide you with four troops."

"That fucking prick. I should go up to that tower of his and beat him around the head until he goes limp," Kalfinar seethed.

"Can't say I haven't had half a hard'un thinking of that myself in the past." Subath grinned and rubbed a calloused hand over his scarred head. "Now, as I don't want you getting all overwhelmed by his generosity, I should tell you he personally selected two of the less effective officer cadets for the trip. Clearing out some dead-wood. As for the other two, he left it at my discretion. Anyone in mind?"

"There is one I can think of. That boy, Thaskil. The one that finished off the assassin in Broden's room. He shows promise. You think he's been toughened up enough for this kind of journey?"

Subath's face adopted a proud look. "Captain, that boy is one of the brightest and best young soldiers I've trained in near twenty years. Since you and Broden, as it happens."

"Good. Let's go fetch them. We don't have much time."

Kalfinar observed the four troops as they readied their horses for the expedition. All of the soldiers selected had recently completed their training, although they had each yet to see their nineteenth year.

Subath stood in front of the four young soldiers and barked commands, "Make sure that coat is on tight. A cold horse is a dead horse, and a dead horse means you're dead. Tie them tight, men, or by Dajda I'll tie you tight around the neck." The winters in the Hardalen Mountains were so extreme that both men and horses were provided with oiled buck leather lined thickly with rich fleece, stained a dark green, in keeping with the rest of the military garb. "These coats will save your lives, men, and those of your beasts. Don't forget it."

Kalfinar strode up and stood beside Subath. He inclined his head towards the sergeant and whispered, "The two selected by Lucius?"

"The big one with the even bigger ears? He's Rallik. The one with the blonde hair, who has his boots on the wrong feet, is Petran."

"Surely not?" Kalfinar squinted towards the cadet.

"No, they're on the right feet," Subath exhaled and shook his head. "But I do wonder sometimes."

"Purchased his place in the academy?" Kalfinar asked.

"Aye, likely. Need to put an end to that."

"I'm sure you would have done by now, if you'd accepted the governor's commission one of those times."

"Piss on it. Who'd tell all you tit-hungry officers what to do then?"

Kalfinar afforded himself a slight smile and then patted Subath's shoulder. "I'll leave you to it. I'm off to see Olmat. One hour, Subath. Have them ready."

"Olmat, are you there?" Kalfinar asked as he and Broden entered the examining room. There was no answer. He called again, "Olmat!"

No response.

They walked towards the bedchamber, passing the covered bodies on the table. As they turned the corner into the darkened chamber, the light from the lone candle touched enough of the small room for them to see him. Olmat sat cross-legged on the floor, his face buried in the palms of his hands. He appeared to be in a trance-like state.

Approaching, Kalfinar reached out and touched his shoulder. "Olmat."

The physician broke from his concentration with a jolt. "Kalfinar! By Dajda, you scared me."

"I'm sorry. You didn't answer." Kalfinar noted the mess surrounding his friend. Scrolls and jars, papers and bags were scattered everywhere. *What've you been looking for?*

"Help a decrepit old soul to his feet now." He raised his arms to the captains like an infant. Grabbing his wrists, Broden pulled him to his feet as though he were of no weight at all.

"What were you doing?" Kalfinar asked him as he stood before him.

"I was praying. Something you would benefit from doing once in a while. When did you last speak to Dajda?" The old physician's tone was irritable and he shuffled to the examining room.

Kalfinar had seen Olmat at prayer countless times as the physician watched over him in the first days in the Hardalen Mountains. Though Kalfinar's memory of the time was hazy, and perhaps mixed reality with fantasy, he did not recall seeing Olmat ever praying in such a manner. They followed his shuffling form into his examining room. Olmat busied himself placing rolled-leather envelopes into an oilcloth bag.

Broden nudged Kalfinar with his elbow and indicated to the examining table beside them. As he glanced across, Kalfinar noticed a fresh bloodstain on the linen at the head of the table and a small, bloodied knife. Beside it sat a small jar, the contents of which he strained to see. He drew his attention off the table and turned towards Olmat. The physician was staring at him flatly.

"I'll get to that in a moment," Olmat said, nodding at the table. "Kalfinar, take this." He handed him a velvet medicine pouch. "It's called falidweed. Take it every morning. Boil it in water, then drink. It will relieve the hurt and keep the black-flesh away. You should have enough for a week, at least, providing you go easy on it."

Kalfinar looked inside the pouch. It was full with what looked like dried red seaweed. Olmat grabbed Kalfinar's good shoulder.

"Listen to me. Make sure you take it every day. No exceptions, no excuses." He looked across at Broden, who was staring at the examining table again. "Broden, pay attention, you lump. He must boil a handful in water and drink it." Olmat took the pouch off Kalfinar and waggled it before Broden. "Here, this stuff, once a day. Understand?"

"I'll keep him right, Olmat." Broden winked at his cousin.

"I can look after myself."

"Yes, I'm sure you can, but a little help from those who care cannot hurt."

"I'm sorry." Kalfinar knew he owed them both so much. Although, some days he wished they had let him go. Let him carry on down that path. "I am blinded by pride." He grinned to the old man. "Any other instructions for us?" Kalfinar was eager to hear Olmat's plans. He inclined his head towards the strange bodies on the table.

"I was getting to that," Olmat said. He looked at them seriously. "When you get to Terna, you must see a physician by the name of Capriath. He has an office in the medical department of the University in Terna. Go to him and take with you this letter." He handed Kalfinar a green leather envelope, rolled and bound by a wax seal. "Give him this. My notes on your wound. He will give you some medicine which I cannot. Without it, you may lose the use of your arm."

"I may lose the use of my arm," Kalfinar repeated, taken aback. "You never mentioned that before."

"Lad, I said you may lose the use of your arm, not you will lose the use of it. If you keep taking the falidweed as I've instructed, you will be fine. Capriath is an excellent physician. I've known him a very long time. I can assure you he will help greatly. He will give you the name of another good man to see in Carte. I must stress that you visit him, also." Olmat's face was serious. "Do you have dispatches for the High Command in Terna and Carte?"

Broden answered, "Yes, Lucius was able enough to give us dispatches. Though I'm guessing they are more a plea for the whole military High Command to come and save him."

"Well, take these also. They are my medical assessments of the bodies. Make sure these are passed to the chief marshals and governors in Terna and Carte. They will surely know what to do next." Olmat's face was grave as he handed across a black leather envelope. Again, it was rolled and bound with wax.

"The governor will not see me," Kalfinar said. "I assaulted the man in public!" *And so viciously, from what the whispers say. I'll be lucky if he doesn't throw me in the cells for showing my face.*

It was this offence that saw Kalfinar being demoted and sent to the garrison at Hardalen. Many within the High Command publicly voiced their concern that it was only Kalfinar's name that spared him the choke of the hangman's noose.

Olmat rested a thin hand on Kalfinar's forearm. "Harruld is a good man, and a forgiving one at that. I've told you time and again that you need not worry on that account." A sympathetic look dawned on Olmat's face, though it did not linger. "Now listen to me. Once you have given the dispatches to the chief marshal and governor in Carte, you must visit the physician that Capriath directs you to. I don't know who he is, but you must see him. When you do see him, give him this." He handed them the small jar. A marked chunk of skin could be seen amidst the pink liquid.

"What is it?" Kalfinar asked, looking at the flesh.

"It's a marking. The mark is significant, as is your ignorance. For now, it keeps you, and others, safe. Give this to the second physician you see, the one in Carte. Keep it from sight until then."

Kalfinar's stomach started to churn with unease as Olmat handed over one last rolled envelope. It was red leather, bound in wax and tied with several knots.

"This is also for the physician in Carte. Make sure it is passed on."

Kalfinar placed the jar into his shoulder pack, and they clasped the old man's hand warmly before making for the stables. From there, it would be into the mountain passes, and into the heart of the storm.

Chapter Three

"PUSH ON, MEN. KEEP MOVING!" Kalfinar roared through the howling wind. The punishing early winter storm they had been travelling through showed no sign of relenting. For two days, the winds had battered them head on. The snow and hail stung with every touch.

"Kal, we must take shelter! We can't carry on. This is hopeless!" Broden shouted, barely audible.

Kalfinar turned to the group and called out through the thick cloth that wrapped around his mouth and nose, "Thaskil, Petran, come alongside." The young soldiers nudged their horses' flanks and made their way towards him. "You two scout ahead for a few miles. Try and find one of the old route caves, if you can. Be back within the hour."

They nudged their horses' flanks once more and rode ahead. It was not long past midday, though the world around was a swirling grey maelstrom. It had been two days since they had seen the sun. Night and day became one endless dark endurance. They trudged on through the bleak weather, with their horses struggling all the way.

They travelled along the natural path of a mountain river that had been carved by a glacier in a time long since passed. Alongside this path, the forces of the Free Provinces had constructed a rough route through the mountains and forests, placing the garrison deep within the Hardalen Mountains. As journeys during winter were treacherous, the Free Provinces command had taken advantage of several natural caves along the route and prepared them as emergency shelters for small parties. Kalfinar hoped that one such cave could provide them with the shelter they so urgently required.

———

"That's been an hour since Thaskil and Petran left," Broden shouted through the worsening weather.

"They'll come. Don't worry," Kalfinar replied without conviction. He looked around, but was barely able to see more than a horse-length in front. "They'll need to be quick. This wind's getting colder and the snow's growing deeper by the minute." Windswept swirls of snow obscured the path ahead.

"There's something coming, Kal! Stay back for now." Broden moved his own mount ahead and drew his sword from its scabbard.

Kalfinar winced as he switched the reins to his left hand, freeing his sword arm. *I'm about as much use as a swinging bag of meat on a hook.*

"Name yourself!" Broden was already lost from sight. His voice trailed out of range in the midst of the storm.

Kalfinar motioned for Arrlun and Rallik to come alongside. Each freed their weapons. Ahead of Kalfinar, a large shape coalesced amidst the swirling blur of the blizzard.

"Found them," Broden's familiar voice issued from the dark shape.

The fleece-lined leather coats of the three mounted men exaggerated their forms, and they appeared as one dark being.

"We've found a cave, Captain. It's about a mile ahead," Thaskil shouted through chattering teeth.

"Let's get out of this hellstorm!" Kalfinar roared. "Thaskil, lead on."

———

Their progress to the cave was slow and steady, but still, they almost passed by the entrance. Thaskil pointed towards a barely visible gash in the side of the mountain.

Kalfinar assessed the scene. There was a long snow-covered ramp leading to the entrance. *The horses should be able to make that.* He dreaded losing a horse, and knew all too well that it could mean death in these conditions. "Well then, let's get in about it." He dismounted gingerly. Holding lightly onto his mount's reins, he edged up the roughhewn ramp. "Take it easy on the approach, it's—"

The intermingled cry of man and horse broke Kalfinar off. Swiftly, he turned to see Petran and his mount twisting and turning as they tumbled down the snow-covered scree. Limbs and hooves flailed wildly before coming to rest in a heap on the drift-obscured mountain track.

"In the name of Dajda," Broden shouted. "You alright, lad?"

The horse had already righted itself, whinnying and snorting as it flicked wetness off its coat in a brief mist. Petran, looking sheepish, regained his feet, and waved up to his companions.

"Fool of a boy," Broden muttered. "Get that horse back up here, and be more damn careful next time! You lose your horse here, you may as well lose yourself. Remember that."

The young man nodded, eyes set downward at his rebuke.

Kalfinar stepped in close to Broden and spoke in hushed tones. "We'll need to check that horse. Can't have any injuries."

"Aye."

Kalfinar moved to within a few horse-lengths of the cave entrance. He flexed his fingers around the grip of his sword. "Best get inside."

"Kal," Broden whispered from beside the cave mouth. "Let me get ahead of you. Just in case."

Kalfinar stepped aside and took hold of his cousin's reins. He watched as Broden pulled his short sword free and approached the cave entrance with well-practised stealth. His deep-green coat broke up his form in the darkness as he moved further, disappearing into the cave and out of sight.

A moment later, he reappeared, sword at his side. "All ours."

"Let's get in and get a fire started." Kalfinar handed back the reins and moved towards the cave. His horse whinnied and recoiled as he entered, the darkness inside unsettling the tired animal. "Come girl. We're better off inside," Kalfinar whispered in the ear of his horse. Looking into the cave, he felt a shudder pass down his spine. The deep pitch-black ahead reminded him of the darkness within his dreams.

A few moments later, the whole troop was inside and moving slowly to avoid any invisible hazards.

"Careful where you step, lads," Kalfinar spoke to the soldiers, his voice echoing off the surrounding cave. "Fetch torches. Broden's afraid of the dark." If the young soldiers laughed, he didn't hear them.

"I can't find my flint, Captain," Arrlun called as he sifted blindly through his pack.

In an instant, orange light flooded the cave, revealing Broden smiling as he held his flaming torch. As each new torch was lit, they saw further into the cave. Although formed naturally, it had been altered and carved many years before. It curved around from the entrance and opened into a large rounded area. It was equipped with a central pit for a fire, filled with dry wood and a narrow chimney pipe cored from the cave roof to the surface, allowing smoke to escape.

Kalfinar craned his neck and eyed the cored chimney. "Hmm," he mumbled to no one in particular, "one of you lads give that a good poking with a spear. We need it clear of any debris."

Several sleeping pallets surrounded the wall, with one side being equipped with grain and bedding for horses.

Kalfinar tied his horse to the beam running along the side of the cave and moved wearily over to his pallet. He said, "Let's get that fire burning. Thaskil, Arrlun, check those drums over by the spare firewood. There should be a cache of preserved food somewhere in here. Let's avoid eating our rations if we can." The troops leapt to their tasks.

His shoulder throbbed. *Shit! Forgot to take the bloody weed of Olmat's this morning.* They had been forced to make camp the previous night. The best shelter they could find had been a thin stand of scrubby pinewoods. Their waxed canvas tents provided only slight shelter from the constant advances of the wind and snow.

"There's salted mutton, sir," Thaskil called out. Kalfinar was pleased to have the young man along, for he appeared well equipped for such an arduous task. He had not appeared downcast or weary, and he seemed to be a hardy soldier. "There's ale too," Thaskil laughed as he called out.

The sight of a cask brought a smile to their faces, Broden's the widest. "That'll do for me. You boys aren't yet officers, so it would be against protocol to allow you to partake alongside me. I tell you what, you can make some pine-needle tea instead," Broden chuckled as Arrlun looked to him in dismay, his eyes wide with injury.

"Captain Broden, sir, you wouldn't deprive us of a little ale. Would you?" Arrlun frowned.

The big captain winked at him and laughed. "Of course I wouldn't—"

"No ale," Kalfinar snapped from by his pallet. "No one drinks tonight."

Kalfinar did not look up as Broden leaned towards him. "Kal, you wouldn't deprive the lads a little—"

"No!" he barked. "No ale. Not tonight."

"It doesn't matter, Captains," Thaskil called out. "It's frozen solid."

Broden frowned. "You all right?" he whispered to Kalfinar.

"The shoulder," Kalfinar said as he looked up. "Now that I'm warming up, it's starting to hurt. I forgot to take my medicine this morning. Reckon I'm paying for it now." Kalfinar felt sweat clinging to the whiskers around his lips and jaw.

"I'll get some water on the boil. We can get some of Olmat's seaweed into you."

"Thanks." Kalfinar handed the pouch of falidweed to his cousin and sat on the pallet on the floor. He sighed with relief as he sank into the thin blankets. Within seconds, he was asleep.

The kind of sleep where dreams reside.

Kalfinar's mind raced as he slept. Images of Carte flashed in his dreams, places he had no memory of visiting, people whose faces he had no recollection of. He saw himself being thrown from darkened doorways into the filth-soaked streets, and waking beside strange faces of women whose name or nature he could not recall. Some faces were more bruised than others. His memories of his last few months in Carte were muddled and confused, like watching players through stained glass, there, but obscured. His many patchy recollections had pieced together an unhappy scene. It seemed a fine tragedy for the stage. From the scenes of Carte, the dream shifted, jolting away from his home city. Once more, there was the creeping blackness and feeling of dread. Hushed words of an unknown language issued from the oily darkness. A sense of frustration and malice accompanied the speech as it grew louder, and closer. The speech changed to hideous screams and the dark erupted into bright, hot flame. Kalfinar tried to wake, but he was trapped within. The flames licked hungrily at his skin like tongues of pain lashing and creeping upwards. The flames died away as quickly as they appeared, and left Kalfinar in the midst of a thick and swirling grey fog. He could see something amidst the murkiness. In the shadowy tones before him were two figures. The miasma around him eased, and then cleared like harbour mist. A hot coil of panic tightened his throat. He was exposed.

Must run. Must hide.

Fear made his skin prickle and his breath came in quick, shallow draws. He was rooted to the ground, surrounded by a ravaged cityscape. Winged beasts circled in a darkening sky above toppled towers. Roofs had collapsed inward and wooden beams sprung from buildings like the ribs of a savaged corpse. Rubble was strewn across the streets and what appeared to be bodies lay naked and scorched all around. Kalfinar tried to move, but his feet were rooted to where he stood. He tried to compose himself, and fight the rising panic.

This is only a dream. It's only a dream.

He focused on the form before him. One tall and wraithlike being stood above another who sat cross-legged. The tall one appeared to be questioning the other, striking it about its shadowy face. Kalfinar felt the frustration and rage emanating from the scene. The spectral being threw its head back towards the sky and roared. The sound was a rank and horrifying cacophony of voices. The howl cut short and the ghostly form thrust its hand into the chest of the sitting figure before tearing out a lustrous heart. The cross-legged figure crumpled to the ground, appearing tiny at the feet of the other. Kalfinar's heart began to thunder and his mouth became dry as he recognised the seated figure.

"Olmat!"

Blinding light.

"Olmat!" Kalfinar shouted as he sat bolt upright from his bed pallet.

"Kal." Broden whispered. "Kal, you're fine. You were just dreaming." *You look terrible.* Broden hunkered beside Kalfinar, trying to obscure him from the worried eyes of the four young soldiers. The big man regarded his cousin in the flickering light of the fire. Kalfinar's hair, brown streaked with grey, was plastered with sweat to the side of his face and neck.

"Reckon you've a fever." He felt Kalfinar's forehead. "You're burning up. Here, take this." He handed him a bowl of water, boiled with falidweed.

I hope that stuff works. Looks like you need it.

Kalfinar's eyes remained wide and wild. He took the bowl and sipped the tonic.

"I've had a few bad dreams lately, worse than the others," Kalfinar spoke in hushed tones.

"Memories again?" *Been with you long enough to hear you live those sorry days in your dreams.*

"No, not memories. The dreams are different now. Something's been growing. It's new…dark. There is something, something that…" Kalfinar's voice trailed off and he looked towards the dusty floor. "They terrify me."

You look weak. The shifting light of the fire seemed to exaggerate the dark circles around Kalfinar's eyes. *You still need it, don't you? You still hunger after it.*

"Do you remember the way we saw Olmat praying at Hardalen? I think he was in my dream." Kalfinar drank the tonic and grimaced.

"Probably nothing. Just nightmares." Broden said. "Come, you'll need something to eat. We've cooked up some of the old mutton."

Kalfinar frowned at the thought of mutton. His stomach was still reeling and lurching from the falidweed tonic.

"Aye, you're right," Kalfinar mumbled, rubbing his bearding face briskly. "It's likely nothing."

"Get up by the fire and get some food into you. You'll feel better for it." Broden watched as his cousin gingerly moved to the fire, offering thin smiles to the troops, and receiving exaggerated ones in return. *Aye, you still crave it, cousin. It's still got a grip on you.*

Thaskil glanced back into the cave. The flames of the fire pit, shifting light and dancing over the party as they slept. The thundering snoring of Broden echoed towards the cave mouth.

Thaskil looked back at Arrlun. "Seems unnatural. Doesn't it?"

"Aye, he'd shake the bones of the dead."

Thaskil laughed and then gazed out into the night.

"How far do you reckon we've come?" Arrlun asked quietly as he watched the snow fall in soft flurries.

"Who knows? It was so bad out there, for all we know we've been going around the garrison over and over."

"Don't even joke about that," the big soldier laughed. Thaskil thought it sounded surprisingly high and gentle for someone so large.

Thaskil had never really known Arrlun as they progressed through their training. Both had arrived in Hardalen since the last winter broke, but had been allotted different troops. The only times they crossed paths was when their respective troops were pitted against one another on the practice field. In the short time he had spent in his company, Thaskil decided he liked the solid lad.

"I can't see a thing through that snow." He squinted into the night. "At least that wind's dropped. Maybe now we'll be able to hear something."

"Something except Captain Broden's snoring would be nice," grunted Arrlun.

"I doubt there'd be many stupid enough to be out in this weather."

Arrlun mumbled in agreement. Both young soldiers had their swords drawn and ready, resting across the tops of their thighs, in spite of their doubt.

As his watch wore on, Thaskil's mind drifted back to the moment the assassin had grabbed at his wrist.

"You saw the assassin, didn't you?" Arrlun asked.

"Aye."

"So, what was he? Solansian?" Arrlun pressed.

"Not really allowed to say, I guess."

"Ach, come on. It's just a face, huh?"

"Can't be so sure. Believe me, I've seen plenty of Solansian faces."

"How so? You from one of the border cities?"

"I'm from Apula."

Arrlun blew out a long whistle, his brows rising high above his eyes. "Aye, well, you'll have seen them alright. Every bloody year. Every bloody skirmish season."

"Bloody is right," Thaskil mumbled, rolling a stone about in the dirt under the toe of his boot.

There were a few long moments of silence before Arrlun spoke again, "So, it if it wasn't Solansian, what breed of sword have they bought in this time?"

"Look, I wish I could tell you. I really do. But the captains have me sworn not to say a thing." He closed his eyes and rubbed the gritty feeling with his finger and thumb, chasing away the tiredness.

"Sorry. Didn't mean to press. Just curious, s'all."

"Aye." Thaskil nodded to his companion, and closed his eyes. Again, he saw those blazing, wild eyes. He shook away the thought and tried to distract himself. He looked across at his large comrade. "So, you're from far up in the North then?"

"How did you know that? You watch me taking a piss and see my massive prick?"

"No," Thaskil replied, a smile drawing on his lips. "I can see you don't shiver much, so you mustn't be as cold as the rest of us warm-bloods. I'm guessing anyone who's not as cold as me must be used to weather like this. And that, well, that must mean you're from the top of the world." Thaskil absently scratched at his bearding chin. "Ultima North."

Arrlun rumbled a laugh. "There's the no shivering, alright, and that they breed us large up there. Large in the prick. Hard to miss, we lot." He chuckled once more. "But you're right enough. Captain Broden and I share a common ability to withstand the cold." The big lad picked up a handful of snow and rolled it into a smooth ball between his two broad hands before tossing it into the blackness. "I'm from Gerloup. You'd be amazed by the winters we get."

"Heard the sea freezes over."

"Aye, the sea, and everything else. You know in Gerloup you can't smell the sea for if it isn't frozen, it is just too damn cold. Don't know if it's because the cold affects the smell of it, or if it is just that our noses are too cold to work. That's why I love it down here. Everything tastes and smells sweeter—"

A deep howl broke through Arrlun's words.

Thaskil felt his throat tighten with fear.

"Wolf," Arrlun hissed.

"Mountain wolf," a voice from behind them said, gritty and slow.

Thaskil turned to see Kalfinar standing over his shoulder. He hadn't heard his approach.

"It's alright. It's not close." The captain turned and headed back into the cave, walking through the passage towards the central fire.

"Your watch is over, lads. Sit and warm yourselves by the fire a while." He beckoned for the two soldiers to join him as he threw more dried logs onto the blaze, sending a shower of sparks and embers out above the flames, bringing it back to life.

Thaskil didn't hesitate, and made his way towards the safety of the fire's glow. "It's nice to get the blood flowing in my hands again."

"What's the difference, Captain, sir?" Arrlun asked.

"Between what?"

"Wolves and mountain wolves."

"I forget how different things are by the coast, lad. Mountain wolves are much larger than their lowland cousins, by a factor of four, or so. And they are solitary beasts, whereas the lowland wolf is a pack animal."

"It sounded near, Captain, sir."

Thaskil regarded Kalfinar in the firelight. Perspiration beaded the captain's brow and his tied-back hair shone with wetness.

"Captain, sir," Kalfinar repeated Arrlun's words. "How very formal indeed." He smiled weakly. "Don't worry. The call of the mountain wolf will carry far when the wind drops. If the storm was still blowing hard, you'd have heard nothing. Believe me. If it were closer, you'd know all about it. Ask Broden." Kalfinar glanced over his injured shoulder to where his cousin lay facing the wall of the cave. "I know you're not asleep, Broden."

The big man rolled over to face the three men hunched by the fire. His brows flexed. "I was asleep until I heard that. Damn near shit myself. Every time I hear one, even when I'm in the keep, it makes the blood stiffen within me." Broden sat up. "About ten years ago, about the time Kalfinar and I were made captains for the first time, we had a rather intimate encounter with one of those bastards. Near ripped me to meat before Kal and another finished it."

Broden rolled up his thick winter tunic. Thaskil gasped as he saw long and ragged purple scars. They were puckered on Broden's side and ribs, clearly visible despite the thick mat of red hair above them.

"Luckily, I've a bit of extra to me," Broden said. "Even so, I don't want another run in, so build that fire high and I suggest that everyone wears their double mail shirts. And wake Petran and Rallik for their watch, Dajda knows how they slept through that."

Kalfinar waited until Thaskil and Arrlun moved to wake the other cadets. When he was sure they were out of earshot, he leaned in beside Broden's ear. "That wolf is closer than I said."

"I know."

Kalfinar glanced towards the others before continuing. "Petran's horse is injured. I've just checked it. It's taken an ugly gash on the hind left fetlock."

Broden's jaw clenched as he glanced over towards the horse.

"Can't have it attracting a wolf," Kalfinar said.

"We can hardly set it loose, or kill it, can we? We need all the horses, even if it's injured."

"You're willing to risk it? You of all people?"

"Damn it, Kal. You know we need it. We'll just have to keep an eye on it so it doesn't fester."

"Aye," Kalfinar grumbled as he looked over his shoulder to the horse. "A close bloody eye."

The sun rose into a clear sky, dead calm and bright. Kalfinar sucked a long draw of icy mountain air in through his nose. They broke camp and set off, eager to make up for lost time.

"How's that seaweed working out for you, Kal?" Broden asked his cousin.

"Why don't you try it and find out." He looked humourlessly at his large comrade. "It works, well enough, s'pose." Nudging his mount's flanks, he trotted out at the head of the group.

Trying to figure out the meaning of his recurring nightmares was useless. He could not help but sense that as the dream progressed, he was being attacked and overwhelmed by something of incredible malevolence. The two figures in his dream had left him confused and frightened. *Shouldn't read too much into it. Nothing but dreams. Or my damn rotting mind unravelling.*

He decided to push it to the depths once more. He turned his horse and rode back to his cousin, noting to himself with mild amusement how the big man looked with his large red beard sticking out of the top of his thickly lined coat.

"Sorry to be short. I'm foul-tempered this morning. I didn't sleep well. Bad dreams, you know."

"It's alright. I'd be in poor form if some blue-skinned, flame-eyed monster just cut me to meat, too!" The morning was still, and the words carried easily in the cool air.

Kalfinar leaned in towards his cousin as they reined in, their horses coming to a standstill. "Damn it."

At the same time, they turned in their saddles, their heads creeping around towards their small troop of men. Arrlun and Rallik sat astride their horses with brows furrowed, suspicion etched across their faces. Petran rode a short distance behind them and appeared oblivious. Thaskil, however, shook his head in disbelief at Broden's slip.

"Fool!" Kalfinar spat the word before turning his horse. "It appears now we have some things to discuss with our young companions. Petran, get back into the squad," Kalfinar shouted towards the young soldier at the rear. *Damn horse.* He cast a knowing glance to Broden, who nodded subtly.

"Men, I'm guessing by the look on your faces you heard Captain Broden. Well, let's keep this short. The two assassins that attacked at Hardalen weren't Solansian, nor were they of the continent of the Cullanain. Their nature is unknown to us still, and so we travel to deliver such a message, and try and learn some more. That's all. No questions." He turned his horse, ignoring the gawping mouths and questions twitching on lips. Both he and Broden continued onwards before Kalfinar shouted back to the party, "And men, don't think too much." Looking back towards Broden, he snapped, "Like you."

The sun set early. The scarlet stain spreading over the sky was an omen ill received by Kalfinar. "Broden, you have the trail map, don't you?" he asked when they reigned in their panting horses. His cousin reached inside his fleece-lined coat and pulled out the rolled parchment.

"Here, catch." He tossed the map over the heads of the four soldiers.

Reaching with his good arm, Kalfinar caught the map. "Reckon we're close to another of the caves. We'd do well to rest up there tonight. Think we may have some poor weather coming." In truth, the storm appeared to have broken and much of the snow was melting away.

Tracing his finger over the aged map and glancing at the

surrounding geography, he assessed their position. "I make it about an hour's riding from here. We're only another day's ride from Terna." He rolled the map and tossed it back to Broden.

"An hour seems about right to me. A little less if we ride hard, though the beasts have had a tough few days, Kal. We don't want to walk the last day to Terna." He patted the neck of his horse, before sliding the map back within his coat.

"Let's keep a steady pace until we're there. Look out for a ridge with three columns rising from it. The cave is beneath it, according to the map." He turned his horse and rode onwards, chasing the rays of the blood-red sun.

It was just over an hour before Arrlun reined in around a corner ahead of the group, the steam rising from his horse in the chill of the night. "The columns, Captain Kalfinar, sir!" he shouted back to the following group. "The cave's just ahead." He turned and looked towards the three columns at the top of a large rocky outcrop. There was just enough light remaining in the sky to cast a striking silhouette.

"Good man. Now, let's rest these beasts before they drop." Broden placed a congratulatory slap on the young soldier's shoulder, almost sending him flying from his saddle. "Oh, sorry. I forget my own strength." He rumbled a low laugh and rode onwards to the cave.

"Fall in behind Captain Broden, men. Single file up that path. Same drill as the other night." *Only more damn careful this time.*

Kalfinar fell in behind the men. He rubbed his shoulder. It had been hard riding and it had taken its toll. But despite the constant aching, he felt as though his grip was stronger. They made their way into the cave and found it too was carved around from the entrance to reveal an open, circular hollow. There was a fire pit in the centre, surrounded by rough beds and straw.

"Home, sweet home, lads." Broden's delight at taking shelter in another cave was clear. "Best get some water for the horses. Petran, Thaskil, the river runs at bottom of the trees beneath the cave. Take the horses down and water them. They'll be needing it."

"Yes, sir," the two young soldiers replied and set off.

Kalfinar watched as the two troops headed off with the horses.

"Arrlun, take one of those spears by the wall and go with them. Keep a watch. Take Rallik, too."

Broden glanced to his cousin as the fire's glow began to spread throughout the cave. The burly lad grabbed one of the spears and assessed its strength and weight. He selected several others before finally settling on one and tossing Rallik another. "You think we're being tracked?" Broden asked, once the others were out of hearing range.

"Just being careful. I don't mean to unsettle you." He approached Petran's horse as he spoke, indicating that Broden should follow him. "You know better than anyone the dangers."

"Aye, I remember all too well. Maybe I just didn't want to think about it."

"Doesn't make it go away."

"True."

"Here. Take a look." Kalfinar knelt down by the horse, muttering soothing sounds to the twitching beast as he reached out to touch its left hind leg. With his thumb and forefinger, he squeezed the darkening, sticky wound, pressing out a stream of stinking brown discharge. He moved his nose closer and sniffed. His face was grim as he leaned back. "Festered."

"Shit! It turned bad quick."

"Aye. Its piss will reek of it. No point doubting it, there's a fair chance we're being tracked."

Broden grimaced. "Damn it." He pushed off his knees and stood with his hands on his hips. "What do you think we should do?"

"It's too late to turn it away from the cave." Kalfinar winced as he too stood. "And in any case, unless she was led away and tethered elsewhere, she'd just come back. The scent will be all over this area now."

"We'll just have to make sure the lads stay alert. We've only one day left. If we can get through the night the horse should be able to carry on until Terna." Broden scratched absently at the spot of his old scars.

Kalfinar held Broden's gaze for a moment as he settled on his decision. "So be it. Fire high and spears low."

"Aye, fire high and spears low."

Kalfinar woke, breaking free from the dark dreaming. He noticed the fire had burned low. The men on watch had not been keeping it high as instructed. He rose, his fury pricking at him, and placed several dried logs on the fire before catching the hiss of hushed words from the front of the cave mouth.

"Did you hear that?" he heard Petran whisper.

Rallik answered in the darkness, "Didn't hear nothing."

Kalfinar could just about make out their words as he moved towards the cave entrance. He heard stones tumbling onto the ground in front of the cave.

"What's that?" Rallik's voice sounded as Kalfinar heard a stream of pebbles landing in front of the cave entrance.

Kalfinar's heart raced. He drew his sword, discarding the scabbard, and quickened his advance.

Rallik cried in surprise and sounded like he stumbled backwards, falling over.

Kalfinar swapped his sword into his weak hand, nearly dropping it, and grabbed a spear in his right. "Broden!" he shouted as hurried towards the cave mouth. Approaching, he heard laughter from the two soldiers. "What is it?"

"Captain," Rallik said as he turned to meet Kalfinar, "it's just a rock grouse. It must have slipped from its nest above the cave, sir. I think it looks as shocked as we were."

As Kalfinar approached the two young men, he saw the grouse standing with a stunned look upon its face. The dozy bird's feathers were ruffled in shock.

"Very well," he muttered to the young soldiers with no small degree of relief. "Stay further into the cave men. I'll keep the fire burning high, seeing as you obviously can't be trusted to follow simple fucking orders. It'd almost died when I awoke." Kalfinar snapped off his words, then turned and moved back towards the cave centre.

Broden approached with spear in hand. Thaskil and Arrlun stood by him. The young soldiers were armed and ready.

"What is it?" Broden asked as he approached.

"Nothing. A bloody rock grouse fell out of its nest asleep. Gave the lads a fright, that's all." He rolled his sore shoulder and moved into the heart of the cave.

Broden laughed, turning and walking back into the cave. "Ought to tell them to catch it. They're delicious, especially served with—"

A high-pitched scream flooded into the cave chamber, cutting Broden off as it reverberated around the walls. Kalfinar sprinted towards the cave mouth. The rest of the troop followed with spears lowered.

Kalfinar skidded in the dust and gravel at the mouth of the cave. A giant mountain wolf stood before him. It was over half the size of a horse. The wolf ravaged Rallik as he weakly swung his fists at its snarling, tearing maw. Rallik's scream cut off abruptly as he succumbed.

The beast released the lifeless body from its blood-drenched jaws and turned towards Petran, snapping its teeth. Petran ducked under its attack and stepped to the side, running his spear between its ribs and punching through the other side. Too deep. Howling, the wolf recoiled. Its movements yanked the spear from Petran's hands before it snapped at the unarmed soldier, nearly tearing free his head and sending forth a fountain of blood. Petran's body slumped into the wall at the cave mouth, as blood welled.

The horror only lasted seconds before Kalfinar and the remainder of the troop fell upon the wounded beast. Their spears pierced the mountain wolf's body repeatedly until it slumped onto the cave floor, paws sweeping at the dust. The beast's tongue lolled from between gleaming teeth as its rib cage rose and fell, then rose no more.

Kalfinar's head dropped and he heaved a long and weary sigh. "Fuck."

Kalfinar felt no pulse from Rallik. He stood from the corpse and looked where Petran lay slumped. The young man's skin was chalk white, his life-blood having rushed from the ugly rent.

"On your feet, men. Retrieve your weapons and get them clean," Broden said. Both Arrlun and Thaskil were hunkered on the ground, their eyes cast off in the distance. "Shake the shock from you. Blood is your life, and Dajda knows you'll see much more of it if you stay the course." Broden strode over and hauled Thaskil up to his feet.

Arrlun rose and hauled his spear from the creature's chest. "Daj-da!" he exclaimed. "It was so quick."

"Should've kept the fire high," Kalfinar mumbled.

"Kal," Broden said, stepping closer and handing him a spear, "we need to get that horse slaughtered. There's no telling if other wolves have caught the scent. We can't risk any other attacks."

Kalfinar scanned the darkness before him.

"Kal?" Broden asked.

Kalfinar's eyes narrowed as he peered into the night. "Do you hear that?"

"Hear what?" Broden asked.

"There's something—Weapons!" Kalfinar roared.

The first runner from the tree line took Kalfinar's spear in the neck. The legs buckled and the body reared forward into the snow.

"The trees!" Broden yelled.

Six more forms broke from the tree line. With a guttural cry, they advanced up the snowy hill.

Broden heaved his spear into the chest of one. Arrlun's spear met another in the gut. There was a squawk, and the runner tumbled.

"Swords!" Kalfinar roared. He widened his stance, awaiting the remaining four runners.

The runners laboured up the distance to the cave mouth, their fearsome battle cries quickly replaced with ragged breaths. Their features became visible. Pointed white teeth juxtaposed from the grey flesh that surrounded open mouths.

Kalfinar watched with bemusement as the attackers laboured up the hill towards them. When they met, he batted away the weakly swung sword with ease, and skewered the attacker.

Kalfinar looked at the dying runner by his feet. Blood seeped from the chest wound and steamed in the chill of the night air. He kicked the runner's sword away and hunkered down. "What are you?"

A pair of blazing eyes narrowed up at Kalfinar.

"Speak!" Kalfinar grabbed the runner's jaw and squeezed. The mouth opened to reveal the burnt stump of a tongue.

"It's no use." Kalfinar stood and placed his sword point on the chest of the runner. Holding the creature's stare, he punched his sword in, twisted one way, and then the next. The runner's head jolted as a final ragged breath escaped. Kalfinar looked at the rest of the troop. "If any are alive, see if they can talk."

"Mine's dead," Thaskil said as he wiped his blade on the black smock of the fallen runner in front of him.

"Aye, mine too, Captain Kalfinar, sir." Arrlun sheathed his sword and hunkered down to the corpse by his feet.

"Took the head off my one," Broden said. "There was no fight in him."

"No," Kalfinar said looking back at the body before him. The eyes blazed still, as did the eyes of the corpse in Hardalen. "There was no fight in any of them."

"Captain Kalfinar, sir," Arrlun called out.

"What is it, lad?"

"The dead. Their clothes are soaked through. My one's pouches are empty. We should check the others for food, Captain Kalfinar, sir."

Broden and Thaskil echoed Arrlun's findings.

Kalfinar stood up after inspecting the pouches of his runner. They were empty, save for a thin slurry of oat dust. "Might be they were desperate," Kalfinar mused. "The wolf provided them with a chance."

A hacking cough sounded from down amongst the shadows of the hillside.

"Broden," Kalfinar hissed, inclining his head to the sound.

They edged down the hill, following the cough. Their swords were drawn. The shape of a man appeared out of the gloom. He was crawling towards the tree line on his hands and knees.

"Don't move," Broden said as he approached the man from the right with his sword pointing downwards.

The man slumped onto his belly, and then, with the sound of great effort, heaved himself onto his back. His flesh was not grey, nor did his eyes blaze. The man was bald and had a long grey beard, stained red down the chin by the blood he had vomited. The darkened patch around his belly, and the protruding grey gut marked where Arrlun's spear had penetrated.

"Well, well, well," Kalfinar said as he strode to the man. "Have you got a tongue?"

"Fuck you, trench rat!" Greybeard hissed the Solansian insult to Kalfinar, before grimacing in pain. His teeth were slick with blood.

"Oh, I'm not from Apula," Kalfinar said as he crouched beside the mortally wounded man. "But one of my friends up there is, and I'm sure he'd love to meet you." Greybeard's eyes stared wildly at Kalfinar, and his chest rose and fell quickly. "But we don't have time for him to hold you to account for all the skirmish seasons you inflicted on his people. No, we don't have much time at all. From what I can see, you are dying, and quick at that." Kalfinar looked at the arm the man had placed over his wound to keep his guts in. Two of the fingers of the left hand were storm-bitten and beginning to blacken. "Your party struggled in the blizzard, eh? Aye, well I suppose it was a bad one." Kalfinar stretched out his hand and placed it on top of the man's left arm. He pressed hard and Greybeard squealed. "Good. Now we know where we stand," Kalfinar said in an even tone. "Who sent you, and what are those things?"

Greybeard laughed between wheezing breaths. His heels weakly scrapped small furrows in the snowy ground. "You're all fucked. Every one of you."

"And why would that be?"

"It's too late. He's risen." Greybeard's bloody smile dropped from his face and he stared hard at Kalfinar. With his free hand, he grabbed at the hand Kalfinar had resting atop his wound, and squeezed. He rasped a sigh of pain before Kalfinar wrested his hand free.

Greybeard's eyes rolled into his head.

Kalfinar swung a backhanded slap across the man's cheek, wakening him. "You'll not get away that easily. Who's risen?"

Greybeard coughed droplets of blood onto his beard. "It's too late. There's a red season rising for you trench rats."

"Who has risen?" Kalfinar shouted.

Greybeard stared into the distance, and then smiled bloodily. "The true God has come to claim you all." Greybeard jerked his head towards Broden, and then thrust himself upwards.

Broden tried to jump out of the way, but it was too late. Greybeard's neck met with Broden's sword point. With a gurgle, he slid from the end of the sword and onto the ground. The remaining life stained the snow red.

Kalfinar stood up and looked at Broden. "We need to move, and quick."

Chapter Four

"WE'RE ALMOST THERE," Kalfinar said as he reined in.

They had been riding for much of the day. The blanket of snow had thinned and then become sparse as they dropped closer to sea level. Kalfinar shielded his eyes from the glare of the winter sun and scanned his surroundings. The landscape around them was dominated by the dull mauve hues of heather, which swept over the many drumlins and spread upwards towards the pine-covered hillsides.

Kalfinar looked back at the map. "A few more hours of riding and we'll be out of the foothills. Should get to Terna before sunset." He slid the map inside his coat and patted the neck of his horse.

Broden edged his mount alongside. "These beasts aren't going to take much more of this."

"Well, they'll just have to. We can't delay getting to Terna. You heard the man last night."

"I heard him, Kal, but we'll be no help if we have to walk to Terna. We shouldn't push the horses beyond a canter. We'll still make it before nightfall."

"Fair enough," Kalfinar said. He rolled his injured shoulder and winced.

"How's it feeling today?" Broden asked.

"Pain's not so bad. Tender in deep, you know?"

"Aye."

"Itching and burning's the worst now."

"Healing," Broden grunted. "I'm sure the physician at the university will be able to do something for that." Broden leant in close. "How do you think the lads are coping?"

The two remaining soldiers had not spoken much since the violence of the previous night. They sat on their horses, staring at the hillsides. Their hands never strayed far from their swords.

"Death comes to us all. They'll learn to deal with it. If they can't, they're in the wrong trade." His own words brought a flush to his face. *Pretending like you've coped with death.*

"Move on!" Kalfinar shouted, changing the subject as he rode off ahead of the others.

They reached Terna at sunset. The outline of the city's buildings came into view as they rounded a hillside, the red light of dusk reflecting on the pale stonework and backdrop of ragged clouds. The city fringed a natural horseshoe-shaped harbour, resting at the foot of the Hardalen Mountains. Buildings spread out from the circular walls of the old city, cluttering the flat land between the foothills and the sea.

"There she is, lads. The most beautiful city in the world," Broden sighed as he gazed upon his hometown.

Kalfinar looked across at his cousin. "How can you love this city? It's all piss-soaked granite, and when it's not raining, it looks like it's going to bloody rain!"

"It's not raining now."

"It will, there're clouds coming in, as usual." Kalfinar raised his hands to the heavens before flinching as his shoulder protested.

"That'll teach you to insult the blessed city of Terna," Broden laughed and nudged his horse onwards to his home. "Dajda judges you. You see?"

Kalfinar watched as Broden shifted beyond him. *I am well aware how Dajda has judged me.*

True to form, it had started to rain. Kalfinar developed a headache as they approached Terna. He felt his palms sweating inside his gloves, in spite of the cold. He had long avoided returning to the cities since he had come to Hardalen, fearing the temptation could grow too great, and he would find how little strength he really had. But the safety of the mountains was gone, and now he had to face his ghosts. As Terna grew closer, the words of the dying man sounded in Kalfinar's head. *It's too late. He's risen.* Kalfinar's headache worsened.

"Reckon there's something strange going on," Broden muttered as they rode through the deserted outer streets leading up to the city walls. "Not a soul to be seen. No one even watching from the windows."

"Aye, it's strange alright." Kalfinar glanced at the shuttered windows above shop fronts. "Very strange."

Broden looked to the walls of Terna through a pall of rain. "Can you see that?"

"The gate," Kalfinar replied, squinting. "Shut." *The gate's never shut.* He turned to his companions. "There's trouble."

Broden reined in his horse at the side of the wide muddy road that lead to the eastern gate of Terna. "Don't much fancy getting shot full of crossbow bolts tonight. Let's think this over a moment."

Thaskil and Arrlun reined in beside them.

"The gate, sirs, why do you suppose they're closed?" Thaskil asked.

"Let's get one thing straight, lads," Kalfinar said. "When it's just us, call us by our names." He glanced back towards the wet walls of Terna. Its gate stood fixed, like unyielding slabs of stone. "In my whole life, I've only ever seen the gates closed when there's trouble."

"What do you think it is, sir? I mean…Kalfinar," Thaskil corrected himself.

You don't look half as young now, lad. "I don't know, and for that very reason we ought to be careful." He felt a sharp strike of pain in his wounded shoulder, and grimaced.

"You alright, sir?" Thaskil asked, falling back into formality.

"I'm fine." He gently rubbed the area around his shoulder. He noticed Arrlun's face fixed in thoughtfulness.

The husky young soldier spoke, his Gerloup accent sounding all the more broad after his relative silence throughout much of the day, "We're only four men, and what's more, we're wearing the uniform of the Free Provinces Pathfinders. You both have your captain's medals. Surely that allows us passage. Don't you think we could just approach as normal?"

"Ordinarily, yes, but this, it seems, is far from ordinary," Kalfinar replied. "Broden's right, we ought to be cautious. Our approach has no doubt been noted already." He peered ahead through the mizzling rain to the gate. "Let's not rush it. I don't want any accidents." *Well, maybe just the one stray bolt.* "Nervous men are prone to accidents."

Broden nodded in agreement. "Aye, nervous men are rash. We're half a mile from the gate. Let's move forward slowly. Once we're within earshot, I'll announce us. Hopefully then we'll find out what's going on." He kicked his heels to the horse's flanks and moved off.

"Nice and steady. That'll do just fine." Kalfinar followed Broden back onto the muddy road.

There were no signs of movement along the battlements of the city walls. The flickering and hissing torches cast a frenetic and dancing sheen across the top of the rain slick walls. They pulled free their medals of rank and stopped well within crossbow range of the shut gate.

Broden rode out several feet ahead and halted. The unrelenting rain fell straight upon his shoulders with great slaps. His hair hung lank, wet through and taking a darker shade.

"Guardsmen of Terna!" Broden bellowed at the imposing walls. "Captain's Broden and Kalfinar of The Free Provinces Command wish to approach the gate. We've travelled from Hardalen with urgent dispatches for the High Command. May we proceed?" He held up his silver chained captain's amulet and stretched it out in front of him, ensuring it was visible.

There was no reply. Nothing broke the silence save for the drumming of the rain and the nickering of their tired horses.

As Broden wiped the gathered raindrops from his brow, he called out once more. "Guardsmen of Terna, may we proceed?" The question hung unanswered in the air. He turned his horse towards his companions and shook his head. "This isn't right, Kal, there's something—"

The familiar thump of a crossbow loosing rung in the air between the walls and their position. Kalfinar's horse reared up, throwing him from atop his horse. He landed in the sloppy filth of the road with a rush of air from his lungs and a stabbing pain in his shoulder.

As he raised himself from the mud, Kalfinar glanced through his horse's dancing legs to where a crossbow shaft had planted itself into the road between him and Broden. Kalfinar stared at it. There was a note wrapped tight around the shaft.

"I'll get it," Broden said, dismounting and splashing through the mud before wrenching the arrow from the road. He unravelled the paper. Squinting in the poor light and frowning at the running ink, he read aloud, "We have your range." He looked at Kalfinar with raised eyebrows. "Approach the gate. Slow. Hands on heads."

"They have our range," Kalfinar said as he rubbed splattered mud from his face. "I guess we do as they say."

"After all," Broden muttered, "they did ask nicely."

"Aye."

Remounting, they made their way across the remaining distance towards the gate. Kalfinar could not fully raise his hands with his wounded shoulder, and instead held his arm out to the side. At a careful pace, their horses plodded through the mud.

"Stop!" The word rang clear amidst the rain. "Far enough." A hoarse voice sounded from a shadowy form between the merlons of the battlement. "Name and business?"

"I am Captain Kalfinar. With me is Captain Broden and two officer cadets, Thaskil Vinsel and Arrlun Brunsa. We've travelled the mountain pass from Hardalen garrison with the most urgent of dispatches for the High Command. We must hand these to the governor and chief marshal without delay, and be on our way to Carte." Kalfinar's shoulder throbbed, making his aching head sway. He let his wounded hand lower.

"Keep yer hands up! That's yer only warning," the voice shouted once more from the battlement.

Fuck you. Shoot me. With an eye watering pain, Kalfinar raised his arm far as it could extend.

The voice called out again, "What you needing to tell the Command?"

"We were attacked at the garrison some nights past, and last night. I'm under orders to only communicate the nature of this attack to the High Command in person."

Silence.

There was no reply for half an hour, nothing but the drumming rain and the hissing of torches. Kalfinar gritted his teeth through the pain. The burning and itching seemed a pleasant memory now. *Keep your hands up! Or maybe I should just let them drop. What's the difference?*

Finally, the gate creaked and moaned as it drew open, pulling Kalfinar from his thoughts.

The voice called out once more, "Slow. Move inside. There're a lot of weapons pointed at you, so I'd suggest you don't make any sudden moves." As the voice spoke, the red glow from torches within flooded out towards the weary group. They moved through the gate into a small square surrounded by high walls on all sides. Wet guardsmen stood atop the walls, lit by fizzing torchlight, and crossbows pointing down. Their faces were set in a grim welcome, and their weapons smiled taut and ready. From behind the gate closed.

The voice sounded again from atop the battlements, "Dismount, take five steps ahead of your horses, and then drop your weapons on the ground. Then take five more steps ahead. If you don't, my laddies here'll shoot you full of sharp things."

They dismounted, dropped their weapons onto the mud, and moved forward as instructed. Footsteps sounded from behind.

"Captain's Kalfinar and Broden." The owner of the voice appeared. It belonged to a tall man. His oil clothes were entirely soaked through. There was a long and ragged scar running from his hairline and down the middle of his face, taking a deep part of his nose with it. He was a gaunt old soldier, with thin, stringy hair framing his pale and pock-marked head. "I'm Sergeant Thosfed. Don't believe I've ever had the pleasure. Know you both by yer reputation, though. Or, in the case of Captain Kalfinar, yer reputations." Sergeant Thosfed inspected the party of men who had just arrived before him. He stopped in front of Kalfinar and stared. "You Kalfinar?"

"Aye."

"Huh," Thosfed grunted. "Heard you kicked the shit out of the governor of Carte."

"Can't say I recall that." Kalfinar's voice remained steady, in spite of the rage and shame that swelled inside him.

"What's wrong with you? Carrying a wound, eh?"

"Aye. When we were attacked at Hardalen. I took a blade in my shoulder," Kalfinar replied in a level tone.

"Attacked." Sergeant Thosfed rubbed at his white stubbly chin thoughtfully. "Aye, no doubting you'd have me present you in front of the High Command, eh?" Thosfed moved closer, the foul rot of his teeth reaching Kalfinar's nose.

Delightful, thank you.

"I would. That's the point of our being here." He held back his reaction to the smell of the old soldier's teeth.

"A man in yer position need not be so clever." The sergeant drew a heavy short sword and moved its tip under Kalfinar's chin. "You'd better be careful and hand me yer papers. Nice and slow, mind, or I'll add another nice scar to yer pretty face. Would you like that?"

As the question hung between them, a tall man with long blonde hair and a neatly shaven face broke between the guards.

Broden glanced across and a smile dawned on his face.

The tall man approached the sergeant and placed a hand on the man's shoulder. "Thank you, Sergeant Thosfed. I received your message. You can relax. They are as they say they are."

"Aye, Major." The old Sergeant sheathed his blade and stood down. He signalled the crossbowmen to lower their weapons.

"Just in time," the newcomer mouthed to the party.

Kalfinar moved towards the tall officer. "Bergnon, it's been too long, old friend."

"Indeed it has. Much too long." He clasped Kalfinar's hand.

"I'm glad you came when you did!" Broden rumbled a laugh. "I thought Kal was going to have another hole ripped in him."

"Aye, Sergeant Thosfed's not known to be one to take chances. That's why he's leading the Night Command."

Thosfed saluted the captains. His scarred face split in an ugly smile, revealing his rotting teeth, blackened headstones in a graveyard of a mouth. "At yer service, sirs."

Bergnon looked grimly at his comrades. "Gentlemen, gather up your weapons and horses. You'd best come with me. We've a bit of a situation at hand, and I fear it has reached as far as Hardalen also."

"What exactly is the situation?" Kalfinar pressed as he retrieved his sword.

"I heard you say you were attacked. So were we." Bergnon stopped and looked about at the many guardsmen gathered about. "This is not the place for such talk. Let's make for the keep. In the meantime, do you need help with your wound?"

"Aye, I'll need to get it seen to. I think I burst a couple of stitches."

Kalfinar remembered Olmat's orders to visit the physician at the University. "Olmat gave me the name of a physician to visit, but perhaps I could take a tonic until then. I've been using falidweed. Not the nicest of remedies."

"Never heard of it. Don't worry, we'll get it seen to. Let's head on, there's much to discuss." Bergnon's face was grave as he led them beyond the guardsmen. A dozen horsemen sat waiting as escort.

"A little old for a chaperon, aren't you?" Broden asked.

"Sign of the times." Bergnon mounted his horse, and they set off.

They rode within the centre of the escorts as they trudged through the rain-slick cobbled streets of inner Terna towards the High Command. The tall buildings of drab, grey granite and dark wood lined the narrow streets.

A crash sounded down a side-street, and Kalfinar turned in his saddle. He peered down the black alley as he passed but could see nothing. The screech of fighting cats issued from the darkness.

"Just a cat." Broden said.

The weather-whipped lanterns that sparsely lined the streets or hung from buildings cast a dull and swaying light.

They rode onwards towards the keep, as it was modestly known. It was, in reality, a massive concentric castle, a huge outer wall surrounding an inner wall and a grim central keep. Built as the Noehmian headquarters of the Military High Command, it also doubled as regional house of government after the sister nations broke from Solansian rule and formed the Free Provinces. It housed the regional governor, Lord Abbonan, and his staff, as well as the main military headquarters for the region, commanded by Chief Marshal Solskaen.

Kalfinar noted his surroundings as their horse's footfalls echoed around the high buildings. There was no one about. Normally the streets would remain busy with citizens. Even later into the night, Terna never really slept; drunks, thieves, and whores going about their business through the swill and detritus. Tonight, there was nothing.

"Bergnon," Kalfinar said. "Why are the streets so empty?"

"Curfew. The Night Command will arrest anyone out after sundown." He looked around to the four soaked soldiers riding behind him. "I can't tell you more until we get to the keep. There may not be bodies in sight, but I've little doubt there are eyes and ears in the shadows."

Kalfinar looked all about him at the empty streets. *This place reeks of fear.*

"Get the horses brushed down and see that they're fed and watered," Bergnon said to a pair of stable boys as they entered the keep.

They dismounted and handed the reins across. Broden fidgeted at a bag tied to his saddle. He unfixed the stubborn knot, and then slung the bag over his shoulder.

"The High Command is waiting," Bergnon said.

Following behind the major, they hurried into the military quarters of the keep. As they passed into the heart of the building, the smell of fresh bread and roast meat hit Kalfinar's senses. His stomach began to protest at the recent neglect.

Bergnon halted and turned to them. "Perhaps it'd be best if the lads here fetched a meal and a bath. They needn't delve into politics just yet. What say you, lads?"

"I would appreciate that very much, sir," Thaskil replied to the tall major. "I'll not deny the journey's been hard, sir." He smiled modestly at the three experienced soldiers.

Arrlun nodded his agreement. "Aye, Major Bergnon, sir. I'd appreciate some food and a bed. I can wash tomorrow." The young northerner smiled.

"Major Bergnon, sir, eh? A man from Ultima North, I presume." Bergnon smiled towards Arrlun. "That's a Gerloup accent, if I'm not mistaken."

"That's right, Major Bergnon, sir."

"Well Arrlun, as much as you wish for a bed, I recommend that you experience our baths. They're very good indeed, and the bed's embrace will be all the sweeter after a soak. Come, we'll find someone to look after you two." Bergnon led the group down a wide stone corridor towards the kitchens. As he entered, he called a housemaid over.

Kalfinar turned back to the young soldiers, "I'll see to it tonight that you both receive your commission."

The two young men smiled.

"I'll have Rallik and Petran commissioned also." *Shitting hell, that's the least you can do for them, you got them into this, got them killed.* He smiled to the lads. "Now go and get some food."

————————————

Bergnon led them up a tight and winding stone staircase towards the rear of the keep. "It's best the lads don't hear too much. We're trying to keep this as quiet as possible for now," Bergnon said as they hurried onwards.

"This isn't the way to Chief Marshal Solskaen's study." Kalfinar felt a nervous twist in his stomach.

Bergnon stopped and turned to his companions, his brows furrowed. "No, it's not. Solskaen's dead. Murdered. Governor Abbonan alone leads the High Command in Terna now. As you can imagine, some of Solskaen's senior staff are a bit upset at Command falling solely to the Governor, now that he's a civilian."

"What? Forty years commanding in the fleet is so soon forgotten?" Broden asked.

"Same old politics." Bergnon grumbled.

They reached a large wooden door flanked by two guardsmen and stopped. Bergnon spoke to one of the soldiers as they approached, "Fetch me the physician at once. Tell him to bring a tonic of, ah, what was that name?"

"Falidweed," Kalfinar supplied.

"And bring some food up. These men are hungry."

The soldier saluted crisply and headed down the stairs. They opened the door and entered. Two dozen men and women sat surrounding a long wooden table in the centre of a large room. The stone walls of the room were covered with many elaborate and bright tapestries depicting sea battles. Their colours danced vividly from the light of the oil lamps lining the upper walls. A large fire crackled and glowed at the rear of the room, and several large grey wolfhounds lay across the rug-lined floor. The senior officers of the Terna High Command were locked in debate. Relations appeared strained. Several officers sat with their heads in their hands. Papers and maps cluttered the large table, and with the room's focus lost in discussion, the entrance of the three men went unnoticed. Kalfinar saw Governor

Abbonan at the head of the table, thick hands rubbing grey-haired temples while the others argued.

Clearing his throat, Bergnon announced their arrival, "Captain's Kalfinar and Broden have travelled from Hardalen to bring us news. It appears the assassins have reached as far as the mountains."

The debate ceased and all in the room turned their attention to the two wet and mud-splattered men in the doorway.

Chapter Five

KALFINAR LOOKED AROUND THE TABLE. *There are so few. It can't be so.* A flush of alarm washed over him as many of the faces he would have expected to see in the Terna High Command were absent. Good soldiers, and some friends. A quick glance towards Broden confirmed that he too had noticed the loss.

"Sit, gentlemen, please." Bergnon ushered Kalfinar and Broden to a pair of seats at the far end of the long table. The officers of the Terna High Command remained seated, each nodding their heads in solemn greeting to the men. Several of those who sat around the table fixed hard eyes on Kalfinar. It was clear the depths of his fall remained fresh within the memory of many of those gathered.

"It's good to see you both. I'm relieved," Governor Abbonan said, his voice weary as he rose, stretching his long, broad frame from his chair with some stiffness. "Bloody knee," Abbonan grumbled as he reached down and rubbed the offending joint. "The old fleet injury has been playing up with this weather."

"Governor. Good to see you. You're looking well, old knee aside." Kalfinar shooed the wolfhounds resting on the floor and moved towards Abbonan.

He grasped the governor's rough, calloused hand. The retired admiral's body bore the stature and marks of one having served long at sea.

His skin was weather-beaten and his steel-grey hair appeared fixed in a permanent stiff sea breeze.

"Ah, kind of you to say. Of course, thanks must go to my new wife, Pila. She keeps my feeling young a priority of hers." He smiled, a feeble effort to inject some good humour into the solemn atmosphere. "Your father does not approve, of course."

Kalfinar's brows furrowed at the mention of his father.

"Broden, I see the mountain living has been good for you. You appear to have lost some of that excess meat about you." Abbonan grinned to the big captain who approached him.

They clasped hands firmly. The bag around Broden's shoulder drew the attention of one of Governor Abbonan's hounds, and it sniffed with interest.

"Indeed it has," Broden said as he shooed the hound away from the bag. "All that chasing after Kal keeps me lean." He gently grasped his cousin's good shoulder and gave it a shake. "He's had a new lease of life up there."

The smiles at the reunion were true enough, however the trouble that had forced such an occasion was palpable. The smiles evaporated quickly.

"Major Bergnon, if you will, please recount to our two travellers what has occurred," Abbonan said as the three men settled into their seats.

"Certainly, sir."

Bergnon cleared his throat and spoke, "This is unlikely to come as a great shock to either of you. Five nights before this, we were attacked. It was discrete, and it was well planned. Twenty-three officers and veteran non-commissioned officers were slain. It appears most were killed as they slept. They were all campaign experienced." Bergnon paused and drank some water, his hand trembling ever so slightly as he raised the goblet. "The Night Command was only alerted by guards who heard the roars of Chief Marshal Solskaen as he fought his attacker, sadly, in vain. If it were not for the alarm being raised at this point, many more of us may not be here tonight."

"Did anyone see the assassins?" Broden asked.

"Fleeting glimpses. Nothing more," Bergnon answered. "The Chief Marshal's guards reported seeing a figure, masked and dressed in black, leaping from the window. The assassin had tied off a rope beyond the reach of the guards and was able to scale down the side of the keep. Before the Night Command could reach him, he was off, away into the night." Bergnon paused and sighed, shaking his head. "These were killers of exceptional skill."

Abbonan spoke up, "Wouldn't have thought what remains of the Solansian forces could manage the level of sophistication it would have taken to carry out such an attack. Their armies were routed and collapsed after the last campaign, and what was left of their navy fled never to be seen again!" Abbonan looked up at a tapestry of two ships locked in fiery combat. "We could never find the bastards. Sailed all around the Yellow Sea and the Salt Coast, and nothing."

Bergnon spoke on, "As you've seen, Terna is on high alert and we've enforced a curfew. Although we've not captured any of the killers, we believe there may still be a chance some have failed to escape the city."

"Were all those attacked killed?" Kalfinar asked.

Bergnon's response was quiet, "Yes. None survived."

Abbonan interrupted, "Thank you, Major, I'll take it from here. We've been sweeping the quarters of the city. We'll find the bastards, if they're still here." Abbonan filled his goblet with wine from a beaten copper jug and slugged at it. "The weather has been treacherous, so there was no point in sending pigeons. They wouldn't have made it five miles. Word was sent to Carte by ship four days ago. We feared this may not have been isolated, and now it seems as though our fears are to be realised." The governor looked to Kalfinar and Broden as they sat before him. "Well, now it's your turn to spill out your tidings, grave as they may be." Abbonan sat into his chair. He rubbed his temples with his thick forefingers. "Damn these days." Abbonan patted the nuzzling head of the hound by his side. He regarded the beast wistfully, "An easier life."

"The governor is correct." Kalfinar's voice felt gravelly. "Our report is not one to cheer the heart, I'm afraid. This attack is not isolated to Terna. It has reached as far as Hardalen also."

The officers of the High Command began to babble amongst themselves. Theory and conjecture hummed around the room.

Kalfinar rubbed at his eyes as the pain of his pounding head cored through them. Flares of bright yellow and white swamped his vision. *Where's that damned physician?*

"Commanders, please!" Bergnon encouraged silence. "Let Captain Kalfinar finish."

As the muttering ceased Kalfinar continued to recount the events of the previous week, "Five nights before this, assassins made their way into the garrison at Hardalen. The attack appears to have only targeted myself and Broden. If there were to be others, they failed."

"You're both alive. What of the assassins?" Abbonan asked. His face revealed a hunger for answers. As did the eyes of the other members of the High Command.

"Dead," Kalfinar replied plainly. "We managed to kill our visitors."

"No harm to either of you?"

"It was a close thing for me. I took a knife to my left shoulder." *A little lower and to the right.*

"And Broden?" Abbonan asked.

Broden was drinking from a goblet. Wiping beads of wine from his beard, he smiled and answered, "No. No holes in me, my lord. I've not been much of a sleeper since I've been at Hardalen. I managed to stick him before he stuck me."

Governor Abbonan returned a thin smile. "Stick or be stuck. The most simple and honest distillation of combat there ever was. Well, blessed be your restless nights," Abbonan replied. "You have dispatches?"

"Aye, sir." Kalfinar reached inside his coat and pulled out both Lucius's and Olmat's reports. He handed them to Abbonan. "Before you read them, sir, I must tell you that the situation developed somewhat since they were written."

"Oh?"

"Last night we had sought shelter in one of the final route caves before Terna. A mountain wolf attacked, and we lost two of our party before we could dispatch it. They were both awaiting commission."

"I'm sorry," the governor said. "If you give me their details before the night is done, I shall see they receive posthumous commissions, complete with a death endowment for their families."

Kalfinar nodded his thanks and continued, "I'm afraid that is not all."

Abbonan's eyebrows raised and his eyes widened.

"It appears the confusion following the wolf attack presented the opportunity the assassins needed to attack. I suspect they were undone by the storm, and, in desperation, sought to complete their mission and obtain shelter. They were weakened by exposure and hunger. It was no hardship to defeat them. One of the party did live long enough to speak."

Abbonan leaned in from his seat. "What did he say?"

"He told me that there was a red season coming for the Free Provinces, and that the true God has risen."

"The true God?" Abbonan asked. "What did he mean by that?"

"I don't know," Kalfinar said, "but he also said that the true God would claim us all."

"For all our differences, the Solansians are still children of Dajda. Did he say anything else?" Abbonan asked.

"No, but there is something else. Whilst the one who spoke was Solansian, the assassins were not."

"Where were they from?" Abbonan asked.

"We don't know," Kalfinar replied. "I suspect there is more to be learned from Olmat's reports. He completed a medical assessment of the dead assassins."

"Yes, of course." Abbonan untied the seal and began to read the report. All eyes within the room watched as the governor's brows met. As he read, the hum of conversation grew.

"Please," Bergnon pleaded for quiet. "For pity's sake, give the governor time before you start with questions."

Abbonan finished reading the report and spoke to the gathered council, "Olmat speaks of men foreign to the countries of the Cullanain, though their exact origin he does not know." Abbonan paused as a frown crept upon his face. "If these men are not of the Cullanain, then surely there must be something of their nature we can discern. In Dajda's name!" Abbonan slammed his fist into the table, startling his hounds. "There must be something about them!"

Kalfinar exchanged a wary glance with Broden as Olmat's warning to keep the nature of the assassin's secret echoed in his mind. "Go ahead, Broden."

Broden leaned down between his feet and retrieved the bag he had been carrying. He placed it on the table and removed the head of the assassin he killed the night before. A pair of flies buzzed off the filthy head as it was drawn from the bag. A foul smell followed soon after. Broden placed the head down on the table, the sticky gore staining the polished finish.

"Dajda!" Abbonan and the rest of the Terna High Command

gasped and leaned in to get a better look. "What is it?" Abbonan asked. "Dajda, it stinks."

"We don't know," Broden said.

"Whatever it is, it's something new," Kalfinar said.

"I think I need to pray on this a while," Abbonan said, his eyes never leaving the head before him. "I think it is best we adjourn for the night and retire. Major Bergnon, take the names of Kalfinar's troop. Make sure the clerk completes a posthumous commission for the two dead boys, and as for any others awaiting rank, see it done." Abbonan inclined his head towards Kalfinar and Broden. "Find yourselves a room. There's no shortfall." His face was wan, and he made no effort to hide his emotion. The atmosphere hung in the room like bad light. Abbonan moved towards Kalfinar and Broden and grasped their hands. "I'm so very glad to see you both." He looked around at his gathered council, all now having risen. Governor Abbonan nodded and grunted to himself, "Good. These are good officers."

There was no trouble locating a room large enough for the three of them. Four beds filled the four corners of the room. In the middle stood a table and four chairs. Broden was busy devouring a plate of roast lamb and fresh bread.

"Kal," Broden said while he rested his hand on his cousin's forearm. "Have some food."

Kalfinar shooed off Broden's offer, his face settling into a frown as he rubbed his sweating temples. "Not tonight. I've no appetite." *At least, not for food.* Kalfinar's mind was in the docks of Carte, remembering the ways to the jalsinum houses, to the dens where he could fill his lungs and shed it all. *Smoke and blood, whores and mud.*

"Here we go!" Bergnon returned from the kitchens with some more Apulan wine. They sat as friends for the first time in four long years.

"Damn, but it's good to see you both." Bergnon smiled.

"Kalfinar." Bergnon's smile dropped off the corners of his face. "I've been wanting to say, I received word when I was in Solansia. I wanted to be there with you. I'm sorry I wasn't."

"Ach," Kalfinar grunted. He immediately felt the flush of heat in his eyes, threatening to spill over. Holding the tears back and looking at his friend, he smiled. It was bitterly devoid of happiness. "I know."

I'm glad you couldn't be there to see me rot into filth. Shaming her memory, shaming myself, tearing our world asunder. "What's keeping this physician?" Kalfinar asked, changing the subject.

"Sorry, I should've mentioned," Bergnon replied. "Our physician was amongst those killed. A case of wrong place at the wrong time, it seems. His apprentice is not fully equipped with the skills. Which is to say the man is more of a danger than the bloody flux. We've drafted in a physician from the university. His name escapes me now. Bastard of a fellow, though."

Broden coughed and interrupted, "Who wants some more—"

Before he could finish, an old man dressed in a long black cloak came briskly into the room. Ignoring the three men who sat before him, he aggressively shook off the rain that had gathered about his thick woollen cloak and then patted down his plain black physician's smock. Puffing and scowling, he was clearly unimpressed at being summoned at such a late hour and in such dreadful weather.

"Shitting weather," the man grumbled to himself. He looked Broden in the eyes as a large raindrop clung to the tip of his long, hooked nose. "I'm the physician, Aslat." His fists rested upon his hips and his foot tapped a ferocious tattoo on the floor. "Well," the old man paused, the air between them crackling as his annoyance spewed out, "which one of you is pissing well sick then?" He looked accusingly at each of them before settling on Kalfinar. "Hmmm, you are, aren't you? I can smell it off you. It's like the stench off a sick cur."

"Take your damn shirt off." The old physician roughly manhandled Kalfinar's leather jerkin and shirt off, before tossing them on the floor by Bergnon's feet.

"Steady!" Kalfinar snapped as he felt his wound bite.

The physician glared, locking eyes. "Big warrior like you complaining about a bit of rough handling. This place really may be in the shit traps if this is what is left to fight our battles."

Kalfinar's eyes hardened.

"I think I'll go and get those baths heated for you," Bergnon said before biting his lip behind the physician's back to stifle his laughter.

The physician, although small in stature, was proving to be somewhat a tyrant, and the atmosphere in the room lurched to the arse-pinching uncomfortable.

Broden, sensing his chance to escape, called after Bergnon, "I'll help!"

"No. He's capable enough without you," Kalfinar ordered his cousin to stay. *I'm not going to be the only one to suffer at the hands of this little crow.*

Aslat cleaned the wound of the grit that had inevitably found its way past the burst stitches and into the flesh, provoking the occasional wince from Kalfinar. The physician's mood appeared to lighten somewhat as he worked. Kalfinar focussed on Broden as he stood gazing out at the thin glass window overlooking the perpetually wet city of Terna.

"You've seen your fair share of sharp edges," the old physician referred to the many small and not so small scars assorted over Kalfinar's upper body. "Or blunt edges. And come to think of it, the odd edge in between as well, I'd say."

Broden called out from his place by the window, "I can never keep him out of trouble, but that's nothing. Take a look at these." He unbuttoned his long jerkin and rolled up his shirt, revealing his raggedly scarred side.

"By Dajda's grace! You're lucky to be alive. What in the frozen hells did that to you?"

"Mountain wolf." Broden rolled down his shirt and tucked it back into his trousers. "He's dead now," he added casually, his gaze again returning to the damp night scene before him.

"Must have been a close bloody call on that front," the physician said, returning to the work at hand. "Good. Despite your best efforts, that appears to be healing well." He applied a fresh bandage to Kalfinar's wound and bound his shoulder once more. "I'd say you'll be using it again, only lightly, in another week. Heed me, just light use. Don't shitting well push it, or the next time I see you, I'll be hacking the damn thing off." As he packed up his supplies, he asked, "Tell me, what have you taken as a tonic?"

"Falidweed. My physician gave it to me to boil up in water. Horrible stuff, it tastes like stewed up pipe leaf." Kalfinar rolled his shoulder as he spoke. "Thanks, this feels better."

"Falidweed," the physician repeated it to himself, as though his tongue was trying on the fit of the word. "I must admit I've never heard of such a thing."

Kalfinar looked across to Broden who peered out the window, though his darkened reflection of knotting brows confirmed he had heard the man speak. Kalfinar returned his attention to the physician as he slung his bag across his shoulder.

"Tell me…"

"Aslat."

"Tell me, Aslat, you teach at the University here in Terna, don't you?" Kalfinar asked the physician as he reached for his shirt.

"Yes. This will be my thirtieth year teaching the healing ways within those walls, mostly to gormless morons and the indolent progeny of the preening classes. But they buy my bread, and so I must educate those vacuous wretches." He helped Kalfinar put his shirt on, somewhat more gently than when removing it.

"Truly a service of merit, Aslat." Broden supplied the compliment from his position by the window.

"Don't be smart with me, boy," Aslat snapped towards Broden.

Kalfinar continued, "Tell me, do you know of a physician who goes by the name of Capriath? An old friend of ours has directed us to this man." Kalfinar studied the face of the physician carefully as he asked his question.

Aslat muttered the name twice as his gaze shifted around the room. "No, I'm sorry, but that name is not familiar to me." Aslat shook his head as he grasped Kalfinar's hand. "I'm sorry I cannot help you with your search, eh…"

"It's Captain Kalfinar, and that's Captain Broden."

"Captain Kalfinar, I see." The physician was silent for a moment, before he spoke again, "Come and see me tomorrow morning, just after sunrise. I'll be able to give you some more tonics for the pain, and perhaps something to speed up the healing. I'm sorry I have few supplies with me tonight. I'm afraid I was caught a little by surprise."

"Certainly," Kalfinar replied. "Where shall I find you?"

"My office is number seven as you enter the medical quadrangle. If you get lost, just ask one of the students. Preferably one who breathes through the nose. There should be plenty about. Not plenty breathing through their nose, though." Chuckling to himself, the physician shuffled through the door and disappeared down the hallway.

Kalfinar and Broden both nodded in silent agreement. Aslat had grown nervous.

He's lying.

Chapter Six

"KAL, why didn't we just take the horses?" Broden grumbled.

"Think about it," Kalfinar snapped. "What would you pay more attention to, two men on foot or two men on horseback? Let's just try to keep our heads down as much as possible." He pulled the hood of his cloak tighter around his face and trudged on through the harbour fog that hung low and cold in the damp, salty air of morning.

The previous night had been restless for Kalfinar. Dark dreams, the symphony of drumming rain and Broden's snoring all served to torment his rest. His limbs felt weary as he made his way through the grim morning.

The sun had been up for less than half an hour and the narrow streets remained unusually quiet. The few tradesmen who passed Kalfinar and Broden appeared too busy rubbing their bleary eyes to pay much heed to the two men. They turned down a tight alley between tall buildings as a shortcut towards the University and narrowly avoided a bucket load of freshly brewed morning filth.

"Shit!" Broden snapped as he leapt back from the splashing excrement. "Think I preferred the rain," he said before carefully sidestepping the waste. Broden ignored the insults cascading down from the narrow window above. "Supposed to be the nice end of town."

"Arse-end of town, more like it," Kalfinar said, eyes scanning the buildings above for any further downpours.

As they approached the ornate University building, a young cleric with short cropped hair and a riot of spots on his face shuffled by.

"Excuse me, Brother," Kalfinar said as he caught the attention of the young man. "Can you direct us towards the medical quadrangle?"

Politely, the cleric accompanied the two captains into the main arcade of the University and led them into the well-manicured herb gardens of the medical quadrangle before hurrying off.

"I'm sure Dajda will forgive him," Broden mused. "At least he's trying to make his devotions." He smiled wistfully. "I haven't been for a week. That's the longest since the last skirmish season three years ago."

Kalfinar shook his head dismissively. "Never mind that. Number seven's over there by the log piles. Let's see what Aslat has to say for himself." He strode onwards, leaving Broden where he stood.

"Oh, I know you care not!" Kalfinar heard Broden call after him. "But I still have my faith."

The voice bidding them to enter the room sounded different than it had the previous night. It was weary and without the same snap. As he opened the door, Kalfinar saw Aslat sitting behind a large desk, buried behind a mountain of charts, paperwork, and maps. His oil-lamp had burned down, its flame moving weakly with the dance of one near done. Aslat looked up at them from behind his desk with blood-shot eyes. The room was not large, though its walls were covered from floor to ceiling with an extensive collection of books and papers, jars, and urns.

Kalfinar scanned the room. *Seems few physicians can keep their house in order. Looks just like Olmat's chambers.*

The heavy green drapes were still closed. They had done a remarkable job retaining the heat from the meagre fire that burned beside the desk, more a bed of embers than any real flame.

"Come in, come in, Kalfinar, Broden." Aslat rose from his seat and moved around his desk. He hadn't changed his clothes from the night before. He broke into a wide grin, one which did not look altogether natural. It hung beneath his hooked nose like a lopsided cut of meat.

"He'd better be careful. His face looks like it's going to break," Broden whispered, leaving Kalfinar coughing to hide his laughter.

"Everything fine?" the old physician asked.

"The damp, Aslat. It's this damned damp city," Kalfinar lied, his features betraying not a word.

Broden's face, however, was not so subtle. The big man lost control and croaked out a bark of laughter. His slip served only to push Kalfinar to the limit, leaving him spluttering also.

The physician looked at the two men before shaking his head, dismissing their behaviour.

"Yes, the damp. Indeed, I almost have gills myself." Aslat smirked at his own quip. "Come, take a seat." He ushered the captains towards two stools by the smouldering fire. "I've not been entirely truthful to you."

Kalfinar and Broden feigned shock.

"For good reason," Aslat continued. "My real name is not as I claimed it to be. Truly, I'm called Capriath."

"We'd guessed as much," Kalfinar admitted.

"You mean my subterfuge failed?" Capriath frowned and took out a wrinkled handkerchief before blowing his nose. "Seems I'm getting out of practice. That will not do." Inspecting his handkerchief, he grimaced. "Piss on it! I'm getting a cold," he muttered to himself, shoving the handkerchief back into a pocket in his gown. "Lucky for me then you are friend and not foe, or I'd be rightly shat on, wouldn't I?"

"You've nothing to fear from us," Broden said.

"Thanks be to Dajda! Nevertheless, to you, and you alone am I known as Capriath. To anyone else, my name is Aslat. Remember that."

"Worry not," Kalfinar said. "We're more attuned to detect a lie than most. Let's call it a special sense."

Capriath did not appear convinced, his eyes narrowing.

Changing the subject, Kalfinar continued, "Our physician, a man named Olmat, told me to seek out a physician in Terna by your name. Your real name, that is. He claimed my arm was at risk." Kalfinar leaned forward a little on his stool. "But something nags at me. Call it this special sense again. There's something more to our visit than my arm, isn't there?"

"Well, there may be, but in time. First, let me take another look at that wound of yours. I really don't want to have to hack the limb off." Capriath moved around his desk, collecting a small pot containing a honey-coloured substance. "Broden, could you swing that pot of water over the fire and boil up some tea?"

Broden obliged, placing some kindling and a pair of logs onto the embers before hanging the pot on the iron arm and swinging it above the rekindled fire. Capriath removed the dressing before inspecting Kalfinar's wound. Applying gentle pressure, he rubbed some of the honey-coloured substance over and around the stitches. "Olmat was right. You do heal quickly."

Kalfinar looked up at the physician. "You know Olmat?"

"I've known him a long time." Capriath's wrinkled face opened up in a wide grin. It sat kinder on his face this time. "I'm just going to apply something to speed the healing further. It's a moss that I've crossbred. Frightfully useful stuff, if I do say so myself." He turned towards his window and pulled back the drapes revealing an array of plants and pots gathering what meagre sunlight they could from the miserable morning.

"If you don't mind my asking, what's the connection between you?" Kalfinar probed further as Capriath returned and applied a green, web-like material over the wound.

"My connection with Olmat? It's fairly mundane. We first met at a young age through some mutual friends, and since then we've kept in touch as and when we could. We're both involved in the same line of work, and have a mutual love of botany, so there are common interests. There! That's looking better." Capriath nodded in approval of his own handiwork. "I'll bind you up again."

Broden sat by the fire, inspecting the water as it heated. He spoke, still gazing at the pot, "You say you've an interest in botany, and indeed that you've dabbled in the breeding of such things." He acknowledged the dressing on Kalfinar's shoulder, "That would require a deep knowledge of the science, would it not?"

"Of course it would," Capriath snapped. "Do you think one can just arrive at the pissing conclusion of how to crossbreed species as I have done on a stroke of luck?"

"Alright." Broden puffed his cheeks and exhaled, his eyes widening in the moment. "I was just arriving at my point."

"Well what is your shitting point then?"

"Well, with respect, how come you know nothing of falidweed?"

"Oh, I know what falidweed is. Don't be a dolt," he muttered, his tone lightening somewhat. "I was just being careful. Some men of my science could be put in grave danger by their knowledge of falidweed. You see, the plant is a potent cleanser for the body. It acts by locating what is best described as a contamination, something foreign to the body, and it enables it to be rooted out. Only a few people know of the plant's uses." His face set in an ominous frown. "Knowledge of falidweed is much desired, and protected." He looked gravely at them, his eyes settling on Kalfinar, giving him an uncomfortable feeling in the pit of his stomach. "These are dangerous times, and I need to be careful. As do you."

"Olmat gave me a letter for you. It's inside my coat," Kalfinar said. "Broden, could you fetch it?"

Broden rose from his stool and retrieved the letter. The physician broke its wax seal and unrolled the envelope. He read the letter and nodded his head, muttering solemnly to himself, "It's as I feared then."

"What's as you feared, Capriath?" Kalfinar asked as the physician lit the corner of the report with the flame of a candle on his desk. It burned away to nothing in a flash of purple flame.

Kalfinar narrowed his eyes at the sight of the rapid conflagration before him. "That's treated paper. That was no report of my wound, was it? It's about those creatures, isn't it?"

"You two are a right pair of deep thinkers, aren't you? Well, you may not be half as smart as you think you are, or need to be. These are grave times, and in grave times, it may be better to remain ignorant. You must trust in Olmat and trust in me. Nothing more can be said to you until you reach Carte. We simply cannot take the risk. Once you reach Carte, you must visit a man named Biscon. Go to him. He will help you understand what is taking place." Capriath moved behind his desk and opened a small cupboard, removing a velvet pouch. He tossed it onto his desk. "There's some more falidweed in there. You'll not need to take very much more of it. One small cup, once a day until you're through with the bag. It should see you to Carte." He began to scribble onto a small sheet of parchment.

Broden and Kalfinar stared at each other with bewilderment.

Capriath rolled up the piece of parchment and tied it. "Take these directions. They'll lead you to Biscon's home. When you go to find him, be discreet. Be very discreet." He handed the parchment to Kalfinar. Looking across to Broden he spoke, "You look like a man who's steady. Make sure you're alert." Capriath gathered up several pieces of parchment on his desk, some of which looked very dated. He tossed them onto the fire and watched as all of the pieces of parchment were consumed rapidly in flashes of purple flame. "It's best that you leave for Carte as soon as you can."

Kalfinar and Broden returned to the High Command's keep in central Terna, avoiding the main thoroughfares. They skulked up the narrow side-streets and alleyways with Capriath's warnings ringing in Kalfinar's ears. They presented their papers to the guardsmen on duty by the outer gatehouse and entered the large paved outer courtyard.

Kalfinar looked up at the inner wall of the castle as he approached the drawbridge leading to the barbican. "This truly is one of the ugliest structures I've ever seen."

"It does the job." Broden sniffed.

"Aye. That it does. The mason's spared no thought for the eyes of future generations though."

"I guess they were in a bit too much of a hurry to consider finesse."

"They managed at Carte."

"Aye, with softer rock."

Kalfinar laughed at his cousin's point. "Fair is fair. I concede."

They passed through the barbican and across the worn paving of the inner courtyard. Kalfinar heard the closing hymn of morning devotions as they made their way up the broad, age-smoothed steps and into the keep.

Kalfinar and Broden avoided the rush as the congregation let out from the church, and made their way to Abbonan's council room. They took their places before the governor returned from his morning prayers.

As Bergnon entered the room, Kalfinar regarded him. He looked exhausted.

"I had to pray to Dajda for you in devotions this morning," Bergnon said to Broden as he took his seat. "My friend, you've been afflicted! I've never heard snoring like it in my life."

Governor Abbonan entered the room and assumed his place at the head of the table. "Morning." The lounging wolf-hounds rose from their place by the fire and padded over towards the governor. His eyes were rimmed red and dark bags hung beneath them. "I didn't see you at morning devotions, Kalfinar. Do you still choose to refuse the welcome of Dajda's house?"

Dajda does not welcome me, and I do not welcome Dajda. "I had to visit the physician, my lord," Kalfinar responded. "He needed to apply some ointments and give me a tonic he didn't have last night."

"Good. What was his name again?"

"Aslat, my lord."

"Aslat, I see. I assume he treated you well?" The governor stroked the long head of one the wolf-hounds as it rested on the arm of his chair.

"Very well, though his manner is a touch abrupt."

"Yes, if I recall, he's a bit rough around the edges. You're well matched." The governor laughed a little and poured some wine into a goblet. With trembling hands, he raised the goblet to his mouth and took a long drink. "I've ordered a ship to be readied. A Noehmian trader. It leaves on the evening high tide from West Jetty Twelve. Can't quite remember the name of it. The Sea Ram, or some nonsense like that. Bergnon, you'll be travelling with Kalfinar and Broden. They'll be expecting you back at the High Command in Carte."

Bergnon nodded in approval.

"Good to hear you're coming along. Nothing quite like a winter voyage from Terna to Carte to liven things up," Broden laughed. "And in any case, Kalfinar's humour has shrivelled up these days."

Kalfinar's face remained fixed. He was in no mood for laughter as his mind wandered the docks. *Smoke and blood.*

"Let's move on," Abbonan said as he refilled his goblet with more wine. "Kalfinar, you confirmed last night that the assassin who spoke was Solansian."

"Aye."

"That ties in with the recent intelligence that Major Bergnon brought back with him. Major, would you mind filling the captains in?"

"Certainly, sir. As you know, since I left my role with the attaché in Canna, I've spent the last three years with the High Command administration in Solansia. Superficially, at least, my role was to implement a marshal system in the outlying provinces. With King Grunnxe's government all run out, we were afraid anarchy would rise, possibly even stimulated by those loyal to Grunnxe's regime. My position enabled me to travel, and gather intelligence. Much of the last three years have been spent trying to identify any pockets of troops or individuals still loyal to the old regime."

Kalfinar's eyes fixed on Bergnon as he spoke, but his mind started to wander. *There you are, old king, cross-guard flush to your belly. I remember the fear in your eyes, the stink of you as you shuddered out those terrible breaths.*

Bergnon paused, causing Kalfinar to look up, noting his friend was looking at him perplexed. Kalfinar realised he had been smiling when lost in his thoughts.

"There was nothing, barely even a whisper for the first two years. But then for the first part of the past year, I travelled the length and breadth of the country. As it turns out, chasing not much else but rumour and lie. Then things started to get interesting. Within the last six months, there've been rumours that two of Grunnxe's generals, Traxal and Altyel, were raising troops in the Eastland regions. Word came to me last spring that the pair were surfacing at villages all along the far eastern Salt Coast of Solansia. They were proclaiming the return of the King. That Grunnxe was back to reclaim the green lands of the Cullanain."

"Return?" Kalfinar spat out his words, "That old viper was as good as a dead man!" He slammed his fist on the table. "I should've taken his head when I—"

Abbonan interrupted, placing a calming hand on Kalfinar's forearm, "No. You got him, and then you got out alive. You did your job. Anyone could see that was a killing wound."

"Sorry. Carry on, please," Kalfinar said, controlling his anger.

"I had to be discreet. You know what Solansians are like. Utter one word to the wrong person and they'll hang you high by your own guts."

"I wonder, can you actually hang someone by their own guts?" Broden mused aloud.

"I must admit, when people started to get that look in their eyes, I never really stayed long enough to find out." Bergnon flashed a grin. "I travelled to a village called Yadil, about fifty miles west from Jerras Port along the Salt Coast, in the Eastland regions. Bloody ugly place, full of salt marshes and barren land. Some old, wine-soaked lord worked the region about it until he fell in the last skirmish season. Seems what semblance of farming they had fell apart. The commoners were distraught, and seemed to be in mourning at Grunnxe's loss. I couldn't understand it. What little land that had been fertile became fallow. It was nothing more than a hand-to-mouth existence." He shook his head. "Most of the hands were empty."

Kalfinar spoke up, "It's hardly surprising."

Bergnon looked confused.

Kalfinar explained his meaning, "Under Grunnxe and his forebears the people were treated like shit. Whether crop yields were rich or poor, they went on feeding the war hordes every skirmish season. But that was their system. That is what generations of Solansians were brought up on. The thought that they were doing their part to strengthen the sword arm of their people, to take back our lands was what bound them together. Misery or otherwise, it was their very bond. It's no wonder they were lost, tyranny was as familiar to them as a mother's love."

"To love one's abuser," Bergnon said, shaking his head.

"And to miss them once they've gone," Broden added.

"Exactly my meaning," Kalfinar said. *That I can understand.*

Bergnon continued, "They seemed to establish some order of things in the last year. Then, in the last six months, there were reports of steady growth in patriotism amongst the outlands regions of Solansia. I didn't think too much of it at first. I thought it just the work of small pockets of troops loyal to Grunnxe, left over from the last skirmish season. Small, but motivated, and well organised. I didn't think they'd be able to do us more harm than perhaps mount a minor rebel campaign. Small attacks here and there to disrupt our administration. But the fervour grew. It seethed in places, and almost spilled over to bloodshed against our administrations in some towns. I knew things were getting sticky when reports filtered in from outlying provinces. It was much worse than we first feared. It appears there were many pockets of Grunnxe's forces operating discreetly within the country. They've been responsible for very subtly bringing whole regions of Solansians to arms."

Kalfinar interrupted, "The entire will of the nation has been bent on taking back the Free Provinces, their 'lands departed.' The day we signed our treaties, and stood united as The Free Provinces, Solansia swore an oath to destroy us. It was in Grunnxe's ancestors' blood, it was in his, and it's in the blood of the people."

"National bloody pastime," Broden grumbled.

Kalfinar nodded his agreement. "Did we really think our adminis-tration in Solansia would heal the wound? No, we closed the wound, and now it's festered."

"Well, I wouldn't believe it until I saw it myself," Bergnon said. "I returned to Yadil a month back. Figured I'd best go quietly, so I left my horse some ways back and headed in on foot. And there they were, as clear as water, General Traxal and that weasel Altyel."

"It's a wonder you even recognised them," Broden exclaimed. "The most I've seen of the pair was their horses' arses retreating back towards Solansia."

"True enough, but it was them alright. Same pair of bastards, sure as my shit stinks."

"Didn't think your shit stank," Broden laughed.

"Well, it does," grumbled Bergnon, not taking on the joke. "Traxal did most of the talking, cursing the Free Provinces for the most part. His big blood boiler was saying how we had no right to split from Solansian rule, claim freedom and unite. It really stirred up the masses when he claimed the Free Provinces' green lands were their lands. All crops, metals and minerals within, theirs too. You know, the usual centuries-old sermon. Altyel stood behind him and he was shaking something awful. His eyes were wild, and shifted all around. I think he's a mad one."

"He always was, and hard on the drink." Kalfinar mumbled.

"Aye, maybe so." Bergnon paused for a moment and sipped some water. "Traxal began to talk of taking back control and mentioned how it was almost time. He was pointing through the crowd, asking each man his profession. They all shouted back that they were children of Grunnxe, and soldiers of Solansia. He whipped them up something terrible. Altyel was gibbering, spitting and thrusting his sword into the air. Traxal picked it up again and called for the village to join him on his march to greatness, and in the service of glorious King Grunnxe. He proclaimed the return of the King and that the Free Provinces would pay for the offences of the past. He was shouting that Solan-sian's kingdom would take back what was rightfully theirs, take back control of all the lands of the Cullanain and make it whole again. He claimed that Grunnxe sat on the throne." Bergnon paused, looking at the faces around him. "Traxal said that Grunnxe had been anointed by God."

"Blasphemy!" Broden exclaimed. "They lie in Dajda's name!

Grunnxe is a damned godless barbarian! We know he offers no devotion to Dajda."

"We know," Bergnon interrupted, "but regardless, I'm telling you the entire village went wild again. There were ones crying, exclaiming God was speaking to them. Others were pulling at their hair and wailing with joy. Grown men were on their knees. It was..." Bergnon paused, searching for the correct word. "It was unreal. As if the words were honeyed and those listening intoxicated by it. I'd heard enough to convince me it was getting a little too hot in Solansia. Looked like the tide was rising and this new word needed to get back to the High Command. Have to say, the journey wasn't pleasant. Had this nagging sensation between my shoulders all the way back. You know, that feeling," he said as his face twisted in a grimace.

"There's a crossbow bolt coming." Broden feigned a shudder. "Do you believe Grunnxe is really alive?"

"I wasn't sure. I saw you, Kal, with your sword up in his guts. The old man should've died. But then with these killings, I don't know. He was always clever, and ruthlessness was never a problem for him. I think we need to tread carefully, not rule anything out. I'm just sorry I didn't come sooner. Perhaps some lives could have been saved."

"Don't blame yourself for that, Bergnon," Kalfinar whispered, his voice quiet and hard. "Bottle it up and spend it where it's due. From what we've all seen of late, there's going to be a lot of blood."

Chapter Seven

THE EVENING TIDE carried the ship away from Terna. The powdery black night sky gave way to rain clouds that sagged heavy and low, before unleashing an angry assault of stinging, cold rain on the ship.

Broden had disappeared below deck immediately after boarding, eyeing the dark waters with queasy suspicion. The remainder of the party stood by the port side and watched the lights of Terna dim then disappear.

Thaskil and Arrlun had retreated below deck, leaving Bergnon alone with Kalfinar. "What're you thinking?"

Kalfinar remained silent for a long moment, staring deep into the black nothing before him before answering. "How could they plan assassinations of our most experienced soldiers at Hardalen? At Terna and Carte?"

"You believe more death awaits us at Carte?"

"You don't?"

Bergnon did not reply. He watched the inky water slide by the ship. "You're probably right. Do you still doubt Grunnxe may be behind all of this?"

"It'd take more than Traxal, Altyel, and an army of farmers to kill so many, so fast. But Grunnxe is dead. His lifeblood spilled out over my hands, over my feet. You were there."

Bergnon puffed his cheeks and heaved out a heavy sigh. "If it wasn't for their damned counter, we'd have watched him die with our own eyes. But we didn't, Kal."

"Aye." Kalfinar's voice scratched in his throat as he spoke. "My guts feel like a bucket of eels. Being back in Terna and now making for Carte has me all turned inside out and upside down."

There was a moment of silence between the men. Bergnon broke the quiet, "I received little word when in Solansia. It's just the way it had to be."

Kalfinar nodded.

"But since I returned, I sought word of you. Came close to doing harm to some with loose mouths on a couple of occasions. What happened?" Bergnon asked as he faced his old friend, the rain slapping with fat drops into the sides of their thick, oiled coats.

"What happened? That's stating the fucking obvious," Kalfinar said with a bitter laugh.

"Aye, well." Bergnon replied.

"When I lost her, and the baby." Kalfinar looked to the wet deck and closed his eyes. "I just fell apart. Never felt pain like it. There was nothing anyone could do. Everyone tried, of course, but you know how it goes. Hurt, anger, blame, more hurt. Endless fucking hurt. I'd just lie on the floor at night, or day, sometimes both. It's not like I could touch our bed." Kalfinar turned his face to the sky and sighed as the rain splashed against it. "That feels nice." He sighed a moment as the wetness of the rain cooled the heat from the tears that were building under his eyelids. "Every foot falling outside, to me, was her coming home. Yet every foot falling outside terrified me. Can't remember how or when it really started to unravel fully, but at the beginning I found that wine was enough. I'd drink myself to sickness, and to sleep, at last. After a time, I couldn't block it out anymore. I was just dying every night." He searched Bergnon's face for some shade of compre- hension, even a flicker.

"I understand." Bergnon's face caved ever so slightly.

"Jalsinum rid me of it. It was quick, complete. It made me forget. Made me forget everything. Who I hurt or what ill I caused in that time, I suppose I'll never fully know." He bowed his head and sighed again. With each word, he felt good. Better. "I know I hurt Harruld. I've been told that much. Don't know what the old man will make of me when I drag my arse before him in Carte. As for the rest, who knows? I've heard rumour, whispers, and I've had dreams or clouded memories, all of which fill me with nothing but shame." Kalfinar felt the wet heat rising in his eyes again. Through clenched teeth, he uttered just above silence, "But that weakness within me is as dead now as she is." *It's easy to lie, when your life is nothing more than a ruined shit. Smoke and blood.*

"Don't worry about Carte. I know she'll welcome you back as one of her finest sons. And don't worry about Harruld, he loves you. He's spoken of you warmly when I've been with him."

"Aye?" Kalfinar asked.

"Aye. C'mere." Bergnon grabbed him in a rough embrace.

"Bergnon." Kalfinar grimaced.

"What?"

"My shoulder."

"Ah! Sorry." He released his friend and stepped back.

"So you truly believe Solansia is mobilising? We're headed for another skirmish season?" Kalfinar asked.

"After what the Solansian you killed said, and with your report, I can only assume Solansia is behind this. Whether we can expect a full scale assault like in seasons past, I don't know. I doubt it, but even if Grunnxe is alive, and his force is weaker than in past years, they've struck first, and they hurt us. Badly."

A gruff voice called from the deck behind them, "Captain Kalfinar, sir. Major Bergnon, sir. There's supper being served below deck, if it pleases you." The accent betrayed the speaker.

"Thank you, Arrlun. We'll be down in a moment." Kalfinar sent the formal young lieutenant back below, then pushed off the rail and made for the hatch himself. Bergnon followed. "Without our veterans, it's going to be young men like Arrlun that we'll depend on, regardless of who we face," Kalfinar said.

Bergnon grunted, "I seem to have lost my appetite."

The weather worsened, and wave after wave heaved against the body of the ship as it battled its way through the sea. They sat at the head of a huge upper storage hold. The hold, normally full of rich sheep-fleeces and beef harvested from southern Noehmia, lay empty. Their accommodation was sparsely furnished with a dining area and crude beds. Rough grained wood lined the floor, walls and ceiling. The lanterns at the head of the hold swung with reckless abandon. With no pattern to their vectors, the light and darkness hounded one another across the space ceaselessly. The five men sat around a central table that was bolted to the floor. They ate a meagre supper of watery stewed beef and hard bread on its way to a week past its best.

"I've had better food in the Solansian salt-marshes." Bergnon tossed a fatty chunk of beef onto his plate where it wobbled offensively.

"What is Solansia like, Major Bergnon, sir?" Arrlun probed the captain about the country which spat forth many childhood horror stories for the badly behaved youth of the Free Provinces.

"This light is giving me a headache." Kalfinar slid his plate into the centre of the table and drank the rest of his water. "I'm turning in for the night." He moved towards one of the beds and, being careful not to aggravate his wound, slid under the thin, moth-bitten cover.

"I'll second that!" Broden stood from his chair and stretched out his heavy arms. Both shoulders popped and joints cracked as he did so. "Looks like Bergnon will be up all night teaching the kids about our beloved Solansia." Broden's face appeared drawn and pale, even in the shifting light of the room. "Dampen that light down, would you? Or better still, turn the bastarding thing out!"

"You don't look so good," Kalfinar said as Broden shifted himself in the bed.

The light faded and went out. "Ah, blessed darkness." Broden grumbled. "You know I hate the water. You should've let me ride. By Dajda, I'd sooner have walked over the Hardalen peaks with my pockets full of offal than be on this ship." Broden slid himself under the sheet, the bed creaking under his weight as he turned his back to Kalfinar.

"Are you sulking?" Kalfinar asked his cousin, a faint smile shifting on his bearding face.

Broden said nothing.

"There, there. You'll be fine." Kalfinar smiled again and laid his head onto the straw-filled pillow.

Sleep was slow to come. The straw nagged at his ears and scratched at his neck. Broden's riotous snoring and the faint whisper of Bergnon's voice accompanied Kalfinar until he drifted off. He had not thought about the dreams at all.

The tranquil blackness of his sleep shattered. It exploded into rage and terror, fire and noise. Before him stood a church, wreathed in flames and smoke, filling Kalfinar's mouth and burning his nose from its acrid stink. The smoke scratched his throat and tore at his lungs. Bodies littered the street, surrounded by rubble and blood. Fear gripped at him. He watched as unearthly beasts of claw and tooth ravaged the remains. The monstrous forms before Kalfinar were almost transparent, but for a shifting iridescence to their bodies. His heart pounded. Blood thundered in his ears.

Just a dream! Wake up! Wake up!

He turned from the burning church and from the savage scene before him. Kalfinar shifted his gaze, but again the horror remained, following where he looked, until at last time the vision faded to black. He rubbed at his eyes, they felt gritty and stung.

Fear tugged at Kalfinar's bowels as a form appeared. Before him stood a shadow of smoky greens and blood reds. The colours shifted and blended. Kalfinar strained to make sense of it. It was no use. The being stepped aside and revealed a sight of horror. Before Kalfinar sat a cross-legged body. It was headless and its heart had been ripped from its chest, leaving a ragged hole which glowed bright, and then faded. It sat as Olmat had done when at prayer in Hardalen. Kalfinar's breath was locked within his lungs and an oppressive weight drove into his head.

Olmat!

Kalfinar tried to scream but his voice made no sound.

The shadow settled into the vague shape of a man, tall and broad. A glowing halo burned red around its head. Within the shifting colours of its hand, it held a dripping heart, shooting beams of brilliant white light from between the long, clawed fingers. The figure turned from the headless body and looked directly towards Kalfinar with blazing eyes. Whatever it was, it could see him.

No!

Kalfinar's skin prickled and burned with dread. He was exposed.

The eyes of fire burned, and its mouth was lined with uneven and ragged teeth. The beast roared with the same dreadful sound Kalfinar had heard in previous dreams, a disharmony of voices, chilling and vile. Its black mouth spewed forth a sensation of hatred. It reached out *with clawed and shadowed arms as it pounded towards him. Its knees seemed to be inverted and it walked with an awkward, alien gait. Large wings unfolded from the being's back, stretching out and flexing.*

Breathless, struggling to escape, Kalfinar remained imprisoned in his dream.

Closer still, the beast bore down on him, and he felt the purest form of terror. Clawed fingers extended, almost touching him.

Dajda! Help me!

A blinding explosion of white burned in Kalfinar's eyes and he bolted upright, awake. He was sweat soaked and breathing heavy.

"Kal?" Broden voice splintered the silence of the room.

"Fine. Just another dream."

The ship was steady and quiet but for the odd creak and knock. It appeared the storm had passed.

"I need some air." Kalfinar stepped out of the bed and reached for his fleece-lined oil coat. "Go back to sleep." He wiped the sweat from his brow with his clammy palm, and headed up the stairs.

Reaching the deck, he walked towards the railing along the starboard side of the ship, avoiding the night-crew, and examined the night sky. Peaceful grey clouds rested above him. He released a long, heavy breath. It rasped and shuddered as it made its way free. The cool sea air chilled him as it met his sweat-soaked body.

"My love, help me. I think I'm losing my mind. What is happening to me?"

The night answered with a weighty silence.

A vision of light flashed just beyond his sight, causing him to spin, his hand reaching for his sword. It was not there. He remembered the sword was hanging over his chair below deck.

"Who's there?" Kalfinar gave himself space for combat. "Show yourself," he called out to the darkness, his eyes searching for the slightest betrayal of movement. "Who's there?"

The vision of light flashed once more, almost out of sight behind him. Kalfinar spun around to face it. There was nothing, just the sea, and a couple of wide-eyed crewmen. Whatever it was had gone.

"Seek us, Kalfinar. Hear our song."

A voice echoed all around him, causing his skin to prickle with warmth, despite the chill air.

"Kal, what's the matter?" Broden called from the hatch leading below deck. "Who were you talking to?"

"You heard that voice, didn't you?" Kalfinar's words trembled as he spoke.

"I heard no voice, save for your own."

"You," Kalfinar called to one of the crew, "you heard that. Tell him you heard that."

"Ain't heard nothing, sorry." The crewman said to Kalfinar, before shooting a worried look to Broden.

"You'd best come back downstairs." Broden said. "You've been dreaming again. Come on, you know I can't bear to be up here."

Kalfinar carefully stepped towards the hatch, his eyes searching wildly. "Broden, I think I'm going mad," he laughed as he headed down towards the cabin.

"Nonsense, it was just a dream."

Kalfinar noticed a sorrowful frown upon Broden's face.

You think I'm going crazy too. "Aye, you're right. Just a dream," Kalfinar muttered without conviction as he descended the stairs.

The morning came with a vicious squall, restricting their movements to the hold below.

"Captain, if I may ask, why is it you don't like the sea?" Thaskil asked Broden as the big man sat pale and drawn on the bed.

"You'll upset him." Kalfinar leaned forward from the darkness, an uneasy smile on his face as he looked towards his cousin.

"Have you ever heard of Nyahds?" Broden asked Thaskil.

"Of course, but that's just a scare-story that all parents tell to their children to stop them going near water."

"They're more real than you would care to know. I can assure you," Broden replied.

Arrlun and Thaskil regarded the Captain with wry, disbelieving smiles.

"Lads, I tell you no lies here. One time, as boys, Kal and I set off onto a swamp glade to do some fishing. I fell in, as happens, and I saw shadows in the water. Didn't think much of them and I swam up towards the surface. I'd just about made it to the surface when I felt myself being pulled down again, and that's when I felt the biting. I looked down, and there was this thing biting into my leg, like a small, pale person. Another one bit me by my shoulder. I managed to get the one off my leg and push to the surface. Kal pulled me back onto our raft with the other one still on me, drinking my blood."

"Horrible creatures," grumbled Kalfinar.

Bergnon chuckled as he sat with his chair tilted and heels on the table. "Broden seems to attract the wrath of most animals he meets, lads. When we had our first post with the pathfinders at Hardalen we had a bear cub as a pet. It was a happy little thing, but it would turn savage at the sight of Broden. It was strange. As a teenager, he was the most bear-like human you'd ever see. You'd think the cub would take to him like one of its own!"

Kalfinar chuckled, enjoying the memory.

Broden looked sullen. "That's it, laugh away. But I was lucky. Others weren't. Nyahds used to be more common in freshwater ways."

"Indeed, they did." Bergnon pulled his boot heels from the table and swung his chair in closer as he spoke, "They'd mostly take animals that drank at water: deer, wolves, and livestock. Even people. They feed on the blood, on any blood they can get."

"But Major Bergnon, sir. How'd they get there?" Arrlun asked.

"Just Bergnon. You lads from Ultima North are too formal. I know this is the command, but as we're sat here cheek by jowl, just call me Bergnon. You lads ever heard of sorcery, or magic?"

The two men nodded.

"Good, it appears the advancement of our military curriculum has allowed the expansion of our young soldier's minds." Bergnon winked at Broden and Kalfinar. "There was no such insight in our day, believe me. I was sent for further schooling in addition to my learnings in the academy. Much good that it did me."

"Don't listen to him," Kalfinar said. "What this man doesn't know about the history of the Cullanain, war-craft and politics, is simply not worth the knowing."

"You flatter me too much. Moving on, you should then know that there are both light and dark forms of magic."

Slowly, revealing some uncertainty, the two young soldiers nodded again.

"It's simple, really. Magic is energy. It is an energy force, and a living thing. It exists in the organic and mineral structures all around us. It's the harnessing of this force which is the difficult part, but once harnessed, it can be used in such a way as to distort the world around it. That's what spells are, distortions of the natural arrangements around us, manipulation of the fabric and structure of life."

Kalfinar looked at the puzzled faces of the young lieutenants. "We ought to be teaching this in more detail in the academy."

"How can we harness the energy?" Thaskil asked.

Bergnon continued, "Good question. Dajda, receives our devotion, and in return certain holy men and women, the Tuannan, have the ability to harness some small elements of this energy force. But like the use of any energy, it can be used for ill. In the past, some followed darker ways, and created the Nyahds, amongst other such abominations."

"Sorry, Bergnon, we can't just will these things into existence," Thaskil said.

"Why not? If that which brokers the energy is powerful enough, it can be bent to whatever will or whim the user wishes."

"Do you lads believe in Dajda?" Kalfinar interrupted.

"I attend devotions when I can, Captain Kalfinar, sir," Arrlun replied.

"I've never questioned Dajda's existence," said Thaskil.

"Good, I'm glad our future commanders are so devout." Kalfinar's face bore no pleasure. "If you believe in the existence of Dajda, then you should probably accept the possibility that there were, and are, other Gods. Doesn't necessarily mean they all have our best intentions in mind." Kalfinar's head began to pound. Hammer blows between his eyes and through his teeth. He clenched his fists.

"So they were created by a dark God?" Thaskil pressed the captains before him, "What was their name?"

"Enough talk of Gods!" Kalfinar's temper snapped as he rubbed his head. "Never mind the name, it's of no moment. Whoever used such power is long gone and should not live in the memory or tongues of any man." Kalfinar sat with his elbows on his knees while rubbing his head.

His companions sat between shock and anger.

"That's enough of a lesson for today," Kalfinar continued. "Head up and see if the Skipper needs any help."

"Kal," Broden said firmly after the two soldiers had left the hold. "I accept your position on faith, but you've no right, none whatsoever, to lay insult to Dajda before those boys."

"You'll all be let down," Kalfinar sighed wearily and sat back, sliding outside the light of the cabin. "Dajda will abandon you all, at some point."

"It is not Dajda that has abandoned you, cousin," Broden said in a low tone. His eyes locked hard with Kalfinar's. "Before your days are done, you'll once again let Dajda into your heart."

Chapter Eight

THE SHIP APPROACHED Carte as the sun began its slide towards the horizon. The crew busied themselves tying off the mizzen mast as the passengers, with the exception of Broden, stood at the forecastle. As the harbour of Carte came into clear view a chaotic scene unfolded before them. Ships of all shapes and sizes were bunched up beside one another at the mouth of the harbour. Crewmen could be heard hurling curses as the ships edged their way into yet another slow moving impression of disorder.

"What in the Dajda's name is going on here?" Bergnon snapped with irritation.

"Booms in the water," Kalfinar grumbled. "They've shut the harbour."

They dropped anchor ahead of the boom, alongside another ship. The neighbouring vessel appeared to be a Cannan trader, judging by its long and decorated bowsprit. Alongside the trade ship sat a Port Command gig with a lone marine guardsman on board the craft. His face looked deathly pale before his body jerked and he retched violently over the side, prompting seagulls to swoop down and squabble for the floating remnants of the man's lunch.

"Ahoy, neighbour!" Bergnon called to the nauseated guardsman. "What happens in Carte?"

The sickened guard looked up as he wiped his vomit-covered chin. A mindless look was firmly set over his pale face.

Bergnon turned to his companions and shrugged his shoulders. "I guess he puked up his tongue—"

"Hold your peace, gentlemen," a high-pitched voice cried across from the trade vessel alongside the gig, breaking Bergnon off mid-sentence. "It won't do you any good to question him. The man's a mute. My guardsmen and I shall be across to you in but a moment. Pray thee have some patience." The owner of the voice was a small man who had surfaced at the stern of the Cannan trader. He was surrounded by a large group of marine guardsmen wearing light leather armour and armed with boarding pikes, short swords and naval axes.

"Since when do the harbour masters of Carte travel so heavily guarded?" Bergnon mumbled his question to no one in particular. "Aye, neighbour! You're welcome aboard at your leisure," he shouted across to the harbour master before thumping his gloved fist onto the railing.

A troop of the marine guards boarded the ship, followed by the smaller man. He arrived puffing and red faced after his climb up the rope ladder.

Kalfinar studied the short man, noting several different shades of fading bruises about his face and amidst his short-cropped silver hair. *A busy, and bruising week for a harbour master can mean only trouble within Carte. Damn these days.*

"Good afternoon, gentlemen. I'm the harbour master. Fergin's my name." He flashed a happy smile and took out a small notebook and quill pen. He uncorked a small horn of ink which hung around his neck and dipped the quill before plugging it once more. "Now, let's get to business, shall we? May I ask who you are, and what of your purpose in Carte?"

"What's the hold up?" Broden called out as he made it to the deck, rubbing his eyes to adjust them to the flood of evening light above deck.

The guard nearest Broden lowered his boarding pike. Recoiling on sight of the levelled weapon, Broden drew his sword. As quickly as Broden's sword appeared, the remaining marine guardsmen had their own weapons readied. Multiple sharp points hovered in front of each member of the party.

"What's going on here?" Broden asked.

"Lower your sword," Kalfinar responded calmly as he rubbed between his eyes. "Let's not escalate things any further. I'd say this has gone quite far enough. Don't you?"

"Aye," Broden said lightly. "I'd say this is about as close to sharp metal as I'd like to get tonight."

"Good," Kalfinar sighed.

Broden shrugged his shoulders and sheathed his sword. He smiled at the nervous marine guardsmen, whose own weapons were still levelled toward the group.

"Harbour Master Fergin," Kalfinar said with a gravelly hint of exasperation in his voice. "You must have spotted our military banners flying from each mast. If you or your men had half the wit of a wet turd, you'd know that it is standard practice to display banners when any military party enters an Alliance port. Surely your men ought to approach their comrades with a little mutual respect and a lot more decorum. Wouldn't you say?"

"In ordinary times, yes, indeed," Fergin agreed. "Your banners were seen, however one cannot allow for the city to relax her stand. Should any enemy wish entrance to our capital, then they could simply hang out a banner of the forces. As I said, in ordinary times, we would not be having such a pleasant debate on such a fine evening." Fergin's thin brow knitted and his jaw set firm. "However, things are a quite a bit more tense than usual, and as such, no one can enter or leave the city without approval from the High Command." The harbour master's face eased and he waggled the tip of his quill pen at Kalfinar. "Now, if you would be so kind as to take a seat for a few moments, my good men here will search your ship. Standard behaviour, you understand."

"Of course." Kalfinar said, indicating to his colleagues and crew that they should comply.

"Thank you." Fergin smiled, seeming to relax somewhat. "Now, may I have your names and business?"

An hour passed before the gig returned. As she ran alongside the

Cannan trader, the high voice of the harbour master could be heard in the failing light.

"I'm sorry, friend, but the High Command has refused you entry to Carte. You shall have to port elsewhere and make arrangements for your goods to be shipped overland. It would be wise not to linger here for much longer or you will forfeit your ship. Good day." The silent form of the harbour master could be seen hurrying the rowing marine guards. Moments later obscenities flew over the side of the trade ship.

Rowing the gig with all their might, the marine guardsmen narrowly missed being struck by an arching spray of excrement, and latterly, the bucket that had until recently been its home.

Some moments later, Fergin boarded the ship again and smiled, as he caught his breath. "I'm getting too old, and too heavy, to be hauling myself up and down rope ladders all day." He wiped some sweat from his brow with the back of his trembling hand. "Those bloody Cannan traders. They think because they've so much gold and grain they should be admitted without question. Ghastly folk, throwing their muck at me like that."

"Just beastly," Bergnon muttered.

Kalfinar noted the faint smiles rising on his companion's faces, and the corners of his own mouth tilted somewhat.

The harbour master cleared his throat. "I am sorry for the delay, gentlemen. As I said, times are tense. There is much trouble afoot in the city and we really must be vigilant."

"We understand," Kalfinar responded to Fergin. "We've not been short of it ourselves. May we pass?"

"Indeed, you may pass, gentlemen. The governor has arranged for some horses to transport you to the High Command once you land. You are to head directly to his study, at his command."

Once we land. The docks. The governor. What merry hell do I present myself before?

Kalfinar chased the thought of the docks away, but the hunger gnawed at him. "Thank you. I'm sorry for my lack of courtesy earlier. There's much we need to speak with the High Command about. You understand, I'm sure." Kalfinar grasped the small man's hand as he apologised.

"Tis of no moment to me, Captain Kalfinar. I am but Carte's humble servant." He smiled to the group. "I've heard of you before, sir. You and your companions. I remember hearing of you lads giving

Grunnxe and those Solansian dogs a fierce few poundings during the last few skirmish seasons. You boys are all heroes in my book."

No hero here. Just a bag of blood and waste is all. Kalfinar brushed the comment off with a wave of his hand. "Many men who live can be called heroes, but it is those men who gave up their lives and litter our borders with graves that we should truly honour. It is those boys that never made it home who are heroes." *But I made sure I got home alright, and to do what? Piss and fuck it all away. Smoke it all to oblivion. A true hero. Smoke and blood, whores and mud.*

"My thanks for your help."

The harbour master bade them good evening and returned to the gig that bobbed on the evening tide below. The boom slowly parted and, after the anchor was raised, the ship ponderously approached the deserted docks of Carte.

They trotted through western gate and into the fish and rot reeking dock area of the city. The neat and even cobbled streets of the city centre had long since given way to pot-holed tracks of mud, interspersed with occasional stretches of poorly repaired cobblestones. The buildings were largely of a similar nature. Stone walls rose a foot back from the clogged drains, and were pock-marked with small windows peering out to the street like watchful eyes. After the first ten feet of stone wall, the buildings stretched another two stories, walls comprising of wood and dilapidated balconies. Flaky painted trade signs swung from groaning metal arms, stretching out from the buildings like the tips of ribs sprung from a corpse. Not a soul, ragged or otherwise, walked the dark and dirty streets. Kalfinar could feel the frightened eyes watching them nonetheless.

"There's been some misfortune here." Kalfinar's words were so quiet they were but ghosts under his breath, fleeting and unnoticed.

"Familiar scene, don't you think?" Broden grunted beside Kalfinar, but his thoughts were elsewhere.

I know it's near, I can feel it. Kalfinar stared as they passed a small run-down tavern with a faded sign above its door. He tried to make out the words in the flickering light from the street. The paint was faded and long past its best, but still he felt acquainted with it somehow. As they carried onward a hazy memory washed over him. *The Rooster's*

Goblet. Fine Ales and Wines. Receding further into foggy memory, Kalfinar saw himself as he staggered from the tavern and fall into a torrent of mud and waste streaming down the street. Wasted on drink and jalsinum, he stumbled towards drunks, lashing out at them unprovoked, but missing widely. He then watched as he was surrounded by the men and the mud, being kicked and pounded, his blood mingling with the filth and his decaying life. *Blood and mud. Hero indeed.* He bitterly shook the painful fragment of memory from his throbbing head.

They rode on towards the centre of the city and found the streets broadening out, with fine paving of cobblestones well-lit with more frequent oil lamps. The buildings walls were universally plastered smooth, where the docklands were of bare stone and wood. Ornate wooden carvings of angels and vines clung to balconies, themselves bedecked with boxes of blooms and lit warmly by small lamps.

Kalfinar's eye was drawn to a puncture of light in the darkness of an upper floor window. He saw the face, before it retreated, curtains snapping shut again. For all the feeling of grandeur, the sense of discomforting atmosphere persisted from the docks. It wasn't helped by the imposing castle of the High Command, looming over the surrounding centre of Carte. While passing several streets, they saw city guards forcing their way into houses and shops, barging into doors and searching for someone, or something.

The High Command castle dominated the centre of the city. Its outer walls were built of black stone. They stood tall and broad, shining like obsidian, with one blocky tower enforcing its authority at each corner. The main keep of the High Command stood taller still, its bleak structure staring down on the streets and courtyards of the city that surrounded it.

They rode through the opulent Cathedral sector, one mile from the High Command. Kalfinar could hear Broden mumble a prayer as they passed the shining copper cupola of the Cathedral. *Empty words offered to an empty house.*

The streets widened out as they approached the outer walls of the High Command, giving way to unbuilt ground before the moat. After a quick exchange between Bergnon and the officer of the Night

Command stationed by the drawbridge they gained access inside the outer walls. Once inside, they unsaddled by the stables, and made their way into the main keep, and towards Governor Harruld's private study as instructed.

Kalfinar ascended the stairs and entered the hallway on which the Governor's study was situated. The broad door to the study was flanked by two guardsmen in dress armour. At his appearance the two guardsmen snapped into a salute.

"Nice to see they haven't forgotten us." Broden quipped from behind.

Kalfinar nodded at the guardsmen and knocked once on the door.

"Who is it?" a shout came from the other side of the iron wrought oak door.

"It's Kal."

There was a sound of movement behind the door followed by the sound of heavy bolts. The door swung open with a hefty groan, revealing a tall man, roughly Kalfinar's height. A neat silver beard framed the man's face, and darker grey waves of hair hung on once-broad shoulders. Kalfinar stared at the older man's eyes. They were the same deep green as his own, however the older man's left eyelid drooped low over the eye, and was surrounded by puckered scar tissue.

Kalfinar's breath held for a moment, as he recalled how he had caused the injury. He gathered himself, and broke the silence, "Hello, father."

"Come in, come in," Harruld said, stepping aside and waving Broden, Bergnon and the two young lieutenants into his study after Kalfinar.

Governor Harruld's private study was by no means a small room. Thick wall hangings depicting woodland hunts, blazing with deep red and rich amber, lined the stone walls. Sumptuous green drapes were drawn across the windows and an array of rugs carpeted the wooden floor. The dark staining of the bookshelves reflected the dancing glow of the two roaring fires, which, at opposite ends of the room, spread the much-needed heat well. The focal point of the room, however, was a large and broad table surrounded by a score of chairs. Like Governor Abbonan, Harruld had several large wolfhounds lounging on the rugs before the fire. Their pink tongues curled as they yawned.

"You're well?" Governor Harruld asked Kalfinar as he made his way to the table.

"Well enough. All things considered." Kalfinar stared at the scarring around his father's eye. "Father, I should have written. I wish you to accept my ap—"

"No need," Governor Harruld said, cutting him short. "I have never, nor will I ever, bare you any ill will."

His father's smile, forgotten to him in his lost times, filled him with an enormous ease he had not expected.

"Tell me, Bergnon, how fares Abbonan?" Governor Harruld pulled his chair in at the head of the sturdy table.

"Well enough, my lord. The governor's marriage appears to have injected some fresh life into him. She cannot be all bad, it seems." Bergnon poured himself a goblet of wine and tucked his chair in.

Harruld patted the head of the hound that nuzzled onto his lap. "All bad, no. I would never think that. It's Abbonan who's the scoundrel in this act." The smiles on the faces were feeble, strained attempts at good humour unable to break the cloud that hung over all. "Anyway, gentlemen, let us get to business, lest the hour grow too late. I can feel it off you like a heat."

"Lord, what has happened in my absence?" Bergnon asked, although, like all in the study, the answer was already apparent.

Harruld's jaws tightened, flexing the sides of his beard. "Thirty-seven veterans of merit have been slain."

The sheer number thumped like a hammer blow.

"It's as I feared." Kalfinar's gaze was lost in the fire as he broke the stillness in the room.

"How many?" A look of grave concern fell upon the governor's face.

Bergnon asked, "My lord, have you not received the dispatches from Terna? A ship has long since been due in Carte."

Harruld sighed and rubbed his eyes. "I'm afraid the seas have been very cruel this last week or so. It appears the ship, and the dispatches, have been lost at sea." The governor slammed his fist into the table. "Damn these days!" He looked up and asked Kalfinar, "Have we lost men at both Terna and Hardalen?"

"There have been synchronised attacks at Hardalen, Terna, and now Carte, also. No man was lost at Hardalen. Both Broden and I killed those sent to murder us. We were dispatched to deliver word to both the High Command at Terna and Carte. At Terna, we found that twenty-three had been lost."

A shadow of massive strain seemed to pass over the governor's face. "I have dispatches for you from Commander Lucius, Governor Abbonan and one from Olmat." Kalfinar handed them to his father.

"Sixty men lost. Dajda, help us."

"Make that sixty-two of this whole sorry mess," Broden added. "We lost two soldiers on the road to Terna. A mountain wolf attacked us. Lucius granted us only four men."

"And these two statues, are they the remainder of your troop?" Harruld asked of Thaskil and Arrlun, who stood silently by the doors of the study.

"Lieutenants Thaskil and Arrlun," Broden replied as the two young men snapped to crisp salutes before the governor. "Freshly commissioned by Governor Abbonan."

Harruld nodded at the news. "Good, that saves me some paperwork at least. At ease, men. Well met." Harruld reached for the dispatches. He opened Commander Lucius's first, snorted, balled it up and tossed it over his shoulder into the fire.

"Funny, Governor Abbonan did exactly the same thing," Bergnon mused.

"He's always prized his own neck above all others. He should never hold rank." Harruld then picked up Governor Abbonan's dispatch and read through it, emitting a pinched sound of loss.

"Solskaen?" Kalfinar asked.

"Aye," replied the governor. "I'll present a list of the dead shortly, but with Solskaen lost, it appears I am to assume rank of chief marshal to command the Free Provinces, at least until an election can be held." Harruld's head rested in his hands for several moments as the enormity of his new burden settled upon him. He rubbed his face briskly, chasing away fatigue, and continued with his update, "Several of those targeted managed to avoid the assassins, myself included. Three other assassins fell upon their own blades before we could disarm them, and several more escaped into the city. One of them managed to climb from my window when my guardsmen entered, and somehow make good an escape. That's why you found the city shut to all without high command approval. The escaped assassins may well still be in Carte somewhere. Curse them."

"Did you learn anything of the dead assassins?" Kalfinar asked his father eagerly.

"There's nothing distinguishing about those who died. Of those which escaped, I know not. I've been told they were dressed in all in black and masked, that's all."

"What of the men you killed?"

Kalfinar said, "The men that attacked Broden and I were not of the Cullanain. They were different."

"Different? In what manner?" Harruld started to break the seal on Olmat's report as he spoke.

"They have skin of grey-blue, and eyes of red and yellow."

"Hair of white and teeth in points," Harruld added as he rolled up Olmat's report.

"Yes," Kalfinar said. "There's more. We were attacked a second time by a party as we travelled to Terna. One of those we killed was Solansian. He told us that the true God had risen."

"No more on this here," the governor spoke with unfaltering confidence.

"No more on this?" Kalfinar said, his voice taking on urgency. "We must act! Something, someone has already struck first. This is the first wave. This attack has taken away our control, our nerve. I've stared into the eyes of these things. There's a madness there!" Kalfinar rubbed his head as he spoke.

"We will react, fear not." Harruld responded calmly. "But we must first regroup and then respond in a measured and comprehensive manner." He had finished reading Olmat's report and absently set flame to it with a nearby candle.

Kalfinar noticed the report was consumed in the conflagration, leaving behind a small pile of grey ash.

"What troubles your head, son?" Harruld asked.

"Headaches. Dull, throbbing. Worsening by the day it seems."

"I assume Olmat recommended a physician?" the governor asked.

"Not Olmat, another. A man of Terna, named Aslat."

"I know him." Kalfinar looked up at his father from his hands. "He'll have recommended a good man. Take some rest tonight and visit him in the morning. Once you've returned, we'll hold council and discuss our position." He looked to the two weary young soldiers standing alongside the wall. "I'm sure you feel the need for some good food and a soft bed. I remember you three being as raw as these lads at one point." Harruld looked at the three experienced soldiers before him. "Go on, the lot of you, and get some rest now. I think you'll need it."

They wearily got up, bid their farewells for the night and made for the door.

"Kalfinar," the governor spoke softly, "would you stay with me a while?"

"Gladly." Kalfinar wished his companions good night and closed the door to the governor's study as his father swung the kettle to boil over the fire.

Chapter Nine

KALFINAR WALKED towards Broden's quarters. He rubbed at his temples as his pounding headache returned. *Should've got some bloody rest.*

In truth, he had enjoyed the time spent speaking with his father, and was even happier still for the distraction from sleep. He strode into Broden's room and shook his cousin awake. It was still an hour before sunrise.

"Get off me!" Broden huffed and grunted.

"Come on. It's time to get up."

"Really? And there's me thinking you were trying to squeeze in beside me to cuddle."

"Not likely. I've seen what you call cuddling."

Broden rose with a grumble and emitted a prolonged series of squeaks and cracks as he stretched his massive frame. "You know, I do love our little morning sorties."

"Shut up and get dressed."

"You shut up."

The dawn was damp and grey. Despite being early winter, there was unseasonal warmth, which brought an oppressive muggy feel to the air. This only served to aggravate Kalfinar's headache further. They set off on a pair of unspectacular stable horses, in light of the considerable distance. Although Kalfinar was uncomfortable travelling through the city so conspicuously, he conceded the necessity, and, in any case, the directions kept them far from the main thoroughfares. To aid their passage through the tense streets of Carte, Governor Harruld had provided them with an order of passage.

They were stopped twice by parties of city guards, and asked to present their papers. The sight of armed men provoked interest, regardless of the recognisable dark green uniform of the pathfinders.

"The guards look like they've seen a few rough days of it," Broden said as he watched a troop of haggard guardsmen exiting a tavern they had just searched.

Kalfinar said nothing, and kept his eye on the street and buildings ahead. The wide streets and open spaces surrounding the High Command had given way to more cramped neighbourhoods. The buildings off the main thoroughfares were of a more similar nature to those of the dockland section of town. Walls covered in plaster comprised less than half of the buildings. The first stories were largely made of stone block work, with any further stories built from wood. Most of the buildings reached three or four stories tall, with fresh paintwork of varying muted colours making for a grim scene in keeping with the quiet and overcast morning. Even though the normal time to commence trading had passed, the shop fronts stood bare and empty with no goods presented outside. The mood of unease in the city had clearly damaged the appetite of many to trade. Aside from their own steady progress, the only movement on the streets was that of the scurrying of slick haired rats as they travelled along the street drains and behind sporadic refuse heaps.

Kalfinar scanned the windows ahead. Occasionally, a resident peered out furtively before stepping away. *Just keep your window's closed, neighbour, and we'll have no problems.*

"How much further?" Broden asked.

"We have another couple of turns to make."

They turned into a tight and tall close that reeked of damp and death. The scant morning light barely penetrated to the puddle-strewn cobbled street.

"Nice place he's got," Broden said as he lifted his cloak edge to cover his nose. "Smells like a dead cat."

"Come on." Kalfinar dismounted and led his horse to a tying pole.

Broden did the same and followed on as Kalfinar approached a small, black-stained door. He knocked twice and stepped backwards, onto Broden's foot.

"Watch it!" Broden joked, shoving Kalfinar in the back.

Kalfinar turned around and glowered at his cousin.

The door opened. An old woman dressed in black stood before them. "What'd you want?" she asked, lifting a pair of optics to her rheumy eyes.

"Ahm," Kalfinar mumbled, "we're looking for a physician called Biscon."

The old woman looked them up and down. Her gaze settled on the pommel of Kalfinar's sword, and she made to shut the door.

"Whoa!" Kalfinar shoved his boot into the gap, stopping her shutting the door. "We were sent by a physician in Terna."

The old woman opened the door. "Why should I care?"

"He gave us this." Kalfinar handed the directions to her.

"What was the physician's name?" she asked.

"Aslat."

The old woman made to shut the door again.

"Wait!" Kalfinar shoved his foot in the gap again, and leaned in. He whispered. "He had another name. Capriath."

The door swung open. The old woman handed Kalfinar a small folded square of parchment, nodded, and then shut the door.

"I'm guessing we're back in the saddle," Broden grumbled. "My arse is starting to hurt."

With some significant backtracking, mixed in with several turns, they made their way to the endpoint of the new set of directions. It led them to the north side of the city, an opulent quarter, and home to some of the wealthiest citizens of Carte. The district was richly appointed with manicured gardens, and wide, tree-lined boulevards. Although the onset of winter had rendered the trees bare, they still presented a grand sight. It was of stark contrast to the run-down filth and squalor that made its home by the docks on the west side of the city.

Kalfinar shifted uneasily in his saddle.

"What's bothering you?" Broden asked.

"Not sure," Kalfinar whispered through his teeth, though the wide boulevard they rode down was empty, save for some dour bird's song.

He whispered again, "I have a feeling we're being watched." His mouth became dry and a tense pressure throbbed at the back of his skull. "Can you feel it?"

"I feel nothing but for the rumble in my belly. I'll be wary of your caution though. Come on, let's press. Judging by these directions, the house is only a little further on the right."

As they approached their destination, Kalfinar turned around in his saddle, feeling something approach from behind. He glared up the boulevard they had just ridden down, awaiting the cause of his unease.

Broden stopped his mount. "What now?"

"Something's coming."

On Kalfinar's words, Broden's sword slid from its scabbard and he nudged his mount in line. The barely audible noise of marching could be heard at the top of the boulevard. A platoon of blue-liveried city guards came into view and halted upon seeing two large men with swords drawn ahead of them. The officer of the guards called out an order to dismount and disarm.

"Aye well, your senses are keen alright. Let's hope our brothers-in-arms are in cordial mood this morning." Kalfinar's response was no more than a surly grunt as they dismounted and sheathed their weapons.

The city guard column numbered twenty men. They quickly approached, weapons ready and faces grim. Kalfinar and Broden shifted their long, grey traveller's cloaks, revealing their dark green military tabards, the sight of which visibly eased the tension amongst the guardsmen.

The officer approached and spoke, "Good morning, brothers."

Kalfinar and Broden returned the greeting.

"Tense times, you understand our need for caution. I'm sorry for any intrusion, but we must remain vigilant. I'm afraid when the only folk on the boulevard have swords drawn they warrant my attention. Your name, rank and purpose." Although young, he held himself well and displayed an air of authority.

"My name is Captain Kalfinar, and my companion here is Captain Broden." As Kalfinar spoke, the officer's face revealed recognition. "We carry orders from the governor, and acting chief marshal, allowing our passage through the city unimpeded. As to our purpose, I seek the aid of the physician, for I carry a wound that needs his specialist attention."

The officer nodded in agreement as Kalfinar silently requested permission to reach into his tabard for Governor Harruld's order. He handed it across. The officer read the order and passed it back.

"I am sorry to have detained you both." The young man saluted Kalfinar and Broden.

"It's quite alright," Kalfinar replied. "How fares the search of the city?"

"It fares badly, sir." He rubbed at the back of his neck and sighed. "The townsfolk are displeased with our orders. We're encountering much resistance searching houses and buildings. Many of our guardsmen have been in the infirmary with various bumps about the head, sustained across the city. There're still no signs of any assassins. They'll likely just have blended in with our people." The officer's face betrayed his weariness for an instant, ageing him, before he took a deep breath and puffed himself up once more.

"Perhaps not. They may stand out more than you think. It's well worth the searching. Keep a strong hand…"

"Lieutenant Mikell, sir."

"Well, Lieutenant, perhaps you'll lose fewer men on this boulevard." Kalfinar glanced at his surroundings. "It looks awfully polite here."

Mikell grimaced. "The north quarter has been the worst yet. The rich seem much more precious about their privacy." Lieutenant Mikell half-laughed as he spoke before adopting a look of feigned thought. "Perhaps they're hiding something."

"Perhaps they are. Good luck in any case. We'll bid you farewell." Kalfinar and Broden turned from the party and made their way towards Biscon's gate.

Broden spoke, "Has that laid your mind at ease?"

"Not half." Kalfinar rubbed his eyes. "I still feel uneasy, and my head is throbbing, worse than ever." He squinted as he led his horse into the grounds of Biscon's home.

The grounds were sprawling and well maintained. Despite the flowers of spring and summer having passed, there were several early winter blooms on show. The house itself appeared from the front to be a low, one storied building with a curved white plastered wall stretching around from the front and suggesting it covered a considerable area. Round windows peppered the wall every few feet, with copper frames surrounded multi-coloured glass. Well established rose bushes, clinging on to their last flowers of the season, grew up on trellises against the walls, stretching out to the green slate tiles of the roof. As they moved farther into the grounds, they noticed a high screen of trees growing around the back of the house, behind which was the suggestion of a copper shine.

"I wonder is this master of the house?" Kalfinar asked as he saw a tall man approach from an outbuilding across the lawn.

"I hope he's a bit less of a bastard than the last physician we saw."

Kalfinar stifled a laugh as the man approached.

"My lords, may I help you?" The man was thin with an ascetic appearance and spoke with an accent unfamiliar to them. He wore a sombre grey wool spun habit and black hose.

"Indeed you can," Broden spoke with a broad smile. "I am Captain Broden and this sour fellow beside me is Captain Kalfinar. We seek the aid of the physician, Biscon. We have been directed here by friends."

The man nodded. "The good physician is my employer. I shall take you to see him." He turned and called to a youth who raked the last remaining leaves from beneath a grand cherry tree, "Boy, come take these horses to the stable and tend to them."

The youngster dropped his rake and crossed the grounds to the gathered men with a lolloping gait before he led the horses away.

"He's a good boy, but kicked by a horse at a young age. It's strange, he has no fear of them now, and seems to understand them better than anyone I've seen before."

Broden glanced wide eyed at Kalfinar and puffed his cheeks, unsure what to say. "Well, that's excellent."

"Quite." The man replied. "Follow me," the man said. "I shall take you to my master's study."

They followed the man into the home of the physician. The floor of the house was polished black wood, and the walls were of white washed plaster. They walked in the direction of the rear of the house, passing by several log fires which burned in fire places within comfortably appointed rooms. Upon the walls hung paintings of unusual landscapes and small tapestries illustrating the life of many species of animal. Amongst the countless book shelves stood taxidermy and terrariums containing obscure plants.

The man stopped them in front of a copper plated door. He knocked once and entered the room, leaving the two captains outside.

Kalfinar could feel his brow was beaded with sweat and he panted as his breath started to quicken.

A short moment later, the serving man exited the door. "He will see you." He opened the door for them and they entered, descending a dozen steps down into the room.

The man stood to greet them from behind a huge desk that was covered in books and instruments of science. He wore a night blue gown trimmed with gold silk, fastened around his slight waist with a heavy leather belt. Upon his head he wore a red woollen cap, from which grey hair poked out of the bottom behind his ears. His eyes were unimaginably blue, and his face was deeply lined, like one that had seen too much sun and cold. "Good morning, gentlemen. I am Sarbien. Or as you may have been informed, Biscon. Just a little ruse to keep us all safe, you'll understand."

Kalfinar was struck by the appearance of the man, his features resembling those of Olmat, albeit considerably more vigorous. They exchanged courtesies as they approached the desk and, in turn, grasped the physician's hand.

He moved to show them to a pair of cushioned leather chairs in front of his desk before himself perching upon its corner.

"I'll not trouble you by asking why you have come to me, I know already. How I know, I will speak of that later. Firstly, Kalfinar, please remove your tabard, any mail and undershirts. I must see this wound of yours." With the slightest of limps, Sarbien walked to a cupboard behind his desk and removed a satchel.

Kalfinar stripped off his garments and hung them over the chair. The physician busied himself with the wound, cleaning and binding it with fresh bandages. "Your stitches can come out tomorrow. Olmat is right, you heal with extraordinary pace."

Kalfinar caught the azure gaze of the old man and held it. "You know Olmat?"

"Aye, I know him well, lad." He smiled at Kalfinar, revealing sparkling teeth before washing his hands in the bowl of petal-soaked water beside him.

Kalfinar looked puzzled for a moment. "I could have sworn Olmat said he didn't know you."

Sarbien laughed, "Ah, yes, he would say that. Now put your clothes on and give me what Olmat sent for me." Again, the directness of Sarbien caught Kalfinar by surprise. The physician moved up the stairs towards the entrance of the domed office and opened the door. He whispered something to someone on the other side before closing the door and returning to his chair. "I've sent my daughter to fetch you some refreshments."

"Wonderful," Broden exclaimed. "Misery Guts there dragged me from my bed without even a bite of breakfast this morning."

Kalfinar dressed himself, pulling his undershirt, mail and tabard on. When he was finished, he reached into his travel satchel and removed the jar. The fluid was clouded somewhat from the blood and tissue within. He handed it across to Sarbien.

A few moments later, the soft footfalls behind them indicated Sarbien's daughter had arrived with the refreshments. Kalfinar looked intently at the jar as it rested in the middle of the desk. A pair of pale hands placed a tray on the desk, and the smell of strong coffee swept into his nostrils.

"Gentlemen," Sarbien spoke, "allow me to introduce my daughter, Evelyne."

Kalfinar nodded towards the lady, not paying any particular attention to her. He rubbed the back of his head and heard Broden greet the physician's daughter.

"Sore head, Kalfinar?" Sarbien asked.

"Aye. It's been throbbing at the back and down the front, spreading behind my eyes. It seems to grow worse each day." Kalfinar noticed that Sarbien's bushy brows were knitting.

"What about your sleep, lad, have you been getting much of that lately?"

Broden remained silent, observing his cousin with concern upon his red-bearded face.

"I've not slept much since I joined the garrison at Hardalen. Lately, it's gotten to be much worse."

Sarbien opened a cabinet behind his desk. It was filled with shelves of glass jars, all filled with multi-coloured powders and substances. He stretched and selected a small jar with a pink powder. He gathered a small measuring spoon and placed one level scoop of the powder into a coffee cup in front of Kalfinar. "Take this. It will sooth the pain."

Kalfinar gratefully drank the bitter mixture and began to take in the nature of the room. The floor was set several feet below the level of the rest of the house, and the walls rose from the floor into a dome. They were entirely coated in copper and windowless. "I hope you don't mind me saying so, but this is a most unusual room, Sarbien," Kalfinar voiced his observation.

"It is my private study. What happens within it is of the highest importance and none who have ill intent must learn of what is spoken. It is very safe." Sarbien smiled to both Kalfinar and Broden as though he had shared a great joke with them.

Kalfinar looked intensely at the physician, not sure how to take his response.

Sarbien continued, undeterred, "As you will both no doubt be aware, there are acts in motion that are beyond your understanding." He pointed a long, wrinkled finger towards the murky jar on the desk. "You seek answers and if you but wait a short while longer, you shall have them."

Pain hammered at the inside of Kalfinar's head. "Wait longer! That's all I damn well hear these days. All this time we are waiting for answers, our friends and our countrymen are dying around us. Someone had better start giving me some fucking answers. Who in the darkness are these people?" He pointed towards the jar, his nostrils flaring with frustration. "Damn it, I don't even know if we can call them people!" Kalfinar looked at the blue gaze of Sarbien, and suddenly felt the impotence of his fury.

Sarbien said, "You can trust me entirely. The forces that work against us have many agents and many means to glean our understandings. This room is secure from most things, but there is another place which is said cannot be breached, by any means whatsoever. It is in this place that we must discuss fully the detail, but that place is not here. This night, at midnight, visit the cathedral. You will find a monk at prayer within the vestry. His name is Brother Anthony. He will lead you to the room I speak of, there you will learn the truths. Until then, my sons, you must have patience in your hearts, and caution in your minds."

"That's twice now we have been asked for trust from those unknown to us, physician," Broden spoke.

"I understand your concern. Admittedly, I do not know you, Broden, but I know Kalfinar."

The two captains' eyes narrowed.

"I was present at his birth." Sarbien looked at Broden as he spoke. He then shifted his blue eyes across to Kalfinar.

"At my birth? Sarbien, I think now's the time for some answers," Kalfinar growled.

"Tonight, gentlemen. Tonight." The old physician stood, indicating it was time for them to leave.

Somewhat hesitantly, Kalfinar rose and left the study.

———

"This whole situation stinks of something, Kal," Broden grumbled as they rode out of the house grounds.

"It stinks alright, but I think he's sound." They exited the gate onto the boulevard again. "Did you notice he looked just like Olmat?"

Broden grunted in agreement.

As they exited onto the boulevard, the column of city guards exited the grounds of a large house across from them. A red-faced man wearing a silk nightgown chased them out, swinging an ornate fire poker.

"Looks like those lads are having a rough time of it." Broden inclined his head towards the retreating guards.

Kalfinar did not respond.

"Kal?" Broden looked across at his cousin. Kalfinar was bent over on his horse, his head in his hands and hair falling down over his face.

"Something's coming," he hissed between clenched teeth. "Someone is watching. It comes!" His voice rose to a shout and an inhuman noises rose from his throat.

Kalfinar bolted upright. His body stiffened and jolted in his saddle. His hands were clutched at the sides of his head and a look of agony squirmed in his tear-streaked face. A sharp cry of pain erupted as his eyes rolled white and dark blood streaked out his nostrils and down his chin. He lurched forward and jerked stiffly upright once more, his hands still fixed to his head, before falling rigid and heavy from his horse into the dirt.

Chapter Ten

WITH THE HELP of Lieutenant Mikell and several of his guardsmen, Broden had Kalfinar brought, thrashing amidst his fit, into Sarbien's study.

"Put him down here," Sarbien directed them to an examination table situated to the side of his desk.

They held his kicking legs still before strapping them down. Kalfinar's hands remained locked to the sides of his head with such force that Broden, even with the help of the guardsmen, was unable to part them. Instead, they strapped his abdomen and chest down, whilst two guards held his arms, should they fly loose and strike out. His jaw was locked and teeth clenched. Spit and foam squeezed through the teeth, onto his stubbled chin. Though his eyes were shut, tears found their release and streamed from his face.

"Everyone but Evelyne, leave the room at once! And shut the door." Sarbien's barked.

Lieutenant Mikell and his guardsmen reacted and hurried out of the room.

Broden made to question, but stopped short when hit with a sudden, icy glare from the physician.

"This room will no longer be safe for you, or anyone else. Leave at once!"

Broden looked in horror as Kalfinar fought against the restraints.

Veins bulged in his reddening face and the cords of his neck strained beneath his skin. Kalfinar's head thrashed and battered against the examining table. The white froth from between his teeth merged with the dark blood that streamed out his nose.

"Save him," Broden said.

"Go now!" Sarbien replied.

Once the room had emptied, Evelyne looked up at her father. "It happened much sooner than we thought."

"Too soon," Sarbien replied, his face grim. "It must almost have him. We'll need to be quick if we're going to save him. Remember your training, my dear. This is no place for doubt."

Evelyne placed seven opaque vials upright on the floor around the examining table. Her movements, direct and exact, were well practiced. She poured a clear powder in the space between each vial, connecting them and enclosing Kalfinar and Sarbien inside the circle.

Sarbien sat cross-legged at the head of the table. His eyes were shut and his open palms rested upon his knees.

Evelyne mirrored her father's position at the foot of the table, but outside the circle.

Sarbien prayed rapidly and Evelyne repeated his silent words.

Their soundless prayer entered and flowed around the circle. Each vial began to shimmer, like dust motes ablaze. The flashes swelled in size and duration, growing stronger, brighter and more powerful with every repetition of their prayer.

With hands still pressed to his head, Kalfinar's body lurched and fought against the restraints.

Sarbien and Evelyne spilt out the words of their prayer at greater speed. The glow spread from the core of the vials, growing so powerful it illuminated the room with brilliant white light.

Kalfinar's thrashing continued, spit and blood spattering over his body, the table and the floor. Juddering, agonised moans escaped from between gritted teeth. One of Kalfinar's legs ripped free from the leather strap, allowing it to rattle and flail as his thrashing worsened.

The thrashing stopped, and his body lay motionless.

Evelyne looked at her father, not quite able to see him, so bright

was the light from the vials. She could sense that he had stopped praying. The light began to fade away.

Kalfinar's chest rose and fell peacefully as he breathed, the room
now still.

"Has it happened?" Evelyne asked.

Sarbien remained fixed in his pose of prayer, his busy brows
furrowed in thought. "I'm not sure. Normally, there's a more obvious
release when—"

Kalfinar's head snapped back, pushing his jaw upwards. His
fingers snaked into his hair and dug into his scalp. Bright blood ran
down his fingers. Spit and cries shot between his peeled back lips and
clamped jaws.

Sarbien and Evelyne resumed their chanting with ferocious
urgency. This time, their voices rang out loud in the room. The glow
from the circle of vials sparked alive. The light grew, illuminating the
room with a brilliant whiteness once more, and then disappeared.

Kalfinar's cries warped and bubbled with the guttural screams of
another, an alien voice bound within his own. The unnatural cacophony
sounded with painful volume. His jaws unlocked and he took one
mighty, ragged gasp of air.

They continued chanting at a frenzied pace. Sweat and pained
effort marked the face of Sarbien as he sat within the circle.

Kalfinar's eyes opened wide and he released a short and chilling
scream. There was none of his own voice in it. The powder between
the vials erupted in a blinding flash of purple flame and Kalfinar's cry
cut off. His arms fell limp at either side.

A formless howl erupted around the room when a stinging wind of
heat and fear flashed by each of their faces before disappearing,
leaving the room in uneasy silence.

Kalfinar's sweat-drenched head rolled to one side, his eyes
vacantly staring to where Evelyne stood, beyond the circle of purple
flame.

"Where is it?" she whispered to her father as he rose.

"Look at me, child," Sarbien whispered to her. "Keep your eyes
on me."

"Where is it?" her voice trembled.

"Up by the ceiling, behind my desk." Sarbien's voice was barely
more than a whisper. "Don't look at it. We must protect Kalfinar first."
He silently incanted a short phrase and opened his palm, within which

appeared a small spherical amulet made of a copper-like metal. He lifted Kalfinar's head and placed the small amulet around his neck. "There, he's safe," Sarbien whispered to his daughter. "You know the prayer." Sarbien turned to face the unseen form cowering near the ceiling behind his desk. His lips parted in preparation for the prayer. "Spirit—"

"Kal!" Broden burst into the room.

"No!" Sarbien cried as the unseen spirit flashed between he and Evelyne, sending a spray of papers in the air and wailing banefully as it flew past Broden and out of the room.

"You damn fool!" Sarbien roared. "You've no idea what you've done!"

"I'm sorry, my lord," the serving man said following Broden into the room. "I tried to stop him, but he was too strong."

"He couldn't have known, Father," Evelyne said.

"What's happened? Is Kal alive?" Broden hurried down the stairs and into the room.

"He's alive," Evelyne said.

"Why in Dajda's name did you enter?" Sarbien asked of Broden.

"There was screaming and then silence. I feared he was dead."

Sarbien heaved a sigh and shook his head. "The spirit won't stop hunting him now it has his taste." He muttered a single word and the glowing vials shimmered briefly, and then were as they had been before the prayer had been uttered.

The circle of purple flame receded and spluttered out, allowing Evelyne to step forward. She softly closed Kalfinar's vacant eyes.

"Fetch some water. His body is parched now," Sarbien ordered the serving man.

Broden moved beside Evelyne. "How is he?" His voice was low.

"He'll be fine, but he needs rest."

"What was that thing?"

"The servant of another. A spirit. It's gone now."

"Will it come back?"

"It will. At some point."

"You are Tuannan? You, and your father?"

Evelyne ignored Broden's last question. "I think you should inform the governor. Go and tell Harruld, and then come to the cathedral tonight. This place is sullied now, and no longer safe."

Kalfinar stirred. His throat was dry and his limbs felt heavy. Yet, for the first time in weeks, his head did not hurt and his mind felt clear. He opened his eyes, but the world around him was clouded, full of hazy shapes and shades. He closed them and tried to focus on his other senses. Dim voices edged around in the darkness. Kalfinar concentrated his efforts on them. As they grew clearer, he recognized the physician's voice.

"It happened much quicker than we thought. One of them found him and was searching deeper. I fear it almost had him fully. We must be quick to—"

"Enough. He stirs."

The sounds of shuffling feet approached Kalfinar as he opened his eyes and sought focus. Nothing but clouds and colours still. "Why can't I see?" His voice was hoarse, and the words scratched at his throat. A hand cradled his head and tilted a cup of water to his dry lips.

"Your sight will return in but moments." The clouded figure standing before him came into focus as her soft, accented voice spoke. Form appeared in a flash and was lost again. He saw remarkable eyes, and was asleep once more.

There were no dreams of dread and hate. Instead, Kalfinar dreamed of his wife and their child. Their daughter was unnamed in her short life, and unnamed still in his dreams. His heart ached with joy. It ached with regret. A life unnamed, and unknown. All he knew was the face was constructed by his own heart's imaginings, and there was no point in naming a fantasy. He cursed Dajda, the one who stole them from him, and dreamt of the happiness he had once felt. No, his dreams were not filled with dread or hate, but they were cruel nonetheless.

Kalfinar awoke.

His eyes opened, focusing on a woman standing before him. She had ice-blue eyes and a pale face. She smiled, though it was clear it was forced. Her brown hair was pinned to the sides and flowed down the back of her head. She wore a simple green gown, bordered with delicate patterns, with an undyed cotton apron tied down her front.

"Hello, Kalfinar," the woman spoke. "My name is Evelyne. I am Sarbien's daughter."

"I remember," he lied. "Hello," his voice croaked.

"You must drink more, here." She handed him a wooden cup of water. "I'll fetch my father." She left the room, shutting the door behind her.

Kalfinar levered himself onto his elbows and looked around him. He was in a small room with one window. It was dark outside. In moments, a shuffling sound came to the door and Sarbien entered. The old man's face cracked from its morose appearance into a wide smile.

"Glad you're awake, lad. How do you feel?"

"Weak, but my head feels as though it was washed clear. What happened?"

Sarbien did not answer.

Evelyne entered and provided extra pillows to keep Kalfinar propped up. As she lent in to place them behind him, he noted she smelled of garden herbs. He shook the thought from his head and focussed his attention on Sarbien.

"Never mind that for now. We must make for the cathedral soon. We have some friends waiting there, and we have much to discuss this night. Do you feel fit to make the journey?"

"I think I can ride." Kalfinar swung his legs out of the bed and stood, swaying like a drunk as he tried to pull on his boots.

"Sit, I'll help you." Evelyne bent to her knees, helping to slip on Kalfinar's boots. He neither looked at her, nor did he offer thanks.

They made their way to the rear courtyard of Sarbien's house. Three horses were saddled and waiting, as were several darkly clad men. Men who held themselves like those who knew the weight of a blade.

Sarbien glanced towards Kalfinar as they sat on their mounts, awaiting departure. "Worry not, these men are friends." Sarbien looked to the surrounding men. "You want answers, well, you'll find them tonight. Though you may wish it were otherwise." His tone was ominous, and Kalfinar's skin began to prickle.

They had been riding for twenty minutes, cautiously negotiating the lamp-lit streets of Carte. Kalfinar measured the shadowy figures who accompanied them. Their eyes were alert, searching shadows and flickering light for the slightest movement.

Kalfinar's guts felt heavy, a sure sign he was in the midst of trouble. He regarded Sarbien and his taller daughter. The words the old man spoke when Kalfinar regained consciousness troubled him. What had found him, and why was someone, or something, searching for him? The weight in his stomach began to burn.

It was a familiar sensation, a warning.

Kalfinar's mouth dried. Movement flashed to his right; something running along the rooftops and leaping from building to building.

"Rooftops!" Kalfinar roared.

Another movement drew his eye to an open window.

"Ambush!"

"Go!" one of the armed escorts shouted. As he cried out, there was a sudden snap of cord.

The sound of a bolt meeting a shield rang out behind Kalfinar.

Evelyne kicked at her horse and rode alongside Kalfinar, her chest flat along the shoulders of her mount.

Kalfinar risked a glance behind to see the guardsman whose shield caught the crossbow bolt falling stiff from his horse. He glanced at the rooftops, but the figure had disappeared.

"Get to the cathedral!" Sarbien roared behind them.

The whistle of another bolt sped through the air.

The cry from behind warned that another of the escorts had fallen.

Kalfinar drove on and leaned low in his saddle.

The figure from the rooftops leapt onto the street ahead and pulled back an arm. Even in the poor light, Kalfinar could see the throwing knife. Kalfinar gritted his teeth and thrashed his horse with all the strength he had, driving his mount over the figure and trampling it beneath its steel-shod hooves.

Another party of armed horsemen appeared in front of them.

Kalfinar pressed his knees into the horse and drove forward to meet the advancing party. He pulled free his sword from its scabbard.

"Kalfinar," Sarbien shouted. "They're ours."

Kalfinar lowered his sword just before the party of horsemen thundered past, toward the hidden enemy. Sarbien, Evelyne, and Kalfinar pressed their horses through the city streets until, at last, they entered the large cobbled square in front of the cathedral. A pair of tall, square-topped towers rose heavenward above the arched entranceway. The copper sheen of the huge cupola glinted between the towers in the faint starlight.

"Keep your pace steady and get inside. The agents of the enemy cannot follow within," Sarbien shouted as they rode across the square. Without another word, he peeled away and rode back to where they had come from.

Kalfinar slowed his horse and glanced behind at Sarbien. "Where's in the hells is he going?"

"Kalfinar," Evelyne called from the gates of the cathedral. "Hurry. There is no time."

He snapped his head towards her, and, with one more glance towards Sarbien, he turned and kicked his horse onwards. They passed through the gates of the cathedral together, their horses gasping for air as they reined in.

Evelyne leapt from her horse and sprinted up the steps into the ancient cathedral. "Kalfinar," she shouted. "Come now!"

Kalfinar jumped from his horse, stumbled, and made his way inside the massive entranceway towards Evelyne.

"Don't worry about my father. He's safe." Her face was calm, but her voice had a hard edge to it. "You however, are not yet afforded that luxury. When he gives you an order, obey it, unless you'd prefer a bolt in the back."

Kalfinar looked at her with astonishment. It had been almost three years since a woman had reprimanded him in such a manner. He found it strangely comforting, and then he felt the familiar sting of grief. "You're right. Sorry." His reply was quiet.

She shook her head before heading deeper into the cathedral, calling back as she went, "Hurry, Brother Anthony will be waiting."

The cathedral was lit by many lamps, which glowed from rings along the wall. They walked between soaring, copper-plated columns and towards the dais at the back of the cathedral. Passing beyond two pairs of heavy oak doors, they crossed a flag-stone-lined corridor to the vestry. It was well lit by lamps and candles.

A young man sat by a large brass candle stand reading some parchment, lips moving as he read. It was clear he had not heard their approach.

"Brother Anthony."

Despite Evelyne's soft voice the young holy man was startled.

"Evelyne, Captain Kalfinar. Forgive me. I didn't know you were there." He rose as he spoke, placing the parchment on his stool.

The youthfulness of the holy man's face surprised Kalfinar, as did his resemblance to Evelyne. Brother Anthony also had ice-blue eyes. His heavy, woollen habit was tied around the waist with a simple twisted-cord belt and he wore simple sandals on his feet.

Brother Anthony embraced Evelyne and kissed her on the cheek.

"Come, we must be with the others. They're waiting." Brother Anthony shuffled past them.

Kalfinar and Evelyne followed behind the brother as he walked through the dimly lit corridors. They ascended a small, tight wooden staircase towards the back of the cathedral. Step after step, round and round, they travelled before coming to a well-lit landing leading to the cathedral's cupola.

Brother Anthony led them to a set of large double doors, gilded in copper and patterned with intricate symbols and several brilliant seraphs surrounding a rising sun

Kalfinar felt he had seen them somewhere before.

"They seem familiar to you don't they?" Evelyne asked.

He glanced towards her.

"There is much you will find has a resonance within you, though you are not aware of it, yet. It is buried deep." Her words caused an unease to creep into his bones.

"Come," Brother Anthony broke the silence and placed his hands on the large door handles.

Kalfinar saw the assassin behind the door as it opened. He leapt past Evelyne and Anthony, his sword hissing from its scabbard.

Chapter Eleven

KALFINAR THRUST, engaging the dark figure within the antechamber. The blood pounding in his ears muffled the shouting around him. He advanced. Steel clashed and rang as his foe parried and conceded ground. The straining face before him mirrored those of the would-be assassins from the mountain garrison at Hardalen. Blazing eyes peered out at Kalfinar from pallid blue-grey flesh. *Like the skin of a drowned man.*

"Enough," the being said, deflecting a thrust and conceding more ground. "I'm not your enemy." The being held one palm out. "Stop this."

Kalfinar glared and held his ground. "Your kind do speak. Save your words, demon!"

Evelyne stepped beside Kalfinar. Applying gentle pressure to lower his sword arm, she spoke, "Kalfinar, he speaks the truth. He's not your enemy. Chentuck is kin to Anthony and me. He means you no harm."

"Kin? This is no man!" Kalfinar spat.

Chentuck sheathed his weapon and stepped back.

Evelyne pushed Kalfinar's sword arm down yet further. "Granted," she raised her voice, speaking into the darkness with irritation, "it's a bit regrettable that Chentuck be here when we entered."

"Sorry about that." Chentuck said in a flat tone, his eyes still fixed on Kalfinar. "Bad timing."

"I don't understand." Kalfinar was less sure of himself, though instinct forced his grip to remain firm on his sword. He glanced towards Brother Anthony as he approached and embraced Chentuck. "Anthony is your Brother?" Kalfinar asked, eyes darting between the figures before him.

She nodded. "Please, put away your sword, dear." She released his arm. "I understand you're confused. Trust me, you're amongst friends."

Chentuck nodded.

Kalfinar said, "I've killed your kind before, demon, and I am ready to do so again." His eyes never left Chentuck as he sheathed his sword.

"Kalfinar," Evelyne snapped, "you'd do well to fear the sight of men such as this, but Chentuck is not deserving of that same fear. Instead, he merits your respect and trust. Count him amongst your dearest allies. Now, enough of this. The others are waiting. Perhaps your scorn will be cooled when you hear the words they will serve you." Evelyne huffed out a frustrated breath before making for the doors at the far end of the antechamber.

Brother Anthony inclined his head towards the doors. "Come, Kalfinar."

Kalfinar could not stop his arm from shaking as the young man guided him. *Do you feel my fear? Can you feel it all?*

Kalfinar and Anthony entered behind Evelyne and Chentuck. The room was dark, and the blackness obscured any sense of space. Kalfinar's hand sought the hilt of his sword.

"Be at peace," Brother Anthony whispered as he squeezed Kalfinar's elbow.

Kalfinar eased his sword arm, but his hand hovered close to the pommel still.

"Forget your sword," Evelyne ordered. "No harm will come to you."

"Kalfinar, do what you're told," a familiar voice called out of the darkness. "The lady has assured you. You're amongst friends." *Father?*

Suddenly, the room was illuminated as dozens of oil-torches flashed to life along its pale stone walls. The floor was of polished wood, lightly stained and reflecting the flicker of the torches which burned from the rough surface of the tall stone walls. Atop the stone walls shone the underside of the huge copper dome of the cupola.

A man leaned casually against the wall before him. He was tall, with a greying beard and eyes of the same deep green as Kalfinar's. The man's left eyelid drooped low and was surrounded by puckered scar tissue.

"Father? What's going on?"

"Answers are coming, Kal. They're coming."

Kalfinar's eye twitched with irritation. *One more time. I swear, one more fucking plea for patience and I'll scream.* He took a deep breath and tried to settle his nerves. "What is all of this?" Kalfinar asked Harruld. "Magic?"

"There are many things you haven't been told, Kalfinar, and believe me, for very good reason."

Kalfinar fixed him with a flat stare.

"I presume by now you're growing sick of people telling you that," Harruld said with a grimace.

"Just a little," Kalfinar grumbled. "Are you Tuannan?"

"Me? No. I'm just a cog in the wheel. There are others who are the masters of the machine. Come. I'll introduce them." Harruld led Kalfinar towards the rear of the hall. He leaned close to Kalfinar and whispered in his ear, "Excuse the dramatic flourishes. Capriath's doing. Now please, Capriath."

"Capriath?" Kalfinar asked Harruld in shock. As he spoke, a horse-shoe-shaped table appeared before him. Sat around the table were several faces familiar to Kalfinar.

"You've met Olmat's brothers, Capriath and Sarbien. Of course, Olmat and Broden need no introduction. Broden of course is as much in the dark you as."

Kalfinar regarded the faces of Olmat, Capriath and Sarbien. "Brothers. I should've tied it together."

"You always knew we were kin," Olmat said. "It was just that we, shall we say, encouraged you not to make that particular connection." The old physician grinned towards Kalfinar, weaving his fingers together over his stomach. "Call it a gift we Tuannan share."

"Magic casters? Since when? How?" Kalfinar's stomach rolled, and his mind raced.

Olmat nodded. "We are Tuannan," he croaked out in a laugh, "and have been for a very long time. As for how, well, we asked Dajda for it. We've been gifted by knowing how to ask, and we were blessed by being answered."

Kalfinar's mind flushed with heat. "And your travel to Carte?"

Olmat waggled a single figure at Kalfinar. "Well that is not quite a gift shared by all of us. That one I've spent an awful long time learning in order to master, and it's one I fear I'll no longer be able to practice, for it's costly to one as old as I."

Kalfinar looked across the faces sat before him. A realisation clicked into place. "The dreams are real, aren't they?"

His gaze settled upon his father's face, and then that of Olmat. He glanced at the grim expressions of the two physicians, Capriath and Sarbien. They nodded. A rush of hot vomit burned in Kalfinar's gullet, though he fought the urge to spill it, and regained his composure.

Harruld said, "We've known that such dreams were possible. We've seen it many times in the past. They are a precursor, a warning of something dreadful, normally a possession by a spirit. However, sometimes, they can forewarn death. A spirit tried to take you. We fear it may have a link to the assassinations, though we cannot yet place it in the scheme of things. If it links, it may mean this is more than just militaristic."

The hot urge struck again, and this time Kalfinar could not resist. He wretched and heaved, but his guts were empty and had nothing to spend.

Harruld bent and offered a cloth as Kalfinar stood with his hands on shaking knees. "Come, sit with us," Harruld said as he guided Kalfinar and the others to empty seats.

When everyone had taken a seat, a dozen hooded figures dressed in grey habits entered the room. Their habits were similar to that worn by Brother Anthony. Each holy person took up a position facing the wall at even distances around the room. They stood so close to the walls that their faces almost touched the stonework.

When they were each in place, like statues of ancient heroes, they began to chant, in unison in a language unknown to Kalfinar. "What are they doing?" he asked.

Olmat responded in a thin, dry voice, "Now that we've all arrived, they are barring the way for any unwanted eyes, ears or bodies. This room will be sealed to all but those within the barriers being erected by our brothers and sisters."

Olmat offered Kalfinar a smile, though it looked forced. Kalfinar sensed the old man was uneasy.

"This is a dangerous time in our proceedings, lad," Olmat continued.

Harruld cleared his throat and spoke, "Some of what we will discuss tonight will shock you, Kalfinar, yet much of it will seem natural to you. Like a forgotten memory brought once more to the fore. Nurture that familiar feeling, and acceptance of what we teach you will come much easier than without."

Kalfinar looked towards Broden. His eyes were fixed on the table. As Kalfinar beheld him, the larger man met his gaze, and then focussed on Chentuck.

Kalfinar spoke, "Can someone answer me this? How does it come to be that this assassin is allied with me?" He pointed his finger in the direction of Chentuck, who sat at the opposite side of the table to him.

Chentuck showed no offence, but his eyes remained on Kalfinar before glancing across the table. "One of you better explain it. He's not going to believe me. Fair enough, really."

Sarbien stood, his chair scraping backwards on the wooden floor. He walked towards the strange being sat at the opposite end of the table. "Kalfinar, believe me when I say that no one here will lie to you."

Funny, seems like you've been lying to me for the last bloody week.

Sarbien carried on. "You feel as though you've met me only this day, but, in fact, I have known you your whole life, and you are most dear to me."

Kalfinar nodded. "Go on."

"The man before you is my son. My adopted son." Sarbien stood behind Chentuck and rested a hand on each shoulder. "The blood in his veins is that of humankind, for his people are as much man as you or I. Despite that, he appears strange, but that is borne of no malice whatsoever, merely an adaptation to the environment of his people. He was born of the Ravenmayne, the same race as those who tried to kill you and Broden. But Chentuck is different, and he is not to be feared by you."

"Ravenmaynes?" Kalfinar looked towards Sarbien in puzzlement, though a heat passed over him as he spoke the name. "I don't know this name. What are these people, and why are they intent on killing us? What ill have we visited upon these men to merit such wrath?"

Sarbien walked back towards his seat and whispered with Olmat who nodded.

"You know there's much good in the world," Olmat said, his voice sounding frail, "but alongside it runs a course of malice. This has always been the way, for without one and other, there would be such a level of inequity as would tear at the seams of the very fabric of our world and lead us into darkness and cold. The Forevernight, the nothingness."

Kalfinar nodded in response. "The Tuannan. The magic casters." He swept his hand around to the hooded beings who remained motionless facing the wall as their chants hummed in the background. "I understand that the Tuannan are on one side, and there are similar beings running the dark course."

"Yes. Well, almost," Olmat replied. "You've known the basics of this for a long time, but it is the level of knowledge which needs fortifying. Those who know even a little are gifted a wisdom that few hold, but even that level of knowledge lacks fibre. The Ravenmayne are amongst the best killers this world has ever seen, or not seen, as the case was. Their ability to go unseen has led to their presence on this world going virtually unnoticed until you and Broden killed the two at Hardalen. They are aided by an unsettling power gifted to them by a particularly ruthless entity. It is my most honest wish that I knew nothing of this monster, but it is a reason for my being. The Ravenmayne are the children of this being. The name is Bhalur."

Chentuck made a sign of protection over his heart at the mention of the name.

Olmat continued, "Bhalur is the Ravenmayne God. Although we thought it was impossible, it appears Bhalur's will is bent on reaching out to you. Be assured, lad, to whatever end, that cannot be good."

The spirit repeated its effort to breach the cupola, but again the protective wards barred the phantom's entry. The spirit shrieked in frustration and terror.

The master sensed its struggle and would undoubtedly punish the failure.

Yet another maddened assault ended with a defeat. The spirit hovered high above the cathedral, desperate to access the cupola.

The master's will urged it forward.

Terror plagued the spirit as it desperately screamed around the dome, seeking a weakness through which to breach the protective ward. The spirit circled again and again, landing briefly to crawl, sniffing for a weakness. There was none.

Chapter Twelve

"I'M SOUGHT BY A GOD." *Quite ironic, given I've been abandoned by my own.* "Why do I merit such attention?" Kalfinar asked Olmat.

"You have certain, qualities," the old physician replied.

A wild howl resounded around the expansive roof, a twisted scream of pain and frustration.

"What was that?" Kalfinar asked. His hand reached for his sword.

"Be at ease, Kalfinar," Olmat said. "One of our enemies tries to access our sacred place, but it cannot. The way is barred. Our wards protect us." Olmat indicated towards the robed Tuannan who muttered chants around the edge of the great room. The old man flicked his wrist and an undulating green wave of iridescent light was visible. Like a spectral fire, it engulfed all edges of the room. With another flick of wrist, the light vanished. "It's the same spirit that had been cast from you. It will continue to seek you now."

"Back to the question of why me?" Kalfinar asked, anxiety taking life in his words.

Harruld rubbed the back of his neck. "Some of what we know is fact, but most we must project from our current understanding and draw assumption. We thought such power and reach was beyond Bhalur. We thought we had caged him, but if Bhalur was under control, it would've been impossible for him to send the spirit to take you."

"Was I possessed?" *It's not as if my mind has been my own for some time.*

"No," Harruld answered, "but it would've taken you, if Sarbien hadn't been able to exorcise it when he did. You've had many a dark dreaming of late, have you not?"

"I have. Many times over the last month, or longer. They became more frequent." Kalfinar's voice trembled as he spoke. "They were more intense, threatening. When they started, it was more of a sense of unease. After a while, they grew in substance. There was more noise, voices, beings—"

"Beings?" Sarbien interrupted. "Tell me, what did they look like?" Sarbien edged forward with his elbows on the table, his eyes searching for detail.

"There were several," Kalfinar said. Another howl screamed out from outside the cupola. "There seemed to be three kinds. I saw beasts flying overhead or feeding on the ruins of a city. Feeding upon the dead. They were hunched and clawed with long, thin limbs. Teeth protruded from their jaws and there were knots of horns along their heads."

Olmat spoke, "Lesser spirits of demon kind. That's the ilk that Sarbien exorcised. They hunt through dreams."

Kalfinar frowned, not quite understanding. "What of the other beings?"

"There were two. One was dead. Killed by the other." Kalfinar locked eyes with Olmat. "It was sat as you were at Hardalen."

Olmat pressed, "The other?"

"It was shaped like a man. A burning red halo sat about its head, and its eyes were like hot coals. It walked with a dislocation, as if its joints were inverted. The colours of the body shifted, like the body of a great squid."

"Desverukan," Sarbien hissed.

"Desverukan?" Kalfinar asked, his guts wrenching again.

"Did it see you?" Sarbien pushed.

"Yes. It screamed something. The voice was terrible. It grabbed out and I couldn't escape until a flash of light. Then, I woke."

"Anulii," Olmat whispered. "What you faced in your dream was no lesser demon. It was a Desverukan. A principle servant of Bhalur's. The lesser demon would've been sent to hunt you, to track you. Once it had control, it would've brought you to the Desverukan. If you have one of them hunting you, then our worst fears are indeed confirmed. Bhalur wants you dead." Olmat sighed.

"Dead?" Kalfinar croaked on the word. "So it's not sufficient that one God has taken my family, but now another wants me dead!"

"Don't speak like that," Olmat warned him. "You only serve to distance yourself further from Dajda with such contempt. Believe me, if what we fear is true, you'll need to embrace, not reject, Dajda's love."

Kalfinar clenched his jaw and stared hard at Olmat. "And why's that?"

"The body you saw in your dream was Anulii."

"What?" Kalfinar snapped, his anxiety bubbling. "What's Anulii?"

"What *are* Anulii?" Olmat replied, unshaken by Kalfinar's temper. "There are many horrors in this world. Murder, rape, and more. Many times, these are the intent of humans. But often, these ill acts are the outcomes of a malevolent design. The action of spirits. They hunt by dreams, corrupted by horrors witnessed. In planting this seed, the spirit has a means of tracking us like quarry, and accessing our souls. Then they feed, and they feed Bhalur. You will have borne witness to a scene carried out at the bidding of some evil. Your nightmares represent the efforts to taste your soul, and the attack outside Sarbien's was the link to your soul being formed. The spirit was aiming to take you for the Desverukan. The Desverukan doesn't feast on souls. It kills. Since the beginning, Bhalur has been looking for any that represents a threat to his existence."

"What threat do I present a God?" Kalfinar asked. "And how does that explain what Anulii are?"

"We are the children of our Dajda. We worship Dajda every day and give our thanks for that which has been bestowed upon us. Among what we give thanks for is the love and protection we've been afforded. The protection from those that would see us harmed and offer nothing but hatred and pain. Each time we give thanks, we galvanise this bond of protection. And so, we are safe against the predators of Bhalur. However, if we cease to offer our prayers to Dajda, the bond between us weakens, and so does the protection. This is not a malice from Dajda, but more of a straining to hear a call in a storm, or to see one in the mist. We simply fall out of reach. You've stopped praying."

"I have. My prayers were empty and unanswered."

"And in doing so, you fogged the bond between Dajda and you.

The protection weakened and the spirit grew closer. You must have called out for Dajda at some point."

"As the being reached for me."

"That's all which is needed to illuminate the darkness. The Anulii are the protectors of the souls of Dajda's followers. They are the shepherds who ward off the wolves. I suppose it's fair to say they are the direct opposite of, and the balance to, Bhalur's Desverukan. Your qualities, Kalfinar, allow you to call forth the Anulii from where they reside within human form. There are many others with your gift, and there will be more after you've passed. It is hoped that no bearer of such a gift should ever learn of it or put it to use, for to do so indicates the coming of dark times."

As Olmat finished speaking, the howl outside sounded once more.

Olmat said, "Hear how the spirit wails. Though it has been cast out of you, it made the link, and as such it shall hunt you still. It will never stop. The amulet you wear should obstruct its link to you, meaning it can never again possess you, or enable the Desverukan to kill you. Never take it off."

Kalfinar toyed with the amulet between finger and thumb.

Olmat continued, "The spirit may be able to use others as a tool to harm you. Anyone who has been hunted by spirits, and who has lost their bond to Dajda, is susceptible to this will. At the moment, our wards prevent it or any other from hearing our words, but you must be on your guard for an attack at any moment from when you leave this protection until we can destroy this spirit."

"The attacks earlier, on the way here, would that have been—"

"Yes, there's no doubt," Sarbien answered. "I searched for the odour of the spirit when I left you. After exorcising it, its stink is known to me. Although it fled, there was still enough of its reek in the air."

"But where do I, or this gift, fit into this?"

Sarbien answered Kalfinar, "The body in your dream was Anulii. The Desverukan was taunting us. They've begun hunting them, and killing them."

"Killing the Anulii is dreadful," Olmat spoke, his voice trailing off with a wheeze.

Capriath leant a hand on his brother's arm and the older man nodded to him to continue.

Kalfinar regarded his old companion with grave concern. He had grown weak.

Capriath carried on where Olmat had left off, "If the image you witnessed in your dream is indeed what we fear, then it heralds the purge of the Anulii. This means somehow Bhalur is hunting the Anulii down and killing them. If this slaughter is left unchecked, it will rid our people of Dajda's protection, leaving both our spiritual and physical worlds exposed and at the will of the beast. The scene you witnessed in your dream, where demons fed on mankind, is the fate that awaits us should the Anulii fall. You, Kalfinar, have the gift of sight, and can see the Horn of the Dajda."

"And what exactly is that?" Kalfinar asked.

"The Horn of the Dajda are the beings that we must find and awaken. Together, their voices call forth the physical form of the Anulii, drawing them from their mortal host, within whom they rest. You must seek them out and set free their song. This will, in turn, raise and unite the Anulii so they may stand by us defeat this enemy. Alone, and hidden in human form, the Anulii will be undone, for as their spirits slumber within us, they are weak. But awaken them, and bring them together as one, and all of Dajda's power will be unleashed upon the world."

Kalfinar stared into the copper dome of the cupola and sighed.

Broden spoke, "You speak of this enemy as if you know more. I don't see what this talk of spirits and possession has to do with the deaths of most of our High Command. I'm not as schooled in the secrets of magic, but I'm a soldier. I know a first strike when I see one. A first strike by men, not demons. Our High Command has been all but wiped out, with the exception of a fraction of senior officers. I want to know how this happened, and what is next?"

Harruld answered, "We appear to find ourselves at the centre of a brewing storm, the strength of which we can only guess at. The Solansian's appear to be on the rise." Harruld shook his head and grunted a laugh rich in regret. "I told the High Command that we could never administer Solansia. We didn't have the resources, and they didn't want us there. It is my summarisation that the assassinations on our High Command have come on the bidding of one of Grunnxe's former Generals, or even Grunnxe himself."

"No," Kalfinar snapped. "I can't accept that. My sword was a foot deep in his gut. The old bastard is dead."

"And you saw his body cold?" Harruld asked. "Of course you didn't. They rallied, we retreated, and they recovered him. Not one of us can profess to have seen Grunnxe dead. You know well enough that there are those who command gifts enough to heal wounds such as that which you inflicted upon Grunnxe."

Kalfinar snapped his response, "Who amongst Dajda's people would heal him? None would maintain or restore that butchering old fuck."

Capriath spoke in reply, "It may not have been one of our Tuannan. There are others who can control energies and cast, perhaps gifted by another God. History is not short of tales of such gifts being used for gain of fortune, power, or simply for nothing short of madness. We who serve Dajda are not alone in our ability to cast energy."

"How many other Gods exist that can offer such power in return for devotion?" Kalfinar asked, his eyes fixed on Capriath.

"That question is beyond my means to answer." Capriath held up his palms. "We know of several extant Gods, and more are referred to in ancient writings in our archives. Some are the work of fantasy, perhaps the wanderings of an unravelling mind. But without doubt, a great many have truth at their core. We know of several hundred such powers. Many were seraphs of Dajda or Bhalur who broke away in the early days. Most are lost to time, but some endure still. But I doubt that any remaining powers have the strength or will to have sustained Grunnxe. That, coupled with the Ravenmayne and the content of your dreams says much. We must assume that Bhalur is somehow behind this."

"But you said Bhalur is trapped," Kalfinar said.

"Captured, and maintained by Tuannan," Capriath said.

Capriath looked towards his brothers, a silent communication passed amongst them. They rose from their seats and walked around the table, moving into the space before Kalfinar.

"Now you'll witness how the energy is sustained. Bhalur is the counterbalance to Dajda. For Dajda to exist, so too must Bhalur."

The three brothers started to chant in an unknown tongue, each of them, in turn, blowing into their hands. A small ball of mist coalesced in their palms. The mist grew as their hands worked its shape. They blew the gathering balls of vapour into one, creating a large form of mist. An image took shape in the cloudy sphere.

Kalfinar was rapt. Before him was a shadowy scene. Three score of tall figures stood dressed in long, hooded robes of dark colours. They stood side by side in a large circle, surrounding a plinth of coarse granite, stained black over time. The image in the mist flickered as the fog shifted in shape. As the vapour reformed, Kalfinar saw another robed figure approach the plinth within the circle. The figure mounted the plinth and stripped off his robe, revealing the wiry frame of a young man. His eyes were hard and fixed with intent. The young man spoke in an ugly language, similar to that which Kalfinar had heard in his dreams. The tumble of words quickened, rising to rapid shouts. The mist shifted again, and image before him distorted. When it settled, he saw the man's naked form juddering upon the granite plinth. The man's eyes bulged and his mouth streamed with bile-coloured froth. The agonised shouts ceased and his arched form fell limp onto the flat surface. The man lay motionless for several seconds before his head rolled to the side and his eyes opened. Black and angry, staring out of the vapour. Staring towards Kalfinar.

He can't see me. He can't see me. "Olmat," Kalfinar hissed, his eyes locked on those of the being in the vapour. *He can't see me.*

"Have no fear, Kalfinar," Olmat said as he broke off from his chanting. "You're safe."

Unnatural sounds spilled from the mouth of the man on the plinth. The man sat upright and pulled himself to his knees. One of the dark figures around him stepped before the man on the plinth, and drew a large knife from the sleeve of his robe. The man's eyes bulged black with hate, and his mouth spat sounds of violence and fury. He threw back his head, his neck cords protruding, and let out a wild howl. As the howl trailed off, the robed figure holding the knife let fly a great swipe towards the neck of the man. Blade met flesh, and opened veins.

The man slumped onto the stained plinth, his life ebbing away. The blood spread over the flatness and into fissures along its edges. As the blood seeped within, a black, spectral fog rose from the fissures, and coalesced into the shape of insubstantial arms. Snaking fingers crept upon the paling body, and, with a jerk, the hands pulled tight. The phantom arms pulled tighter still around the dead form of the man, sucking every drop from it. An unrecognisable, withered husk was left upon the plinth before the phantom arms dissipated and sunk back within the blood-stained altar. The image in the mist shifted once more and disappeared.

"What was that?" Kalfinar asked Olmat. His steady voice did not betray the anxiety that churned within his guts.

"You saw the harvest of dark energy, which allows Dajda to grant us our own gifts." The matter-of-fact nature of Olmat's delivery set Kalfinar ill at ease.

"We killed that man?" Kalfinar voice was rich with disgust.

"We did," Harruld said. "It is a necessary act."

"But that man, what happened to him? Where did he come from?"

"That man dedicated himself to that order, and had volunteered his life. He knew what it entailed, and his sacrifice represents one of the greatest that anyone can offer to Dajda."

"What order?" Kalfinar asked. "Are they Tuannan? And was that Bhalur?"

Olmat looked at him. "Those you saw are they who maintain the balance, which is all the name of them you need. They are Tuannan, yes, but they are set apart from us. Their order dedicates itself to imprisoning that which was in the altar. That was the beast, Bhalur."

"So we've been feeding him worship and keeping him trapped in this tomb?"

"Yes," Sarbien answered. "We trapped him, and we thought we had caged him still. By rationing the worship, it allows him no real strength. That way, we maintain the balance, yet remain untouched by the horrors he would reap, if he were not contained."

"But what of the Ravenmayne people? Don't they worship him still, giving him strength?"

"The wards prevent any worship from outside the altar room from entering. The Ravenmayne people's prayers go unanswered," Sarbien replied.

"So if Bhalur can see his will done, then there must be a betrayal within the order. We must go to them and root out the traitor."

"No," Harruld replied, "we can't. Our order hasn't had contact with them since the caging of the beast. And in any case, where would we find them?"

"But we just saw them!" Kalfinar snapped.

"What did you see?" Harruld asked. "All I saw was the inside of a cave. That could be anywhere across the Cullanain, or beyond."

Stupid. He's right. "Can we send a message?"

"They're barred from us. If there is a betrayer amongst them, we must trust that they're revealed to our brothers and sisters."

"I can't just sit here and wait!"

"And you won't," Olmat said. "There are many threads in this unhappy tale. Here," he said, passing some parchment to Kalfinar, "read this."

It was stained with age and felt brittle in Kalfinar's hand. He looked towards the parchment and then to Olmat.

"Go ahead," the old man encouraged. "Read it aloud."

Kalfinar unpicked the leather thong which bound the old parchment, before unrolling the document. The bile still burned in his gullet after his earlier evacuations. He cleared his throat and began to read the small, antiquated print before him.

Here follows the written record of the dreamings of Teporan Mane, by the hand of Magnarus, primary scribe of the Great Holmon I of the Noehmiana, Chief Marshal of the Peoples of the Free Provinces.

Kalfinar ceased his reading and looked up, brows furrowed. "This parchment must be at least four hundred years old. Holmon was the first chief marshal of the Free Provinces."

Olmat nodded. "Holmon did command four hundred years ago. Bear it in mind that the words of this parchment are older still. What you hold is a replicate, for the original was undone by time. Teporan Mane first scored these words some time before the age of Holmon. Carry on please."

I, Teporan Mane, primary son of Baltron Mane endow unto thee, my brothers and sisters, these words, humble as they are, for they be all that I have. May they entangle thy soul and fortify thee against the storm that lays ahead in the days of my bones beyond dust.

I, Teporan Mane, have been the recipient of a wondrous blessing. Nae, a terrible curse, bestowed to me by an accident of my birth to being. The true God, Dajda, above all, has deemed me the vessel for divine dreamings, light, or dark, as they may be. Withheld from the parchment most have been, for I had not the skill of the quill. I awoke this morning with tools and means to write the divine dreamings, these gifts bestowed by a spirit of our Great Dajda, I believe.

The dreamings said to me these things. Heed them well, or heed them not.

The woes of man will be felt as the earth weeps black tears and a dead king rises, rejuvenated by the powers of a dread lord, chief among our terror and wielder of our bane. First unto thee shall be cast hunger and chill, and hunger redoubled.

Hark!

The Betrayer has placed the dagger afore your breast. They have marked the course. Chaos will reign when the rudder of the ship is cast lose in the sea of turmoil. The grey cloud and blue chill of night will stab deep into the heart of men, and the armies of a dread lord will smash upon thy ship in the storm of the seas, in the sea of blood, in the season of blood.

Woe unto thee!

Feared men shall walk the world, and the children of a dread lord, usurper, will rise up and claim their place in the balance of all. Children of tooth and claw, children of fire and pain, shall legions form.

Fear them!

Hope lies with the sleeping ones, they alone shall deliver unto thee a salvation, calling forth the proclamation, the trumpet song, to bring *unto thee the turning of the tide. Release them from their slumber, and free upon the world Dajda's voice. Such is thy deliverance.*

Wary thy must be!

The Great Mother, Dajda, will sleep as her servants search for the masked children of the divine, the salvation. Watchful as thy go, for when the Dajda doth sleep, thy souls, and the souls of all Dajda's children, are wanting of divine embrace, and are vulnerable to the dread lord.

Seek them!

Look ye for the servants, granted to them the light and the vision, for it is within these spirits that thy peace shall reside. The servants shall awaken the saviours, and as one, two and three pillars fall, so shall their song soar.

Seek them!

Woe unto thee my brothers and sisters. Heed these tellings and cast thy lot against the design of the foulest dread. Stay thy course marked by the servants, and ye shall be delivered salvation by the shining ones. Stay this course not, and thee shall suffer eternal under the yoke and lash of the dark and cruel usurper.

The dreamings said to me these things. Heed them well, or heed them not.

Here ends the written record of the dreamings of Teporan Mane, by the hand of Magnarus, primary scribe of the Great Holmon I of the

Noehmiana, Chief Marshal of the Free Peoples of the Free Provinces.

Kalfinar looked up after reading aloud the ancient script before him. "Well, that was cheery. What in the hells does this mean?" He looked once more at the parchment. "As the earth weeps black tears? What am I to make of this?"

Harruld answered, "We've held this parchment, amongst many others by Teporan Mane and other such seers, for many ages. Tuannan amongst us, archivists, have consulted them in times of threat, hopeful of insight. It's when we met and discussed all matters that this parchment became a little clearer to us. You know well enough there have been poor crop yields these last two seasons. The farmers in Ilsinuer are calling it a famine. The grain stores have suffered all over the Free Provinces as a result. We're only just keeping the bellies full with reserves, and imports from Canna, but the cost is bleeding us dry. The most recent reports coming out of Ilsinuer and Noehmia were of a black discharge weeping from the fields. I've seen it with my own eyes. It's a blight throughout our principle agricultural lands." Harruld's face bore a tired and worn look.

Kalfinar glanced back to the parchment. "'A dead king rises. That must mean Grunnxe. Children of tooth and claw, of fire and pain. My dreams." Kalfinar shook his head. "What must we do?"

Olmat answered, "It is you who must find the Horn of the Dajda, find the sleeping ones. There'll be those who will hunt you down. You must evade them, and return to us with the horn of Dajda."

Small beads of sweat formed under Kalfinar's eyes. *I'm needed. No. I need. Smoke.*

"They are our salvation," Olmat said. "They are the Anulii, the children of Dajda."

"But why? If these are the children of Dajda, can they not simply be awoken by the will of their God?"

Olmat rubbed his bald head. "The Anulii had to reside within us to protect us. Man is free willed and may choose to worship, if he wishes. Many of us have chosen not to worship, or, for whatever reason, have been unable to do so, and, as a result, that link has been broken. We need to find them and bring them back, for without them all, their power is not complete."

"How many have been lost?" Kalfinar said.

"Innumerable," Olmat responded. "And it appears many more have been isolated and destroyed by the Desverukan."

"What of the light when I was saved from my dream on the ship?"

"You were one soul in need at that point in time, and you called for Dajda. If many more, thousands, or millions, called for Dajda's salvation, then there may not have been the strength to do so. Souls would be lost in such a way, food for the demons, as yours could have been."

"How am I supposed to be able to find these people?" Kalfinar asked.

"You don't need to. You just need to find the Horn of Dajda. It will call them forth."

"And where exactly is this fucking horn?" Kalfinar rubbed the sweat from under his eyes and then the gathering beads on his forehead with the back of his hand. *Get yourself under control, damn it. Forget it. It's nothing but poison!*

"You must seek them"

"Them?"

"The Horn of Dajda is three souls."

"How am I supposed to find them?"

"There will be help for you in this task. Both this and your strength will see you succeed. I'm sure of it," Olmat said.

Kalfinar shook his head. "You need someone of strength? Well, everyone in this room knows I'm not strong. What strength did I display when I lost her and the child? I was weak and wretched, and spilled my sorrow upon the streets!" He shook his head. "No, I'm not one of strength. You'll have to find another."

"Your role in this act is already marked, Kalfinar," Olmat said. "As are the roles my brothers and I will fulfil. I interpret Teporan Mane's writings of the three pillars as my brothers and I. What it means to say the pillars will fall is for any one of us to guess. But I think it is clear what that is to mean."

"Not that." Kalfinar said, the words feeling thick in his throat.

Olmat dismissed the words with a wave of his hand. "We have been around for a rather long time. Longer than most, in fact. Our primary focus has been to protect Dajda from her enemies. To do so, we have sought to learn of our world, to interpret ancient texts, and so seek out the gifted and watch over them as they grow. Sometimes, some are born who are granted the gift of sight. The sight to see the

Horn of Dajda. You've suffered a terrible loss, but the dark days you lived after it should not torment you, and you shouldn't mistake grief for weakness. You need to free yourself, free yourself from your fears. There is no other way. You must accept your part in this, as we all must."

"Then the choice is not my own," Kalfinar said as he bowed his head. "Show me what I must do."

———

The spirit trembled before its master. The rebuke was fierce. It was, however, surprised not to be obliterated. If it had not been for the link made with the manthing, it would surely have been destroyed. No longer was it the charge of the spirit to take control of the manthing's soul. Now, the spirit had to take others and possess manthings to do its master's bidding. If the actions of the manthing could not be manipulated for its master's will, the spirit would see that others would strike. The spirit gathered its subordinates and set off for the cities and lands of manthings, searching for weakened bodies, and vulnerable souls.

Chapter Thirteen

THE OLD KING'S face split in a grin as he beheld his reflection in the mirror. His teeth showed no sign of the blackened decay that, until recently, they had held. His skin was tight and pink, no longer sagging and dull. His short beard sprung white on his chin still, but the braids in his hair, worn long at the back of his head, were brown and shined, instead of the tired grey which had crowned his head before. Although pleased on the whole to be revitalised in such a manner, Grunnxe was still disappointed to see the ragged scar which ran from his left eye and across his cheek remained, blinding him still on that side. He recalled the handsome face of his youth, before the governor of Carte, Harruld, stabbed out his eye. His thoughts turning to his enemies, Grunnxe pulled up his smock and rubbed his stomach, his muscles firm once more. Over the area above his navel, a lumpy, star-shaped purple scar remained.

He laughed to himself.

The governor's son had thought him dead, for his sword had slid deep within his guts, mangling his innards. Grunnxe knew he should have died, and doubtless would have been had the priestess not come to him after the governor and his men were forced to retreat. His laughter ceased as he recalled the cold burn and stinging shock of Kalfinar's blade ramming its way through his body.

He shook his head, chasing the memory away. He cared not. The governor and his son would already be dead if his plan had been realised. The fast riders would be back soon with news of the mission's success. He would savour that news. Turning, he regarded himself once more in the long mirror. He turned his face fully to the left, and stared long at the unscarred side and smiled at what he saw.

"It pleases thee, your highness?" the small holy man in the dark habit standing behind Grunnxe spoke at last.

"It pleases me more than if I were dead, yes. You said I'd be young again, yet you fail to give me back my eye. What manner of success is that?" Grunnxe had turned from the mirror and bent with his face pressed close to that of the trembling man.

"We could only go so far back, great king. It is harder to undo the injuries. We had to work around them. Any further and we risked losing our grip on the process and you could have been undone. My master said this would be so." The small holy man's hands clenched tightly below his chin, offering meagre protecting from the snarling face of Grunnxe.

"Pah! You fear much, little man."

Grunnxe knew the small holy man was correct. His master, the priestess, had indeed warned him there was only so far they could take him back. Despite it, his ego yearned for his once unspoilt face and, in his disappointment, he effortlessly shoved out his hand and pushed the trembling holy man over onto his backside before turning toward the mirror once more. He approached it and raised his arms wide above his head. His fingers spread, and his head tilted back towards the roof of his pavilion. Grunnxe, the once old and beaten king of Solansia, descendant of the great kings of the Cullanain, and long-time enemy of the Free Provinces, proclaimed himself returned. He would sweep bloody vengeance and devastating pain onto whoever remained alive to oppose him. His ancestor's lands would be reclaimed once more, in the name of the Kingdom of Solansia, the rightful rulers of all the peoples of The Cullanain.

Kalfinar put down the parchment as his father spoke.

Harruld summarised their thoughts, "So we've concluded that Teporan Mane's word depicts the crop failures throughout our main agricultural regions in Ilsinuer and Noehmia, and it appears, from what

Bergnon has reported and from our own logic, that Grunnxe is alive. That makes two accuracies from the parchment. Now, we've a number of areas we need to puzzle out if we're to be sure, and ready."

"If we're going to gamble on the entire piece," Broden interrupted.

"Yes, quite," Harruld acknowledged. "Let's work through this as best we can, so at least we've considered our options."

Kalfinar said, "Somewhere and somehow we've been undone by betrayal."

"It could refer to the assassinations, perhaps the hand of the assassin was guided," Broden said.

"Yes, perhaps so," Governor Harruld said as he stroked his grey beard. "It was a stunning strike if we look at it coldly."

The severity of the betrayal dawned on Kalfinar. "It had to be someone who knew everyone who was targeted. They knew where we were barracked, even down so far as to where we slept! This had to be someone who knew our command, and it had to be someone close."

"I fear you're right," Governor Harruld grumbled, rubbing his eyes. "This is a grave theory, indeed. I'll get Bergnon to compile a roster of the senior command that lives. In fact, we'll need to take it down so far as sergeant. I think we'll be in need of some promotions."

Kalfinar consulted the parchment once more. "The Field of Storms," he said.

"What was that?" Broden asked.

"The Field of Storms, to the east. It used to be a huge lake, an inland sea around about a thousand years ago. This was known as the Sea of Storms. This may be what 'storm of the seas' refers to."

"But there's no sea today," Broden said.

"No, there's no sea today. But the land that used to be the sea is covered at this time of year in winter poppies."

"The Sea of Blood," Governor Harruld mused aloud. A grave look etched across his wrinkled face. "Solansia is going to strike at Apula."

The rejuvenated king admired himself in the full-length mirror. His armour of freshly burnished steel and polished leather, complimented his invigorated body. He flexed his arm, strong once more, and smiled.

"Traxal, are they ready?" he called to his general, who waited outside his pavilion.

"Your Highness, they are," the response returned through the canvas partition.

"Then let them behold their king reborn," he whispered to himself as he appreciated his flexing arms. Grunnxe placed the crowned helmet over his head, careful not to dishevel his hair, and slid his sword into its ornate scabbard. Pausing in front of the exit, he exhaled and smiled to himself.

The cheer was enormous as Grunnxe strode out.

Thousands of loyal Solansians rejoiced. Once feared to be dead, the beloved Grunnxe, patriot and hammer of the Free Provinces, stood before his people with his muscled arms aloft.

The priestess stood in the shadows of the tent behind Grunnxe. Clothed fully in black, the crowd were not able to see her form.

Grunnxe turned his head and cast a glance back to the shadowy figure. "Spread my words. Make them loud. They all must hear what I speak."

"As you command, master."

"Soldiers of Solansia!" Grunnxe addressed the mass, his voice booming with unnatural power. "The hour of darkness is passing, for King Grunnxe has come to lead you into the light!"

There were more thundering cheers.

"Solansia will at last, after four hundred years of fury, crush the traitorous alliance and reclaim our place on the throne of the Cullanain. There is no doubting that this is the hour of our glory, for I have been told so by a great and powerful God. A God who is rising from the shadows and will reward our loyalty with power."

With his arms aloft and voice resonating across the vast plain, Grunnxe received the adulation of his subjects. He knew he had their devotion. They would do anything for him. The disciples of the priestess, the wretched holy men, had gone forth and spread the word of their new God to the masses. Prayers and benedictions were taught and worship conducted. The Solansian forces gripped their love of their new god with a ferocious and hysterical enthusiasm.

"Children of Solansia, let us pray together now to our God, and may he bless us with strength and courage against the demons of the west. Let us offer our spirits to the great and true God!"

As cheering gave way to silence, Grunnxe felt engorged with pleasure.

It was perfect.

Chapter Fourteen

BERGNON HAMMERED on the governor's door. "My lord, I have the roster."

The heavy oak door swung open and a tired-looking Governor Harruld ushered Bergnon into his study. Thaskil and Arrlun followed behind and stood at ease by the door. Long-limbed wolf hounds sniffed at their boots and legs before settling.

"How'd you get on?" Harruld asked as he sat behind his paper-strewn desk, fingers knitting behind his head.

"We were only able to review the rosters as they were delivered from Hardalen and Terna, so there are no further changes to our knowledge in that respect. We did, however, manage to secure a full rollcall of the senior command here in Carte, down to campaign-experienced corporals."

"Fair enough. We'll be needing the bodies." He sighed a long and ragged breath. "Go on."

"My lord, all who were present after the attack remain present. That is, all but one." Bergnon paused, his eyes fixed on the governor.

"Yes?"

"Chief Administrative Officer Johnstane is missing."

"Have you confirmed this for certain?"

"We have, my lord. I sent Arrlun and Thaskil out to the church, infirmary, his offices, and just about everywhere else he was known to frequent. Johnstane has no family or other homes within the city. I've had the city scoured this night and no one has seen him. He appears to have vanished."

"How on earth did he get out?" Harruld asked no one in particular. "Damn these guards." He slammed his fist into the desk, startling the dozing wolf hounds. Harruld rubbed his face and sighed. "Well, that's something to go on at least. Good work. We'll have to dispatch a team to bring him in. If that's all, Bergnon, go and rest some. I'm organising a council for midmorning. I'll need you there. You two," the governor addressed the two raw soldiers.

"Yes, my lord," they answered.

"I want you both in attendance. From what I can judge, I believe you both to have the making of fine officers. I'll be giving you command of your own men, under Major Bergnon. You'll assist him in leading the battalion he'll be assigned. Ironically, the paperwork was sent to Johnstane's offices last night." He looked down as he stroked one of the hounds. "In fact, both of you go and chase this matter up with the administrative department." Harruld scribbled a note and stamped it with his seal of office before handing it to Arrlun. "Give this to the duty clerk and make sure they assemble your sergeants. Ensure they see to it that the companies are mustered. I want this battalion ready in the morning. That's all for now. Go and get some rest."

"How did Sarbien come to adopt him?" Kalfinar looked beyond Olmat to the head of the long mess-table where the Ravenmayne, Chentuck, ate with Evelyne and Brother Anthony. Kalfinar sat at the other end of the table with Broden and Olmat.

"He kidnapped him," Olmat said as he heaped another mouthful of lamb into his mouth. Kalfinar and Broden both stared at the old man.

"He kidnapped the monster?" Kalfinar asked. "From where?"

Olmat chewed his mouthful, swallowed, and then answered, waggling his fork in front of him, "Chentuck's not a monster, as you would say it. That's the last time I want to have to tell you that. He's a human, like you and I. The differences are few. They are a result of environment wherein the Ravenmayne people evolved. I suppose that is the 'where' in your question."

"You've lost me already, Olmat," Broden admitted.

"The Ravenmayne people are from the Hagra Peninsula. This ragged landmass is virtually inaccessible, by land or by sea."

"I've read it's entirely impossible," Kalfinar said. "A thin isthmus at the far north of Solansia, surrounded by treacherous seas and rocks. I've not read of anyone having explored the area."

"You're ill-informed, but that is no slight on you, for few know the truth about Hagra. It's remote and virtually impossible to reach, that's a certainty. Hagra is dominated by ice and snow, great mountains and deep trenches in the earth. Although there are no reports of a successful expedition on record, Sarbien has been there. He was more vigorous in his youth, and was a very hardy traveller." Olmat shoved another forkful of lamb into his mouth and chewed intently. He continued, "Sarbien was capable of feats of great endurance and fortitude. He travelled to Hagra to verify the Ravenmayne existence. It has been long his course to uncover the truths and consolidate our understanding."

"So he was chasing a myth in Hagra?" Broden asked.

"We Tuannan have been privy to archives and records that would make your head spin. We've come across many records of races, creatures, spirits and Gods. We've investigated many, and yes, on that particular occasion, Sarbien mounted an expedition to uncover the truth of Hagra. This undertaking almost cost him everything. Next time he walks, watch him; the limp. It's caused by the loss of several toes, taken from him by the cold."

"But him?" Kalfinar said, again indicating towards Chentuck. "How did he come to take him?"

"Opportunity. Impulse. Sarbien was able to observe the activity in a Ravenmayne village. He reported that they lived a normal, hunter-gatherer existence. However, one night, not long after sunset, the mood in the village shifted and aggression spread amongst the Ravenmayne. Sarbien reported that there was a savage fight between families over their huts. It appeared most unusual, for none of the other villagers would offer up refuge in their huts to their neighbours. It soon became apparent that to be left last outside at sunset was a horrible fate. The last family that Sarbien saw without a shelter that night was made up of a father and mother, with an infant. He reported to me that the mother hid her young towards the outer edge of the village amongst the snow and rocks, before running back to the side of her mate, just in time for a glowing beast to stalk into the village. He reported that it seemed to interrogate the pair, speaking some guttural tongue, before it ripped the twosome to shreds, consuming them and leaving only the hidden infant."

"For whatever purpose?" Broden exclaimed.

"It's a mystery. Sarbien did not choose to stay around too long to observe, for he feared the presence of the hounds he trekked in with would alert the villagers to his presence. For some reason, they had been growing agitated that day. Perhaps a sense of what was about to come. Subduing them was becoming a difficult task. Sarbien waited for some time and when he realised no villagers were leaving their shelters and that the creature had gone away, he sneaked towards the forest edge and retrieved the infant. So, he gathered him up and retreated, being careful to cover his tracks in the snow. Lucky for Sarbien, one of the bitches in his sled pack had given birth along the journey, with all the pups having frozen near instantly. The bitch let the infant feed and so he was sustained."

"Incredible," Kalfinar exclaimed. "So he was raised by Sarbien?"

"Yes, almost entirely in secret, for obvious reasons. We've learned a huge amount about the Ravenmayne people and their ways from Chentuck. It appears that they are born with an innate understanding of what it is to be Ravenmayne. They are aware of their customs, their ancestors, and, most frighteningly for us, their God and Undergods."

Kalfinar slammed a fist into the table. "If he was born with devotion to Bhalur, then how can we trust him?"

"This man has been given a choice, Kalfinar. Chentuck was not driven only by instinct, like many of his unfortunate ancestors. He has never had a bond with Bhalur. Evelyne is correct. You would do well to count them dear amongst your allies, so my advice to you is that you set aside your own animosity, and forget your own instincts."

Kalfinar held the old man's gaze, unconvinced still. *Nothing but a rotten treachery sat amongst us.*

"We can't claim to understand their ways, for we have only been able to learn from this limited first-hand experience, and what small studies Sarbien was able to record of them in their natural setting. When we first became aware that there could be something to the writings of Teporan Mane, we didn't think the Ravenmaynes people were those spoken of. It was felt they were too limited in numbers, and too impotent."

"And you think now that your original theories were wrong," Kalfinar asked.

"It seems that way, yes, perhaps," Olmat replied. "We may have misjudged them. We knew they had been gifted the use of energies by their God and his Undergods, such as it was, but we had never believed that it could be used in force against us. We never felt it was sophisticated enough. We didn't think their God had the strength."

Kalfinar heaved a heavy breath. "It seems they may well have been underestimated."

"Indeed," Olmat agreed. "Sarbien reported an impressive degree of stealth, pace and agility when hunting. Now, we can only presume such skill is influenced by the energies gifted by their God to ensure what limited game is available in the extreme north was successfully caught. This set of skills seemingly lends the Ravenmayne the ability to make excellent assassins, as demonstrated so tragically."

Kalfinar's cold stare locked on Chentuck.

"So, how has it come to be that these people look as they do?" Broden asked, interrupting Kalfinar's thoughts. "You said that they are a product of their environment. What does that mean?"

"Well," Olmat answered, "the environmental conditions in Hagra appear to be the cause of the people's appearance. Their skin colour, eyes, and hair, for example."

"How does the land they live in affect this?" Broden asked.

"We've studied Chentuk as he's grown in a bid to unravel what the Ravenmayne are and how they've come to be. It seems to be that the surface of their skin receives less blood than the core of their bodies, likely to keep the main organs warm and functioning, and so the grey-blue tinge. Now, their hair is very interesting. You'll see it is thick, each strand twice the thickness of our own. The paleness of it draws the sun all the way down to the surface of the skin, providing more warmth. Amazing, isn't it?" Olmat called out to Chentuck at the end of the table, who simply shrugged his shoulders.

"If you say so," he said with a modest expression.

"No need to be so humble, lad," Olmat laughed. "Now, their eyes are also a product of their environment. They especially are fantastic. When Sarbien travelled in Hagra, he suffered terribly from snow blindness. It's a reaction caused by ice and snow reflecting the glare from the sun, and is a terribly painful and troublesome condition. To manage in the glare, Sarbien cut a flap of leather from his coat to cover his eyes, slicing the thinnest of slits to see through. That seemed to minimise the extent and frequency of the bouts he suffered. Admittedly, to us, the Ravenmayne eyes look rather sinister, like burning coals, but it seems as though they have small metallic deposits, likely iron and copper, within the irises. This appears to reflect the majority of the glare and enables them to thrive in the environment."

"What about their teeth?" Broden asked. "Chentuck doesn't have the same pointed teeth as the ones we killed."

"It may be a social trait. Perhaps of warriors or adults; we don't know. But, on the whole, it's fascinating, isn't it?" Olmat asked.

"Truly," Kalfinar muttered, glancing once again towards Chentuck. "A man like you or I."

"Like you or I."

"Keep digging, damn you." The foreman sat astride his horse and shouted orders to his workers as they tried desperately to recover the turnip harvest before winter fell on the Free Provinces.

The foreman's skin prickled as anxiety mounted. The crop yield was poor for the second year in a row, and he was failing to return his quota, as were most others throughout Ilsinuer and Noehmia.

He shifted in his saddle and reached into his saddle bag, pulling out an apple. "Here we are, the bread basket of the Free Provinces fumbling in the cold dirt for a harvest of neeps. How has it come to this?" he muttered solemnly to himself. He took a bite from his apple, grateful at least for the imported food. "Can't keep shipping in from the bloody Cannan's," he mumbled through the mouthful of apple.

"Boss," a labourer shouted from the field. "It's no use. The crop is spoiled again." The man bent and scooped up a handful of putrid neeps. They were black and ruined.

The foreman dismounted from his horse and trudged through the mud towards the workers. "Move! Out of my way!" he shouted at the labourers crowding around the digging party.

As he lumbered towards his man, one of the more distant labourers cried out, "Boss, I've found something." The labourer waved towards the foreman as a crowd of fellow workers fell in and surrounded her. "Boss!"

The foreman made his way towards the agitated worker. "This had better be good."

The labourers parted as he approached, revealing the discovery.

"What is it?" The foreman asked to no one in particular as he stared down on a mucky urn fixed within the earth.

"It appears to glow," the labourer whispered. He pointed to the urn as a white and purple light faintly pulsed within its centre, forcing its light through the dirt caked around its exterior.

"Wipe that off and let us have a look at it then," the foreman ordered to the labourer who uncovered the urn.

As mud was wiped clear, the power of the pulsing light was revealed, reflecting on each of their faces.

The foreman knelt down towards the jar. "It's beautiful," he exclaimed, mystified by the colours before him.

"Boss," the labourer said. "Boss!"

"What is it? Damn it!" the foreman snapped, tearing his gaze away from the nimbus.

"Your apple."

"Dajda!" the foreman exclaimed, stumbling backwards away from the urn and dropping the apple to the ground. The apple had withered to a putrid black mass of slime. "Dajda, help us," the foreman mumbled. "What is this witchery?"

Chapter Fifteen

KALFINAR SAT on the edge of his cot and rubbed his bleary eyes. He pulled on his boots and, stretching out a long leg towards Broden, shoved his snoring cousin in the arse.

"Get up, you lump." He shoved Broden a second time. "Get up. We have to meet with the others. I don't know how you can sleep at times like this."

"I wasn't just sleeping. I was having a nice dream," Broden grumbled sullenly.

"Oh really? Which old conquest was she?" Kalfinar replied as he stood up and pulled on his deep-green buckskin breeches.

Broden stood up, his joints protesting noisily. "I was dreaming of Evelyne. Dajda knows, I'm getting too old for these cots."

Kalfinar looked up at his cousin. "Evelyne?"

"Aye." Broden pulled on his undershirt.

Kalfinar eyed him with raised brows.

"What? No! It wasn't like that!" Broden blurted defensively.

"I believe you!" Kalfinar raised his palms in surrender. "So, you like her?"

"She's nice to look at, isn't she?"

Kalfinar tucked in his undershirt and buckled his belt. "I suppose so," he said absently.

"It's her eyes. Never seen eyes quite like it," the larger man said as he fastened his jerkin.

Kalfinar grunted as he fastened his sword belt around his jerkin. "I'm going on. I'll meet you in my father's chambers," Kalfinar mumbled as he made for the door, swinging his arms into his long-coat as he went.

Harruld and the three old brothers had assembled by the time Kalfinar arrived in his father's chambers. He was shortly followed by Evelyne and Chentuck, and the two newly promoted lieutenants, Thaskil and Arrlun. Broden entered a short while later, and was grateful to see the fresh bread, jams, fruits and coffee on the large table. After helping themselves to a warming breakfast and attempting some light-hearted small talk, the conversation turned to more pressing matters.

Harruld commenced, "I must inform you all of some news which arrived from central Ilsinuer late last night. A fast rider arrived with the news as quickly as possible, and he brought with him something which I must show you. Have you all had your fill of the food this morning?"

Everyone nodded in contentment.

"Very well." Harruld signalled to one of the guardsmen who exited the room for a few moments before returning with a large sack. "Please remove the urn and place it over on the table. Observe the food," Harruld said.

They watched as the guardsman pulled the faintly glowing urn from the sack and placed it in the table's centre, by the breakfast platters.

"Dajda!" Broden exclaimed, pointing as the food putrefied into rotting slime.

"It turns black before us! What is this?" Kalfinar asked.

"It was found buried in a field in central Ilsinuer," Governor Harruld said. "I've sent dispatches via fast riders to all of the main agricultural regions where we've had reports of crop failure and blight. I fear we may find more of whatever these things are." He looked to the three old brothers peering towards the urn and asked, "Have any of you any idea what this is?"

The three men looked at each other before each shook his head.

Olmat spoke for them, "I fear, despite all our learnings, none of us have seen the like of this before." He scratched at his head absently as he thought. "It has to be some form of energy, but this is manipulative. Destructive. Not like the energies we Tuannan have harnessed or seen utilised by our own. This is something altogether more treacherous." Olmat paused in thought, all eyes observing the old man as he assessed the situation before him. "I fear we find ourselves at the centre of an established and coordinated threat. There have been failures for two years, so if this is the cause, and there are more of them, then surely they must have been implanted within the earth before that time. It seems now it is all coming together."

"Olmat's right," Kalfinar followed on. "I think it's clear that we're now entering into a dangerous phase of whatever plot this is. Look at all that has come to light recently: coordinated strikes on our High Command, a rising in Solansia, two years of crop failures, our treasury bled dry, and widespread food shortages. This is a grave circumstance."

"Grave indeed," Sarbien agreed. "Whatever it is, whoever's behind it, to sustain such widespread destruction, and for so long, would take an immense amount of power." Sarbien stared intently at the glowing urn. "Whatever the source of this energy is, we need to locate and destroy it."

"Sarbien is right," Harruld said. "We must act decisively. I fear the endgame of this terrible design is upon us. Our response must be set in motion. Gentlemen," Harruld addressed the brothers, "can you guide us in our actions?"

Olmat and his two brothers rose from their seats and gave instructions to the guardsman by the door. The man disappeared and returned after several silent minutes, followed by two servants carrying two large jugs of water and three washing bowls. They laid the items out before the three brothers, who poured water in each bowl before shifting things about until they were content with the arrangement. They stood, holding hands while facing Kalfinar and Broden, with the water-filled bowls between them. The three older men repeated in unison a long musical incantation, a harmonised throaty humming noise.

"What are they doing?" Broden asked as he leaned towards Kalfinar.

"Shush!" Kalfinar responded, raising his hand to his cousin, his gaze never shifting from the scene before him. "Look at the water," he directed.

The water started to steam and bubble, its temperature rising as the incantation proceeded.

"It's starting to boil," Broden said. "Another vision?"

The steam became thicker and transformed into a sheet of vapour. The incantation broke off and the vapour fixed in the air, boiled water frozen in time, mid-evaporation. An image, hazy at first, became visible before them.

"Observe. Your mission is before you," Harruld whispered.

"This is ludicrous!" Kalfinar exclaimed as the water ceased boiling and the vision faded away to nothingness. "You're to send us out into the world, to landscapes and cities we don't know, to recover individuals no one can recognise, using nothing but our wit! This is obscene." Kalfinar rubbed at his healing shoulder as he ranted, "You're asking us to return to you special grains of sand from a desert." He shook his head and exhaled a breath heavy with frustration.

"I agree with Kal," Broden said. "How can we be expected to find these people, and with what time? If our logic is correct, then Grunnxe and his forces are readying for an assault as we speak."

Governor Harruld raised his hand towards the two men. "I understand your concerns, but this must be so. We've been unable to react until now, for it was not the time nor the mission. Without fully knowing what was occurring, and with the spirit closing in on Kalfinar, the mission would certainly have failed. We stand a chance now, for only now can we take the risk."

Kalfinar felt a vein throbbing at the side of his head. "Risk! Do you want to know about risk? Risk is taking Broden and I, and whoever else you send with us, to the four corners of the world when we would be better put to use commanding the defence of our country!"

"Still yourself, Kalfinar," Olmat said. "Your mission is the key to the defence of our country, and our faith. For if you fail, we all fail. You have all got roles to play in this design." The three old brothers returned to their seats as Olmat spoke, "You will not be alone or without guidance. You saw a stone in the vision, did you not?"

Kalfinar and Broden affirmed they had witnessed such.

"That is the key to your success, for it will grow brighter the closer you get to the horn of Dajda; they are linked," Olmat said. "The vision showed you the lands that they were born into. These lands mark your path and it is in these places you shall find them, all being well."

"And I suppose we will be able to see them walking around with a nimbus around their heads as well," Kalfinar said, referring to the locating of the beings from the vision, his tone thick with disbelief.

"Yes, as a matter of fact, you will, in a manner of speaking," Olmat replied, with no sign of his patience flagging whatsoever. "You have that gift amongst your many other skills, lad. You have never experienced it before, because you have never seen one of such light, of such spirit, before. But when you do, oh, what a site it is to behold."

Kalfinar's brows furrowed as Olmat revealed more.

"You will use the stone to guide you, to draw you close to them. Now, remember the horn of Dajda are not consciously aware of their being. They are like you or I, simply flesh and bone, but when you see them, you will know it. What you saw in the vision does not do their beauty justice at all. You will see their true form before you, and you will do well not to weep."

Kalfinar nodded slowly.

"So what is this stone? It must be special somehow," Broden said, referring to the fist-sized rock which pulsed and glowed in the vision.

"It is special," Olmat answered. "It is the most precious thing you will ever behold. It is the Godstone."

"I'm sorry, the what?" Broden asked.

"The Godstone." Olmat looked at the confused faces before him. "I think I ought to speak plainly."

"Please do," Kalfinar and Broden spoke in unison.

"The Godstone is essentially the heart of Dajda." The brows on the faces before Olmat furrowed further still. "To enable us to get close enough to locate the horn of Dajda, and to awaken that consciousness within them, we need to have a link to them. They are the children of Dajda, and so they are linked through Dajda's heart. From the instant you receive the Godstone, our world becomes threatened yet further, but it is a risk we must take if we are to break what evil floods us. For the Godstone to manifest itself on this world, Dajda need to, essentially, go into a form of stasis."

"A what?" Kalfinar asked.

"Dajda must sleep. It will mean we who worship will enter a period of grave risk. Our souls will not remain protected as they were, and our prayers will go unanswered. We Tuannan will have no gifts. It is a time of darkness for our people."

Kalfinar nodded.

"Once you locate them, in order to awaken them, as you witnessed in the vision, you are required to touch the Godstone to their heart. I mean this literally." Olmat looked at the men, fully expecting another question, but none came. "Do you understand what I've just said?" the old physician asked.

"I understood what you said, Olmat," Kalfinar said. "I think it may be best to just accept it all now, whether I comprehend or not."

The old physician nodded. "I see. Do not worry about harming the individual when you make for their heart. The Godstone will undo any physical damage inflicted."

"So when do we get the Godstone?" Broden asked.

"You will not get it," Sarbien spoke up. "Evelyne shall carry it."

"What?" Kalfinar and Broden barked in unison.

The guardsman entered and saluted the governor, who was surrounded by paperwork following the High Command's earlier council. "Governor Harruld, Captain Albright from the City Guard has some news to report concerning Chief Administrative Office Johnstane."

"Send him in." The governor placed down his quill and sat back in his chair.

The blue-liveried officer strode stiffly into the room and saluted the governor.

"What news have you for me, Captain?" Harruld asked as he stroked the head of his wolf-hound.

"My lord." The captain's stare fixed on the embroidered tapestry hanging behind the governor's desk as he spoke, "We have located Chief Administrative Officer Johnstane."

"And?" the governor prompted, frustration displayed on his face.

The captain glanced down and held the governor's eyes. "His body was found in a boarding house by the port this morning. Strangled."

Governor Harruld nodded his gratitude for the receipt of the news. "How long had he been dead?"

"My lord, the landlady said he checked in two nights ago and hadn't been seen since. She said he seemed anxious. He paid her for two nights upfront and claimed he was a merchant waiting for a ship to Terna leaving this morning. She said that when the key had not been left for her in the morning, she grew concerned and that when she went to the room, the door was locked. It was after she used the spare key to access the room that she sent for the City Guards."

"Had he any visitors that she could report of?" the governor asked.

"None that she mentioned, my lord," the captain replied. "But it appears there were no signs of a forced entry. He had to have let them in somehow."

Governor Harruld nodded his agreement.

"Also, my lord, it appears Johnstane did not die without a fight."

Governor Harruld rose in his chair, eager for some good news.

"We think Johnstane wounded his killer, although it seems as if there was some rushed attempt to cover this up. There are smeared stains on the floor of the room that is certainly blood. Johnstane was strangled, so the blood is not his, and the landlady claims that they were not there before. I think the killer has been maimed. Johnstane's side arm is missing. I believe the killer took the weapon upon leaving."

"No one can leave the city without the clearance of the Command, so there is a good chance that the killer remains within the city walls." Governor Harruld thought, absently gnawing at a rag nail. "Captain, fetch me a list of all those who have left the city in the last two days. And, Captain, keep an eye out for that key. If the door was locked from the outside, it has to be somewhere," the governor ordered.

The captain saluted and turned to leave the room.

"And, Captain," Governor Harruld called after him. "Good work."

Chapter Sixteen

"WHERE'S KALFINAR?" Evelyne asked, storming into the room where Broden sat in conversation with the three old physicians and Chentuck.

"I think he's gone to our chambers. I got the impression he was a bit put out of joint by the idea that you and Chentuck would be joining us."

"So I've heard!" she snapped each word off. "I've had enough of his shit. One of us needs to say something. Seems you're all quite content to indulge his attitude." Sarbien's daughter flashed out of the room.

"My, she is a feisty one isn't she?" Broden quipped.

"You have no idea," Chentuck replied with a good-humoured grimace.

Evelyne's buckskin-soled shoes padded quietly atop the flagstones lining the accommodation wing. She had found Broden and Kalfinar's shared chamber to be empty. Evelyne chided herself for having barged into the vacant room and voicing her annoyance at nothing but the walls.

"Self-pitying prick," she muttered to herself as she searched. "Needs a good kick up the arse."

Evelyne wasn't quite sure how long she had been searching, having got lost amidst a maze of stairs and hallways. Upon hearing a strange sound, she stopped in front of a shut door to a distant apartment. Leaning her ear against the door, she listened.

———

Kalfinar clenched his teeth and squeezed his eyes shut. His skin burned and he felt the perspiration merging, creeping towards his hairline. His fists balled by his temples as he hunkered in the darkness of the empty apartment he once shared with his wife.

Tears fell freely from his eyes and soaked his face. The mounting pressures and conflicts of his heart and mind washed over him. Only now did the pain find its escape.

"I'm sorry. I tried not to come." He slouched onto the floor, his back to the cold stone wall. "Why? Why did you leave me?" Kalfinar's words were coughed out between sobs and the crackling of mucus. "Why did you go? Why did you go away? I'm not able for this. I'm wasted. I'm at my journey's end, love." His spluttered words fell into the blackness of the room around him. "Call me home, my dear. Call me home and I'll come."

His mind raced, flashing from one thought to the next. The task before him, vast and beyond his understanding. The burning need to return to the docks, to his relief, constantly nagging, itching, tormenting him. The pain of his loss, stabbing at his heart, over and over. His shame, so much shame, and the pain. His secret wish to rest at last, leaving all the burdens aside. And, finally, his duty to those about him. Those whom he still loved. He released an agonising moan, banging the back of his head repeatedly onto the wall. A maelstrom of sorrow enveloped him, and his heart ached.

———

Evelyne stood silently against the door, tears brimming her eyes and rolling down her cheeks as she felt the full force of Kalfinar's pain.

The moan from the other side of the door trailed off into a pitiful whimper. It was wrong, she knew, that she should bare silent witness to this grief. She carefully removed herself from the apartment and left Kalfinar to his agony.

"Thaskil, make sure the sergeants have the men ready. Each soldier must have all of the personal equipment on this list. No exceptions and no excuses." Bergnon handed a rolled sheet to the young officer. "Arrlun, see that the quartermaster and his men have loaded the provisions tonight. I want the ships to be moving down the Valeswater by sunrise."

They saluted and set about their business.

When the young lieutenants had vacated the room, Bergnon opened up the map of Ilsinuer, and looked at his objective: Sail down the Valeswater and then push ahead with the battalion to the city of Apula and make ready the defence against Solansian raiders.

"Apula shall bleed for the sake of the Free Provinces once again. Another red season dawns," Bergnon sighed. He squeezed his eyes shut and cradled his head in his hands. "And so to blood."

Kalfinar opened the door and entered the office where Broden sat with Governor Harruld, the three physicians, Chentuck and Evelyne. His face revealed little of his earlier grief.

"Where have you been?" Harruld asked. "We've waited for some time."

"I needed to think." Kalfinar said as he took his place at the table. "I must apologise for my earlier behaviour. Been a little short on manners of late. I can't profess to understand fully this path we tread, but I know we each have a role to play in this. I'll accept what I don't understand. Chentuck, please accept my apology. I've behaved with ignorance and little grace."

Kalfinar leant across the table and shook the hand of the Ravenmayne. As he sat back in to his seat, Kalfinar caught the eye of Evelyne, who smiled at him, nodding her thanks almost imperceptibly.

Olmat produced a map and spread it over the table. "Pay attention to me now, for you will have to remember what I show you on this map. Remember well, for you may take nought but memory, for fear it falls into the hands of our enemy."

Each of the members of the expedition edged closer to the old physician.

"There are three that make up the Horn of Dajda. They will each need to be awoken. You must be so very careful, for the Godstone will be the most desired object in the world, and many will try to claim it. Doing so will put the soul of every man, woman and child in a position of the gravest danger, and leaving them exposed to those of dark motives. Once you have located them, you must touch the Godstone to their beating heart to awaken them. Do that as soon as you find them, for in mere human form they are more vulnerable than once they have been awoken. Do it quickly, for I fear you will be tracked and enemies will try to steal away the mortal life before they can be brought into the world as whole. Be wary of this, for if the body dies, the soul is lost to us until its rebirth."

"How will the Godstone come to us?" Kalfinar asked.

"It comes now, Kalfinar. When we pray to Dajda, and it is known that we are ready, Evelyne shall receive it. Let us pray, in whatever words you wish. They will be heard all same."

They bowed their heads and offered silent words to Dajda.

After several interminable minutes, Olmat spoke, "Dajda is coming."

A flash of hot wind gusted around the room, blowing out candles and flame, leaving the room in total blackness.

"Dajda is here," Olmat continued.

Light exploded into the room, and was gone again. The glare blinded everyone with a kaleidoscopic storm of pulsing colours.

"That is all," Olmat said in the blackness.

"Someone fetch a light," Harruld called to the one of the guardsmen outside of the room.

As the room was illuminated, Kalfinar gasped. "Evelyne!" he shouted as he pushed his chair back. His actions were mirrored by all. "What's happened?" he roared as Evelyne lay slumped backwards in her chair, a smouldering mark in her dress above her breast.

Olmat spoke, "Fear not, for she has received Dajda."

"What?" Kalfinar opened her closed eyes, checking for signs of life. He felt for a pulse. "What are you talking about?" Kalfinar asked.

"Trouble not, Kalfinar. Evelyne will be fine." As Olmat spoke, Evelyne stirred, her eyes flickering open.

"Father," she coughed. It was a dry and wracking noise. "Has it happened?"

"Yes, my love." Sarbien's smile was unable to fully mask his concern.

Broden produced a mug of water for Evelyne. "This will help your throat," he said as he wrapped her fine hand around the earthenware mug. She lightly nodded her gratitude. Broden returned to his seat with a timid smile.

"Olmat, what exactly has occurred here? I thought we were to receive the Godstone?" Kalfinar asked.

The old man stared at Kalfinar for a brief moment with an amused look on his face. "We have received it." He glanced towards the stricken woman and back to Kalfinar. "Evelyne is the Godstone."

"Get that first ship moving! We can't linger here all bloody morning!" The sun crept above the horizon as Bergnon shouted ahead to the first ship transporting men and supplies along the Valeswater. "Damn it, but we're already behind schedule," Bergnon cursed.

"Relax," Kalfinar said, clapping a hand on his friend's shoulder. "You'll be in Apula before you know it."

"Aye, perhaps so," Bergnon replied as he stared at the sailors fumbling with the lead ship's tethers. He made to shout at the sailors, but then returned his focus to his companions. "I wish I could come with you."

"I too." Kalfinar smiled. "But you're needed at Apula. If our theory's correct, Colonel Albasi and many others are already dead. There'll be few remaining skilled enough to ready the city's defences," Kalfinar replied.

"And there's no one better for the job," Broden said. "Listen to everything Major Bergnon has to say, lads," Broden addressed Thaskil and Arrlun. "You'll be serving under one of our best. There's much you can learn from him."

"So, farewell?" Bergnon offered his hand to Kalfinar, but was embraced instead.

Sensing his friend flinch within their embrace, Kalfinar stepped back. "You alright?" he asked.

"Fine." Bergnon smiled. "I just pulled a muscle loading my armour last night. I guess we're just getting that little bit older. Should've left the labour to these strapping lads." He laughed and slapped Arrlun on the back.

"In that case, I'll settle for a handshake." Said Kalfinar as they shook hands.

Broden laughed as he stepped up towards Bergnon. "Be careful, friend, we've much more wine to drink together."

"Until the wine then, good luck." Bergnon said before he turned and ascended the gangway, followed by his lieutenants onto the ship.

Kalfinar watched as the gangway was hauled up and the ship pulled away from the dock. The sun climbed high into the morning sky, silhouetting Bergnon at the stern of the ship as it slid away on the Valeswater. "Until the wine then, my friend."

———————

"Are you sure she's able to travel?" Kalfinar asked Sarbien as they waited in the courtyard. Their horses were fully loaded and ready to depart.

"Stop fussing over her, both of you. She's harder than her frame shows. You'll learn that soon enough, I'd think," Sarbien said before heading off to find his daughter.

"Remember, son," Harruld said, "there's much in movement all around us that is beyond our understanding. All that you can do is accept what is taking place and carry on."

Kalfinar nodded his acceptance.

"You must find the horn and return to us here within the month, for I fear the tide is coming quickly," Harruld said gravely.

"A month! Father, we must travel much of the Cullanain, and who knows where else, searching for people we don't even know. How can we possibly be back in Carte in a month?"

Olmat replied, "There will be a way. It is possible."

More doubt, trust, blind faith. Faith, what faith have I left? I'm wretched. All I have faith in is the docks, the smoke and filth of it all.

"This is goodbye for now," Broden said as he embraced Harruld.

"Look after my boy, Broden."

"As always."

"You both need to look after each other," Olmat said, "for the road will be dangerous. There are many who will now seek the Godstone, and the horn too. Be very cautious."

Kalfinar embraced both men and pulled himself into his saddle as Evelyne and Chentuck made their way into the courtyard. Sarbien, Capriath and Brother Anthony followed after them, and to each they bid their farewell.

———

Kalfinar and Broden rode side by side at the head of the party; Chentuck and Evelyne at the rear. The air was chill and damp, as an evening mist rolled down from the heather-clad hills around them and slid, phantom like, across the drumlins lining their route.

"It's been a long day," Kalfinar said over his shoulder to the others. "We ought to stop and make camp for the night."

"Over there?" Broden pointed towards a cluster of stubby trees which clung sickly to their last remaining leaves.

"Should do," Kalfinar grunted. "Best scout around it first," he instructed.

Broden galloped off to inspect the wooded area whilst the others approached at a more conservative pace. Broden signalled a short time later and the others made their way towards the woodland. The sun began to slide towards the horizon and the hazy light of dusk painted oily shadows in the sky.

"I'll be glad to get amongst the trees," Evelyne said from behind Kalfinar as they approached the woodland. "It seems my eyes play tricks on me."

"It's just the light. Don't be concerned," Kalfinar replied without emotion as he approached the trees. He slid off his saddle and led his horse in amongst the stand of stunted birch and pine.

They found a small clearing in the centre of the stand of trees. The party cleared away the rotted mulch of dead leaves and needles before laying out meagre bedrolls.

"I hate a cold camp," Broden complained as he began undoing his saddle to remove it from his horse.

"Don't! For night's sake!" Kalfinar snapped, a little too sharply, causing the whole party to turn suddenly. "I'm sorry," he apologised. "Best we keep the horses ready, in case we need to leave in a hurry."

"Don't dim your words on account of me," Evelyne said from the other side of the camp. "I'm all too aware of the dangers we face."

Kalfinar acknowledged her and addressed the whole group, "I think we ought to heed the warnings we have received. We'll need to be cautious when we stop at night. To that end, we'll keep the horses saddled and ready to move in a hurry, if needed. It must be a cold camp. I'll not risk giving away our position with fire or smoke."

"Sorry, Kal," Broden mumbled. "Just wasn't thinking. You're right."

"Right, well that's agreed then," Evelyne said. "Fear not, Broden. I've learnt a trick or two which will make the camp along the way somewhat more hospitable." She smiled to the big captain.

"What do you mean?" Kalfinar asked.

"My father is a skilled manipulator of the energies that exist within the world and he was able to school me in some of the more natural of these tricks. If you can find me a large, flat rock, I can concentrate a mix of mineral powders and elements that, when exposed to air and a little water, will cause the rock to heat up enough to allow us to cook on it. It will not give off any light, so we'll remain unseen."

Kalfinar caught the slightest glimpse of a wide smile through the gloom of the dusk.

"A large, flat rock. Leave it to me," Broden announced happily as he stalked off amongst the trees.

As Broden moved out of earshot Kalfinar turned to Evelyne. "A large rock? You could use his head."

They had been sailing down the Valeswater for over twelve hours. The sun had set and the ships had laid anchor for the night, rather than negotiate the fast-flowing river in the dark. Arrlun and Thaskil stood on the poop deck and watched over the soldiers as they ate their evening meal.

"I'd never have expected to be commissioned so soon," Arrlun said. "I'm just sorry it's come at such a heavy price."

"Just hope I'm ready for it." Thaskil leant his elbows on the deck rail and cradled his head in his hands. He straightened himself up and vigorously rubbed his stubbled face. "Enough of this heavy talk." He smiled to Arrlun and nudged him in the side. "I think you'll like Apula."

"Oh aye? Why's that then?" the Noehmian lad asked in his distinct accent. "I didn't think you got any snow there. I'd feel out of place."

"It's a beautiful city," Thaskil said as he turned towards his comrade and leant on one elbow. "The smell of fresh sweet-breads and coffee fills every winding street you walk through. Your mouth will be watering."

"I doubt there'll be much baking of bread with the poor harvests," the big northerner countered with a half-mocking grin.

"Alright then. The view from the city walls across the plain will drop you to your knees. The winter poppies should be flowering by the time we arrive. From late autumn, they coat the plain beyond the city like a sea of rubies. They sway in the winds like the swell on the surface of the sea."

"Poetic, but not likely. If I know anything about agriculture in tough times, which I will hasten to add, I do," Arrlun said as he adopted a thoughtful look, "I would suggest your kinfolk will have recognised the fertility of the soil of the plain and sown crops there."

"Not a chance of it. The poppy is on the city's coat of arms. I'd say you're wrong on that count. Apulan's are a proud people. We'd rather go hungry than plough up the poppies!" Thaskil said as he shifted his weight. "Right, I've got it."

"Come on, what is it?"

"It's the women!" he laughed. "The women are the most beautiful in both Ilsinuer and Noehmia."

"That's quite the claim!" Arrlun remarked.

"They are dark-haired, with warm, golden skin, and have eyes like emeralds." Thaskil smiled to himself for a moment. "Ah, they are just beautiful."

"I think I may like this city after all. It's so damn cold in Gerloup that most of the time our women are so well wrapped-up in furs that you'd be skilled to tell them apart from the men!" He patted his friend on the shoulder and then turned to watch over the soldiers. "How long has it been since you were home, Thaskil?"

Thaskil emitted a long sigh. "Six years. I was twelve winters when I first went to Carte to start as a cadet. It's been a long time."

"You've missed your family, haven't you?"

"I have. I know how fortunate I am to be with this battalion and to be going home. I've dreamt of it. Just wish the circumstances were different."

"Never worry about that, aye. We can't change it now, so it'll do you no good sitting on it. Imagine their faces when they see you ride into the city. At the head of a battalion, no less!" Arrlun spread his open hand before their faces as though spreading the image before them. "Aye, not a bad sight, huh?"

"You're right." A grin spread over Thaskil's face. "My sister's face will just drop. She always used to say I'd not make it beyond pot cleaner!"

"You've a sister, aye?" Arrlun interrupted as a not-so-innocent smile spilt his face. "I love sisters."

"Don't even think about it! I'll send you back to Gerloup with your seeds in a coin pouch!" Thaskil punched his friend in the shoulder and both men struggled to stifle their laughter in front of the men of their new command.

"That's a handy trick to know," Broden commented as he rubbed his stomach. "I always feel better after having a hot meal, don't you?" He reached across and gave Kalfinar a playful slap on the thigh. "What do you say, misery-guts?"

Kalfinar ignored the playful taunt and instead sought out Evelyne with more questions about the Godstone. He could not see her for the blackness of the night, but he knew she sat no more than two metres from him. "So how is it we will determine our course of travel if the Godstone cannot be seen to be leading us towards the sleeping ones? Have you been gifted some insight?"

"My understanding of how this will work is that I'll be drawn to each location, as I feel drawn now to the south. I must place my trust in that sensation, for I've been instructed to do so by my father. More of this design will reveal itself to us as we progress."

Kalfinar grunted in the darkness. He was thankful she couldn't see him shake his head with frustration.

"So you," Kalfinar addressed Chentuck. "Tell me, how have you found common folk's reactions when they see you? I mean, the initial reaction can hardly be welcoming. Granted, it may not be as hostile as my own." He coughed a short, uncomfortable laugh.

Chentuck replied from the darkness, "I was schooled by our father at home, along with Evelyne and Anthony. We did not live amongst your people as everyone else would. The home we grew up in was not in Carte, but in the foothills near Terna. Here, I had some friends, mostly children of men and women who worked with our father on his matters. I'm sure they were uncertain of me initially, but in short time, I suppose they realised that we are just the same in most ways. Old tales of monsters and Gods seem easier for children to forgive than adults. And so, I keep my face hidden for the most part."

"I'm sorry for that," Kalfinar said with a slight flush of shame. "Tell me of your God, or your Gods, as I understand it."

"What do you want to know?" Chentuck replied.

"So far all that I have learnt is really what Olmat has told me. That there is one overall God and a number of Undergods, the Desverukan. Is this the case?" Kalfinar asked into the darkness.

Chentuck replied, "Our understanding of the Gods of our people is instinctual. We are born with an appreciation of it. That does not mean we submit to it or understand the reason." He paused. "But yes, Olmat is correct. There is a controlling power. His name is Bhalur, as you have learned." Chentuck paused again. "I would suggest the utterance of these names be limited. If his creatures are hunting us, which I suspect they are, the speaking of these names could conceivably draw attention to us. Let us not take unnecessary risks. I will refer to the Master God. I assume Olmat told you of how our Father came to adopt us, correct?"

"He did," Kalfinar replied.

"Well, the creature that stalked into our village and killed my parent-folk was one of the Undergods. I understand there to be several dozen of these, each with a relevance to different tribes of the Raven-mayne. They are worshipped out of fear. I believe the Undergods demand sacrifice for the Master God when the devotion of the people has slackened. That is what must have happened to my parent-folk. I do not fully comprehend all aspects of our Master God, or indeed the Undergods, but one thing which is inherently clear to me, born as Ravenmayne, is the Master God was insulted and outcast by the other Gods of men in the days of the beginning, and the Master God has been thirsting for vengeance ever since."

"So we are at the centre of a timeless grudge then," Broden said.

"There have always been clashes amongst the Gods," Evelyne spoke. "Their egos, built on power and creations, clash time and time again, one attempting to outsmart the other, and the next trying to create something stronger, more beautiful, more deadly. They have warred since they exploded into existence."

"How do you know of this?" Broden asked.

"I can feel it. I can—I can understand it," she stammered as she replied.

"The Godstone," Kalfinar muttered.

"Yes," Evelyne said. "I think it has given me insight. The one Chentuck speaks of, the Master God, created the Ravenmayne people, as our Dajda made us. It appears they created us as one. Equals before the split tore it all asunder." She paused for a long moment, her heavy breathing the only noise audible over creaking trees. "Man and the Ravenmayne were to live amongst each other as brothers, and the same people. Their dual worship was to be received by both Gods, but then a rivalry was born with a need to obtain more worship and become more powerful. At this point, I see our Dajda created the Anulii and the Ravenmayne God created the Undergods, the Desverukan. They did battle and the Ravenmayne God was defeated. They were cast out to the wastelands of Hagra, and our Dajda, and the Tuannan bound the Ravenmayne God so he could not grow to that power and compete again. That is what I can see."

"So how has it come that we are under such threat. Has he grown in power again?" Kalfinar asked. "And if he has, how has this come about?"

"The Undergods were not bound. They received the worship of the people on his behalf, and it appears somehow that the Master God has been able to receive this and grow in strength," Evelyne said.

"How is this so?" Broden asked.

"Betrayal." With that, her voice trailed off and a she slumped to the ground, the soft thud of her head hitting the earth announced her state to the group.

"Evelyne?" Chentuck asked, rising and feeling for his sister in the dark. When his hands found her, her head was soaked with sweat, and her skin was cold to the touch.

Chapter Seventeen

"HOW MUCH LONGER DO YOU think it'll take us to get there?" Evelyne shouted ahead as the horses galloped along the road, heading towards the southern port city of Enulin.

"We've travelled about one hundred and fifty leagues," Kalfinar shouted over his shoulder. "We should be at Enulin by midday tomorrow if we maintain this pace." He reined his horse back a little, so as to come alongside Evelyne. "How are you feeling?" he asked, concerned she suffered exhaustion from the relentless travel and burden of the Godstone.

Evelyne smiled, "I'm feeling better today. A little saddle-sore. I'm not used to such travel, so I suppose that's to be expected." She feigned a look of grave pain as her backside landed upon the saddle once again, provoking laughter in the man.

"And of your head? How do you fare?" he asked, speaking of the momentary blackouts she had been suffering after interpreting the ancient memories.

"Much better. The pain is almost gone. Perhaps I'm getting used to carrying this gift. Thanks for your concern."

Kalfinar grunted and nudged his horse's flanks. The horse trotted ahead and he reined in alongside Broden, casting a sidelong glance to his cousin who sat with a smirk on his face. "What's so funny?" Kalfinar asked.

"Nothing!" Broden replied. "Just think it's nice to see your soft side every now and then."

"Oh, shut up."

"But women are great, aren't they?"

"You're hopeless," Kalfinar grumbled. "Perhaps you can do me the honour of getting your head out of your prick and give me your thoughts on that woodland ahead." He pointed towards the trees, which were bisected by the road they travelled along.

"I see it," Broden replied. "What's the matter? You see something?"

"Logical place for an ambush, isn't it?" Kalfinar replied.

"You say this at least ten times a day and still there's been nothing to bother us. I thought Sarbien said that amulet would protect you from the spirit?"

"He did," Kalfinar's brows furrowed as he whispered through clenched teeth, "but it's not my possession that concerns me. We can be tracked and the spirit can turn our own people against us." Kalfinar held his hand up in a signal for the party to stop. "Caution as always."

Broden reined his horse in beside Kalfinar and leaned close to him. "Do you think our own people could be possessed?"

"You heard Olmat and the others. If we don't pray, the link is broken, as in my case, it seems. When the link is broken, we're exposed, and when we're exposed, we can be corrupted. There are many who do not have your strength in the faith. And on top of that, they said that with Dajda in a state of stasis, all souls are exposed to some extent."

"Caution it is then," the larger captain said.

No sooner had Broden finished speaking than a projectile became visible moving through the air towards them.

"Arrow!" Broden roared and wheeled his horse around, followed by Evelyne and Chentuck.

"It's short." Kalfinar sat calmly astride his horse.

"Kal!" Broden shouted. "Get down!"

The arrow thumped into the road about fifty yards in front of Kalfinar's horse. Kalfinar dismounted from his saddle and undid his longbow, which was fastened to the rear of his saddle. He strung it and rolled his injured shoulder to loosen out the stiff muscle. He untied the cover of his quiver as another arrow thumped into the ground several yards ahead of the last, sending forth a plume of dust.

"Kal! What are you doing?" Broden called out.

"Never worry, we're out of range for now. We can wait here a moment and then pick these dreamers off. Interested in joining me?"

A third arrow smashed into the ground just behind the first.

"See? We'll be fine here. They don't have our range, and they've lost their advantage."

"Alright." Broden trotted his horse back towards Kalfinar, before dismounting and untying his longbow.

"Look!" Evelyne shouted, pointing towards the trees.

A group of six men came running out of the woods. Five of them ran towards them waving swords, while one followed behind holding a bow.

"Seems a little unusual, don't you think?" Broden commented.

"No appreciation of strategy," Kalfinar said as he pulled an arrow from his quiver and readied his bow. His cousin mirrored his actions. "Broden, you're a better shot than me."

"So you finally admit it," the big captain grumbled with a throaty laugh.

"Shoulder's still a little stiff, that's all. Be a good man and take out that bowman when he makes it to range, would you?"

"It's done." A moment later, he pulled his arm back, so the feather flights sat by the side of his face. Broden waited a moment, and then let fly his arrow. "Wait for it."

In the passing moment, Kalfinar fired off an arrow at one of the onrushing attackers.

"Got him!" Broden shouted as his arrow slammed into the throat of the charging bowman, fletchings flush to his skin and sending a mist of blood into the air before the man crashed to the ground in a stiff heap.

One kick. Two kicks. Dead.

"Nice work," Kalfinar said, as his own shot fell wide of his mark.

"You take the left and I'll take the right," Broden apportioned the targets. "We'll meet in the middle."

The two men fired off several arrows. Broden's found their mark expertly, while Kalfinar only made his target once out of four shots. One attacker remained, and continued his mad charge along the road they travelled.

"Wait!" Kalfinar ordered, his bow laid across Broden's. "He attacks alone."

The onrushing man yelled nonsense as he charged the final two hundred yards towards them.

"Seems strange, don't you think?" Kalfinar said as he dropped his bow and drew his sword. "He's just seen his comrade's fall dead around him, yet he still charges, outnumbered, outmatched. It's not normal. Let's take him alive."

The man, dressed in the plain clothes of a farm labourer, charged towards them holding a rusted and nicked short sword above his head. His screams were seemingly nothing but random noises, though they were disturbing nonetheless. As the man bore down on the two captains they stepped a short distance apart.

"Let him come," Kalfinar said.

The man stopped a few strides from the men before him. His wild eyes flashed from Kalfinar to Broden, and then back. His face bore no significant expression until his eyes rested on Kalfinar. The man's face broke into a savage cry as he charged, his sword aloft. Kalfinar deftly sidestepped the rush, parried the blow, and spun around the man in one movement. Kalfinar's hilt crashed onto the back of the man's skull, sending him face-first into the hard dirt of the road.

"Fetch me rope," Kalfinar instructed. "Let's bind him before any more come at us."

Broden and Chentuck reined in their gallop.

"The stand's empty." Broden said. "No more of them in there. Looks like there was a camp of sorts. Seems they'd been waiting a few days."

"Bandits?" Kalfinar asked.

"Don't think so," Broden replied. "Let's go wake this one and ask him just what he and his friends were doing shooting arrows at us." He walked towards the bound man, who lay slumped by a rock at the side of the road.

The party stood around their captive as Broden aimed a kick at the man's thigh to wake him. As he stirred, the man's eyes flickered and he groaned. He moved his bound hands to the back of his head, searching for his blood-crusted and swollen wound.

"Just who the fuck are you?" Kalfinar asked, looking down on the man.

As he spoke, the captive's eyes flashed open and he exploded into action, leaping towards Kalfinar's leg with his mouth gaping. Springing backwards, Kalfinar avoided the rabid man, who now hunkered before them, posed ready to strike like a wild animal. His mouth was open wide and he hissed. A faint green discharge crusted around his eyes.

"What's wrong with this man?" Broden asked.

"He's been taken," Chentuck replied, eyes fixed on those of the man.

"Who are you?" Kalfinar asked.

The man answered in a foreign tongue, alien to Kalfinar, but not unfamiliar.

As the man answered, Chentuck's face twisted in revulsion. "This man's soul is tainted. It is twinned with something evil."

"This man is possessed," Evelyne said.

"He speaks the tongue of the Undergods," Chentuck supplied. "He just said there are more and that we're all going to die this very day."

"That's encouraging," Broden muttered.

"He's lying," Evelyne said. "The spirit is frightened."

"Frightened of what?" Kalfinar asked.

"Frightened of me." Evelyne stepped forward.

As she did, the possessed man fell backwards and tried to scramble away, spitting words in the guttural tongue. She hunkered down beside the man and looked into his eyes. A stillness passed between them and the possessed man's rabid face relaxed and became calm. In almost the same instant, the savage look returned and he leapt at Evelyne.

She deflected his face with the back of her hand before wheeling around on the balls of her feet and kneeling on the man's shoulders. Her middle and forefinger pressed firmly into the man's forehead. The skin of his head began to hiss as she pressed her fingers. The man screamed. She pressed firmer still until he emitted a shrill cry, which shot out of him and shrieked skyward from the party. The man looked into Evelyne's eyes, exhausted, and then passed out of consciousness.

Evelyne whispered a short incantation into a closed fist before opening it to reveal a small copper-like amulet, similar to the one Kalfinar wore around his neck. Fastening it around the unconscious man's neck, she said, "Wrap him in some blankets and let's take him with us. He poses no threat to us now."

"Evelyne, that's really quite amazing," Broden exclaimed, enraptured by her ability. "Did your father teach you that also?"

"This is not something I've been taught." She looked solemnly towards the man as Chentuck wrapped a blanket around him. "I felt compelled to do this. I believe it to be something I've gained, along with the insight."

"Damn it," Kalfinar spat as he turned from the scene and headed toward his horse.

"What is it, Kal?" Broden asked.

"If Evelyne can free a man from a spirit, then those other men didn't need to die." Kalfinar looked at the five bodies that littered the open ground between the stand of trees and them. "Those men could have gone home to their families tonight."

They tied the unconscious man across the rear of Chentuck's saddle and started off again.

"Let's avoid the roads from here on," Kalfinar said. "Too easy to lay an ambush."

"We've made good headway up until now," Broden said as he shifted in his saddle. "A bit of cross country won't do us any harm."

"Evelyne," Kalfinar said, "can you orientate us accurately to Enulin across wild country?"

"Yes. I can lead us wherever I feel the draw is strongest. I'm sure I can keep us on track," she replied.

"Good, let's get going then. We've hours yet until sunset."

They rode on through the open, rolling countryside of southern Ilsinuer, avoiding the road and keeping a keen eye for any further signs of ambush. The captive man remained unconscious.

"If all's well, we should reach Enulin by tomorrow. Sometime after midday," Kalfinar said as they reined in. "We should check that area out." He pointed towards a rocky outcrop in the distance. "If it's clear, it'll make a good spot for us to rest up for the night."

After they cooked their evening meal, the captive man began to stir. He awoke and let out a ragged groan, followed by a low and quite sob. His eyes adjusted and settled on the faces before him. He snivelled and began to cry once more.

"Enough sorrow," Broden said.

"Who are you?" Kalfinar followed up, looming tall above the man.

The captive's body trembled and tears began to stream freely down his dirt-smeared face. "Name's Yaren. Yaren Hobbs, my lord. Just a farmer. From Helvensfoot Brook." A bead of spit coalesced on his lower lip as it wobbled like hooked meat on his face. "My lord, I dunno what I've done to cause you offence. Dunno why I'm here."

Evelyne picked up a cloth and moved towards Yaren, hunkering down beside him and placing the cloth into the pot of the recently warmed water. She wrung off the excess and began to wipe the dirt from his face as he sobbed with fear. Her touch, unnerving at first, seemed to relax him and he stared at her, fixated by her eyes as she cleaned his face.

"Do you remember trying to kill us?" Kalfinar asked.

Yaren's eyes widened at the mention of his crime. His whole body started to judder.

"Cease that!" Kalfinar shouted. "We'll do you?" he pressed.

Yaren shut his mouth and tried to control his panic-struck body.

"No, my lord, I don't remember that." He looked up at Evelyne. "Last I recall, I was digging out my rotten neeps. I remember a feeling like I was going to be sick…feeling afraid, and then a pain in my head. After that, dunno what happened until I woke here."

Kalfinar thought for a moment as he fingered the amulet around his neck. Yaren watched him before realising he too had a similar one around his own neck.

Kalfinar looked at the man. "Have you had dark dreams? Dreams where you felt something was coming for you. Have you sensed dread in sleep?"

Yaren nodded his head slowly, a frightened look dawning in the man's eyes. "Aye, my lord. I truly have."

They provided Yaren with some food and sent him off in the direction of his home, which appeared to be about two days walk to the north of their position. They set off just before sunrise and made good time. They crested a tall hill of dry, thick-bladed yellow grass, and looked down upon the southern Ilsinian city of Enulin.

"It's beautiful," Evelyne exclaimed. The city sparkled in the midday sun, making it a fine sight when paired with the glittering sea by which it was situated.

"What do you feel?" Kalfinar asked Evelyne.

"We're near. I can feel a pull towards the city. The urge has grown stronger and more defined. I can feel it now as we sit here, tugging at me."

"What do we look for?" Kalfinar asked.

"We'll know soon enough. I believe that when the time comes it will be unmistakable," Evelyne answered, her eyes fixated on the city before her. Focused like a hunter's eyes upon prey.

They set off again towards Enulin, the final stretch of the first leg of their journey coming to a conclusion. Ever alert, they approached the city a short time afterwards and were greeted by an explosion of spices and colours as they passed through the bazaar outside the sandstone walls.

"Things seem normal here," Broden said as he observed the hubbub of the marketplace.

"It's not," Kalfinar spoke quietly. He indicated with his eyes. "The City Guard are everywhere. I have to deliver dispatches to the Command when we get in here. I want to keep our visibility as low as possible, for as long as possible. We should take a room at the command safe house. There's a cosy, somewhat-underused inn over by the eastern gate that is sometimes used by agents not wanting to be seen entering the High Command keep. That'll be a good place to lay low until we work out just what we need to do."

They wound their way through the noisy and hot streets of Enulin. The streets teemed with traders and customers alike, all bartering in great animated gestures, as was the Enulinian way. Kalfinar and his companions formed a protective knot around Evelyne as they led their horses through the busy streets, believing passing on foot would draw less attention. They watched the hands and eyes of the passers-by as they went, ever watchful for the slightest sign of trouble.

They entered into the courtyard of an unspectacular inn. "Head in and take a room with a view of the street," Kalfinar ordered. "I must deliver these dispatches. I should be back within the hour."

Kalfinar knocked three times on the heavy oak wood door. "It's Kalfinar. Put your weapons down."

Chentuck opened the door and Kalfinar strode in.

He slumped into a battered wooden chair by the grubby window. "We've lost twelve men here."

"Twelve." Broden shook his head sorrowfully. "Did they catch any of the assassins?"

"None." Kalfinar rubbed his bearding face as he felt dust clinging thickly to it. "Command sits with a major by the name of Maltasi. I've never heard of him before. He seems unsure of himself. All the more senior officers are dead." The weariness in Kalfinar's voice was palpable. "After the assassinations, the more senior major, Major Coltsmoot, was to assume command."

"What happened to him then?" Broden asked.

"Seems the shock brought on a falling sickness and he dropped dead." Kalfinar stepped over to a wash bowl and proceeded to splash his face. Dirt dripped from his chin, creating whirls and spirals as it merged with the clean water. "Maltasi's dispatches should have reached Carte by now." He dried off his face and neck. "Any food?"

———

Kalfinar ate the modest meal of hard bread, cheese and ham without complaint. "Evelyne, how do you feel now?" he asked as he finished his meal.

"I feel as though I am being pulled towards them, and I think they are coming to me also." She sat by a window. It was clouded with age-old dirt, obscuring the view onto the street below.

"So you think the horn comes to us?" he asked.

"Yes," she replied without looking away from the window. "I can feel the draw getting stronger, they are getting closer." Her voice had adopted an almost monotone drone and she focussed intently on the street.

"Why don't we just wait here then?" Broden asked. "It's probably safer, don't you think?"

"Aye, you're probably right," Kalfinar responded. "Fine, it's decided then. Let's wait until we see them, then we'll make an approach."

They surrounded the window overlooking the street and waited.

"I can't see through that damned thing," Broden said as he reached out to rub the dirt away with the cuff of his sleeve.

"No!" Kalfinar grabbed his wrist to prevent him from clearing the time-gathered filth away from the pane of glass, "Let's not make it too obvious that we are watching the street. We don't know who else is out there. Watching. Waiting."

They waited for what seemed an eternity, with no signs of any approach.

"Are you sure they'll come to us?" Broden asked Evelyne as the light of day began to fade. There was no reply, and Broden looked quizzically to Kalfinar. "Guess she's not listening to—"

"They are here," she replied, her eyes closed and her voice almost lifeless.

"You alright?" Broden reached over and touched her shoulder. "Evelyne?" he asked again.

"It's beautiful," Kalfinar murmured. Before him he saw a glowing light, about the size of a man, moving up the centre of the street towards the inn.

He was struck with an overwhelming mix of emotion. "So beautiful."

"What can you see?" Broden asked.

"The one before us shine bright with Dajda's love. This is called the reverie," Evelyne said. "This is what draws them home to Dajda's heart."

"I can only see the people below." Broden said.

"What of the light moving up the middle of the street towards us?" Kalfinar asked.

"I see no light. There's nothing, save for a child. A little beggar girl walking towards us," Broden replied.

Evelyne interrupted them, "It is time. We must bring them here. They must be awoken." Her eyes snapped open and she turned to face Kalfinar. "Hurry. Danger comes."

Kalfinar and Broden bounded down the stairs, hands fixed on sword hilts, ready to draw should the need arise. They burst out of the back entrance to the inn and through the courtyard into the street. Kalfinar froze at the sight of the glowing light hovering in place outside the entrance to the inn.

"Come on," Broden snapped, hauling at Kalfinar.

As Kalfinar made the final steps towards the nimbus, the light faded, revealing a weak and dishevelled little girl, no more than five years old. Her eyes shone a deep green, complemented by a shock of rich brown hair. Kalfinar choked as his throat swelled up at the sight of her.

"Kal, pull yourself together!" Broden snapped. "Come on, let's get her inside."

The little girl appeared to be in a trance-like state and offered little resistance as Broden picked her up. A number of onlookers stopped and watched as the two men hurried back around to the courtyard with the small girl. Kalfinar opened the doors and allowed Broden to storm in and up the stairs towards their room. As he followed his cousin up the stairs, the small girl, being held over Broden's shoulder, looked at Kalfinar with her skin still sparkling, and smiled the faintest little smile. Kalfinar's heart broke.

"Lay her here, on the table," Evelyne instructed as they entered the room with the girl. "We must be fast. She will not be safe until we turn her. We have to awaken her now."

"What do we do?" Kalfinar asked as they laid the child onto the small table.

"Everything I tell you to, without question, without hesitation. Do you understand?"

They nodded.

"Chentuck, hold her legs down. Broden, you take her arms. Be firm, and don't worry about hurting the child."

The small girl groaned and blinked.

"Hurry! She is coming out of the reverie," Evelyne barked.

Footsteps could be heard bursting into the inn, causing all to look towards the door.

"Broden, lock the door," Evelyne commanded.

He quickly saw to it as footsteps and shouting could be heard down the stairs.

Evelyne tore open the small girl's ragged dress from neck to her belly. "Kalfinar, take this blade and make a hand-width incision here, just above the heart." She handed Kalfinar a long, sharp silver blade. His face reflected a troubled look. "Broden, take this clamp and insert it between the ribs once Kalfinar has made the incision."

As the shouting grew louder, the little girl stirred once more, her eyes flickering open. Footsteps could be heard coming up the stairs now. They flashed looks to each other.

"Draw your weapons," Kalfinar said.

"No!" Evelyne barked. "There is no time, we must see this through now! Make the cut!"

Kalfinar looked at the little girl's eyes as they flickered open and closed. He hesitated as a nearby door was kicked open.

"Here, give it to me." Broden grabbed the blade of his cousin, placing the clamp in his hands. He placed the blade tip on the little girl's chest, causing her eyes to flash open, an emerald explosion. She unleashed an almighty scream as she stared at the alien being holding her legs down and the strangers around her.

"Do it, Broden!" Evelyne shouted. "Do it now!"

The door to the room crashed open in a shower of wooden splinters and a half-dozen blue liveried city guards poured into the room, their swords drawn. The blade sliced deeply. The little girl screamed as the city guards stormed forward.

Chentuck released the girl's legs and, in an instant, had his twin swords free. He parried the guard's blows with a speed and savagery that forced the guards backwards.

"Don't kill anyone!" Kalfinar shouted as the Ravenmayne engaged the guardsmen.

The little girl's scream subsided as she passed out. Broden finished the incision.

"Clamp it, Kalfinar," Evelyne ordered.

Kalfinar clamped the incision, exposing the little girl's beating heart before them, pounding its rhythm. "Help him," Kalfinar said to Broden. The ring of steel and voices in the room was fearsome. He cast a quick glance at the melee that had unfolded.

Broden waded in to the fight, crashing the pommel of his sword behind the ear of a guardsman, sending the man crumpling face-first to the rough wooden floor. He stepped up beside Chentuck and set about driving the remaining guardsmen tight into the corner of the room.

"Hold her," Evelyne cried over the noise. The urgency of her voice tore Kalfinar's attention back from the fight before him. He pressed down on the small shoulders of the child and gazed into her face. *I've seen you in my dreams, little one.*

Evelyne repeated an incantation and placed her mid and forefinger onto the beating heart of the child. There was an explosion of light and force, sending all in the room backwards onto the floor and blowing the panes of glass out into the street in fragments.

Kalfinar pushed himself onto his elbows and looked towards the source of the light. He felt an instant mix of emotion, both sad and joyous at once. Tears welled in his eyes and he gasped at the brightly glowing child that floating before him. A spear of white heat radiated from her heart.

"Secure the room!" Evelyne cried out. Her words prompted a scramble for weapons.

By the time the guardsmen had gotten to their feet, it was over. Kalfinar, supported by Broden and Chentuck, had the advantage.

"Let's just go easy, lads." Broden grinned at the city guards who remained conscious and able-bodied. "No one needs to get hurt. Well, no one needs to get badly hurt."

"Broden, don't waste your words," Kalfinar said, sheathing his sword. "Their minds are elsewhere." He regarded the guardsmen before him. Their mouths were slack and open, their eyes brimmed with tears as they stared mesmerised by the small child of light before them.

"She is with us now. She is the first of the Horn of Dajda." Evelyne wept as she received the child. The intense light from the girl's heart faded as she was enveloped.

Kalfinar saw there was little need to concoct a believable cover story for what had just taken place. The guardsmen, now bound and sat in a corner of the room, stared at the small girl who slept soundly in Evelyne's arms, a look of deep peace settled on her face. The explosion of terror and then light that had met them as they entered the room had given way to an air of serenity. They were captivated by the child.

"They can't hear a word I'm saying." Kalfinar turned from them and sat by Evelyne and the others.

"They are in awe of her grace," Evelyne whispered as she rocked the child back and forth in her arms.

"What of her wound?" Kalfinar asked.

"It sealed the instant she was awoken by Dajda's touch. She is safe now from most dangers on this world." She looked up at Kalfinar and held his gaze with her ice-blue eyes. "Do not ever hesitate again when I give you an order. They are fragile in human form. We could easily have lost her."

Her reprimand was delivered gently, but Kalfinar felt the power of the command all the same. "My lady," he accepted her rebuke demurely.

As he spoke, the little girl's green eyes flickered open and gazed directly at him, before she shut them and fell back asleep. Once more, Kalfinar felt his throat tighten with emotion.

"What will we do with the guardsmen?" Broden asked Evelyne.

"Leave them here. They are entranced for the meantime and when they come around, they will probably be hit with an overwhelming urge to speak to Dajda. They offer us no threat. I suggest you untie them before we leave."

"And when will that be?" he asked again.

"I suggest we leave now. We must travel south," she said.

"South?" Kalfinar questioned. "Across the Yellow Sea? To where? Canna?"

"Yes, I think so. We must leave tonight."

Kalfinar nodded grimly back. "Tonight it is." *South. South to jalsinum and baking sun. If ever there's a dark hole rotten enough for my wasted soul, it'll be in the south. Smoke and blood, whores and mud.*

"Let's just lead the horses out of the city street," Kalfinar said as they gathered in the courtyard. "No point in making ourselves too obvious."

He led the party out of the courtyard gates and into the lamp-lit streets of Enulin. The customary hubbub from the merchants had died down and was replaced by the desperate side of the city. They hawked what wares they could, mostly cheap wine and even cheaper flesh.

"Anyone in need of comfort tonight?" a thin whore called out from the sickly light of an upstairs window across from the inn.

"Not tonight, sister," Kalfinar said in a low, gravelly voice. His hand rested on his sword's pommel under his cloak.

"What a beautiful child," the whore croaked from above.

Kalfinar exchanged a look with Evelyne and carried on walking.

"I said, what a beautiful child," the whore rasped again.

"Just ignore her," Evelyne whispered.

The whore cackled from above. "She's going to burn." The whore's head shook in a brief judder as Kalfinar looked up at her.

"What did you say?" he growled.

The whore laughed a ragged sound and leaned out of her window, her thin, veiny breasts nearly falling out of her threadbare dress. "You're all going to fucking burn." She waggled a long black tongue at them and leapt up onto the window sill in a crouch. "You're all going to fucking burn. Take them!" the whore called out to the night and was answered by inhuman howls from the streets and alleyways around them.

"Back to the inn!" Evelyne shouted.

They turned and sped towards the inn's gate, covering the short distance in a moment.

Kalfinar glanced behind as they began to close the gates and saw a group of around three dozen men and women sprinting towards the inn. He slammed the doors shut and locked them before turning to Evelyne. "Are they more of the possessed?"

"Yes, but the whore was different. Did you feel it?"

Kalfinar rubbed unconsciously at his amulet. "The spirit?"

"Yes. It has followed us."

"It said the child would burn. Can she be hurt?"

"No, not in this world. But we can, and without us, the horn cannot be found."

"We're badly outnumbered," Broden called over from where he tethered his horse.

"The gates are narrow. They should prevent us being over-whelmed," Kalfinar said, drawing his sword and hatchet.

"The guardsmen will fight with us," Evelyne replied. "Chentuck, bring them down."

"You should go with him, and take the child," Kalfinar said to Evelyne.

"The child will be safe enough down here. As for me, we need every blade we have. I stay where I am."

"But-"

"Save your breath, Kal." Evelyne drew a long, gently curved sword from beneath the skirt of her saddle. "If I fall, Dajda will find another. Just stay out of my way."

The banging of steel against wood rang loudly throughout the courtyard. The wood splintered and brief flashes of glinting steel and teeth could be seen.

"I wish some more of the city guard would turn up," Broden grumbled as he stood with his sword in a two-handed grip.

"We've got the sector patrol right here," Kalfinar said, looking at the six stern-faced guardsmen beside them. "Others will come, but perhaps not in time. Fight hard."

"Only fighting I know." Broden flashed a smile at him.

"Good. Get ready. Here they come." Kalfinar spun his hatchet in his left hand and tightened his grip on his sword with his right.

The courtyard door burst open and bodies spilled in. Steel whirled. Kalfinar parried an overhead blow with his sword and smashed his hatchet blade into the face of the possessed. A mist of blood plumed up from the wound and the body crashed to the cobbled courtyard, already slick with blood. The body kicked out twice, and then lay still.

Another possessed barged into him from the side, catching his aching shoulder and almost sending him reeling to the corpse-littered stones. As he spun to engage the possessed, the man stiffened and fumbled at the blade point that protruded from his chest. A line of blood spilled out of the man's mouth and down his chin as his eyes tried to search behind him. The blade withdrew and the possessed dropped onto his knees and then fell sideways. A guardsman stepped from behind the corpse and nodded at Kalfinar before re-joining the fray.

Kalfinar stepped past the possessed as her fingers played at the rent in her throat, a broad wave of blood flowing from the wound in pulses. He heard the rattle of breath behind him and a thump on the ground. He stepped up to a knot of possessed as Evelyne and Broden engaged them.

Evelyne's fighting style was more fluid than he had thought her capable of. She fought with a flurry of kicks and spins, her blade slicing in quick arcs, taking life as easy as limb.

"Help!"

Kalfinar's attention was drawn by Chentuck's cry from the other side of the gate. He was being hard-pressed by four possessed. The whore was amongst the attackers, swinging a vicious-looking cleaver at the Ravenmayne, who was struggling to parry the onslaught of blows from all sides.

Kalfinar threw his hatchet into the back of one of the attackers and sprinted towards Chentuck. The weapon dropped from the possessed's limp grip, and the functioning hand searched his back for the hatchet. Kalfinar's sword cut through the searching hand and into the gap between shoulder and neck. The wound fountained a dark spray of blood, catching Kalfinar in the face. The possessed keeled over, and Kalfinar stepped past the body and towards the whore.

She waggled her black tongue at him and screamed a high and unearthly sound, "Your wife and daughter curse you in the frozen bowels of the barren hells!"

Kalfinar froze at the offence, shock dawning on his face only to be replaced with hatred as the whore laughed a vile noise at him.

She leapt into her frenzied attack, swinging the cleaver with redoubled speed and rage. "They know your shame, Kalfinar, and they curse you for it."

Kalfinar gave two steps back, and then a third as he struggled to parry each blow. The whore kicked, catching his knee and sending his right foot scraping on the gore-slick cobbles.

"I'm going to cut that fucking amulet from you and finish what the Master demanded. He's going to feed on your soul, and all your fetid souls for eternity. Like he feeds on your daughter's soul now."

The fury burned so hot in Kalfinar that he felt for a moment he was going to pass out. He sprung from his prone position and feinted a blow to the right, his sword thrust being parried by the whore. His left hand came around in a fist and smashed into the jaw of the possessed, sending a spray of black blood and teeth out of her mouth. His left boot came up in a kick and crunched into the whore's crotch, sending a whoop of air from her. She stumbled backwards and tripped over the corpse of a possessed, her cleaver skittering away.

The whore sprawled out on the stones as Kalfinar stood over her. "Say hello to my family for me." He raised a boot and stamped it down on the whore's throat, crushing it under his heel.

—————

The last of the possessed was cut down by the only guardsmen remaining alive. The courtyard was littered with bodies and the gaps between the stones pooled with blood.

"Everyone else alright?" Kalfinar asked as they fell in, blood-spattered and chests panting for breath.

"Aye," Broden grunted. "Was tight there for a time, wasn't it?"

Evelyne wiped the blood from her face with the sleeve of her shirt. "We can expect more attacks like this. They'll grow more desperate, and so we must be ready."

"You fought well," Kalfinar said. "Didn't appreciate you had such skill."

"Well, now you do." She smiled at him. "Come, we must hurry. We must leave for the south. The pull is urgent."

Chapter Eighteen

"BLOODY SHIP," Arrlun cursed as he stared at the wooden-beamed ceiling of the cabin.

He had not slept easily at any point of their voyage down the Valeswater towards Apula. Despite having spent many nights sleeping on his father's trade ship as a boy, he was not used to the gentle, rhythmical motion experienced on such a river voyage. He stirred in his bunk and swung his legs over edge above where Thaskil slept. He softly landed on the cabin floor in front of Thaskil's bunk and noted his friend's eyes were open.

"Can't sleep again?" Thaskil asked. He propped himself onto one elbow.

"Aye," he grumbled a quiet reply. "Perverse as it is, the rougher the water, the better I sleep. This passage is too gentle for a rough-cut soul from the north like me."

"A strange people, you Ultima North folk."

"That we are." Arrlun tucked his shirt into his trousers and tightened his belt. "Think I'll go and give Major Bergnon some company for the last of his watch."

"You just can't call him Bergnon, can you?" Thaskil laughed quietly. "A formal lot too."

"It's a survival mechanism for us. A six month winter without manners can lead to a lot of bloodshed in the north. Get back to sleep.

No point in us both having eyes like piss holes in the snow come the morning."

As he made his way out of the cabin, he thought ahead to Apula. He was looking forward to seeing Thaskil's home town. Though he was keen not to admit it, he had long dreamed of seeing the bloom of the famed winter poppies. He considered his own home of Gerloup in Noehmia's Ultima North and hoped that one day he could show Thaskil the shapes created by the snow and ice, like a forest of spiralled ice towers reaching towards the magical dance of the aurora.

Arrlun moved quietly to avoid waking any of the troops asleep on the deck. "You see the major?" he asked the old sailor at the wheel.

"Think he went down to the stern, sir," the old sailor replied in a hushed, gruff voice.

Arrlun patted the sailor on his shoulder as he moved past him toward the shadowy rear of the ship. He approached the stern and saw the form of Bergnon illuminated by the gently swaying lamp hanging above. His head was bowed as he inspected something in his hands, hidden from view.

A warning flared in Arrlun's mind and he ceased his approach, remaining unseen, hidden in the shadows. Bergnon muttered something and shook his head as he extended his hand over the rear of the ship. As the light swung, Arrlun caught sight of what the captain held in the brief moment before he released it into the disappearing blackness of the ship's wake. It had winked in the glare of the light. A flash of metal, and an unmistakable shape: a key.

Arrlun's heart jumped to a quicker beat, something felt wrong. He shouldn't be watching. As he stepped backwards, the ship beneath his feet creaked, and although it only made the slightest noise, it seemed like a jarring shriek in such a still night. His face winced and he froze where he stood, his presence masked by the shadows still. For an endless moment, Arrlun stood still, holding his breath, unsure fully of why he even hid. Bergnon had not moved, he appeared not to have noticed the creak as Arrlun backed away. He waited another moment, and finally, deciding all was well, he carefully crept away, and back to the cabin.

"Did you speak with the major, sir?" the old sailor asked as Arrlun hurried past.

"Yes, thank you," Arrlun replied as he walked on. He paused and stepped back towards the old sailor. "He asked that he not be disturbed," Arrlun added before stepping past the sleeping troops and entering the cabin below decks.

He climbed back into his bunk and pulled his woollen blanket up towards his chin, his heart rate lessening. Not entirely sure what he saw, if indeed he saw anything, Arrlun closed his eyes and pretended to be asleep, and a strange feeling of fear gnawed at him.

The Valeswater flowed into a large lake called the Night Sea. The ships had docked and unloaded at the trading-post town, Nightown. They prepared the battalion for the remaining leg of their journey and set off to cover the distance around the mountain ranges and south to Apula. Although it remained unspoken, all knew that if the Solansian forces were to attack at the eastern border of the Free Provinces, it would ultimately mean having to take Apula.

Arrlun forced himself to pay little mind to the nagging feeling that followed him since he watched Bergnon on the ship. He was careful to make sure his mood reflected nothing, although he was not entirely sure why.

They approached Apula with a battalion of exhausted soldiers shortly after the sun had set on the third day. The lights of Apula shone in the dark of the night, marking the broad walls and gently rising shape of the inner city. The plain before the city was cloaked in darkness.

"Pity you can't see the bloom," Thaskil said to Arrlun. "It'd be a sight for sore eyes, I tell you."

"Sure it would," Arrlun responded wearily, his words tinged with disappointment. "Aye, but for now, I'll be content with making camp and getting some rest. And maybe even an ale!"

Thaskil sounded his agreement, "Sounds good. The plain is an even greater sight at sunrise." He reined in his horse and looked back at the exhausted soldiers of the battalion. "Suppose we're fortunate we've not had to march the entire way like the rest of the men."

"Right enough," Arrlun replied. "The poor bastards will be exhausted. Alright, let's get this camp organised. Sooner we get done, the sooner they can rest up." Arrlun nudged his horse's flanks and trotted towards Bergnon. "Major Bergnon, sir."

"Ah, my formal Noehmian deputy. Remember, when out of

earshot, you can call me Bergnon. Nice and simple, eh?" He smiled at his young friend. "Now, how can I be of service?"

"Well, Bergnon, Sir," Arrlun continued awkwardly, "I was thinking perhaps as the men have travelled hard this week that we give them some reward. Perhaps we should send for some wine or ale from Apula for them?"

Bergnon laughed. "A very kind gesture my young friend, however I think with experience you'll soon learn the folly of such a kindness. The marriage of eight hundred tired and bored soldiers with wine and ale is indeed an unhappy one. You can expect trouble, and lots of it. No, let's not encourage a rowdy spirit in the lads. At least not until we have some visitors. Let's just concentrate on getting the camp up, perimeter established, and the men's grub on. You and Thaskil know the drill by now. I'll send one of the corporals into Apula with dispatches for the Command there. We'll present ourselves tomorrow morning. Now set to it." He leant over and gave the husky youth an encouraging slap on the shoulder before turning in his horse and trotting off to seek a corporal.

The night had passed peacefully and Thaskil woke Arrlun shortly before sunrise so he could show him the famed sight of the winter poppy bloom on the plain of Apula. It was a particularly cold morning and as the sun crept up above the mountain range that framed the Sea of Storms to the west, Thaskil felt a frost underfoot and saw his breath before him.

"Here it comes," Thaskil excitedly said to his friend. As the sun inched over the mountains and cast its first rays of light onto the plain, the reality before him caused Thaskil to inhale sharply. "The bloom," he cried. "What happened to the bloom?"

Before him now was not the spectacular sight of bright red winter poppies, but instead a vast expanse of swaying wheat. The sea of wheat, fit for harvest, danced to the caress of the wind as it glided across the plain before them. The scars of previous battles, trenches and bulwarks, palisades and pits, caused the waves of golden sea to sporadically break. Yet beyond the scars of war, the wheat stretched out across the plain, alongside roads and edging forests and villages in the distance.

Arrlun put his hand on his friends shoulder to reassure him. "Major Broden spoke of some poison in the earth that was causing crops to fail. Perhaps with the ground being so strong here they needed wheat more."

Thaskil stood in silence and watched as the red light of the sun washed over the city walls. Arrlun felt a shiver creep down his back. The light of the sun held no warmth this morning.

———

Arrlun poured Thaskil a cup of steaming coffee. "Here, get that into you." Thaskil was clearly troubled by the apparent decimation of the famed poppy fields of Apula. Arrlun touched Thaskil on the elbow and indicated that his friend should follow him away from the more crowded elements of the mess tent.

He had been thinking about what he had witnessed on the ship that night. Why would Major Bergnon be upset and throw a key overboard? Before they had departed, there had been rumours that the senior clerk within the High Command had been murdered when on the run after the assassinations. Although he could not be sure, or place faith in rumour, Arrlun had absently heard a city guardsman mention how the clerk was found in a room in a bunk house by the docks, locked from the outside.

Arrlun lurched from one thought to the next. He admired and respected Major Bergnon. The man had been as a mentor to both he and Thaskil. He had shown nothing but pure devotion and commitment to the cause of defending the Free Provinces, even now working tirelessly, and forgoing food to prepare the defence of Apula.

"What is it?" Thaskil said as he slurped down a gulp of the bitter brew.

Arrlun rubbed the back of his neck nervously and looked up holding his friends gaze. "You'll think me mad when I tell you. Promise me you will hear me out, and tell me what you think, because I don't know where my own mind is anymore."

"Of course," Thaskil replied, his expression shifting to one of concern. "What is it?"

"Well, I wasn't able to sleep one of the nights we were sailing down the Valeswater, when Major Bergnon was on watch, so I got up and went above deck to give him some company. You know what a long watch can be like."

"Aye. Was that the same night I was awake?"

"Aye, the same. I saw him at the stern of the ship looking upset by something." Arrlun paused.

"These are troubled days. Shouldn't think there's anything unusual about that," Thaskil interrupted.

"There's more," Arrlun mumbled, before carrying on. "He was talking to himself, looking at something he held in his hands. I couldn't hear what he was saying, nor could I, at first, make out what it was he held. It was when he went to throw the thing in the water that I saw it. It was a key."

Thaskil looked confused and snorted, "So? It was only a key. I don't see the significance in that. What's your point?"

Arrlun avoided Thaskil's eyes and looked at the ground. He felt the blood beginning to pulse in his ears. "You see, I...I overheard the City Guard in Carte say that the command clerk who was murdered was found dead in a room locked from the outside. The clerk is linked to the assassinations."

Thaskil lowered the mug of coffee from his mouth as a look of cold anger dawned on his face. "Arrlun, you can't be suggesting what I think you are?"

"I can't honestly tell you what I think," Arrlun replied. "I'm not even sure I fully know myself."

"Not another word on it." Thaskil's words were low and deliberate. "I'd advise you, as your friend, to shake those thoughts from your head and get yourself together right now. Stop being such a bloody fool!" Thaskil spilled his coffee as he pointed at Arrlun with his mug. "That man is probably the greatest chance we have of defending Apula, and with it, the Free Provinces. The last thing he needs, and the last thing the Free Provinces needs, is for her defenders to lose their heads. And the last thing I need is for you to lose yours!" Thaskil's moment of ill temper passed as quickly as it came to him and he regarded the doubt in his friend's eyes. "It's a hard time on us all. Just try to keep your head straight." He slapped Arrlun on the shoulder and headed back towards the main body of the camp, leaving his friend looking over the sea of wheat before him.

Arrlun breathed in deeply through his nose and muttered to himself, "You're a fool, Arrlun. A damn bloody fool."

Bergnon stood flanked by his lieutenants, Thaskil and Arrlun, as he addressed his stern-faced company sergeants. "Sergeant's Wulff and Threftan, I want your companies to start work on the reinstatement of the palisade by the time I return. Salvage what you can of the last compound. Dispatch platoons into the woods for what you need. Sergeant's Holleck and Felfarnen, I want your companies to set to work opening up any of the old trenches that have collapsed in on themselves. Let's get this city battle ready."

The sergeants saluted and withdrew to their business.

"You two, follow me," Bergnon said to Thaskil and Arrlun before galloping off in the direction of Apula.

They rode for ten minutes through the edge of the plain and into the buildings and stockyards that radiated outward from the city walls. They slowed as they ascending the broad access ramp which led into the main body of the city through the portcullis.

"The gate's not normally shut this long after sunrise," Thaskil said to no one in particular.

"Words like 'normally' don't apply here. Nor is it likely to apply in many places, if our fears are to be realised," Bergnon responded with a neutral tone. He cleared his throat and then called out to the unseen watchmen who had undoubtedly observed their approach. "Ho there, officers of the High Command seek access to deliver dispatches to the city Command. I am Major Bergnon."

His address was greeted by silence.

"May we enter?" he shouted at the portcullis once more.

After several more minutes of silence, a reply came from behind the cover of the gatehouse walls. "Major Bergnon, Major Metvani addressing you. Please excuse the caution, but we've had a spot of trouble here of late. I noted your arrival last night. Figured you were friend when you came from the west. Then your corporal arrived with word."

Bergnon whispered to the two lieutenants on either side of him, "I know Metvani. He's an ass. No scouts posted last night, and he allowed a battalion of heavily armed troops approach his walls on the assumption because they came from the west they were friend and not foe. It's not good news at all if he's leading the Command here, and Dajda help us if he sets the standard for a defender of our border." He turned back toward the walls and greeted the major, "Major Metvani, we come with dispatches from the governor of Carte, Lord Harruld. He is acting chief of the High Command. There has been a coordinated strike across the Free Provinces High Command. We have lost many men. I carry urgent orders."

There was another prolonged silence before the portcullis groaned into life, opening before them.

Major Metvani called out as the three officers trotted towards the entrance, "Nothing rash until we confirm your identity. We have archers on you."

"Isn't it a bit late for caution?" Bergnon mumbled.

They made their way inside the walls and looked up at the dozen bows aimed down upon them.

Bergnon looked around him and smiled. "Good morning, chaps."

"Sorry about the hostile welcome, old boy," Metvani said as he descended the stairs from the ramparts. "Just being careful. You understand, I'm sure." He approached as Bergnon stepped off his horse, and offered him a trembling hand in greeting. "You mentioned a coordinated attack on the High Command a moment ago." Metvani leant in close to Bergnon and lowered his voice, "We've lost a significant number here also."

"As I feared, Major," Bergnon replied. "We can discuss this in more depth in private, but first I must deliver dispatches from Carte to the commander."

Metvani extended his open hand. "I'll take them," he said solemnly. "There is no one more senior left alive."

"Colonel Alabasi?" Bergnon asked about the esteemed siege expert.

Metvani shook his head. "The colonel was killed."

Bergnon sighed. "Well then, we have much work to do." He guided Metvani towards Thaskil and Arrlun. "My lieutenants, Thaskil and Arrlun. Thaskil here is a native of Apula."

The major greeted the two lieutenants with a raised eyebrow. "Aren't they a little…fresh?"

"If we are to stem the coming tide, it will be largely done by the hands of young men such as these, Major. After all, we have lost much of our experienced men," Bergnon replied.

"Quite," Metvani replied. "We've lost fourteen senior officers and veterans here alone. I dread to think what our combined loss is. Come, let's have a look at these dispatches and perhaps you can enlighten me as to what on earth is going on here." He ushered a young soldier over with his horse and mounted it. "Do your men need any supplies or assistance pulling the old encampment together?" Metvani asked, his disinterest edging out any hint of sincerity in his voice.

"Not necessary, Major," Bergnon replied as he and his lieutenants mounted their horses. "The men are well drilled. They should manage just fine." Bergnon's words smacked of his own disinterest in the major's fragile offer.

"Excellent," Metvani replied. "Let's be off to my office then." He spun his horse on the cobbled street and trotted off with Bergnon and the two young officers riding behind in silence.

The revelation of the intelligence and evidence, both solid and circumstantial, seemed to leave Major Metvani cold. His hand trembled as he poured himself a glass of chilled wine.

"Grunnxe is alive," he murmured to himself. "I though Kalfinar ran him through? He was dead, was he not?"

"He did. And he's not. Or so it appears," Bergnon responded, not bothering to look at Metvani as he spoke. "Kalfinar himself is quite adamant about the extent to which he put his sword into him. He gets all misty eyed talking about it." Bergnon afforded himself a slight smile as he watched Metvani's grimace grow.

The coward's eyes searched the surface of his desk, as if an escape route would somehow appear and offer him freedom.

"Nevertheless, it appears Grunnxe has the assistance of someone or something of great power. The thought on the matter is that he has aligned with another, and is utilising their strength." Bergnon had not yet mentioned the discovery of the Ravenmayne, fearing it would be too much for Metvani. "It seems some Gods must be quite adept at undoing the odd skewering."

"Dajda," the major gasped. "That's preposterous." His face bristled with righteous indignation. "Despite their flaws and madness, the Solansian people are still children of Dajda. Setting aside our differences, they are still our brothers in God. How can that vile monster abandon our faith for another?" The major was furious, his religious fervour being until now unknown to Bergnon.

"I fear his conversion was somewhat opportunistic and borne out of a rather pressing necessity," Bergnon replied. "When three feet of steel have passed in and out of a man, I would think one's conviction could be swayed a touch more easily than normal. Don't you?" Bergnon glanced slyly to the young lieutenants and rolled his eyes as the major fumbled with his thoughts.

"Not I!" Metvani barked. "I myself received a wound during the last skirmish season. Here." Metvani rolled up his chain mail and pointed to a short, thin scar running above his hip. "See. A Solansian spear thrust in the trenches. No, Major, my conviction is like oak. Perhaps with weaker men the heart can go in such times of war."

The most glancing of touches from a spear, if indeed. What a blustering prick. "The dispatches." Bergnon handed the scrolls to Metvani.

Metvani's face set piously as he began reading the dispatches. His brow furrowed and his bottom lip trembled before he coughed and spoke, "Governor Harruld's dispatch states that if there's to be a follow-up strike, it is likely to come here at Apula." He glanced down again. "The command also reads that should Colonel Alabasi fall, that you, Major Bergnon, are to assume full command of the defence of Apula. Well, it appears I must hand over authority in light of your superior knowledge and skill in such matters of defence." Metvani's face was a conflicted mask of relief and damaged pride. "I'll do all I can to assist you. Just ask and I'll see it is so."

"Thank you, Major," Bergnon replied. "Your understanding is appreciated. We should receive regimental backup within the next four weeks. Until then, we'll have to prepare all that we can in order to withstand any initial attack. How many men have we garrisoned in the city full-time?"

"We have around eight hundred permanent troops in the City Guard."

"That makes sixteen hundred, counting my battalion." Bergnon thought momentarily. "Major, mobilise the local militia and have them stationed within our encampment. I want them all brought in within three days."

Metvani scribbled the orders down.

"And major, can you ensure an administrative officer sends me a list of all retired soldiers known to live within or near to the city. We'll be wanting the veterans brought in, too."

The major scratched his quill to paper again. "I'll see that you get this information before sunset," Metvani promised.

"Now, what's the situation regarding food stocks and water within the city? We'll need to make sure we can pull as much in from the countryside as we can in the next two weeks."

"We are due to begin our harvest of the Field of Storms next week."

Bergnon noted the furrow of Thaskil's brow at mention of the once poppy-filled expanse before Apula. "Ah, yes, a sea of wheat where once a sea of poppies stood. The decision must have been hard on the Apulan people."

"No more hard than the second winter of hunger and delayed imports from the Cannan's," Metvani replied in a weary voice. "Colonel Albasi and the Council made the decision with great reluctance. We weren't sure if the crop would take, but take it did, and in spectacular form."

"Well the harvest had better be quick. There could well be a force of Solansian raiders on their way here as we speak, and I'm in no mood to offer them a feast on the plains. Get it harvested and in store. Start tomorrow."

"Major." Metvani nodded, scribbling his orders.

"What of water. How many wells are there within the walls?"

"The city has eight wells including a major one within the inner castle walls itself. It should be sound for some time," Metvani replied, seeming to be more at ease.

"Good. We'll need to ensure that livestock is brought into the city. I want platoons dispatched to the hamlets to ensure the provisions are secured."

Thaskil whispered to Arrlun as they walked behind Major Bergnon, who was engaged in discussion with Major Metvani. "You got your head straight?"

"Aye, don't worry. My imagination was just running away with me. Feel like an idiot. Forget I mentioned it."

They carried on toward the stables where their horses awaited them. "Thaskil." Bergnon turned and spoke to the young lieutenant,

"Perhaps now would be a fitting time to visit your family, don't you think?"

Thaskil fizzed with excitement, but kept his emotion in place. "Sir, what about my duties tonight? What about the men?"

"Fear not about the men tonight, lad. The sergeants can more than handle them. It's been a long few weeks for you. Go and see your family. And for goodness sake, will you take Arrlun with you! He looks like he could do with a home-cooked meal." Bergnon laughed at the raw northern youth as he looked awkwardly towards his friend.

"I wouldn't want to intrude upon Thaskil, Major Bergnon, sir," Arrlun stuttered.

"Nonsense! There'll be no intrusion at all," Thaskil said.

"There, it's settled." Bergnon clapped. "Make sure you're back at the camp for sunrise tomorrow." With that, Major Bergnon put his heels to his horse and rode down the cobbled streets and out of Apula.

Arrlun turned towards his friend. "Perhaps Major Bergnon is right. Maybe a good home-cooked meal is what I need."

"Well, you'll eat like a king." Thaskil smiled and slapped his stomach. "Come on, I'll lead the way."

"Do you think your sister will be home?"

Chapter Nineteen

GRUNNXE'S WRATH WAS TERRIBLE. He panted as he bent over and grabbed a fistful of the unconscious officer's jerkin, drawing the broken and bloodied face of the man towards his snarling mouth.

"This is what happens when my soldiers let me down," Grunnxe exclaimed, looking around his pavilion at the faces of his commanding officers.

Several men trembled visibly, whilst many others had long since gone beyond the stage of fear. The old king, now rejuvenated, was more dreadful than ever before.

"Take him away and finish him, and take your time with him," Grunnxe ordered two guardsmen at his side before picking up a cloth and casually wiping the blood and flesh from his knuckles and rings.

He pointed in the direction the officer was dragged out. "That man failed me. He failed us all. I ordered him to destroy the High Command of the Free Provinces and he tells me all were not killed! He failed me! Failure cannot be tolerated." As he stormed, he heaved his breath like a warring bull thundering rage from its nostrils. "The governor and his boy live. Harruld and Kalfinar, they live!" His voice rose in a scream and Grunnxe suddenly slammed his fist into the nearest face.

A short-lived chorus of gasps and winces sounded in the pavilion from Grunnxe's commanders as the unfortunate officer crumpled to a heap, his nose splattered pulp-like across his face.

Grunnxe cast a glance towards the priestess, who watched from the rear of the pavilion. The sight of the hooded priest sent a shiver down the back of Grunnxe's skull. He withdrew his gaze and focused on the officer who squirmed at his feet. "Get up! Get up and don't bleed on my rugs." He paced around the circle of officers. "I'll not accept any more failures. No more. Do you understand? None!"

The entire body of officers shouted their emphatic response in unison.

"Now, as you are aware, we've dispatched warships to the Yellow Sea. All grain imports to those hungry bastard rebels will be commandeered for our own use. Any ships that remain in port in Nabruuk will be scuttled. Soon, our separatist neighbours will find that Canna will no longer answer their call for aid, and if their beloved Father of the People knows what is good for him and his flock, he'll stop resisting my generous overtures." Grunnxe paced in front of his senior officers with his hands knitted behind his back. "If the Father of the People still resists, well, the raiders have been ordered to—" Grunnxe paused, searching for the right word, his wicked blue eyes flashing across the gathered faces. "Encourage the fucking Father of the People to ally himself to our cause, if he knows what is good for him." Grunnxe smiled a wicked smile. "I have no doubt that the message will be delivered most soundly by our brothers."

The commanders cheered loudly and spat curses on the families of the Cannan people.

"Yes, our fleet will leave them in no doubt as to whom they are aligned with!" He laughed a crackling, barking sound and regarded the fervour that grew in his men. "Now, my children, we sit here, massed on what has been anointed by the separatist hand as the limit of our dominion, and we are poised to strike into their heart and take back our lands. We are ready to rip them from the seat of our ancestors and reclaim our rightful kingdom. With the power of our forefathers, we will make them pay a price in blood and soul!"

A savage cheer exploded from the throats of all the Solansian commanders, their battle lust peaking as Grunnxe invoked their fallen ancestors.

The old king felt his heart thunder and his throat swell. His sword arm bulged as he gripped the pommel, and he himself was ready to become death. "Yes, my children, with the hand of Bhalur guiding our sword and his children at our side, we will sweep through our stolen lands like a terrible plague and we shall have our vengeance!"

Drawn swords were pointed towards the pavilion roof as Grunnxe's commanders drank fully on the king's words.

Grunnxe stared through the throng of arms and swords and into shadow beneath the hood of the priestess. The priestess nodded imperceptibly towards Grunnxe. It was time.

Kalfinar sat awake in the cabin as they sailed towards the Cannan capital of Nabruuk. His companions all slept around him. He found their rhythmic breathing soothing. Kalfinar regarded the small child who slept silently, clinging to Evelyne as she dozed in the chair opposite him. He stared at the child's brown ringlets, his eyes tracing the spiralled mass. *I've seen you so many times before, little one. Are you as she would have been? Is this how we could have lived? Together? Happy?*

"Kalfinar," Evelyne whispered.

His eyes snapped onto hers in an instant.

"I'm sorry," she said quietly. "I took you by surprise."

A heavy silence thickened between them. Kalfinar felt Evelyne searching for the words to draw him out of his cloud.

He glanced back at the child and broke the silence, his gritty whisper having lost its edge. "You know, I've seen her a thousand times." The faintest hint of a smile flexed his lips as he regarded the sleeping girl.

"What was her name?" Evelyne whispered.

Kalfinar looked to the floor and his brows furrowed. His sigh was grave.

"A funny thing," Kalfinar muttered. A humourless smile cut his face. "I never named her. They were both there, and then they were gone from me. I never even held her." He closed his eyes for a moment and the bitter smile faded. He flexed his jaw, and fought away his sorrow. "I hold her in my dreams. I've even wiped her runny nose and picked her up when she has fallen. Even shouted at her as a teenager, once." Kalfinar's eyes dropped to the scuffed toes of his boots. "I see my wife call to her, telling her that supper is ready. But when she calls her name, her voice always falls away to nothing." He fell silent and the quiet hung empty in the air. He looked up and saw that Evelyne regarded him sadly. "What kind of a man am I never to have named or held my own child?" Kalfinar leant with his elbows on his knees. His palms slid over his face.

Evelyne stretched out an arm and rested it upon Kalfinar's head, causing him to flinch as her palm pressed down upon his crown. She spoke gently, "Grief is not something which follows a predestined path. We each have to let it find its own course and take root somewhere within us. It is in denying grief that you tear open wounds and create scars. We must accept it, and let it pass without burden. Otherwise, it will consume us."

Kalfinar raised his head from his hands and looked at Evelyne for a long moment. He noticed her eyes, and how unusually blue they were.

She smiled at him as the small girl stirred. "Here," Evelyne said. "Why don't you hold her a while?" She gently leant towards him with the child in her arms.

Kalfinar felt nervous. He stared into Evelyne's eyes as a wave of panic swam over him.

"Kal, don't be frightened of her. Hold her," Evelyne insisted as she softly placed the form of the little girl into his arms.

As he placed his arms around the warm little body, the girl latched tight onto his sides and nuzzled her little head against the soft suede of his jerkin. Kalfinar looked down at the small form and, in that instant, it was not pain or sorrow that he felt. It was joy. He looked up at Evelyne. She grinned and clenched her hands by her mouth.

"That's a look that suits you." She whispered.

Kalfinar could not help but smile and laugh, being careful not to wake the sleeping child. The sleeping child with the brown ringlets who slept soundly in his arms at long last.

"That really was one of the finest meals I think I've ever tasted," exclaimed Arrlun as he and Thaskil trotted in to the encampment an hour before dawn.

"My mother can blend spices to make even a dry old shank of mutton taste like it was Dajda sent!" Thaskil laughed.

"Mutton's my favourite," muttered Arrlun. "We practically live off dried mutton in Gerloup over winter."

"Sometimes I forget quite how different the lands are we come from, my friend. Next time I'll get my mother to prepare some for you."

The two young officers laughed as they approached their tent.

"Who's that?" Arrlun hissed, drawing Thaskil's attention to the shadowy form sneaking into the tent they shared with Major Bergnon. "Quick!"

He and Thaskil dismounted, drawing their swords while charging into their tent.

Arrlun was the first to burst in, his sword levelled to the back of the hooded stranger. "Don't move or I'll have you run through, neighbour," he growled to the form before him.

Without turning, the intruder spoke in a voice familiar to the two young men, "Well, I'd know that accent anywhere. My formal young friend from the far north, may I be permitted to turn around?"

"Major Bergnon, sir! I'm so very sorry, sir," Arrlun blurted, recognising the major's voice. He lowered his sword and slid it into its scabbard. "I thought you were an intruder. Or worse, an assassin."

"You did just right," Bergnon said as he threw back his hood and untied the neck of his cloak. He smiled at the two youths and ran his fingers through his fair hair. "We've a lot to do today. I've just been to check in on the lumber work. Most of the salvageable palisade is up, and now I want the new stuff dug in today. We'll need the gardens of stakes dug in around the encampment as well. Sergeants Wulff and Threftan have the companies working on this. I want you both to oversee. I'll be overseeing Sergeant Holleck and Ferfarnen's men as they set to reinstating the trench networks outside the city." He sat down on a stool and pulled off a boot to rub his foot. "Go on, off you go and get yourselves some breakfast first." He shooed the two officers out of the tent. As they pushed out past the flaps, he called out, "And bring me back some coffee."

Arrlun's face was sullen as they collected their breakfast and coffee.

"What's the matter with you?" Thaskil asked his friend as they sat down alone at a table to eat.

"Nothing," Arrlun mumbled as he sniffed and then began to eat his meal.

"I don't believe you," Thaskil said. "You're still worrying about Bergnon, aren't you?"

Arrlun paused for a brief moment and exhaled before looking his friend in the eyes. "Don't you find it a bit strange that Major Bergnon would be sneaking back into camp at this time of the morning?"

"Dammit!" Thaskil snapped. "He said himself he was checking on the lumber parties. That's what a good commanding officer does, takes charge of all elements of his troop! He's preparing the defences, as Bergnon does best!" Thaskil slurped some hot coffee down and huffed his exhale.

"But don't you find it odd that he was sneaking in? It was as if he didn't want anyone to know he had been away," Arrlun said, with doubt eroding his conviction as he spoke.

"No, I don't!" Thaskil snapped. "Shit! I thought you'd wised up!" He stood and stormed off.

"Where you going?" Arrlun called after him.

"To get Major Bergnon his coffee," Thaskil shouted back, striding off into the amber light of dawn. "And then to set to work, like I've been instructed by my commanding officer. I'd suggest you do the same." Thaskil paused and stepped back to Arrlun. He leaned over the table and stared hard into his eyes. "I think it best you get your head straight, and forget your fantasies about the major. You need straighten up, or I'll damn well see it done myself. You understand me?"

"Aye," Arrlun said, swallowing the lump forming in his throat. "I understand."

***

"Thaskil," Bergnon called out to the young lieutenant as he cut stakes alongside Arrlun and their work party. "I need you to take a dispatch to Major Metvani in Apula. Can you do that for me? I'll be heading off to oversee Sergeant Holleck and Felfarnen's work at the trenches in a few minutes and can't spare the time to deliver it myself."

"Of course, sir. It's no problem," Thaskil replied, wiping the sweat from his brow.

"Good, the major will be expecting you in half an hour, so you'd best set to it."

"Sir, I'll attend to it straight away."

With that, Bergnon handed a message pouch to Thaskil and left the work party.

"I'll see you later, alright," Thaskil said as he wiped down his hands.

"Thaskil," Arrlun said, speaking in a hushed tone. "Look, about earlier—"

"Arrlun," Thaskil interrupted and leant in close. "I think you need to stop your imagination running wild here. Let's just get on with our job. No more fantasies." Thaskil's tone was abrupt, and he turned.

Arrlun watched as his friend stalked off towards his horse. He felt his face flush with the rebuke, and he cursed himself as a fool once more.

Arrlun rested his axe against a hefty pile of sharpened stakes and stretched out his back. Something caught his eye and he squinted into the low, bright sun. "Where in the frozen hells is he going?" He watched Bergnon ride off towards the back of the encampment in the direction of the woods where the lumber party would still be at work. "That is most certainly not in the direction of Holleck and Ferlfarnen," he mumbled to himself.

"What was that, sir?" Sergeant Wulff asked.

"Nothing, Sergeant," Arrlun replied. "I was just thinking aloud. I'll be back shortly. Make sure and keep the men working. I want to see these stakes in place before nightfall."

Arrlun pulled his jerkin and coat on and ran over to his horse. He mounted it and discreetly followed Bergnon's route towards the woodland in the distance. Being careful to keep a good distance behind, Arrlun quickly covered the ground and was soon approaching the tree line at the point he saw Bergnon enter. He reined his horse in to a trot and scanned the ground for Bergnon's trail. The leaf and needle litter betrayed the major's track. Arrlun's heart began to race as he followed the tracks leading away from the sound of distant chopping.

"Where you going?" he muttered to himself as he followed the tracks deeper into the woodland.

The trail left by Bergnon's horse wound around the mixed stands of ancient oak trees, and tall, red barked pines. He carefully led his horse through patches of marshy glades fringed by white barked birch, and thick, dark sections of pines that shut out the morning sun. His mind raced as he followed further, coming to sunlit glades amongst the pines. He chose to skirt along the edge of the sunlit patches rather than cross the open ground.

It was at the far end of such a clearing that he spotted Bergnon's horse tied to the branch of a twisted granny-pine. Deciding on stealth, Arrlun dismounted and likewise fixed his reigns to the branch of a gnarled old tree. He withdrew a dagger from under the skirt of his saddle and shoved it under his belt at the back. Arrlun walked slowly along the edge of the clearing towards Bergnon's horse, being careful not to spook the beast as he closed the distance between them.

Arrlun's eyes searched through the branches of the trees and brush ahead of him for any sign of Bergnon. He rubbed at his eyes, sure they were playing tricks on him, when, like a falling shadow, the major stepped out from behind the trunk of a broad pine and into the dappled sunlight pouring in golden beams to the forest floor. Arrlun froze as he saw him.

"What are you doing here, lad?" Bergnon asked of his young companion.

A lump rose in Arrlun's throat and he quickly answered. "Major Bergnon, sir, I was just making sure you were safe. I saw you ride off alone and, well, I thought I had best watch your back, what with the assassinations recently."

"You're watching my back, lad?" the major responded with a thin smile.

"Yes, Major Bergnon, sir."

"Then why is your hand upon your sword? And tell me, why do you shake? It's not especially cold," Bergnon challenged him.

Arrlun felt his breath rasp quickly in and out. He felt fear.

"Tell me your concern, lad," Bergnon continued, slowly stepping towards the young soldier.

"I have no concerns, Major Bergnon, sir. I only followed to make sure you were safe." Arrlun's voice wavered as he spoke. He inwardly cursed exposing his fear.

Bergnon approached a little further, his pace measured and exact. "Yet you still have your hand on your sword, lad."

Arrlun looked at his hand and towards Bergnon. He wanted to remove it, but he found he could not.

Bergnon spoke again, "You weren't asleep on the boat that night, were you, lad?"

"I don't know what you mean, Major Bergnon, sir." Arrlun's heart thundered.

"You watched me. I know. The pilot asked me if the young lieutenant had spoken to me. Your fine northern accent gave you away, lad."

Arrlun's hand tightened on the hilt of his sword.

"You've gotten too close, been too clever. Haven't you, lad." Bergnon approached slowly as he placed his hand on his sword hilt.

Arrlun stepped backwards as he spoke, "Why did you throw away the key? The City Guards said that the chief administrative officer was locked inside his room, and that whoever killed him did it to stop him talking." Arrlun felt the sweat sticking under his arms and its cold touch on the back of his neck. "You murdered your own people, your own friends. You tried to kill Captain Kalfinar and Captain Broden. Why?" Arrlun was emboldened by his fear.

Bergnon's face was struck with regret. "Lad, you cannot understand. Dammit! You're hardly more than a boy! You're too green to understand this world."

"I'm enough of a man to understand betrayal. I'm old enough to see a traitor when he stands before me," Arrlun spat his words with venom. "I looked up to you, Major." Arrlun steadily stepped back towards his horse. If he could reach it, he could make an escape, for the major was walking further away from his own mount.

"And I am fond of you, lad. Very much so."

"But you betrayed your nation. You murdered your commanders, friends, that officer, and now I suppose you mean to murder me too. Shit on you, Bergnon, you fucking traitor!" Arrlun cursed.

Bergnon laughed, but it was tinged with a mournful frown. "Always so formal, my lad, and now you call me Bergnon. I wish it were not this way. I truly do."

Arrlun heard rustling behind him. He spun and found a group of four armed men approaching from behind, cutting him off from his horse. They rushed him.

"Fuck." The word tailed off in a ragged grunt as his muscles tensed.

Arrlun's sword flashed from its scabbard. In a wide sideways arc, his blade slashed out the throat of one of the approaching men. The moment seemed to slow down and the spray of blood caught a beam of sunlight and sparkled for a moment like a scattering of rubies. The throatless man stumbled with a wet gurgle and fell to the ground face-first, tripping one of his colleagues and sending him crashing to a heap.

The remaining two men spread out and engaged Arrlun. Bergnon remained at his distance as the fight unfolded.

Arrlun spun and parried a deft blow from a one-eyed man, before kicking the tripped man in the face, preventing him from rising. The grounded man's nose made a satisfying, squelching crunch.

A roar sounded from the left. A big man with a flat face swung a spiked mace at Arrlun's head. He ducked under the hefty swing and aimed a swipe of his sword at the man's leg. It bit home along Flat-face's thigh, causing him to stumble back with a pig-like squeal.

"Give it up, lad," One-eye croaked to Arrlun. "Yer gonna die one way or another. No point fucking us off, eh?"

One-eye set himself to attack again while Flat-face hobbled around to Arrlun's left. One-eye pulled a throwing knife from his belt and flashed it towards Arrlun. He ducked, avoiding the blade as it sped through the air, being lost somewhere in the leaf litter behind. One-eye followed up with a lunge.

Arrlun quickly deflected One-eye's sword point and, in the same moment, grabbed his dagger from his belt. One-eye stumbled forward, his momentum meeting Arrlun's dagger as he thrust it forward into One-eye's one good eye. The hilt met eye socket and One-eye wheezed and sagged onto Arrlun.

Flat-face shambled forward as Arrlun struggled to shove off One-eye's corpse. Flat-face swung his evil mace, but missed Arrlun and tore into the trunk of a pine, wedging his weapon into the flesh of the tree.

Flat-face's expression was one of slack-jawed surprise as Arrlun thrust his sword up and into the man's chest. The big man stiffened on his blade as Arrlun twisted and heaved upwards, before withdrawing, leaving the man to drop on his knees. He vomited out a stream of dark blood before he hiccupped, and fell to the ground.

Arrlun turned to face Bergnon as he charged, meeting his thunderous blow and only just keeping his feet under the older man's strength.

"I'm sorry it's come to this, lad, truly," Bergnon said through gritted teeth as he stepped back and thrust.

"Save your apologies. You fucking disgust me." Arrlun parried the blow and slashed at Bergnon with his dagger.

"Disgust myself, lad, truth be told." Bergnon grimaced, leaning away from the dagger slash.

"Bastard!" Arrlun spat at the major and launched a vicious flurry of overhead blows.

Bergnon conceded ground before Arrlun unleashed a hopeful kick at the major. His boot found its home in Bergnon's balls and sent the major coughing to the ground. Bergnon spluttered and rose to his feet.

A noise sounded from behind. Arrlun turned, but already knew he was too late. Tripped-man. Arrlun tried to dive out of the range of the Tripped-man's sword stroke, but the sharp edge buried deep into his thigh. The blood fountained from his leg in flashing jets of bright red. Arrlun roared before he swept the Tripped-man's legs with his good leg, sending him prostrating on the ground. With a grimace of pain, Arrlun slammed his sword edge down onto the back of Tripped-man's neck. Bergnon approached Arrlun as the young officer struggled to rise, blood spurting rhythmically from his wound.

"That's a death wound that one, Major." A fifth man appeared beside Bergnon, one Arrlun hadn't seen. The fifth man pointed to Arrlun's wounded leg with his sword. "Let's just be leaving him and get on."

Arrlun felt panic as his lifeblood fled from him with ferocious pace. He felt cold.

"No! Leave us!" Bergnon shouted to the man.

Arrlun struggled up, but slipped to the ground. His head swam and his vision faded to cloudy and back. He watched as the other man removed himself and stood across the glade from them. As Bergnon approached, Arrlun feebly tried to raise his sword, though he was too weak and so his grip faltered. His sword tumbled into the leaf litter. Bergnon caught him as his head fell backwards.

"Ach, lad. I'm sorry." Bergnon gathered Arrlun into his arms, propping the young man's broad shoulders against his leg.

"No. I'm not ready to—"Arrlun struggled to form his words between his laboured, shallow breaths. He glanced at his hand; the skin was pale and waxy. "I'm not ready to go."

"Ach, lad. I didn't want this." Bergnon choked on the words.

Arrlun was sure there were tears brimming in the older man's eyes.

"Didn't want any of this."

Arrlun pursed his drying lips together and tried to utter something, but Bergnon could not make out his words, so weak was his voice.

"What did you say?" Bergnon put his head closer to Arrlun's mouth, his ear almost touching Arrlun's lips.

"Fuck you!" Arrlun roared with all his might and then struck. His hands gripped Bergnon's head as his teeth clamped shut on his ear.

Bergnon roared as Arrlun shook his head, teeth cutting into flesh and gristle alike. Bergnon screamed and punched out at Arrlun, striking him firmly in his wounded thigh, the pain of which caused Arrlun to release his hold on the major's ear. Bergnon shuffled back from the dying lad and felt his ear burn.

Arrlun smiled at him with blood-stained teeth and blood streaked down his chin. He leered at his former mentor, and then spat the ragged chunk of ear at Bergnon with all the force he could muster. But there was hardly any strength left in him, and the chunk of ear flopped onto the ground, where it lay stuck to leaf litter. Succumbing to his wound, Arrlun fell back to the forest floor, caught a glimpse of a pocket of blood red winter poppies at the edge of the glade, and then slipped out of consciousness.

Bergnon held his bleeding ear and knelt into the leaf litter by the body of Arrlun. He regarded the lad as he lay before him, his lifeless eyes staring off towards a small pocket of winter poppies. He leant over him and closed his eyes, whispering a final apology to him.

As Bergnon rose, the other man walked towards him. He spoke as he approached, "That bastard put up a hell of a fight, didn't he? Still, he got his in the end." The man released a foul laugh and kicked leaf litter onto the body.

Bergnon's shoulders and head began to shake. He felt his fury build as he stared at Arrlun's pale face.

"What's the matter with you, eh?" the man asked.

Bergnon turned towards the man and grabbed him by his gambeson, drawing him close into him, their noses almost touching. "He was a friend of mine. Mind yourself."

"Get yer fucking hands off me!" The man shoved Bergnon's grip and adopted a defensive stance. "Careful now, Major. If you harm me, who'll deliver yer message to the old man, eh?" The man smiled a decay-filled grin. "The old king's relying on you to ease his passage. Without my word, he'll be most displeased with you, won't he? In fact, he may even be so displeased that yer lady friend could find herself in some fairly permanent trouble, eh?" The man laughed wickedly.

Bergnon knew the man was right; there was nothing he could do. He dusted himself down and proceeded to pick up the scattered weapons. "You'll have to lead the extra horses away." Bergnon directed the man to assist him. "Lead them a good distance off and then slaughter them."

"And what am I meant to do with them?" the man asked, pointing to the four bodies strewn across the forest floor.

"I've no time to bury them. I must get back to the city. You'll have to tie them to the saddles, and when you're done with the horses, burn them. Make sure it's far enough away that we can't see the smoke from Apula."

"Yer the right bossy prick, aren't you. Man like you shouldn't be in the position to tell a man like me what he—"

Bergnon cracked a punch into the man's face, sending him tumbling onto his arse. "Listen, you fucking nameless wretch, if you don't do as you're told, you can forget about whatever ego you have here and now. We are both dead men if you don't do as I say. And if we are dead, she's dead, if that murderous bastard king of yours hasn't killed her already."

The man looked as though he was about to protest, but then appeared to change his mind. He grumbled as he stood and dabbed at his bleeding lip with his cuff. "Name's Mulan," he grunted.

"I would say it's a pleasure to make your acquaintance, but we both know that would be a lie. Just get on with it," Bergnon continued as he dragged one of the dead men over towards Arrlun's body. "Do you remember the message?" he asked Mulan.

"Course I remember," the man snapped defensively as he hauled Arrlun's body over the saddle of his horse.

"Then tell me."

"Dawn, five days from now, yer going to set a signal fire atop the cathedral spire. That's the signal to assemble on the plain. After the signal fire's been lit, the outer western wall will be primed with charged oil. It'll be ready to open up a breach as we approach. Yer going to foul the wells in the inner castle walls and make ready the surrender of the city, leaving the old man's way clear to Carte."

"Good," Bergnon replied. "Now get the rest of the bodies out of here. I've got to be getting back." Bergnon retrieved his water skin from his saddle and wet a rag. He wiped away the blood on his head and neck, as well as that which was hardening darkly in his fair hair.

"What about yer ear?" Mulan asked. "They'll sure be seeing a wound like that."

"My hair should cover it," Bergnon said as he withdrew an ointment from his saddlebag and smeared it onto the jagged edge of his ear. He winced as the thick, oily substance smothered the exposed flesh. "Just you worry about your own role in this rotting fucking design, alright! I'll be bloody careful of mine."

"Just make sure you are, aye! Remember, you fail the old man, she dies." The man revealed a bloodstained smile, a hangman's mocking grin.

Bergnon held the man's stare coldly. "I won't fail."

Chapter Twenty

HARRULD SEALED his dispatches and handed them over to a newly promoted captain who stood solemnly by the governor's desk, wolfhounds sniffing at his mud-spattered boots. "Make sure that Governor Abbonan receives these personally, do you understand?"

"Yes, my lord," the young captain responded.

"I want you to make two copies of these orders and have them sent on ships alongside you. I want a full withdrawal from Hardalen and a fifty percent troop extraction from Terna to Carte. Governor Abbonan is to dispatch ten galleys to accompany our protection fleet for the Cannan grain ships."

"At once, my lord."

"And one last thing, make sure the governor knows Captain Merkham and Sergeant Subath are to come here to me at Carte without delay."

The young captain saluted and left in a hurry, almost bowling over another messenger as he entered Governor Harruld's study.

"My lord," the messenger said breathlessly, "two more of the urns have just arrived from the lands in the north."

Harruld nodded towards the messenger. "Make sure they're placed with the others."

"Yes, my lord."

"Once you have placed the urns with the others, fetch me Olmat."

He paused before looking up. "And best bring Capriath and Sarbien whilst you're at it. They'll be with him, no doubt."

"What in Dajda's name are we going to do with them?" Brother Anthony asked to the gathered crowd of Governor Harruld, Olmat, Capriath and his father, Sarbien.

He gazed over the near three dozen clay urns that had been brought to Carte from the surrounding regions of the Free Provinces. The urns pulsed with a cool, uneven light, casting an eerie glow across the faces of all as they stood around them.

"They can't stay here, locked away in the basement." Anthony scratched at the thin collection of brown whiskers that sprouted from his boyish chin.

"Why not? This is as good a place as any?" Sarbien replied.

"It just...doesn't seem right. I don't quite know why," Anthony said.

"Well, perhaps when you can ascertain why you feel such, you can enlighten us," Sarbien said with a grin. He clasped his son's shoulder through his rough habit. "What is most urgent is that we learn what sustains them. We need to know what the power is, and, if need be, nullify it."

Capriath approached the neatly piled urns and crouched to his knees, groaning as his old joints creaked. "I probably have the most knowledge out of the three of us on charging inanimates. From what I've learned of remote charging, when dealing with multiple inanimates, whatever is sustaining them should ideally be placed equidistant between each object. In doing so, one can ensure a balanced distribution of charge. This, in turn, ensures a greater likelihood of success in one's aim. So, what we need truly is the location that each of the urns has come from and we will be closer to the source. If indeed I am correct in my assumption, that is." Capriath creaked to his feet and looked at his companions.

"Fair enough," Harruld spoke. "It's a worthwhile hypothesis to pursue, but we've no telling how many of these urns there are, and indeed the location of them all." Harruld paced a short distance back and forth, his hand stroking his silver beard as he thought. "Without locating all of the urns, I suppose we have to be accept that we may not be able to establish a precise location." Harruld considered his own words for a moment. "I see the strategy behind these strikes. Combine the loss of so many leaders amongst our ranks with the effects of wide-spread and sustained crop failure, and you have a military on the brink of collapse. I think we can assume that the urns have been placed strategically only to target the yields of the Free Provinces, and that Solansia remains free from blight."

Harruld's companions nodded their agreement as the governor outlined his logic.

"It is quite plausible that our main crop regions have been targeted and that some more outlying provinces have been untouched. That would narrow the range down further. Guard, fetch me a map and a quill, and hurry," Harruld instructed the young guard who stood outside the door.

The young man darted off on his errand.

Harruld continued pacing. "Canna has no blight, for we've imported much of our grain over the last years. Which means, to our knowledge, the blight is restricted to the Free Provinces. Enulin and the other southern regions have reported extensive failures in all but the immediate lands surrounding the cities. The same can't be said for Apula. The blight has ruined all the lands, but the poppy bloom was strong again last winter, so I believe the decision was to make use of the good ground for crop. If it's taken as well as they hoped, it will save us some heartache, and gold to boot."

The young guard entered the room once more, breathing heavily as he handed the map and quill to the governor, saluting before returning to his post outside the door.

"Now, gentlemen, let us puzzle this out as best we can," Harruld said as he spread the map out on the table. "Now, where did this one come from?" he asked, pointing the quill to one of the many urns.

"Have we got them all?" Harruld asked as he regarded his map. It was covered in crosses and notes, marking out the known or estimated location of each of the recovered urns.

His companions leant over the table, reviewing the annotated document.

"There have been none in from the east," Olmat muttered.

"None, indeed." Harruld rubbed at his chin as he thought. "We can assume the western lands of Apula have been poisoned too. The blight there is consistent with everywhere else we've seen it, but with the surrounding plain cleared of the bloom and the good soil put to use, I think we can expect trouble. I think we can say with certainty now that Grunnxe's aim is to take Apula. Why else would we find our croplands blighted in the west, but not entirely in the east? Grunnxe means to use the grain resource as provisions for his own troops. He has then a stronghold in the east of the Free Provinces and a springboard from which to strike west." Harruld heaved out a shuddering breath. "Bergnon will see to it that the city doesn't fall easily."

"But if it does, Grunnxe will strike us here." Brother Anthony said. "Where he will find us hungry and weakened,"

"We have grain shipments due from Canna, Brother," Harruld said.

"But if the shipments don't make it," Brother Anthony added quietly, "then Grunnxe has the capital, and he has the command."

"I've already dispatched ten of our Carte fleet to Nabruuk. Ten more will join them from Terna. The grain should be secured."

"My lord." Anthony bowed subtlety. "Forgive me. I spoke with haste. Fear is my weakness."

The four older men looked up at the young holy man.

"Fear is not weakness," Sarbien corrected his son. "To have fear is to have wisdom. Know that we have Dajda on our side and we will face this coming storm and weather it."

"Yes, father," Brother Anthony conceded, his eyes dropping to the floor.

Capriath bent over and looked closely at the map on the table. "It doesn't make sense to me." He regarded the crosses marked on the map of the Free Provinces. "I would judge the equal distance between each of these crosses to be somewhere east of Carte." He pursed his lips a moment and waggled a finger in front of his face. "But it's not exact, not quite right in my mind yet. There are a few of these locations where crosses seem to throw me somewhat. There must be more of these urns towards the north, north-east, and south-east." The old physician rubbed his watery blue eyes.

"Can we extrapolate these onto the map by marking down known areas where crops have failed with signs of blight? Once we do that, we can mark the point at the core, surely?"

Capriath nodded. "Aye, it's worth a go."

"Here." Harruld offered the quill.

Capriath took the quill. His hand hovered above the map as he puzzled out locations in his head. Carefully, he marked small circles in the assumed locations of the urns, as well as the known sites of large-scale crop failures. He placed the quill on to the table beside the map and looked towards his colleagues. "There you are." Capriath took a step back from the table to allow his companions to look at his work. "Now, in that circled area, where would you think would offer a sound place to sustain something best kept secret?"

Harruld leant in to the map, and, after a moment, he let out a weary sign. "Shalima," he muttered.

"Shalima mines, indeed," Capriath sighed.

Harruld sighed. "Under our fucking noses."

———

"We must understand their nature before we move too fast," Capriath urged Governor Harruld in his study. "Give me some time to study the urns. We'll be better equipped to face whatever is sustaining them if you spare me two days and nights with them."

"Capriath, time is not a luxury we can afford at the moment. We must move now." Harruld cast a glance to Olmat, who shook his head subtly in disagreement. Harruld regarded the old physician for a moment and deferred to him. "You may have your two days and nights, but on the third morning, we'll ride out to Shalima. I'll have a unit of troops readied. Brother Anthony, return to your order and send me your abbot. We must have a company of your Tuannan."

"At once, my lord." Brother Anthony swiftly left the room, his sandaled feet slapping on the stone floor as he hurried off.

"You'd best get to work, Capriath," Governor Harruld added before he too set off to make firm his arrangements.

———

Anthony slept uneasily. His mind flashed with images of the urns, of rotting matter and barren fields. He saw starving children, ragged and filthy. He saw children begging in the streets, and at the feet of invading troops. The troops laughed and kicked at the unfortunates. He saw sorrow and pain.

Anthony screamed silently in his dream. He tried to lash out at the savage men, but he had no power there.

His eyes flashed open and he sat up straight in his bed. The plain nightshirt clung to his thin frame such was the sweat that streamed from his body. The chill of the winter met the wetness of his skin in a treacherous union. He lay down within his cot, and drew his blanket tight. Anthony fell back into sleep, and fell deep. An intense heat spread from his feet, and rose up his legs and around his middle. The heat spread down his fingers and up his arms before swamping up over his neck and onto his head. Although at first the sensation intimidated him, it coaxed a sensation of comfort. It intoxicated him. Anthony fell deeper within sleep, and he gave himself up to the warmth. He drifted into a dream of heat, of light, and of celestial music.

Then came a vicious flash, and intense, hateful flames. Something snapped and clawed in his mind. Then there was fury, and pain. So much pain. More than he could endure. Anthony felt his dry throat scream, but it was useless. His cry fell silent. The warmth that had intoxicated him now burned at his limbs and scorched his mind. He fought to waken, but it was no use. He was trapped. *Surely he would die*, he thought. Anthony's mind turned to God.

I give myself to you, Dajda. No sooner had he formed the thought than a burst of violent flame and savage, guttural screams crashed over him. The ferocity redoubled. His mind reeled after the most dreadful of assaults. But then calm, and light. Ease of breath and looseness of limb.

"*Anthony, my child,*" a voice spoke to him. Although it soothed, he felt his skin prickle as the voice spoke. "*Thou art safe here in the embrace of my love. I will not judge thou or cast dim light upon thine face for thy failings, for I am God, thy Father.*"

"*Dajda, Mother,*" Anthony spoke in his mind.

Flames collided over him. He felt the vicious rebuke of the presence in his mind.

"*Curse this name, child, and utter it not. Do not thou durst to utter that name as thy Mother God. Dajda does not love thou, child. Dajda thinks of thou a wretch, naught but a rank cur. Why else hath thou been cursed? Why else hath thou been denied the gift? Dajda, does not love thou! Thy father and sister are held in a fulsome embrace by the betrayer Dajda. They hath been granted the gift and can call them-*

selves amongst the Tuannan. Aye, child of mine, Dajda loves thy weak
father and whore sister, but she does not love thou."

Anthony felt his mind break and emotion flood over him. Fear and
sorrow. Betrayal and uncertainty.

The voice continued to woo him; a sweet seduction of honeyed
words arousing Anthony. *"But I love thou. I love thou fully enough my*
child to protect thou. I love thou fully enough to bless thou for all thine
days in this world. I wilt bless thou for all eternity. I love thou enough
to bestow unto thou my gift. Thou wilt sit by me as one of my most holy
and powerful Tuannan, and receive all of my love and my gifts."
Anthony felt a flush of warmth. *"Set thy spirit unto the palm of mine*
hand, child. Come live with love in my house. Thy Father's house."

Anthony's eyes flashed open. His nightshirt was dry and warm. His
body felt strong and his mind alert. He swung his legs from the cot and
placed his feet onto the stone floor. He pulled on his habit and kicked
aside his sandals. An urge to go to the urns washed over him and he
made his way out from his bedchamber and into the dull, flickering
glow of the oil lamp-lit corridor.

He quietly navigated his way through the corridors of the High
Command, slipping into shadows when the sounds of movement
drifted nearby. Carefully, he made his way to the basement, to where
the urns were stored. Anthony felt his heart begin to race, only for a
flush of warmth before calm washed over him, his Father's encouragement.

He descended the final steps toward the basement and carefully
stole a glance towards the room from around the corner of the hall.
There were no guards. Anthony strode forward towards the room in a
dozen purposeful steps. Without breaking his stride, he reached for the
handle and turned, his momentum causing him to slam his head into
the rough grain of the locked door.

In that brief moment, Brother Anthony remembered himself, and a
flush of terror washed over him. "Dajda, help me!" He burned.

"Dajda cannot hear thou! There is nought love but that of the
Father. Abandon thy false betrayer. Use thy power, child. Use the gift I
grant unto thou."

Anthony was aroused by the urge to use it, to realise at last the power gifted to Tuannan. All his life he had dreamt of mastering the power. All his life he had dreamt of being in such favour to receive the gift, and to follow his father and sister as one of the Tuannan. His breath heaved with lust.

Anthony held his palm open before the lock of the door and concentrated. He asked his new God for the power. In that instant, the lock fizzed away in a puff of noxious gas and was no more. Anthony's eyes rolled up in his head and he indulged in the spasm that ran down his body from his skull. This gift was great indeed.

Still panting, he shoved the door open and beheld the urns that sat before him. The faintest whispers rose from them through the air towards him, and asked him to set them free. Anthony knew what he was to do next, and he walked steadily towards them.

"Anthony, what are you doing, lad?" a voice called from behind.

He turned toward the door and looked upon his uncle, Capriath.

"You shouldn't be in here," the old physician said.

Anthony stood panting heavily, his head bowed towards the floor.

"Is there something wrong? Speak to me, lad." Capriath urged as he stepped forward, stopping suddenly as his nephew lifted his head.

Anthony's ice-blue eyes were bloodshot and his mouth gaped. His lips hung like the hungry maw of a great moloser and dripped pink saliva.

"By Dajda, child. What is wrong?" Capriath asked, edging back a step.

Anthony began to rock from side to side. He fidgeted with himself and muttered as if he spoke to someone in the shadows.

"My lad, who do you speak with?"

"I speak with the Father." Anthony leered. "The Father says you are a betrayer; nothing more. He says you mean to take my power from me and send me back to the feet of the Mother of Curs. He tells me to set forth my brothers and sisters, and purge you all of your weakness and sin. If I do this for the Father, I shall feel the strength of his love for me."

"No, Anthony, you are betrayed," Capriath said as he backed away up the hallway. "These are words of deceit."

"Yes, Father. I will see thy command done."

"Anthony? Dajda!"

"Say not that name!" Anthony shrieked.

"Anthony, no!" Capriath cried. He quickly wove what power of protection he could, though it was no use. Dajda could not answer.

Anthony bounded the few steps between them in an instant and shoved the old man, sending him crashing into the wall of the corridor with an explosion of breath from his lungs.

Capriath slid down the wall onto the stone floor. He looked up to the form of Anthony panting above him, his face a mask of violent lust. Before Capriath could find any words, blows began to rain down upon him and the world for Capriath turned to blackness.

Anthony turned from the bloodied and battered body of Capriath and entered the room. The urns sung to him and his ecstasy peaked. He approached the clay vessels and rubbed his cheek with the back of his hand, smearing sticky blood onto his face. He reached down and picked up the nearest urn to him.

Holding it tight under his left arm, his began steadily trying to dislodge the plug holding the urn shut. He requested the power of his new God to open the urn, but his plea was unanswered. As he struggled, light flooded the corridor, and sent shadows stretching along the wall in front of the door.

"Child, the strength of man must set thine siblings free. Dost thou not love me?" the voice questioned.

Anthony redoubled his efforts in time to see a party of command guards rush to the bloodied body of Capriath before casting the light of their lamps into the room with the urns, revealing Anthony.

"Stop right there," cried the first guard into the room, his sword levelled to the blood-spattered Anthony.

As the guard's colleagues joined him in the room, Anthony freed the plug. A hiss of pressurised gas filled the room with a thick, smoky mist. Next to fill the room was the choking and retching of the guards as they fell to their knees, eyes bulging and faces distorted in agony and terror.

Anthony did not see a mist. Instead he saw only the beautiful fae beings that danced around the room, singing their heavenly songs. He had set his brothers and sisters free and was wrapped in the love of his new God. The children of the betrayer, Dajda, would pay for their sins.

The eyes of the guards bulged in their blackening faces. Their tongues protruded purple and swollen from their mouths. Their skin burst with blood and dark, lumpy vomit flowed from their mouths.

As the final guard choked out his last breath, Anthony hurriedly opened the rest of the urns, setting free the children of his new God. Such was the delight that enraptured him, he did not care that the corpses that surrounded him developed black and bulbous boils, some bursting and sending plumes of spores into the air. Nor did he care for their flesh rotting in places and sliding from the bones.

Anthony's rapture was so great, and his praise so rich that he did not even care as patches of flesh sloughed and fell from his own face and hands.

"Have you seen Capriath or Anthony this morning?" Harruld asked of Olmat as he shuffled into the governor's chambers. Sarbien was already sat by the table.

"I've not seen either," Olmat said as he lowered himself into the seat with a groan.

"I was just saying it's unlike either of them to be late," Sarbien said as he patted his older brother's hand in a greeting of the morning. "How are you brother?" he asked.

Olmat smiled and, in turn, placed his hand on that of his brother. "I'm well enough to come and speak. Well enough to tend the sick and injured, but I came this morning to tell you honestly I am not well enough to travel to Shalima with you. As much as the heart is willing, my body is failing me. The last transport from Hardalen to here took much from me, brother. To travel now, across land, well, that, I fear, is a journey I cannot make. My time comes." The older man's startling blue eyes misted over as the wetness of tears formed on the lids.

"I didn't want to be the one to say, brother." Sarbien smiled. "Not that you would have listened to me anyway."

Olmat laughed, a dry and wheezing noise. "Of course I wouldn't have. I wiped your backside as a child. I'll not take orders from you."

A knock thundered on Harruld's door. Before Harruld had the chance to answer, a young guardsman burst in, such was his urgency.

"I'm sorry for my intrusion, my lord, but I have grave news."

"Speak man!" Harruld barked.

The guard snapped his eyes forward and relayed his report, "My lord, someone broke into the room you ordered the urns be stored in."

Olmat glanced towards his brother, and then towards the guard.

The guard paused, his lips shook, as if the words trembled in his mouth. "I'm sorry, my lords," the guard answered, keeping his eyes fixed on Harruld. "Lord Capriath's body—"

Olmat and Sarbien emitted strangled moans, halting the guard.

The young guardsman continued, "Lord Capriath's body was found in the basement, by the storeroom. Within the storeroom, there were four more bodies."

"My son?" Sarbien looked up as he fiercely wiped the tears from his eyes.

"No, my lord. Brother Anthony was not amongst the dead."

"Thank Dajda," Sarbien said as he placed his arm around his older brother.

Harruld got up from behind his desk and moved towards the door of his chamber, opening and calling in the nearest guardsmen.

"Fetch Brother Anthony from his chamber. If he's not in his chamber, then he must not have returned from the order house last night. If so, go to there and bring him hear at once."

"How did he die?" Sarbien asked.

"I'm sorry, my lord." The young guardsman avoided the eyes that searched him. "Lord Capriath appears to have been beaten to death, perhaps by many assailants."

Olmat released a sorrowful sob.

"My lord," the guard continued, "that is not all."

"What then, damn it?" Harruld snapped.

"The bodies, sir, they are sickened with something. Some kind of illness."

Olmat suddenly broke from his sorrow. "What do they look like? Have you seen them?"

"No, not with my own eyes. The message had been passed to me that there were blacked lumps upon each of the bodies. These lumps burst open, even in death."

"Did you go near the bodies, or one who did?" Olmat asked of the guard.

"Corporal Yannis, my lord, who bid me pass on this message,

discovered the bodies." The guard's voice had taken on a panicked edge.

"Did he touch you?" Olmat's bony knuckles turned white as he gripped the table before him.

"My lord?"

"Did Corporal Yannis touch you at any point?"

The young guardsman began to shake from his hands up, and his breaths quickened as fear gripped him.

"Speak!" Harruld barked.

"My…my arm, my lord. Yannis gripped my arm."

Olmat shook his head almost imperceptibly to Harruld before he took a breath and slowed the beat of his heart. He smiled. "What's your name?"

"Guardsman Herrick, my lord."

"Herrick." Olmat looked thoughtfully at the guardsman. "I recognise the name. Your father was also in the household guard, wasn't he?"

The young guardsman's hands ceased to tremble and he relaxed a little. "Yes, my lord. You knew him?"

"Aye, lad. Is he well?"

"He is, my lord. He was given his pension and now runs a small stoneware shop with my mother."

"Excellent. I should like to see his shop." Olmat smiled. "Until then, however, be sure and pass on my regards to your father, would you?"

"Of course, my lord." The young man smiled, his fear seemingly having diminished.

"Guard Herrick," Harruld commanded the man's attention. "When does your watch end?"

"Sunset, my lord."

"Good. I'll send someone else to fetch Brother Anthony. You seem a steady lad, so I have another task for one such as you. I want you to stand guard at the basement of the keep. No one gets in or out without my command. Clear?"

"Yes, my lord."

"Good. Now, you know that talk of this will cause those of a weaker heart to fall to fear. There is no need for this, so I want you to remain steadfast. Keep your head, man, and for the love of Dajda, make sure others keep theirs. Touch no one, and don't let yourself be touched. It's just a precaution."

"Yes, my lord." The guardsman saluted and left the room.

As the guard closed the door behind him, Olmat looked to his two companions. "That lad is already dead. Our enemies have brought plague on our city, and delivered us death."

Governor Harruld's order to lock down the High Command spread quickly, as did his instruction for every guardsman who had entered the basement, or those that were in contact with them, to assemble at the lower level of the High Command. Soon, near forty mean stood in rank before the governor, amongst them, Guardsman Herrick. Some men's brows glistened with beads of sweat, whilst others tried their best to stifle coughs, causing their companions standing beside them to shift uncomfortably, a fact not lost on the sweating men.

Governor Harruld stood before the men as Olmat and Sarbien wove their symbols in the air in front of them, requesting Dajda's aid to protect these young men. He knew it mattered not, for there was no power forthcoming whilst Dajda slept, and so each of their chances came down to the hand of fate.

"Men, we have had to shut the High Command from those outside. It will no doubt be clear to you all that we have been attacked, once more by stealth and guile. Our enemies have brought disease into our house and we must now fight it before Carte falls into death by this ill doing."

Some of the men sobbed, whilst others stood tall, their faces set in an unwavering display of calm.

"Carte needs her sons and brothers to protect her against this enemy. Carte needs your sacrifice." Governor Harruld looked upon the men, his challenge laid out to them.

Some of the men nervously eyed the stone and mortar that rested by the corner of the large room they occupied.

"What must we do, my lord?" one guardsman asked, stepping forward from his rank.

"What is your name?" the governor asked.

"Corporal Gillen Habston, a man of Carte, my lord," the guardsman answered proudly.

"Gillen Habston, a man of Carte," Governor Harruld repeated.

"Yes, we men of Carte are proud and strong." The governor approached the younger man. "I need you to help contain this enemy within these lower reaches of the High Command. We must block out the basement. Seal up the passageways and staircases," the governor said.

"And then we must block ourselves within the lower level, my lord," Gillen added, smiling calmly at the governor as all others stopped and stared at the steadfast guardsman.

"You are heroes of Carte, as much as those who bleed on her battlements," Governor Harruld said. "Tuannan have cast powers of protection over you. Some of you will succumb to this foul enemy, whilst some of you will survive. Those of you who get sick, please, take yourself away from those who are not. We ask you to do a most brave thing."

A brief sob could be heard. Guardsman Herrick wept with fear before one of the more resolute men stifled the sound.

Governor Harruld continued, "Those who succumb must take themselves to a remote part of the lower level. There are large fire places in the armoury. It's ideal." He paused a moment and looked into the faces before him. "What you will need has been set aside for you. There is enough fire oil here to soak your clothing, and there are daggers waiting."

More sobs escaped from the ranks before him.

"If you are ill, you must take yourself to the armoury, and set a flame to yourself. Once you have done so, use the dagger, and commit the ultimate sacrifice. Set loose your spirit, rather than suffer the flames. Sarbien will show you how to do this quickly." Governor Harruld looked upon the men before him, his face and heart clashing with a mix of pride and sorrow. "If by the next passing of seventh-day you have been fortunate, we will set you free. We will have men on hand to help you if you signal. If not, my brothers, then may Dajda take you into her embrace quickly and without pain."

With that, Governor Harruld saluted his men and left the lower levels of the High Command.

Chapter Twenty-One

"I CAN FEEL A PRESENCE. One of them is near, within the walls of the city," Evelyne said to Kalfinar as they stood together on the forward deck of the ship.

They approached the harbour of Nabruuk in the mid-hours of morning. The sun was hot, despite the early hour, and it glittered off the water with dazzling effect.

"It's truly a sight to behold," she said, looking at the stunning white that glared from the walls of Nabruuk. The shine of blue glaze and mother of pearl tiles that coated the roofs of the city set the city scene ablaze with almost painful intensity.

Kalfinar grunted in response, his focus set on the many merchant ships that sat low in the waters of the harbour. He felt Evelyne's question before it passed her lips. "More grain ships bound for Carte, Terna, and everywhere else there is hunger in the Free Provinces." He reflected upon the nationwide need for imported grain, and the ruthless profiteering of the neutral nation of Canna. "A rich nation grows richer still on the hunger pains of another. Doesn't seem right, does it?"

"We need to eat, Kal. The people need to eat," she said. "What else can we do?"

He changed the subject. "Can you sense where we ought to go to await the coming of the next one?" Kalfinar asked, drawing his eye from the harbour as they were piloted in.

"I know of a safe house in the east quarter. Some of my Tuannan brothers and sisters use the house from time to time. If the sensation is as it was last time, we should be able to rest there and await their coming."

The group donned headscarves and long white robes, as was the custom in Canna. Chentuck drew a veil across his face to hide his unusual appearance, lest he draw too much attention to their party. Evelyne and the child were dressed like Chentuck, masking their gender, should that serve to reveal too much to seeking eyes.

They rode through the bustling streets towards the safe house in the east, with every street of Canna's capital awash with commerce. Exotic smells and sounds met them at every turn. Kalfinar remembered the thrill he experienced when he previously visited Canna, although this time he was not able to relive the feeling, such was his raised sense of alarm.

The streets were cramped, with busy stalls of fruit, bright mounds of spices and silks on either side, all being towered over by tall white-washed buildings. Their progress through the busy streets was slow and Kalfinar shifted uncomfortably as they passed the countless individuals wearing long, robes and headwear. The many open balconies and narrow alleyways off to the side of main streets only served to swell Kalfinar's unease. *Perfect for surprises.*

As if sensing his discomfort, Evelyne nudged her mare up beside Kalfinar's. Being careful not to take up too much space on the crowded streets, she leaned in to him and whispered, "We're not far. It's at the end of this street and then the next left. The entrance to the courtyard opens onto a square. We should have a good vantage point from the roof."

Kalfinar nodded in acknowledgement and carried on, his eyes ever watchful.

They passed the remaining distance in minutes and approached the safe house without any fuss. The house was a three-storied affair, and like all the buildings in Nabruuk, it was washed in pure white. Evelyne shared some hushed words with the man guarding the entrance to the courtyard, and they quickly passed within the walls.

"One of your Tuannan?" Kalfinar asked as they made their way to a room within the lower reaches of the building.

"Yes," Evelyne replied, still holding the child to her body. "Everyone you see within this building is Tuannan."

"We'd best keep watch for the coming of the next one," Evelyne said. "They draw ever nearer. We must be ready."

Kalfinar looked at the small child who clung to Evelyne's leg, fingering the material of her skirt and looking up at Kalfinar with her deep green eyes. He absently toyed with the amulet around his neck with one hand and rubbed his head with the other. His headache was beginning to return, albeit slightly. *Jalsinum, I can smell it. Drift away, drift away to sleep, and no more pain.*

"Come, let's go to the roof and keep watch. Chentuck, you stay here and keep a watch at the entrance to the yard. Let us know if it looks like there's anything happening," Kalfinar ordered before heading up the narrow, winding wooden staircase towards the roof.

Hours passed as Kalfinar, Broden and Evelyne waited patiently on the roof of the safe house. The child remained present, inseparable from Evelyne from the moment she was awoken back in Enulin.

"Something's wrong," Evelyne softly said.

"What is it?" Kalfinar asked.

"The feeling I had, it has somehow diminished."

"Diminished? As in they're not coming?"

"Perhaps so. I don't sense the coming together as I did in Enulin." Evelyne's face was a puzzle, her ice-blue eyes unsure and searching for answers. "There is more. I sense alarm within them."

"What can we do?" Broden asked as he surveyed the emptying square. The bells of the holy houses tolled as the sun set on the bustling capital. "It'll be dark soon and the Cannan's will be at prayer."

"Perhaps we should move towards them?" Kalfinar supplied.

Evelyne looked at Kalfinar, locking eyes with him, although she did not voice any disapproval.

"We can sense their presence, and we can see them," Kalfinar made his case. "If they're not coming to us, then we should go to them."

"I'm not so sure, Kal," Evelyne added.

"There's no telling how long we could be sat here," Broden said, his eyes imploring Evelyne to act. "We can't simply sit about and wait if there's a problem, can we?"

Evelyne's silence seemed endless as she sat considering the best course of action. The night could be fraught with danger, for their enemies could send foes against them at any time. However, the longer they waited with no understanding of what was taking place, the worse the situation could be. She considered their options, looking down at the child who clung to her. Evelyne smiled at the two captains and inclined her head towards the child. "Which one of you wants to tell her she can't come?"

Kalfinar shifted his belt and sheathed sword uncomfortably under his Cannan robes. Despite the long garments restricting the quickness of his draw, he was reluctant to expose the weapon lest it draw unwanted attention to him and his two companions as they negotiated their way through the dusk-lit early night.

The bells of the holy houses had ceased to toll and now the air was filled with the faint hum of reverential chanting from all around. Despite his present unease, Kalfinar enjoyed the song of the city.

Evelyne stopped from time to time as they came to empty street corners, the Godstone drawing her ever closer to the sleeping one. Kalfinar and Broden kept a steady watch of the roads, balconies and alleys. They shifted around her randomly as they walked. If there were to be a strike against them, they would see that there would be no easy targeting of Evelyne.

"You two are making me dizzy!" she cried, rubbing her eyes. Their blue shine leapt out in contrast to the white veil and headdress.

Kalfinar found himself distracted by her eyes, and shook his head, clearing the thought. "Evelyne, with the greatest respect, it is not your becoming dizzy I am concerned with, but that of the crossbowman who watches us from above," Kalfinar retorted.

"Where?" Evelyne asked, her voice an urgent hiss.

Broden answered, "There is no crossbowman that we know of." The two men continued to circle Evelyne, swapping directions errati- cally. "But what we are doing, although making you dizzy, is preventing any crossbowman from easily planting a bolt in you." The big captain smiled apologetically.

"Come, we must move on," Kalfinar said. "What way?" he asked.

"Towards the south. This way." Evelyne pointed at the street to the right of the crossroads ahead.

As she finished speaking, an explosion sounded in the distance, flashing an orange haze across the fully darkened night sky. Another explosion followed, flaring in the sky, followed by several more. The gentle hum of reverence was torn by a rage of noise and light.

"What in Dajda's name was that?" Broden exclaimed.

"It came from the docks," Kalfinar snapped as he shot off in the direction of the blasts, the opposite of where Evelyne directed. *The docks, the docks. Yes! At last.*

"Kal!" Broden called after his cousin, but it was no use, he had set off at pace and was not stopping.

"Kal, you damn fool! Why did you run off?" Broden asked, arriving by his cousin as he glanced around the corner of a building overlooking the harbour front. "You could've got yourself killed." Broden heaved for breath.

Kalfinar regarded his cousin and then Evelyne. She breathed lightly, untroubled by her exertions. "Sorry. Knew something ill had happened. Look," he said, pointing to the scene unfolding upon the water of the harbour.

Broden's eyes widened as they beheld the scene before him. "Dajda! The grain!"

The Cannan merchant ships heavy with grain were on fire and sinking. Ragged looking corsair ships manoeuvred within the harbour alongside vessels baring the banner of Solansia. They cast explosive naphtha barrels onto the remaining ships. Explosions birthed flashes of light and noise into the sky, sparkling on the water and shining light onto the enemy forms revelling upon their decks.

"The fucking Solansian fleet!" Kalfinar whispered.

Evelyne tugged at Kalfinar's robe. "Kal, come on! We can do nothing here. Let's go." She placed her hand on his shoulder and squeezed, urging him to draw his eyes from the harbour and press on with their objective.

"You're right," Kalfinar said, his eyes fixed on the harbour. "We'd better be quick," he muttered, finally turning his head towards his companions, "they're coming ashore."

They moved swift and quiet through the lamp-lit streets, avoiding the many Cannan's filtering out of holy houses. Cries could be heard behind them as the raiders made their presence felt, most likely bringing death to any in their way.

Evelyne directed them as quickly as she could to where the sensation was strongest. She barked an order, turning them down a dimly lit side street. The back of Kalfinar's skull burned. He exchanged a knowing glance with Broden.

Trouble.

The two captains and Evelyne had just enough time to shift their robes and draw their swords before the assault came. Their attackers had made a fatal error, spilling out onto the alley from narrow doorways on either side. The skirmish was brief. In an explosion of noise and blood, it was over. Six bodies lay heaped in the doorway recesses at the feet of the captains, lengths of wood and lumps of stone for weapons.

"They're not Solansian's," Broden grumbled.

"No," said Kalfinar, "nor are they pirates."

"They're Cannan," Evelyne whispered. "The spirit still hunts us."

They continued along their path driven by the urge that continually washed over Evelyne. After the chaotic attack in the alleyway there had been no further trouble, save for the cries ringing out all around them as the raiding parties laid waste to all in their path. They kept to the back streets, their eyes hungrily searching for the slightest betrayal of movement, ever ready to strike out in defence. They had been darting from alley to alley for nearly half an hour when Evelyne whispered for them to stop.

"What is it?" Kalfinar asked.

"The feeling is strong, we're very close," Evelyne said, her eyes troubled.

Broden sneaked a glance around the corner of the last building on the alley and turned back in, exhaling a long sigh, heavy with frustration. "It's no less than the palace of fucking Canna," the big captain said, leaning back against the wall with his head tilted towards the starry night sky.

"The palace?" Kalfinar questioned. "Evelyne, is there no indication of who exactly we're looking for?"

Evelyne pulled down her veil and gave Kalfinar a tired look. "I don't have such insight. All I can feel is a strength, a bond. It grows stronger or weaker. Right now, the bond is very strong, and stronger still when I turn towards the palace. They are within its walls, as we will soon need to be."

"Wonderful!" Kalfinar huffed, earning a flat stare from Evelyne.

"How are we to get inside the palace?" Broden questioned, raising his palms to the sky in exasperation.

"We'll work that out," Kalfinar responded, his eyes darting up into the darkness of the alleyway, "but for now, we need to get off the streets. We'll shelter in one of these merchant houses." Kalfinar made towards the nearest door recess of a merchant house exiting onto the alleyway.

"Kal," Broden whispered towards his cousin through his teeth, "what of the owners?"

"The owners will comply." Kalfinar's response was deadly low. He did not look up as he spoke and continued, gripping the door handle and finding it locked. "I suppose I should at least knock," he muttered before stepping backwards and slamming his foot hard into the door, sending splinters shattering into the darkness inside.

In the next instant Kalfinar had someone in a firm grip. The assailant, invisible in the darkness as Kalfinar entered, leapt forward, only for Kalfinar to pin him against the wall, his sword to his throat.

"Drop the weapon and I promise you the morning light will meet you," Kalfinar said, switching to flawless Cannan.

The man held his wicked curved dagger tight in his hand, his wrist held firm by Kalfinar's other hand. "Dog, you shall have to kill me and have my blood on your soul."

The man struggled again as Broden and Evelyne entered. Evelyne tried to shut the door behind them, though it could not be closed fully due to the trauma of Kalfinar's kick. The hinges were bent and twisted from the force of his entry.

"Are you alone?" Kalfinar asked.

"Answer me or make your peace with the world." Kalfinar pressed his sword edge to the man's throat, emphasising his point.

"Kal, stop it!" Evelyne hissed.

"I am alone, Solansian," the man sighed, releasing his wicked blade as he did so, sending it clanging on the wooden floor with a soft metallic din. He spoke in the tongue of the Cullanain.

Kalfinar eyed the man in the dark of the room, his eyes adjusting within moments. He watched the man's eyes as he spoke. "We're not Solansian. We're from the Free Provinces, of the Cullanain." The man's eyes betrayed his relief. Kalfinar continued, "Now, don't lie to me. Are you alone?"

"I am. I swear upon holy Nabruuk."

"Don't try anything stupid," Kalfinar said as he released his grip.

The man quickly lit a candle lamp, casting a warm glow around his modest shop floor. Kalfinar and his companions watched in silence as the man repaired his door lock, pulling a hammer from a bag and driving long metal nails through the door and frame.

"What are you doing?" Kalfinar asked. There was a hint of alarm in his voice.

The merchant turned to him with nails protruding from his mouth. "There are raiders afoot tonight. Surely you can hear the screams and the explosions. That is why I believed you to be Solansians. I do not want any more unwanted visitors this night." The man turned and hammered home further nails, securing the rear entrance to the building.

"What is your name?" Evelyne asked, stepping from behind Broden.

"My lady," the man ceased hammering and turned to Evelyne before executing a sweeping bow. "My name is Rondo Alaman al' Hastimun."

"Well, Rondo Alaman al' Hastimun, it is a pleasure to meet you this night. I apologise for the manner of our intrusion, but I am afraid we were in rather a rush." Evelyne smiled apologetically to the merchant before shaking his hand. She nudged Broden before casting a scowl towards Kalfinar.

Broden introduced himself and shook Rondo's hand, likewise apologising for the abrupt nature of the entry to his home. Rondo dabbed a rag to his neck, stemming the slight blood flow from the small cut in his neck.

"That one is Kalfinar, and he is sorry, Rondo," Evelyne said, her words snapping Kalfinar from his concentration as he listened to the distant cries beyond the merchants shop.

Kalfinar spoke, "You must understand I had no choice." Kalfinar shook the merchant's hand and offered a dismal smile.

"No choice. Right." The merchant sounded unconvinced. "Come, follow me." Rondo guided them upstairs to his living quarters and lit a small fire, warming some water to make chai.

The floor of the room was lined with rich rugs and several fine velvet chairs lounged beneath gold-framed paintings. The nature of the room seemed to contradict the means by which the merchant operated, if his small shop was anything to go by, Kalfinar thought. *There's more to this man than meets the eye.*

Rondo was a small man, an inch or so shorter than Evelyne. His beard was long and black, trimmed to a fine point, which waggled from his chin as he spoke, a style typical of Cannan men. Unusually, he wore a set of polished glass lenses upon his nose, improving what must have been poor vision.

The three companions sat on low cushioned seats whilst the small merchant busied himself with the tea. Kalfinar and Broden shifted uncomfortably, there was no time for such matters, however Evelyne cast them both wicked stares, and so they remained seated, albeit fidgeting. Once warmed, Rondo poured them small mugs of sweet, spiced chai and a plate of sugared dates. He smiled and drank his tea with his uninvited guests.

"Rondo, why did you assume we were Solansian?" Kalfinar asked.

The small merchant shifted almost imperceptibly, though Kalfinar caught it. "I didn't realise I had," Rondo said.

The silence hung heavily in the air between them as Kalfinar locked eyes with the merchant. He did not to need to utter a word.

Rondo broke his stare and spoke, "Sorry, my new friend, but in my line of work I need to be careful. I can tell you are a man of sound intentions, I can feel it." Rondo smiled uncomfortably, he shifted again and leaned forward. "I am sometimes employed in the less permissible trades in Canna. In your tongue, you would call me a smuggler, but that is insulting. Your language is crude and ugly. What I do for a living is much more refined than that."

The three companions looked at one another and then back to the small merchant.

He continued, "Towards the end of our last harvest, I received some other uninvited guests. They greeted me much the manner you did this night. They were the same men who visited me some months earlier seeking me to do some ill deeds for them."

The merchant paused and shifted uncomfortably after he spoke, which Kalfinar took as the man assessing if he was too free with his words. "We are friends of Canna's, Rondo," Kalfinar reassured the man. "We are here on a cause so grave that it will impact upon us all should we fail." Evelyne's stare snapped hard on Kalfinar, and now he felt perhaps he had revealed too much. Kalfinar nodded and acknowledged his fault before continuing, "What ill deeds are you speaking of?"

The small merchant poured some more chai into his cup and drank. He coughed as the hot brew caught his throat. "My friend, I was requested, at first, to, ahem," Rondo coughed once more, "to use my maritime contacts to intercept any grain shipments to the Free Provinces ports and to redirect them to the Salt Coast in Solansia." Rondo wiped the sides of his mouth with a napkin.

"What do you mean by 'maritime contacts'?" Broden asked.

"Pirates," Kalfinar added, jumping in ahead of the small merchant.

Rondo's face adopted a grimace. "Well, I would call them privateers. My privateers." The small man laughed, though it was a sound devoid of all humour. "Well, they were my privateers. You see, I did not agree to such a doing. Why would I? The Free Provinces and Canna have been on good terms thee last years, and is a valuable trade partner. As I was not agreeable, the Solansian's returned and tried to force my hand. They kidnapped my daughter, Eshanta, and took her off with them." The merchant's face became drawn with sorrow. "She is lost to me now, but still I did not bend to their will, and so they bought my crews with riches beyond my means. Now they raid their own homes alongside those Solansian dogs." Rondo cocked his ear to the sounds of chaos outside in the city. "There, the sound of sons stealing from their own mothers; killing their own neighbours. Curse the dogs." The small merchant spat onto his rug in disgust.

"I am sorry to hear of your daughter, Rondo," Evelyne said. "I am sure we have been sent here to your home by fate, not fortune. You have a role in what plays out before us."

The small man looked up at Evelyne, his eyes watery behind his polished eye lenses. "What is truly unfolding then, my lady?"

"We've found ourselves in a position where Solansia has grown to some significant strength and has attacked the Free Provinces, and now appears to attack Canna. There is some power at work granting them strength and we are working to prevent this," Evelyne spoke quickly, for screams and sounds of steel clashing grew closer.

"My lady, how do you mean to prevent this?"

"There are some key elements we must collect that together will break the back of the source of the enemy's strength. Right now, I am seeking an element within the walls of the palace."

The noises grew closer still, the voices becoming identifiable as being accented in Solansian.

"You seek something within the walls. Do you know what it is and where it lies?" Rondo asked, his shoulders beginning to shift uncomfortably as the sounds of the raiders drew closer.

"I know, I just need a way in—"

Kalfinar cut off Evelyne as he rose to his feet and moved to put out the light before heading to the small window overlooking the alleyway.

"What is it?" she asked.

"Rondo, six men just cut down a pair of Cannan soldiers and appear to be coming our way." Kalfinar drew his sword and a hatchet as he spoke, his actions mirrored by his large cousin.

The small merchant rose in a flash and lifted two curved short swords that hung on his wall. "Let them come," the small man whispered ominously as the banging on his door started.

They ran down the stairs to meet the thunder that fell upon the shop door.

"Let them come," the small Cannan muttered once more, adopting a crouched stance beside the two taller warriors, his curved short swords glinting as his hands twisted and rolled, anticipating the breakthrough of the raiders.

And come they did.

The raider's crashed through the backdoor to the shop. The raiders spilled inside, their accented shouts blending cruelly into screams as they met flashes of blades in the dark. The six men fell swiftly, though it was a certainty that their cries would draw more raiders soon.

Rondo wiped his blades clean on the vest of the man he felled, the one raider not dispatched by the swords of the two bigger men beside him. "Come, I know of safe passages. We must go now!" Rondo said hurriedly. "

They began to filter out of the backdoor, Kalfinar first, glancing side to side, his eyes acutely adjusting the shifts and tricks of the night shadows. Bodies lay like tumbled piles of rags in the street. Suddenly, a crash came from behind as the front door of the shop exploded into a cloud of splinters, sending Evelyne to the ground, struck in the back. Rondo quickly dragged her from the frame of the rear door as further raiders spilled in. Kalfinar and Broden dashed inside.

"Watch her!" Kalfinar barked to Rondo as he met the attackers, his and Broden's swords wheeling in the dark, cutting deeply and taking life before them as though it were but a wheat harvest.

The fight did not last long and the shop floor was now treacherous, such was the clutter of blood and bodies. Evelyne had come around by the time they had retreated from the shop. She groaned as Rondo helped her to her feet. They moved off into the night.

"Are you alright?" Broden asked as he came to Evelyne's side.

"I'm fine, Broden," Evelyne replied. "Just banged my head as I fell."

"We'll need to take those splinters out and treat them or they'll fester," the big captain said, nodding towards the thick arrows of wood protruding from the back of Evelyne's arm.

She smiled and nodded weakly as they moved forward.

"Is there somewhere close?" Kalfinar asked as he walked in front of his companions.

"Just there." Rondo pointed to a warehouse door before them.

"That's handy," Kalfinar snapped, his paranoia beginning to get the better of him.

"I am a man who must be careful, friend, trust me," Rondo replied, his voice showing no sign of the offence. "Come, help me open it."

They opened the door and squeezed everyone inside before shutting it over with a creak.

"Come, I have a passage to somewhere safe." The small merchant moved purposefully in the dark, his feet knowing exactly where to step in the blackness. His invisible shuffling stopped and he risked striking a fire stick before them. "Down here." He stood on a near-invisible lever before him and the stack of heavy pallets holding clay pots shifted by some strange mechanics, revealing a staircase winding below the warehouse floor. "Come, my friends," Rondo said, ushering them down the stairs before following, his hand pressing an unseen button, drawing the pallets back over.

The spiralling staircase was encased in blackness and they fumbled their way down the first few steps uncomfortably until Rondo lit another fire stick and quickly shed light all around as he brought it to contact with an oil lamp slotted within a wall hook.

"Here." Rondo passed the lamp to Kalfinar who was at the head of the party. "Take this and keep on going until you reach the first level below." The small man struck another fire stick and lit another oil lamp.

"The first level below? What is this place?" Broden whispered to his companions, though the closeness of their quarters earned him no discretion.

Rondo chuckled, "This is where the other half of Nabruuk lives."

The next ten minutes were spent in relative silence as they made their way down the winding staircase, stopping at apparent crossroads in the stairs only to be directed further by Rondo. The staircase appeared to be a descending maze, impossible to navigate unless one was familiar with its secrets, or at least in its good favour. They finally arrived at a vestibule before a thick wooden door fortified with iron straps.

"Think it's time you told us more about this place," Kalfinar grumbled in the flickering lamplight.

The little merchant smiled and approached the large door, hammering a practiced tattoo upon it. Moments later, a slat was drawn back and a single ugly eye stared out at them.

"Who are they?" the voice called out in Cannan, its tone aggressive and unfriendly.

Rondo replied, slipping back to his native tongue, "Friends of the Free Provinces. Lords Kalfinar and Broden, and the Lady Evelyne."

"You vouch for them, Rondo?" the voice questioned again. "You know it will mean your life?"

"Agurk, just open the damned door," Rondo replied, his tone becoming irritated. "We have business that must be attended to." There was silence behind the door for long moments before Rondo finally exhaled heavily, "Yes, I vouch for them at the forfeit of my life." He turned to his companions. "Hear that?" he asked. "Don't go picking any fights in here or I'll be strung up for shish in the market!"

The locks of the heavy door were systematically undone, a process that seemed to take considerable time. The door grudgingly swung open, revealing an orange lamp glow that lit an antechamber and seven unwelcoming faces within. The man Rondo had conversed with,

Agurk, moved from behind the door, his massive frame filling it. The giant stood before them, the dark skin of his arms flexing as he folded them before his chest. Kalfinar observed the man had lost an eye through some violent event in the past, leaving a ragged scar across his cheek, eye and forehead.

"Remove your weapons." Agurk growled with a thickly accented voice. He nodded towards their swords. "You too, Rondo," the huge man added.

Rondo adopted an offended look, his arms spread in front of him. "Agurk, there's no need for this. You know me. We took chai together just yesterday."

"I know. Don't blame me. Boss says so," the big man said, his tone betraying frustration. "Anyway, there're raiders in the city. You can't expect me to let armed strangers in, can you?"

"I'm not hostage to these people and I'm no traitor to Canna," Rondo said with a plaintiff tone.

Agurk shrugged his shoulders and crossed his broad forearms in front of his chest. He nodded towards a woven basket in the corner of the antechamber. "Weapons in there."

Kalfinar undid his sword belt and wrapped the leather around the scabbard before placing it in the basket along with his hatchet and two knives. His companions complied, appeasing Agurk and relaxing the other door guards who waited within the antechamber.

Agurk walked towards the door at the other end of the antechamber, indicating for Kalfinar and his companions to follow. As they did, half the remaining door guards formed a rank around them.

"Nice welcome they're giving us," Broden quipped.

"Who's the boss?" Evelyne asked Rondo, drawing Kalfinar's attention from the guards.

"Her name is Ohasha," Rondo replied under his breath. "She's what I would call the administrator of the less official side of Nabruuk's society. She'll assist you."

Agurk led them through another secure entry. They entered into a bright and comfortably appointed waiting area.

"Wait." Agurk grunted as he left them standing in the centre of the room. He headed through a heavy, black-stained door into a side chamber.

Agurk came out from the side room and motioned for them to follow. "Come, the boss will see you."

They entered a large, round room lit in a soft light by several oil lamps and candles. The ceiling hung low and curved into a dome. Along the walls of the room, stood a dozen armed men and women. As with Agurk, their weapons and armour were mismatched, more personal collections than uniform.

Kalfinar's focus was drawn to a huge, polished wood table and the woman who sat behind it. She was of late-middle years and possessed a hard-edged beauty. Her shining black hair was shot with grey and hung thick on her shoulders. Her dark skin was smooth, and wrinkle-free. The eyes that watched them as they walked towards the middle of the room were those of a wolf. Cunning and ruthless.

Her dark-lined eyes narrowed and a smile played across her lips as she beheld Evelyne.

Kalfinar felt a strange desire to step in front of Evelyne.

"That's Ohasha. Follow my actions and watch your tongue." Rondo whispered to his colleagues before executing an extravagant bow.

They each followed suit and bowed to the woman behind the desk.

She looked steadily at each newcomer as they stood in silence before her. Her eyes rested on Evelyne.

Again, Kalfinar felt the unusual urge to step before Evelyne and block the older woman's stares.

At last, Ohasha spoke, her eyes locked on Rondo's. "You know the rules about bringing strangers to us when there is trouble afoot. Why then do these three stand before me?" Ohasha rested back into her tall chair and swung her feet up onto the polished surface of the table. She wore knee-high leather boots with black leather trews tucked into the tops. The shine of metal was apparent down the outside of her left knee, though Kalfinar could not quite determine its function.

"My lady, these three come with only a plea for aid. They are of the Free Provinces. Captains Kalfinar and Broden."

Ohasha nodded, but her eyes stared long at Evelyne, tracing the shape of her hips and breasts with a hungry lust. "And what of the woman? She's a fine thing," she interrupted Rondo.

"Ah, Lady Evelyne. She is Tuannan," Rondo added.

"A woman of skill," Ohasha said. She smiled, revealing teeth stained from years of tabac. "I'd be most keen to learn of your abilities, my lady." Ohasha's eyes made it obvious what she was interested in learning. She pulled her gaze back to Rondo. "And how do they come to be before me?"

Rondo answered, "The raiders came for me again. They came to my home, but my companions came to my aid and we were able to escape. No one saw us enter the tunnel."

"And for what purpose are they here in Canna? We know there are rumblings of war. We're not veiled by ignorance here. We too have agents embedded within your societies, as your friend Major Bergnon was embedded within ours."

Kalfinar did not flinch.

Ohasha's eyes locked with his. "I know of you, Kalfinar. I know of your people, and of whom your commanders send to spy on us. What I don't know is why you are here in Nabruuk."

Kalfinar's eyes flicked to Evelyne before he spoke. "We seek someone within the confines of the palace. We must speak with them. If we cannot, then the trouble with Solansia will not be for the Free Provinces alone."

Ohasha burst with rage. Her feet flashed off the table as she stood. Her chair screeched backwards and she slammed her hands down hard on the desk. The rings on her fingers clanged loudly as they met polished wood. "Do not presume we Cannan's are defenceless against the like of the Solansians! What makes you think we would allow you access to our royal house with such ease?" Her face was reddened. She breathed slow, resting herself back into her seat. Ohasha looked closely at the surface of her desk before smoothing a hand over the surface where her rings had scuffed the finish. "Shit. I just had that fixed."

Rondo discreetly whispered under his breath, "Let it pass. She's dangerous when angry."

Kalfinar did not react until the woman looked back at him. "I don't presume anything. I know what comes and it comes to us all. That includes me, you, and all the people of Canna. The same people who are right now fighting for their lives out in your streets." Kalfinar stared hard at Ohasha as he spoke. "Whilst you sit here in your hole."

Rondo groaned.

"How dare you, dog!" Ohasha roared, slamming her balled fist into the table before him.

The guards around the room stepped forward and placed hands to weapons.

Rondo shrunk as Ohasha stepped out from behind her desk.

The raging woman picked up a metal-plated club as she rounded the desk. She walked with a heavy limp on the left side. An articulated metal frame rounded her knee, providing support to some injury. "I'll have the tongue torn from you and have you eat your fucking balls for—"

Kalfinar cut the enraged woman off as she shouted, his own voice dead calm, "If you maintain this course, then you condemn countless to death. Likely yourself along with them."

"Guards!" Ohasha screeched, prompting her men to close a circle of sharp edges around Kalfinar and the party.

"No, not countless." Ohasha pointed the scuffed metal end of the club towards Kalfinar. "Just you and your friends. Except maybe the girl. I could find some uses for her."

The guards stopped within several feet of them.

"Kal, I hope you know what you're doing," Broden said as he set himself in a defensive stance.

"Think this through, Ohasha," Kalfinar said, raising his hands in supplication. "Why should we fight amongst ourselves whilst Grunnxe ravages our people? Our kin? Our lands? Ohasha, if you love Canna, then we must work as one. We can put an end to Grunnxe or we can shed blood amongst those who should be standing side-by-side." His eyes never broke from Ohasha's.

"We need your help," Evelyne said.

Ohasha blinked and her club arm lowered. "You have a beautiful voice. The perfect package, it would seem."

"We need your help," Evelyne repeated. "There is one within the palace that we must speak with. They hold the path of all our fates."

"This thing you require, will it stop the Solansians?" Ohasha asked.

"It is greater than that," Evelyne replied. "Without our work being done, there is only darkness. All will fall to death or slavery, from the beggar to the Father of the People."

"The Father of the People?" Ohasha's gaze was uncertain before faltering. "Stand down." The fury had yet to fade from her face as she stared hard at Kalfinar and pointed her metal-shod club at him. "You'd do well to show some respect, Captain. I've had more dealings in blood than you'll have had horse miles. I don't usually allow such words to be issued towards me."

Kalfinar nodded his head respectfully. "I apologise, Ohasha. Our need is urgent and we don't have much time. I let it cloud my manner."

"Many things cloud our minds from time to time. I too am known to be hasty," Ohasha said, her rage dissipating. "If what you say is true, then my anger is best being spent elsewhere. What would you have me do?"

Kalfinar outlined the need for access to the palace whilst Ohasha had servants bring them coffees and maps of the complex.

Broden looked quizzically at Ohasha after scanning the detailed schematics of the palace complex. "How is it someone such as you has come by such detailed plans of the palace?" he asked before slurping the bitter coffee.

"Someone such as me?" Ohasha repeated, one thick, dark eyebrow arching. "You mean a criminal? A thief?"

Broden raised his hands. "I meant no offence."

"I'm not some simple Queen of Thieves. I served for many years in the Cannan Fleet. It was when the fleet met your Governor Abbonan that I got this." She tapped at the metal scaffold around her knee. "Before my forced retirement into this life, I served under the Father of the People. We were close, as comrades often are when they bond over blood. I swore to give my life for him, and that oath stands more true today than my leg. I hold such plans that I may serve him and his, should I ever have need to protect them. It seems tonight is that night."

Kalfinar interrupted, "Ohasha, the tunnel leads to the armoury in the basement?"

"Yes."

"And we can access the armoury through an old vent?" He pointed towards the annotated diagram before him.

"It's an old chimney," she replied. "It's easy. Some of my men will come with you. They're former palace guards."

"My thanks," Kalfinar replied.

"Perhaps it would be wise to leave the Lady Evelyne here," Ohasha suggested, her eyes glancing back along the curves of her body. "It would be a great shame to place one so beautiful in such harm."

"I'm afraid she's the most important person we can have within. She is to guide us," Kalfinar said.

"I see," Ohasha said as she pulled on a leather shoulder-webbing.

Kalfinar watched as she picked up two hatchets and slipped them into their respective holsters. "I presume this means you're coming with us."

"I swore an oath." Ohasha's grin was devoid of humour. "I intend to see it fulfilled."

"Are we close?" Kalfinar asked as they made their way along the dimly lit tunnel, crouching low.

"Yes, we're moving closer," Evelyne replied. "The sensation has not shifted for some time. They haven't moved."

"Shhsh," one of the guardsmen hissed. "We've passed the outer wall. Still your voices."

Kalfinar grunted in response as they continued deeper into the tunnel.

A short while later, the guardsmen in front froze and raised his hand, bringing Evelyne to an abrupt stop. Kalfinar bumped into her from behind.

He felt himself flush. *Get a grip on yourself.* Although it was dark, he could sense Evelyne was looking at him. *Is she smiling?*

"We're here," the guard whispered, breaking Kalfinar off from an awkward desire to say something. "Wait a moment." The guard melted into the darkness before returning moments later. "Come. The way is clear."

He led them into a dark alcove off the tunnel. It was lower than the rest of the passage, causing them to stoop so they could fit.

"See, the hole." The guard pointed to the small square of lighter dark before them. "That leads to the chimney of the armoury. The fire's no longer in use. Just pull yourself through and land in the fireplace. I'll go first and make sure the way is clear. Don't hesitate; we may not have much time." He pulled himself through the gap and disappeared out of view.

Broden shrugged, though the motion was almost lost on Kalfinar in the dark passage. "Don't see how I'm going to fit in there," the big man said.

"Come, now," the guardsman urged from beyond sight.

"Suppose you'll just have to find a way," Kalfinar grumbled as he, in cumbersome fashion, pulled himself through the gap and landed in the fireplace with a soft thud.

Rondo came next, without emitting even the faintest of sounds.

Evelyne's slender figure slipped into sight whilst Rondo was still patting himself down. She landed in a crouch, her hand on the hilt of her sword.

Kalfinar gave her a nod and received a smile in return.

"Nothing to it," Broden's voice could be heard through the space.

Kalfinar looked around the armoury. The room was small, but every wall was lined with weaponry. An assorted array of blades, spears, axes, and bows were contained within, as well as barrels stacked in the far corner.

"Volatile compounds," Rondo whispered. "Explains why the fire is out of commission."

"I think we should have a talk about these compounds—"

Grunts from the fireplace stole Kalfinar's attention. He and Evelyne approached and bent to look up the chimney. They were met by Broden's red face as he struggled to shift his frame through the gap.

"Don't say a word," Broden hissed, his voice straining as he shifted and wriggled.

"Move it, fool!" Ohasha's voice could be faintly heard beyond Broden's wedged body.

Kalfinar rolled his eyes and stood upright, followed by Evelyne with a smile creeping on her lips.

"How do you feel?" Kalfinar asked.

"They remain close. I've not felt any change in distance. They're in the same location."

"Still alarmed, as before?"

"More so. We must be quick." Her eyes held Kalfinar's with urgency.

An almighty crash sounded from the hearth. The noise resounded around the armoury and caused the guard listening by the door to jump. They approached where Broden lay sprawled on his back, covered from head to toe in soot.

His face contorted in pain as he pulled himself to his feet. "Think we may need to find another way out." He smiled, his bright white teeth juxtaposed against his soot-stained face.

"You make much noise, Red-hair," the guard said in his accented tongue as his colleague softly landed behind Broden, soon followed by Ohasha.

"Come now. Put these on," the first guard said, reaching for black pantaloons and a blue smock, the customary uniform of palace guards. "Take the sash and wrap it around the waist twice, navel height. Tie it off in a knot at the left side." The guard tossed a maroon silken sash to each of them, followed by a maroon headscarf. "We'll tie your head-wear for you. You two, cover your faces," the guard spoke to Broden and Evelyne.

Ohasha looked at Kalfinar before saying, "You I think can perhaps pass for a Cannan. A light skinned Cannan anyway." She chuckled to herself.

They worked fast and were soon dressed in the garb of palace guards. Kalfinar looked towards Evelyne, who closed her eyes, seeking the sensation that would mark their course.

"Let's move," she said, prompting the first guard to open the armoury door.

They slipped into a lamp lit hallway of broad paving slabs and decorated walls. Fine tapestries of renowned Cannan weave hung along the entire length, a considerable distance in each direction. The air smelled of incense and perfumed oils.

Evelyne pointed to the right and, with silent steps, they made their way to the end of the hall. The space opened into a large hall with broad stone staircases rising on opposite sides. A sentry stood by the base of each staircase, spear in hand.

The first of Ohasha's guards walked across the open area, exposing himself to the two sentries.

"Keep on. Don't break stride," Ohasha said to the rest of the party.

They obeyed her instructions, moving into the open space. The first guard approached the nearest of the two sentries and greeted him in Cannan. As the sentry replied, the guard spun on his toes and brought his rear leg around in a smooth circle. His heel crashed into the back of the sentry's head and sent the man to the stone floor in an unconscious heap.

Before the sentry hit the ground, the first guard charged the second sentry. He sprung forward in front of the sentry and completed a full forward roll before springing upwards with his feet driving into the sentry's body.

"Impressive," Broden said. "You people know how to make a fight look good!"

"Surely your Governor Abbonan told you that already?" Ohasha grinned. "Come on." She cleared the rest of the distance between the unconscious sentries.

Kalfinar and the remainder of the party covered the ground in seconds. Evelyne paused momentarily before pointing up the farthest staircase. The first guard bounded up the steps, ensuring the top was clear before motioning for the others to follow.

"We must move further," Evelyne whispered. "They're towards the top of the palace."

"My lady," the second guard said, "the top of the palace is the royal quarters. We cannot access at that point. There will be too many guards."

"I may be able to sway some opinions," Ohasha said, her hands resting on the handles of her hatchets.

"It'll hopefully not come to that," Kalfinar said as he looked to Evelyne. "What do you feel?"

She sought a way, her eyes fixed shut. In an instant, they flashed open, her ice-blue eyes locking on Kalfinar's. A scream ran out in the distant reaches of the palace, followed by the clash of steel and further cries of pain and fear.

"Quick! Something's wrong! We must protect the Horn!" Evelyne hissed. She ran up the stairs, bounding them two at a time. She had made it up the first flight before the others caught up with her.

"Damn you people," the first guard grunted as he ran. "You better know what you're doing or we're all dead this night."

Bodies of raiders and palace guards lay tangled in death, their blood married on the cold stone steps as Kalfinar and his companions bounded towards the Cannan royal quarters.

"We must hurry. I sense them moving," Evelyne shouted from the rear as the party moved swiftly, their weapons readied. The sound of commotion and conflict grew as they leapt up the final steps. "We must protect the Horn. They are still vulnerable."

Kalfinar had his hatchet held ready as he burst onto the onyx and gold landing and rounded the corner. He was met by a flash of steel. Instinctively, he fell to his knees in a fluid motion and slid beneath the advancing blow.

The first of Ohasha's guards didn't even see the strike, rounding the corner in time to meet the raider's blade with his throat. He halted with a soft gurgle and fell on top of Kalfinar.

The body of the fallen guard obstructed the raider's follow-up thrust, allowing Kalfinar enough time to swing his hatchet into the leg of the attacker. Before the raider could slam his sword point into Kalfinar, Rondo rounded the corner and, with one artful stroke, sent the man's head arcing towards the reddening floor.

"Quickly, get up!" Rondo snapped as the second guard and Evelyn made it to the landing. Rondo grabbed Kalfinar's arm and hauled him to his feet.

"Thanks. I was done there."

"Return the kindness, if we come to it," Rondo said as he flicked the blood from his blade.

Kalfinar turned towards commotion up the hallway. His eyes focussed to see a brilliant light surrounding the faintest shape of a person. On either side of the light stood three shadowy silhouettes, two tall and one smaller.

Screams echoed over them from further up the corridor. The scene before Kalfinar was a clash of exquisite decor, gold and onyx, and the chaos of bloody death. The rich scents of fragranced oils were overwhelmed by the stink of blood and bowel.

"The Horn must be one of the two girls!" Evelyne barked. She clutched her sword and ran past her companions, leaving Kalfinar and the others scrambling to catch up.

"Evelyne! Wait!" Kalfinar roared, panic swelling in his gut.

She advanced on the four raiders as the form of light was bundled out a wide window. Evelyne cried out.

Kalfinar charged, leaping over the hacked and bloodied bodies of palace guardsmen, but he was too slow.

Without breaking her stride, Evelyne flicked a throwing knife, catching one of the raiders in the eye. He touched his face and then slumped against the wall. Evelyne dropped to the floor, avoiding the next raider's sword swing. She used her momentum to slide through his legs and stab a dagger home, leaving it embedded in the man's crotch.

The remaining raiders focussed on Kalfinar and the others as they bore down on them. Kalfinar smashed his sword down on to the blade of a raider as Ohasha cut down the other. Kalfinar crashed his crossguard into the man's face, once, twice, sending a spray of blood and teeth against the wall before bringing his hatchet down into the space behind the raider's ear with a hollow click. The man's eyes widened and then rolled white.

Kalfinar freed his weapon and ran towards where Evelyne stood, looking out the window. He reached the open window and watched as a carriage sped off, led by a team of four horses. The glowing light of the Horn disappeared into the distance.

"That was reckless," he said to her.

Evelyne had tears in her eyes as she looked up at him. "I can hear her screams. There's great fear within her."

Broden joined them at the window. They looked upon the cityscape as sporadic fires burned throughout and the sound of Cannan's wailing haunted the warm night air.

"My friends," Rondo said, "come with me."

The small Cannan ushered them to a doorway near the dead raiders. Kalfinar stepped over the crumpled bodies and entered the bright and ornate room. Ohasha stood inside the door. Her face was contorted in sorrow. On the floor in front of Ohasha sat a man of late-middle years. He cradled the body of a beautiful woman. Her bright, embroidered gown was soiled with blood, which spread from a single chest wound.

The man wept, rocking with the woman's body. He appeared to pay no heed to Kalfinar or his companions as they entered. The man was so lost in grief that he seemed oblivious to the wounds that bled freely from either side of his head, where his ears had once been.

Rondo whispered subtly to his companions, "Esra, Father of the People, and Suna, Mother of the People. But the Daughter of the People, Natalya, is missing."

"They took her," an accented croak of a voice issued from the Father of the People. "They killed my beloved." He grimaced as another wave of grief crashed over him. His tears and mucus merged on the tip of his nose and dripped onto the body of Suna. The Father of the People appeared to fight back the grief for a moment. "They killed her and then they took my child." He looked up with sodden eyes.

The pain-stricken man stared helplessly at each of them before settling on Kalfinar's face.

Kalfinar returned the man's gaze. *You and I, we are players in the same tragedy.*

The Father of the People fell back into his crushing grief.

"We can't linger," Evelyne whispered to Kalfinar as he tore bed sheets for fresh dressings and handed them to Rondo, who tended the

Father of the People's wounds. "We must move after the Horn. I can feel them travel further away.'

Kalfinar sheathed his knife. *I know. They're taking the Horn to the docks. Back I come to a smoky embrace.* "I know," he grumbled.

Ohasha stood from where she had been crouched beside the Father of the People. "Take me with you." The sorrow that had previously lined her face had been replaced with a hard calmness, though fury appeared to prickle not far beneath the surface. "Kalfinar, we must get the Daughter of the People back." She stepped up to him. "And they owe me blood."

Kalfinar nodded. "We need a ship. Any in the harbour will be burned."

"My daughter," the Father of the People croaked from where he sat huddled on the floor. His knees were pulled tight to his chest. "Bring me my daughter back."

Kalfinar looked at the pleading eyes of the Cannan Father of the People, ears hacked from his head and a dead wife before him. Now the man stood to lose his daughter too. *I know the bitterness of your pain all too well.* "We'll bring your daughter home."

"I have a fast-sail in my private dock. It was being painted for the Festival of Sails," the Father of the People said. He coughed a racking sound. "Take it. Bring my daughter home to me."

Kalfinar flashed a look between Rondo and Ohasha. "Do you know where that is?"

"I know," Rondo replied.

"Kalfinar, bring my daughter home." The Father of the People croaked as he buried his head into the neck of his wife.

"Your daughter will return. I swear it." *Promises, promises.* "Come on. We must hurry!" Kalfinar ordered. He set off with the others in tow. His mind was awash with darkened dens full of rich, powerful smoke. *To the docks, at last. Yes!*

Chapter Twenty-Two

GRUNNXE DID NOT CARE about the cold rain that lashed against the side of his face; such was the depth to which he was lost in a fantasy. He rode within the central column of his vast army as they marched upon the Free Provinces. It felt better than he had ever dreamed.

In his mind's eye, he watched the enemy fall, his sword opening their veins and showering him in blood. Blood he tasted from the glinting pommel of his sword. He carved his way through hordes like a farmer harvesting wheat. Chop, chop, slice, and slice. Closer he came towards those whose black hearts he hated most: the father and son he swore to kill. Grunnxe watched as he swept all enemies aside and finally stood before the terrified forms of the governor of Carte and his son. He absently rubbed at his stomach, the wound throbbing its near constant reminder. He watched as he raised his broadsword and smashed it into the space between Harruld's neck and shoulder. He watched again as his fantasy shifted and the Priestess stood before him with Kalfinar bound and kneeling. The son of Harruld wept tears of blood.

"End him," the Priestess hissed.

Grunnxe watched himself step forward and, with a slow and casual progress, he slid his sword into Kalfinar just above the navel.

"My Lord," Grunnxe snapped from his fantasy as the Priestess hissed from the horse beside him. He shifted in his saddle and noticed he was aroused; his first erection in years.

"What is it, Priestess?" Grunnxe asked as he drew his oiled-leather hood tight to shield from the rain.

"Some of the spirits have been freed. We have reached someone within. Now death will ravage them for their sins against our Lord God." The Priestess hissing voice trailed off and disappeared back into the black shadows of the hood.

Grunnxe smiled at the revelation. It would work. The Free Provinces would fall. The Master God's embrace was warm indeed. In return for his devotion and that of his people, Grunnxe would return Solansia to its rightful place as lord of the old empire. He would be restored as king of all the peoples of the Cullanain, as was his birth right.

Grunnxe's massive army marched through the western salt plains of Solansia, trudging endlessly across vast, flat emptiness. Grunnxe observed the rider from several miles away and watched as the mirage-wrinkled form bled into clear detail. The rider was intercepted by a minor officer before he approached Grunnxe. The men spoke a moment before the officer turned and announced the arrival.

"Messenger, Your Highness."

"Send him on," Grunnxe growled, the hunger for more news stirring in his belly. "Let's see who comes to bring me fortune," he muttered under his breath.

As the messenger approached, Grunnxe recognised the man: Mulan, whom he had dispatched to pass the final plans to the traitor. Mulan's horse was near death, panting ragged breaths as blood from its nose merged with froth around its mouth.

"You've ridden that beast near to death, Mulan," Grunnxe spoke, though he cared nothing for the animal. He scratched at his whiskered chin and relaxed his pace. "Your news is urgent, yes?" Grunnxe leaned over the extravagant silver, bear-headed pommel of his saddle, leering towards Mulan, such was his eagerness to hear his news.

Mulan stopped beside the king and bowed in his saddle before kicking his heels into the dying horse's flanks and keeping time alongside his king. "Indeed, Highness," Mulan answered. The man's jaundiced face was a patchwork of motley bruises and his nose had been broken of late. He cracked a weary smile. "The traitor Bergnon is ours, Highness."

"You're sure he has the stomach to see it through?" Grunnxe asked.

"Yes, Highness, more'an sure," Mulan replied, his tired smile awakening into something altogether uglier. "He's got such a hard-on for tha' girl he'd wade through liquid fire to keep her prime."

The messenger appeared to draw energy from the rich flavour of pain. Grunnxe decided he liked that quality in the man.

"He killed one 'is own to keep his neck and follow through. He'll stay the course." Mulan sucked on his blackened teeth stumps as Grunnxe savoured his news.

"Yes, he'll stay the course," Grunnxe responded after a long moment tasting another victory. "He'll stay the course or that bitch whore of his will bear me sons and then service my brave men." He barked a laugh. "Take your leave, Mulan. Replace that horse and get a meal from a grub cart."

"My thanks, Highness," Mulan said as he bowed from his saddle before turning his horse and heading towards a meal cart.

A moment after the messenger had moved off, Grunnxe heard a whinny and a crash. He turned to see Mulan's horse had succumbed and lay dead on the ground with Mulan pinned beneath its weight.

Mulan pushed weakly at the bulk of the dead horse. He coughed and blood spattered his chin. "My Lord," he wheezed, "help."

The old king turned to the shadowy Priestess and shrugged his shoulders. He chuckled and said, "I suppose we're lucky he told us that much before that damned beast gave up."

The Priestess remained silent and Grunnxe snorted indifferently before riding on.

Grunnxe waited until his retainers had erected his tented pavilion before speaking again to the Priestess. Ever present, she stood on the edge of Grunnxe's vision, in the corner of the pavilion's central chamber. Grunnxe drank deeply on the wine whilst servants brought fresh food.

"Leave me," he growled, sending the servants scattering through all four exits of the chamber with a wave of his hand. When alone, he swallowed the remaining wine and poured some more. He rose from the cushions piled in the chamber's centre. He paced around the pile and rubbed the back of his neck, reddened by the strong sun that

blasted them as they progressed across the salt desert. "Tell me, Priestess, what do you sense of the girl? Have they captured her? Not much
good with just the traitor." He stopped and glared into the heart of the
shadow under the Priestess' hood. "I want Canna too. I need the bitch."

The Priestess hissed a slow breath in and a rasping breath out.

Grunnxe felt uneasy; unsure of himself. Perhaps he had spoken to
boldly, he thought. He shifted his weight and felt his confidence sag.

The Priestess lurched into a slow pace, walking around Grunnxe
and wheezing sibilantly between words. "Yes. I sense there have been
many pains within the Father of the People's heart. The princess is
within your grasp and pray to our Lord God that she be soon in your
arms, for the girl is ripe for your seed and she will bear thee strong
sons." The Priestess ceased pacing in the corner of the chamber and
fell silent as Grunnxe regarded more good news. "Canna will
be yours."

"Yes! Excellent," Grunnxe said. Turning, he clutched his crotch
and shook it towards the Priestess. His tongue waggled as his foul
laughter filled the chamber. "Ripe, you say!" He laughed and poured
himself another goblet of wine. "That is timely indeed. I'm starting to
feel the old vigour in the blood as before. I think I may even enjoy
some new children. The others were all such disappointments," he
barked before quaffing the wine in one go. "Yes, ripe indeed," he
repeated, his voice lowering as wine fuzzed his head. "Let's hope she's
still full of the fight when I get my hands on her. My old prick always
liked a fighter." Grunnxe cackled as he plonked himself down onto the
pillow pile.

His thoughts drifted as he rode the drunken tide. The Master God
was a kind god, kinder by far than the foul god Dajda had ever been.
Dajda did not share her love with Grunnxe or his people. The Free
Provinces was the favourite child in that unhappy family. Now they
would stare up in fear and awe of the great Master God, with his foremost servant King Grunnxe's boot upon their throats.

Chapter Twenty-Three

BERGNON WASHED his wounded ear in salted water. He daubed off the ragged end, being careful to stop his trembling hands from removing too much of the sticky black blood for fear of it bleeding heavily again. He paid close attention in the mirror to make sure all the blood from his face, neck, and hair was removed. He dried the washed areas, applied a small herbal poultice to stop it turning bad, and placed a gum-backed muslin strip over the wound.

Regarding the area in the mirror, Bergnon observed he had done a remarkable job. His heart rate slowed as fear lessened. He dried his wet hair and pulled it over the injured ear, noting it was almost obscured from sight. He puffed out a breath heavy with emotion and mixed himself a tonic to ease pain and lessen stress.

Bergnon thought of his love, Natalya, and what he must do to ensure she lived. Within seconds, his resolved stiffened. Even so, Arrlun's eyes burned in his thoughts. He cursed himself, chased away sorrow, and left the tent. His mind was straight and focussed, and his smile was ready to flash easy in an instant.

The noise of a horse trotting up behind caused Bergnon to shift nervously as he spoke to the assembled troops.

"Major Bergnon, sir."

The familiar voice made Bergnon's throat tighten and pressed his guts. He turned from where he was arranging fortifications and, with a practised coolness, smiled at the young officer. "Lieutenant Thaskil, how did you get on?"

Thaskil looked distracted, Bergnon thought. The young man's brows were furrowed as he replied, "Fine, sir. No problems with your orders."

Bergnon nodded in response. "How can I help you this morning?" Bergnon acted concerned, knitting his angular blonde brows and rubbing his light beard. "Tell me, where is that formal friend of yours?" *You bastard, you utter swine. The boy's blood is all over you. You stink of it.*

Thaskil's face reflected the slightest uncertainty and then relaxed. "I was going to ask if you'd seen him, sir." He rubbed the back of his neck. "Haven't seen him since I left."

"I've not given him any different orders from this morning," Bergnon responded. "Have you checked with the troop?"

Thaskil nodded. "Yes, sir."

Bergnon laughed as he approached the young officer, ensuring he was out of his men's earshot. He leaned closer to him. "Between you and I, Thaskil, I've had the feeling recently that our friend was perhaps feeling a little pressure. He spoke to me about being afraid some night's back." *Lie, lie away. Lying comes easily after murdering friends.*

Thaskil's eyes flashed upwards to meet Bergnon.

"I know, I know," Bergnon whispered. "Doesn't seem like him. Dajda, he seems as brave as a mountain wolf, that boy." *That's it, breathe life into the fear. Open up the wound.* Bergnon shook his head and grumbled. "I don't know. I just felt uneasy in my gut. That's why I gave you both the night off." Bergnon locked his gaze on Thaskil's. "You'd tell me if he said anything to you about running off, wouldn't you, Thaskil?" Bergnon caught the flicker of doubt and fear in the young man's eyes.

That's it. Plant the seed, you evil bastard. You despicable shit, you don't deserve her. Kill yourself, fucker. Bergnon heard the words over and over in his head as he watched Thaskil ride off, except this time it was different. This time the voice belonged to Arrlun.

Thaskil entered the tent he shared with Arrlun and Bergnon. He looked around. Nothing appeared to have changed. He looked under Arrlun's neatly made cot for his belongings and found what few possessions his friend had. Nothing appeared to have been moved.

Thaskil lifted a leather bag onto the cot and undid the loosely knotted thong. He spread the bag's neck and upturned it, forcing the contents onto the bed. Spare clothes, gloves, a small notebook, an ink pot, and whetstones rested amongst various other mundane items.

Surely you'd have taken clothing, or at least your whetstones. You'd never have left without these.

Dropping the whetstones onto the cot, Thaskil regarded the notebook. It was about the size of a block of butter, bound in blood-red leather, and wrapped shut with a braided hide band. He undid the tight knot. As he picked at it, Thaskil noted the craftsmanship in the leather: a blazing sun surrounded by rows of tangled vines and flowers. As he opened the small book, he saw page after page of tightly scrawled writing. Arrlun's flowing script tattooed every sheet of parchment. Thaskil read a few lines.

'neath the stillness of my hand,
my love,
rages the tempest of my heart,
my dear,
you send the waves of your spirit,
a crashing o'er the rocky shores of my barren soul,
and breathe life into it,
breathe life into me,
and take me into your poppy fields.'

"Your poppy fields," Thaskil muttered before he heard someone approach the tent. His heart leapt; what if Arrlun caught him rummaging through his belongings? He shoved the items into the bag and pushed it under the cot. When he looked up, the red leather book remained on the blanket. He crammed it inside his jerkin before turning to his own cot and making himself look busy fixing the tightly made folds of his bedding.

"Ah, Thaskil," Bergnon said.

The major's voice caused Thaskil's heart to drop. In the same moment, he felt an unusual flush of alarm.

"Bergnon," Thaskil returned the greeting. "I was just making sure our quarters were in order should there be an inspection." He smiled towards his major.

"Now, now, lad." Bergnon put his hands on his hips and smiled. "I imagine you've not had an inspection since Hardalen, isn't that right? And besides, you're an officer now, on merit too. And in case you'd forgotten, we share these quarters. I'm not likely to spring a surprise inspection on myself, now am I?"

"Old habits, suppose," Thaskil replied, matching his smile. There was a moment's pause as both stood in silence, smiles burning out as each waited for the other to speak.

Bergnon broke first. "I was thinking after we spoke that it may be best to check Arrlun's belongings to see if anything was missing. You know, in case he has fled." He held Thaskil's eyes, as if prompting the young man to follow his lead.

"Sensible enough, suppose," Thaskil responded without reservation, glancing to Arrlun's cot. "His stuff should be under there." He nodded his chin towards the cot.

Bergnon crouched beside Thaskil, reaching under the cot and pulling out the leather bag. He placed it on the cot and opened the neck wide to reveal its contents.

"Not a very tidy job," Bergnon tutted as he peered inside the bag. Reaching in, he drew out its contents onto the cot.

"Not like him," Thaskil added, crossing his arms to obscure the notebook beneath his jerkin.

"No, it's not," Bergnon said without looking around. "He left his whetstones. Seems strange he would leave without these." He turned around holding the stones up before Thaskil.

"He can't have left," Thaskil replied. "He's forever sharpening his blades." Thaskil coughed out a feeble chuckle. "He keeps me awake at night grinding on those stones."

"It's strange, for sure" Bergnon said, refilling the bag with Arrlun's possessions. He stuffed the bag under the cot and turned to Thaskil. "I'll ask around, see if he's been seen anywhere. If not, I'll make sure they keep an eye out for him."

Thaskil nodded. "I need you to take some further commands for Major Metvani. They're orders for the city guard, running out tactics in response to being besieged."

Bergnon reached inside his jerkin and pulled out a rolled leather envelope before handing it to Thaskil. He stuffed them within his own jerkin, not uttering a word.

Bergnon continued, "I'm placing you in charge of the training of these men."

Thaskil nodded again.

"Metvani won't interfere; he's not got the stomach for this. You'll need to run the men through the tactics today and tomorrow. Drill them hard."

"I will, sir," Thaskil replied.

"No need for the sir, lad. Only in front of others, remember?" Bergnon smiled. "Now, you know the city better than any officer. That's why I'm sending you. You may find some of the older hands cause you difficulty, so I'm sending Sergeant Birch and Corporal Arroch with you."

Thaskil feigned a shudder, causing Bergnon to laugh.

"Aye, they certainly aren't going to stand for any trouble. Right then," Bergnon said as he patted his stomach with both hands and sighed. "I'm overseeing the finalisation of the fortifications this morning and receiving the men called to arms this afternoon. If they don't arrive sooner, that is. I'll not be able to come to Apula until tomorrow midday at the earliest. I'll catch up with you then."

"I'll have the men in order by then." Thaskil saluted as Bergnon moved to leave.

"For Dajda's sake, always so formal, you lads," he tutted and left the tent.

Thaskil exhaled a breath he didn't realise he was holding before being caught by surprise as Bergnon's head popped back into the tent, causing Thaskil to jump.

"Sorry, didn't mean to startle you," he said.

"No, not at all, sir."

"I just wanted to tell you not to worry about Arrlun. I'm sure he'll be around."

"Yes, of course, sir." Thaskil lied.

Bergnon left the tent, leaving Thaskil alone.

He puffed out his cheeks, exhaling deeply. Turning his thoughts to his duty, Thaskil gathered his belongings and headed out towards his horse. He mounted and rode off towards Apula, still uncertain as to where his friend was.

Bergnon slid like a shadow along the outer wall of Apula, his long dark coat rendering him invisible to the searching eyes of city guards on the battlements above. He paused, pushing his body tight to the wall until the guardsmen moved along, finding the idle chatter of a companion. He broke from the wall, his feet falling silent as his movement entwined with the night's shifting darkness.

Upon reaching the southern face of the city walls, Bergnon crouched between clusters of exposed bedrock out of which the expansive walls rose, embedding himself within the blackness they cast. If all was going to plan, his man should be waiting for him upon the battlements.

Bergnon's heart thundered in his chest. The blood flushing around his ears seemed so loud it could betray his presence to the night. The pressure also brought a great throbbing pain to his ravaged ear, though it was not the wound itself that pained him most. His mind cast back to Arrlun's face when his betrayal was exposed. Those eyes.

I'm sorry, poor lad. I'm sorry. Sorrow gripped Bergnon and his eyes surrendered tears to the ground below.

The signal sounded. The call of a whoop owl.

The mournful sound broke off Bergnon's regret and he remembered his duty, steeling himself to his task. He clasped his hands around his bearded mouth, creating a horn, and returned the call from the darkness far below the battlements. A short moment later, a knotted rope unfurled and slapped him on his shoulder as it made its way to the ground. Exhaling a heavy breath, Bergnon moved out of the shadows. Gripping the rope in front of him, he climbed up the south face of the outer wall of Apula. The unseen owner of the whoop owl call aided his ascent, pulling as Bergnon climbed. Swift and quiet he progressed towards the battlements, ready to greet the faceless person above. Within a matter of moments, Bergnon grabbed a proffered hand and was hauled the final few feet by brute strength.

"Major Bergnon, welcome." The voice was like a whisper poured over gravel. The man's face peered out from the shadow of his hood. He had an ape-like face; jutting jaw and beady black eyes. His thick mane of black curly hair all but merged with the densely haired ridge that made up his eyebrows.

"Name's Brostoff," the brute of a man said as he pulled up the rest of the rope, coiling it around his shoulder neatly as he went.

Bergnon scanned the battlements around him for bodies. They were alone. "We should move fast. The watch will be back any minute now."

"Hold your horses, Major. I ain't leaving no rope lying 'bout up here," Brostoff whispered over his shoulder. "We'll be on our way soon enough."

"Sooner the better," Bergnon muttered, pulling his own hood over his head.

"Follow me," Brostoff hissed as they set off, his footsteps falling soft as he nimbly darted along the battlement.

Bergnon followed, amazed at the stealth displayed by the big man.

Brostoff peered over the edge of the battlement, checking for guardsmen on the level below before leaping the distance and landing into a crouch.

Bergnon followed suit, landing with an awkward stumble. Brostoff wasted no time and moved onward, leaving Bergnon to hobble after him. His ankle throbbed after his clumsy landing. The big man moved with the practiced furtiveness of one given to a life of creeping and shadows. Bergnon regarded the careful movement of Brostoff and was glad that the mercenary guild did not entertain politics; he knew otherwise he would be hard pressed to find someone else capable of sharing such a wretched betrayal with him.

"Across there," Brostoff whispered as Bergnon crouched down beside him.

"The rooftops?" Bergnon asked while peering into the darkness.

"Aye, we'll have to be quick. There's a watch unit due on the street soon."

Bergnon spied into the blackness, hopeful the faintest flicker of movement would herald the approaching patrol on the street below. The black night made things hopeless.

"Now!" Brostoff darted across the thin beam linking the battlement to the rooftop of the building across the street.

"Dajda!" Bergnon was caught off-guard by the mercenary's sudden burst and tried to catch up. His first step onto the beam almost betrayed him, but his speed bought enough momentum to step forward onto the ankle he hurt in his earlier fall. He winced at the pain and felt the ankle go.

Bergnon's eyes locked on the shadowy face of Brostoff ahead of him, hiding behind the building's chimneystack. The moment felt like it lasted for an age.

But it didn't and he was falling two levels to the street below.

Bergnon twisted his body and shot out an arm. He managed to wrap his arm around the beam, halting his fall. From his hanging position, Bergnon swung his legs and propelled one heel over the beam's upper edge. The other followed and he knitted heel over foot. A shift in the blackness below drew Bergnon's attention at the same moment he heard Brostoff's ragged whisper.

"Don't move. Below."

The words crashed into Bergnon with terror and his face flushed and burned. His head craned backwards over his shoulder and he watched the shifting darkness form into a four-man watch party. They moved slow and without much sound, observing the sleeping city night around them.

Bergnon's fear began to peak. His muscles burned and his arms trembled under the strain. He felt his wounded ear throb from the pressure of being upside down.

What if the wound bursts? What if it bleeds?

A shift in the darkness caused his eyes to dart towards the battlements he had moved from. Another watchman.

Fuck. Fuck. Fuck.

Bergnon hung tight, hoping the embrace of the blackness would conceal him.

The painful moments crawled by. Bergnon's arm's twitched and ached, and he felt his treated ear wound burst under the strain, causing a hot spread of fresh blood. The watchman on the battlements drifted on, but the party of four lingered below, having lit tabac pipes.

The four watchmen finished their pipes and walked far enough away for Bergnon to strain his weary limbs and haul himself along the underside of the beam. Reaching the end point, he was hauled onto the roof without grace by Brostoff's calloused grip.

"You're one lucky bastard, y'hear," the big man whispered before scurrying along the rooftop.

You've got one part right, at least.

Bergnon stood and caught his breath before chasing the mercenary's shadow. He followed, leaping after his man into the darkness of Apula's rooftops.

A leaping, creeping bastard.

Sticking to the shadows between cramped rooftops, Bergnon and his ape-faced mercenary guide moved undetected towards their goal: the western limits of Apula.

Hunkering behind a rooftop shed, Bergnon surveyed the area, though the moonless light did nothing to assist his appraisal. "Are your men nearby?" Bergnon whispered over his shoulder towards Brostoff.

The man's fetid cheese breath washed over Bergnon in waves as the brute breathed. "Close enough," he grunted. "Once you've found your place and give me the word, then we'll transport the stuff in. Until then, I'll be damned if I tell you anymore."

Bergnon felt his face flush with anger. He turned to face the man. "Now you listen here—"

Brostoff grabbed Bergnon's jerkin with one hand and pulled him in close. So close the mercenary's breath flooded Bergnon's pores. The brute's voice was deadly calm. "No, you listen to me. With a flick of my little finger, I could have the bones of your body broken and the milks of your eyes rolled. The guild is key to any success of yours, so mind who you're speaking to or I'll fucking kill you." Brostoff released his grip and straightened out the creases in Bergnon's jerkin. "There's a good major, eh."

A flash of boldness. Bad idea. Bergnon cooled his anger and smiled towards the heavy-browed man. "Sorry. I've much at stake and forgot myself a moment. Quite right you don't tell me where your men are. Forgive me."

Brostoff grunted his reply, "Shit on forgiveness. You'll need more than that, fucking traitor."

Bergnon felt the stab of the word. *That's rich from a hired sword. A murdering assassin. Mind you, what's the difference between us?* "We need to get to ground level and find a good location," Bergnon whispered, diverting his thoughts.

Brostoff moved towards the edge of the roof, fixing the coiled rope from his shoulders to an iron ring in the masonry with a self-releasing knot before lowering it into the shadowy alley.

"Come," Brostoff whispered to Bergnon before his massive frame slipped into the darkness.

Bergnon wasted no time springing towards the rope and was hunkered in the deep blackness of the alleyway in no time. Brostoff held the rope and gave a couple of flicks of his wrist, causing the rope to shift and snake towards him and clattering Bergnon on the side of his head. The explosion of pain as the wound dressing was ripped from his ear caused him to gasp. Instantly, the rough hand of Brostoff clamped over Bergnon's mouth.

He looked up at the assassin, who scowled. "Silence," he mouthed.

"Ahead there." Bergnon pointed towards the outer western wall. "There must be a building backing onto the wall. We need to find the location tonight. We've little time if we're going to be ready for them." Bergnon reached out and gripped Brostoff's thick forearm. "Remember," he whispered, "we can't have any guardsmen die tonight. We don't want to draw any attention to ourselves."

The big man shook Bergnon's hand off and snorted. Brostoff spat chunky phlegm onto Bergnon's boots. "You worry too much," he grunted.

Bergnon's face prickled as his blood rose. *One chance, shit-eater, and I'll cut your stinking head off. One chance.*

Brostoff leaned around the alley corner and peered his beady black eyes into the night, scanning shadows for hints of movement. The alley and inner-side of the western wall were a quick sprint away. If they could make it across unobserved, they could stick to the darkness along the walls as they sought the most suitable building.

Brostoff whispered, "On my signal, we run. Don't hesitate. If you do, you die alone."

Bergnon waited for what seemed like an age, his palms sweating. His body shook with a mix of night chill and nervous energy. Natalya's face flashed before his eyes and his heart quickened. Her dark skin, the deep black and shining curls, and her bright green eyes. *This is all for you, my love.*

Having let his mind drift, he almost missed Brostoff's signal. By the time Bergnon realised, the mercenary had sprinted almost halfway across the distance between the alley and the buildings of the western wall. Springing forward, Bergnon felt his ankle burn in agony. Despite the flush of pain and restricted movement, Bergnon made it across. He fell into the shadows alongside Brostoff.

Silence.

Made it.

The big man turned and pressed a knifepoint into Bergnon's chest. The ape-like mercenary whispered into his face with the stale stink of old wine, "If you foul this up again, I'll waste no time in killing you. Do you understand?"

"I understand," Bergnon replied, pushing the blade of the mercenary's knife away from his chest.

"Let's move on," he whispered before limping ahead of the mercenary and gliding along the shadows of the western wall. There had to be a suitable area to store the explosives that Brostoff's men were holding in the woodlands.

A flash of slaughter, of sorrow and smoke to come, filled Bergnon's thoughts as he pressed on through the darkness. *I'm doing this is all for you, Natalya, all for you, my love.*

For thirty minutes, Bergnon and Brostoff darted through the shadows of Apula's western wall, searching for a place that would bring the wall crashing down and allow Grunnxe's forces to storm the city.

At least this way there will be fewer deaths.

They came to a stop in the recess by one such building and appraised its structure and position. It was built directly against the inside edge of Apula' outer wall. There were no windows at street level. The door to the building opened onto a small porch with steps leading down to the street. They were hunkered in the piss-stinking darkness of a recess between the gable end, the next building, and the inside edge of the western wall. The recess was covered with a timber roof and a ladder ran from the ground up through a gap in the roof and towards the ramparts above.

"It's a city guard building," Bergnon whispered. "Think it's an armoury. If I remember right, there are two armouries placed at each side of the outer walls." He paused for a moment and thought, scratching at the dried blood from his injured ear before turning to Brostoff. "This is perfect."

"Perfect?" Brostoff hissed. "You're just done telling me you don't want anyone to die tonight. How can we remain unnoticed and not kill anyone if we take up lodgings in a damned armoury?"

"Trust me. I know what I'm doing."

"Don't know about that."

"How soon can you get your men here?" Bergnon asked.

Brostoff hesitated in the darkness, his heavy brow knitting. "Can be here within the hour. What you thinking?"

"There'll be men in there. A quartermaster and perhaps a pair of guardsmen. Go and get four of your men and bring them. I'll wait for you here. When you arrive, we'll enter. They'll not be expecting an officer to descend on them at this hour, so they'll be taken aback. Chances are they're drunk anyway. You follow me with your men after I'm in a few moments. Wait a short while and then enter. We'll overwhelm them and take charge of the building."

"Risky," Brostoff muttered. "What if they get loose? The whole plan is undone then."

"They won't get loose. I think you understand my meaning."

Brostoff's ape-like jaw split the darkness, his rotting, tabac-stained teeth fouling the air between him and Bergnon.

"Changed your tune. So much for no one dying tonight, eh?" The brute laughed, "You're a real treacherous bastard, aren't you? Was wondering when you'd start to play my way."

Bergnon ignored the comment. "Go now. Be back with the four within the hour and make sure the rest of the men are dressed as militia with a mix of city guard uniform when they come to the encampment in the morning, just after sun-up. They must bring the naphtha and, for Dajda's sake, make sure they're subtle. They'll have to be registered with me when they arrive. I'll make sure they know where to break from the rest of the troops they get assigned with."

"Leave it to me," Brostoff grunted. "I'll be back within the hour." With that, the mercenary checked the street and dashed off into the blackness.

Bergnon stood alone in the shadows with nothing but the reek of piss and the shitty taste of his betrayal.

The hour dragged, leaving Bergnon to wrestle with a maelstrom of emotions. His unflinching love for Natalya, his betrayal, and the rising aggression as he grew more and more to hate the man he was transforming into. The man he had transformed into. He hunkered down in the darkness, surrounded by the stench of piss, and wept for the things he had done and the things he had yet to do.

As he dried his face, Bergnon heard a subtle shuffle of feet coming towards him. He drew his sword and primed himself, ready to spring into action. His caution was unnecessary, as the frame of Brostoff slid into the recess, followed by the shapes of four others.

Bergnon relaxed. "I was just getting worried," he whispered.

"No need; the guild's reliable," Brostoff replied. "But then, you know that already. That's why you came to us."

"Quite," Bergnon responded as he tried to make out the faces of the four new men hunkered before him, their gentle breath the only really sign of their presence in the blackness.

"No need for introductions," Brostoff whispered. "Best be getting on with it, hadn't we?"

"Quite," Bergnon found himself repeating. "Remember, follow in a moment."

With that, Bergnon shifted out of the stinking recess and slid towards the armoury, his sword sliding back into its scabbard. He stepped up towards the door and listened. There were no sounds within. Taking a deep breath, he raised his gloved fist and gave a solid knock, before leaning his ear against it. Muffled voices. Stepping back a pace, Bergnon adopted an authoritative look and made his uniform and emblem of rank clearly visible. As the door opened, gentle lamp-light flooded Bergnon's face.

"Who the hell are you?" the faceless silhouette in the doorframe asked.

"Major Bergnon. I command this city and, by consequence, I command you." His tone left the man with no room for doubt. "Now step aside before I have you on charges."

The startled guardsman's jaw dropped as he regarded the uniform and registered the name.

"Apologies, Major. Just being vigilant an' all, sir."

The guardsman stepped aside, allowing Bergnon to pass into the armoury. He was greeted by the screech of chairs as three other men leapt from their card game and snapped to attention.

"Shut that door," Bergnon shot over his shoulder to the guardsman. "I've come to inspect your duty. These are times of grave threat and I find you here playing cards! Disappointed doesn't even cover it." Bergnon's voice rose to a growl, "What level of vigilance is this?"

The guardsman who opened the door fell into rank alongside his colleagues, his body locking in rigid attention.

Bergnon paced along the rank of four men, staring at them so hard they directed their eyes to some safe place in the wooden ceiling. "You're not fit to wear that tabard. The crest of the Free Provinces should be worn only by men who are ready to die for her sovereignty."

The guardsmen swallowed and shook.

"Take them off! All of you," Bergnon barked as he came to a stop behind them. "Off with the mail also."

As one, the guardsmen undid their sword belts and pulled off their tabards, and mail shirts, before standing in front of Bergnon in only their undershirts and leggings.

"Throw them in the corner over there," Bergnon snapped, pointing towards the room corner piled high with chopped wood for the stove.

The guardsmen complied and tossed their tabards, chainmail and sword belts into a pile in the corner of the armoury. "Now, close your eyes and pray to Dajda for forgiveness,"

The guardsman who opened the door looked over his shoulder at Bergnon, his expression uncertain at such a command.

"Major," the guardsman croaked, "you're bleeding."

"Do it," roared Bergnon, kicking at the back of the guardsman's knees and sending him crashing onto the floor. "All of you, on your knees."

As the last guardsman's knees met the floor, Brostoff and his four accomplices crashed into the armoury, their short swords drawn. It was savage and without mercy. Before the guardsmen had even let loose a cry of alarm, they were bleeding life out onto the floor.

Bergnon wiped his sword clean on the shirt of the guardsman he had just run through, the man who questioned him. He shook his head in regret and chased the emotion from his mind. *All for you, my love.* "Move the bodies upstairs and then put on their tabards," he muttered towards the smiling form of Brostoff and his men. "You're now employed as guardsmen of Apula."

Bergnon slipped back into the night, leaving Brostoff and his crew to act out the roles of guardsmen playing cards, but ready to dispatch anyone who looked too close. The upper floors of the armoury had plenty of space for more bodies, should the wrong questions be asked.

With caution, he made his way back over the rooftops, limping due to the ankle sprain. He formulated an excuse for having incurred the injury as he slid from rooftop to rooftop, retracing his steps from earlier. There were still a couple of hours before sunrise, so Bergnon knew he could afford to be cautious. Realizing his ankle would slow him, he chose his moments to dash wisely, ensuring he remained unnoticed.

Reaching the rampart of the southern outer wall, Bergnon removed Brostoff's rope from his shoulder and tied the self-releasing knot to a merlon. He climbed over the edge and, with slow and gentle movements, made his way down. After a short time, he reached the outcrops of bedrock he had hidden amongst earlier and, with two careful flicks of his wrist, he undid his knot, causing the rope to fall.

After recoiling the rope around his shoulders, Bergnon set off within the shadows alongside the outer wall back towards the camp. Within the hour, he would be back in his tent, washed, and fed, sipping on a morning coffee. Within the next day, he would have the explosives placed and, before long, Grunnxe would take the city and Natalya would be free. Within the week, Bergnon would be with his love and he could forget all of his treachery, his murder, and his shame. In one week, he could start again.

One week. One week and this will all be over.

Chapter Twenty-Four

HARRULD STOOD by his study's window, peering out at the rank morning. Thick-spread grey clouds hung low and heavy in the sky, obscuring the weak sun and casting a cold light upon the slick rooftops of Carte. Thin, misty raindrops varnished everything with a slippery gloss.

Harruld stepped away from the cool air and sagged into his chair. He poured himself a cup of water and drank from the glazed clay vessel. His shaking hands caused him to spill some onto himself and then the floor.

"Damn it!" he cursed, startling the hound dozing by his chair. Harruld sat up and brushed the beading water from his tabard.

"You need to rest," Olmat said in a thin, tired voice.

"We all need to rest, old friend. Even one with such gifts as you must take a moment from time to time." Harruld smiled to his companion. "How are you both?" he asked, directing his question to the two remaining brothers.

Olmat pursed his lips and nodded to Harruld.

"He was not deserving of such an end," Sarbien grunted. "Though I'm sure he faced it with every ounce of courage he had."

"Aye," Olmat muttered. "A stubborn, argumentative courage. That was his way of it."

The atmosphere in the room was heavy with the weight of burden.

Harruld broke the quiet. "The tactics of the enemy are as treacherous and dark as any we've ever faced. I can't recall as comprehensive, as damned thorough, an attack. I fear with the convergence of all our woes, we'll simply be overwhelmed when the time comes to stand fast."

"Harruld." Olmat creaked to his feet and moved towards the governor. "You must not—"

"Lose hope," Harruld interrupted. "I know. I see it. It's just that it seems with every step we take, we face yet another enemy; yet deeper losses."

"It is war and with the highest stakes ever," Sarbien chipped in. "We'll each endure much worse before we see the end, I fear. We must shake ourselves and regain our focus. I'll take a team of Tuannan and head for Shalima, and root out whomever, or whatever, is sustaining Bhalur."

"You can't go alone," Harruld said.

"I won't be," Sarbien replied. "I'll be accompanied by our brothers and sisters of the order."

"You know what he means," Olmat interjected.

Sarbien's smile cut a faint crease across his thin mouth. "I know what he meant, brother. What other options have we? You're too weak to travel and the road will be hard riding for two days, not to mention the passage in the mines, however long that may take us. As for you, my dearest governor, accept it. You aren't just acting chief marshal, you are the only chief marshal of the High Command. Who else is going to stem the tide; repulse the enemy?" Sarbien's smile faded. "No, there is no other way. Capriath is gone and so I must do this. I'll leave as soon as I ready the party."

Sarbien stepped towards the door of Harruld's study, stopping short as Harruld spoke behind him. "At least take a body of troops with you," he pleaded. "A half-dozen more or so will not hold you up."

"As you command it, Chief." Sarbien nodded, smiled towards his brother, and then swept from the room.

As the door clicked shut behind him, Olmat rubbed at his watery eyes and spoke, "Harruld, you're going to have to tell him and tell them all."

Harruld looked at the hound by his side, stroking the long, wiry hair on its neck. "I know." He looked back up at the older man. "I just keep hoping if I stay busy, if I forget about it, it will just go away." He smiled, knowing it was foolish. Sadness touched the faint curl in his lips.

"It won't."

"I know. I'll tell them. I'll make the arrangements."

Anthony shambled towards the horse tied at the back of the tavern. The commanding voice ringing in his head encouraged him, guided him with every step. It praised him, honeyed words intoxicating to him, filling him with love, and redoubling his commitment to his master's way.

Anthony hummed and gibbered to himself as he undid the bridle of the horse and heaved into the saddle. He was not aware of the efforts that were played out as he hauled himself up, nor the smears of dark, clotting blood and bits of flesh that were left on all he touched. To Anthony, all he saw was his own majesty, his rich strength, and his worth finally recognised.

He kicked his purpling, blistered, and peeling ankles against the flanks of the horse and trotted out from behind the tavern and into the open road.

"Yes, Master, to Shalima," he muttered before kicking the flanks of the whinnying beast once more and speeding off unsteadily along the northern way.

The spirit rested atop the prayer tower, befouling the spire of the weak Cannan god as it watched the flames in the harbour grow tall and then recede, black water washing over the man-things' vessels as they sank. It purred at the blood spilling and the pain being unleashed. The Master would be pleased.

The searcher was nearby. The spirit could smell his fear; could taste his essence still. The master wanted his soul and so the spirit needed to be closer, close enough to strike out at the trinket the searching one wore about his neck. Trinkets were weak, frail like the bodies of the man-things. Sooner or later, the trinket would be gone and the spirit would be there, waiting to claim the soul, ready to take it and gift it at last to the Master. And, once more, the spirit would be in favour and in receipt of its Master's love.

It swooped down from the prayer tower and swept above the streets, sniffing and turning, flying high above the black and flame-red city below. The spirit tasted the scent again and hovered above, there was the searcher. He ran below, followed by others. None of the other man-things would do, they couldn't be taken.

They were all too strong.

Except.

There.

The small one in front.

The servant of the Cannan god.

The spirit swooped ahead, sniffing at the air above the small man leading the way of the searching one. Perhaps that one would do. The spirit tracked them from above, sniffing, tasting for a way in, and waited.

Bergnon shifted his weight uncomfortably onto his other foot and winced. Damn it, but he could not find any way to stand that didn't aggravate his sprained ankle. He shifted once more and settled in a crooked stance by the entrance to his tent. He felt more akin to a crippled wretch than an officer of the Free Provinces.

Probably closer to the truth.

He sipped at his coffee and watched the rain heaved down over the many tent roofs. Soldiers went about their business, saluting as they churned up the red earth underfoot.

Blood-red earth, how very apt.

Bergnon cast a glance toward the Field of Storms. The wheat was cast in a grey hue before him as the heavens expelled their contents. He sipped at his bitter brew and nodded at a passing group. A rider approached along the track from Apula and caught his eye through the sheets of rain. The rider sat tall in the saddle. The figure made Bergnon's throat tighten for some reason.

You look like trouble.

He shifted his body and straightened up, taking a deep breath to settle himself. With some effort, he tried to lighten his demeanour. The smile he faked sat uneasy on his face.

The rider came closer, his hood drawn low over his face. Stopping before the tent in front of Bergnon, the figure swung down and tied off his horse.

"Major Bergnon," the familiar voice of Thaskil greeted him, followed by a crisp salute. The young lieutenant pulled back his hood as Bergnon stepped aside to allow the sodden man into the tent, a look of surprise still etched on his face.

"What brings you back here, lad?" Bergnon asked, barely attempting to hide his shock. "Weren't your orders to remain in Apula and train the city guard? Who's with your men?"

"Yes, Capt—"

"Just Bergnon, damn it!" Bergnon snapped, his frustration getting the better of him. He regretted it in the instant. The reaction was over the top.

"Sorry, Bergnon." Thaskil showed no concern by Bergnon's loss of calm. "I left the men with Sergeant Birch and Corporal Arroch to run through a morning drill."

"And what then brings you here?" Bergnon flicked his wrist and sent the rest of his cup's contents out of the entrance of the tent and into the blood-red earth. "It can't be the coffee." He tried to force a weak smile.

"I wanted to update you on the guard's progress. Let you know how they were getting on." Thaskil's face adopted tell-tale signs of guilt, his lower lip twitched and he blinked too much before staring at his feet.

"Sure it has nothing to do with seeing if Arrlun has turned up?" Bergnon asked.

Thaskil glanced up. "It had factored into my thinking, yes." He looked hopefully up at Bergnon.

"I'm sorry, Thaskil. No one has heard or seen from him." Bergnon stretched out a hand and placed it on Thaskil's sopping shoulder. "Try not to worry," Bergnon added. "Soldiers run off all the time. Come on, let's get some of that filthy coffee into you."

He led Thaskil out of the tent and into the pouring rain, using every ounce of control to numb his mind to the pain that shot through his leg as he moved.

Thaskil swallowed the last of his coffee as Sergeant Rushnall came storming into the mess tent, snapping to sodden attention before Bergnon.

"Major, we've some militia reporting from the surrounds. What you wantin' me to do with 'em?" The old sergeant cast his eye across Thaskil as he sat beside Bergnon, the greying warrior no doubt questioning the merit in placing one so young in such a position of authority.

If Thaskil was being honest, he doubted the wisdom in it himself with almost every decision he made. His doubt had redoubled, now that he was without Arrlun. *Where are you, friend. Come on back, I'm foundering here.* Thaskil's mind wandered back to their last exchanges. Bergnon's behaviour had made Thaskil think again, there was something odd. *I'm sorry, Arrlun. I should have at least listened to you, I should have at least.* His mind then wandered to the book he had found. To the words Arrlun had written. *Why did you write of the poppy fields? Did you mean me?*

"Lieutenant," Bergnon's voice said, snapping Thaskil from his thoughts.

"I'm sorry, sir, what was that?" Thaskil stammered.

"Mind somewhere else, lad?" Bergnon gave him the narrow eye. "Were you listening?"

"No, Major Bergnon. I missed that, sorry," Thaskil apologised, fumbling his words like he'd been caught dozing by the schoolmaster.

"Get yourself together, lad," Bergnon scolded, his tone firm in front of the other troops. "There's a damned war coming. Get your head in the right place before I drag it back to reality kicking and screaming. You hear?"

"Yes, sir. Sorry, sir."

"Good. Now come with Sergeant Rushnall and me. We're to review that troop of militia and assign men to supplement the city guard. You'll take the men for the city with you when you return."

"Yes, sir."

Thaskil pushed the bench back and stood, allowing Bergnon to get out before following after the sergeant. Bergnon winced at the sudden movement.

"Sir, are you ok?" Thaskil asked.

"Fine, lad, just a sore leg is all," Bergnon replied, clenching his jaw and standing before stiffly following into the driving rain.

Thaskil approached the militia standing at ease in haphazard ranks. Dozens of men sported grim faces. They wore mismatched uniforms of old alliance army, city guard, chainmail and boiled leather armour, procured from careers and battlefields of old. The weapons, however, winked in the morning gloom, their edges kept keen, no matter what years had added to their owners. Thaskil observed those assembled as Bergnon barked at them. Their faces were hard-bitten, eyes low and dark.

Exactly the men we need. Men with appetite.

Bergnon reviewed the newly arrived militia as he stood before them. "My name is Major Bergnon."

Four men in the back rank, in filthy and tattered city guard uniforms, stared hard as he shouted his name. *There you are. Evil-looking bastards, aren't you? S'pose it takes one to know one.*

"I have assumed full control of the defensive command here at Apula, under the orders of the acting chief marshal of the High Command." *Sold my countrymen and my soul.*

"I am your commander. You will place your trust in me, above all else, as I will place my trust in you." *Don't be so foolish as to trust me. I barely even trust myself.*

"Together, we will be able to hold back the tide of Grunnxe. We will break the enemy as it comes forth and we will keep our people safe." *Together, you bastards back there, you assassins and I, will rip these walls apart and send our people to the ravenous teeth of that evil old fuck.*

"I'll be splitting you up. Some of you will remain here as part of the front line. The others will be sent to augment the city guard. Now, I ordered food supplies to be brought in this morning. Which of you lot brought them?"

One of the men from the back rank raised his hand and called out to Bergnon. "T'was my men and I 'at brought the supplies. They're over there in 'at wagon, Major."

Of course it was you. I could tell what kind of men you were when I saw you. Exactly the men I need. Men with black appetites.

Thaskil looked at the men along the back rank as they outlined their food supplies brought in from their township. *Hard-looking men. Look like they've seen their share of action. Men well placed to face the horde on the front line.*

"You lot will head into the city and augment the guard," Bergnon commanded. "Place your supplies by the armoury along the western wall. The quartermaster there will take charge of them. Make your way back to your rank at that point."

Thaskil felt uncertain for a moment, glancing between the militia and Bergnon. *Would've thought the strong veterans should stay at the front. They've got the nerve.*

"Lieutenant!" Bergnon roared, his voice as loud and rough as Thaskil had ever heard it. It tore him from his musings with a cold snap that ran from his arse to the nape of his skull.

"Major," Thaskil said, jolting to reality.

"Take the back five ranks into the city with you once we have their names. I want them to begin their training with the city guard immediately."

"Yes, Major, sir." He snapped to attention.

"I want these supplies left with the quartermaster at the western armoury. Allow these men to do so before they commit to their training. Best allow them the opportunity to take part in one of the later training drills. Understood?"

"Loud and clear, sir." *As clear as if my head was up my arse.*

"Good," Bergnon mumbled, his eyes scanning the militia. "Sergeant Rushnall."

The old soldier snapped to attention.

"Get the men's names in."

"Sir." Rushnall stepped towards the ranks and began scratching names onto a large recruit book.

Bergnon stepped towards Thaskil and leant in close.

"Thaskil, I want you to make sure the men are able to deposit their supplies to the quartermaster at the western armoury. These men have served as city guard here before, they know the way. Make sure they are able to do so, understood?"

"I'll make sure it's done," Thaskil responded, his eyes focussing on a small red then pink stain spreading on the exposed edge of the quilted undershirt of Bergnon's chain mail. A reddish drop ran down his neck and joined the growing stain.

"Bergnon," Thaskil muttered.

"What, lad?"

"You're bleeding."

Thaskil didn't notice the rain slapping against his face in thick, cold sheets as he rode back to Apula at the head of the new ranks of militia. He couldn't even recall entering the city, or the militia splitting off for the western gate armoury. No, Thaskil's thoughts were entirely elsewhere. Bergnon's reaction to his bleeding head was a puzzle for sure. He ignored Thaskil's question; paid no heed whatsoever to his wound and simply walked off with an obvious limp in his stride. *What could have happened to him? Had he been in a fight?* A weight grew in Thaskil's stomach with every tangled, brooding thought.

Something's wrong, Arrlun. Something's very badly wrong.

The afternoon sky turned from lead grey to black as the storm rolled in. Peals of thunder crashed as the rain hammered down into flash floods that gushed in the drains at the sides of Apula's streets. A rank, dismal-looking hound stood in the middle of the cobbled street, levelling an aggressive challenge as the militia bore down on it with their cart.

"Get outta here, dirty mutt." The brute beside the cart horse swung a heavy boot, narrowly missing the miserable cur as it tucked its rear end in and bolted away with a yelp.

The man looked ahead as lightning flashed above, casting the streets in momentary greasy white light.

"Reckon that'll be our place over by that wall, eh?" the man leading the cart asked his companion.

The brute beside grunted something, but did not move.

"Well," the man leading the cart snapped, "go and fuckin' check!"

The brute grunted again and spat, half of which fell in snotty beads down his own filthy tabard, before setting off towards the building. He reached the door and hammered on it.

Silence. There was light coming from the building, no doubt, but no answer.

The brute turned his heavy-browed head towards his companions and shrugged his massive shoulders. The man with the cart horse urged another knock from the brute, who shrugged, dribbled yet more spit, and pounded again. One knock, two knocks, three—

"What the fuck do you want?" An equally large and ape-faced city guard opened the door, his features knotted into a mask of aggression before easing and splitting in a wicked grin of tabac-stained teeth. "Eck," the city guard barked with a smile, "reckon you're lucky I didn't gone and have you run through, eh!"

"Brostoff," the brute called Eck muttered, "got stuff." He nodded over his shoulder towards the cart.

"Bring the cart down here. To the front." Brostoff waved his hand towards the rest of his men, who shambled the cart towards the building.

The man leading the horse aimed a kick at the shivering mutt as he passed. The cur barked half-hearted defiance before slinking off into a dark alleyway.

"Glad to see you arseholes made it." Brostoff clapped the man on the shoulder as he stopped the cart outside the armoury. "So that bloody Bergnon didn't get you all killed then? S'pose that's something, at least."

"He's cold, I reckon," the brute grumbled as he stepped into the armoury.

The rest of his companions followed in after him, nodding to their comrades dressed in fresh city guard uniforms.

"Psst," Brostoff spat. "He's wetter than a fish that's gone pissed itself." He laughed at his own joke and led the men towards the back wall of the armoury. "Come here." He guided the brute by the shoulder. "Take a look and see what we've been busy with." He smiled and nodded his head to one of the men who stood by the wall, one hand holding onto the corner of a huge sheet that hung against it. "Go on."

The sheet fell down in a flap.

"Aye," the brute muttered, "nice big hole you've made."

"Right into the western wall. She's keyed right in." Brostoff grinned.

"Guess we'd best get the stuff then, eh?"

"Aye, guess you should and all."

Chapter Twenty-Five

"YOU'LL SIMPLY HAVE to wait a moment!" the bandy-legged officer snapped.

Sarbien looked at the six soldiers with exasperation. "Captain Tyrnan, not that you'd know, lad, but time is somewhat precious." Sarbien pressed, leaning over the horn of his saddle. "Perhaps you're not fully aware, but there is a war coming!" Sarbien almost screamed the last words, such was his frustration at the rest breaks.

Captain Tyrnan turned away from Sarbien, who sat astride his horse, surrounded by the party of Tuannan. He plugged the cork on his waterskin and fastened it to the skirt of his saddle, tying off the loose tongs of leather. When Tyrnan spoke, his voice was calm and steady. "For a man reputed to have travelled far and wide, you've a distinct lack of appreciation for the levels of endurance of your beasts." Tyrnan turned and faced Sarbien. "We could keep pressing the horses, as you wish, and we would reach Shalima before long, but you would soon find yourself walking home."

Sarbien held Tyrnan's cool gaze. It had been a long time since anyone but Evelyne had chastised him so.

"You'd hardly be much use to the war effort if you walked all the way back to Carte."

Sarbien's face didn't flinch.

"I've worked with horses my whole life, as did my old man, and his father before him. Now, we've been pressing them too hard, and made good pace for that price, but rest assured, there will be a price."

Sarbien grumbled and leaned back from the horn of his saddle, his shoulders dropping. He turned and looked at his companions. Several shrugged their shoulders in supplication as he caught their eyes.

"How long will they need?" Sarbien conceded.

"Allow them to drink and feed," Tyrnan replied, his tone showing no sign of irritation. "They should be fine after an hour, but we should stop again after supper and rest for the night. If we run them through the night again, it would be foolish."

Sarbien grumbled and winced like he smelled something foul. "I suppose we can rest up in that case. We should still make Shalima by mid-morning tomorrow, shouldn't we?"

Tyrnan nodded. "By my reckoning, if we leave at sunrise we should be there by mid-morning, yes." He offered a smile to Sarbien. "It beats arriving in that place at night," the bandy-legged man added with his smile widening on his thin face. "I hear spirits reside in the dark reaches of that place."

Sarbien tried to return a smile, but felt the cringe corrupting it. *That's exactly what I'm afraid of.*

Hot, foetid air wafted upwards into Anthony's path as his feet fumbled in the dark of the abandoned mine shaft. His ragged whispers slithered out ahead of him and into the black, leading the way for him into the bowels of the place. The Master's words of encouragement were his only companions, blackened whispers sustaining his dark desires. Soon enough, he would at last be gifted the enormous strength his former god, Dajda, the liar, refused him. Soon enough, Anthony would serve the great and kind Master God, and drive the disbelievers into a sea of blood. Soon enough. Soon enough.

"What's that?" Sarbien asked Captain Tyrnan.

They sat on their horses looking down the track ahead of them.

"Dead horse," Tyrnan replied, his hand fishing in his satchel for his eyeglass.

"Is there a rider?" Sarbien's eyes strained towards the distant carcass.

"Don't think so," Sarbien muttered.

Tyrnan found his eyeglass and snapped it to full length, the brass polished and glinting in the sun. He shifted the end around the area of the horse and then snapped it shut with an efficient click. "No one about. Can't see any obvious wound on the beast. Reckon I'll go take a look. You all stay here." Tyrnan nodded to his second and drove his heels into his horse's flanks, trotting off down the track towards the dead animal.

A few minutes later Tyrnan returned to the group of Tuannan and soldiers.

"Looks like it died from exhaustion," he grumbled. "Bled out of the nose and mouth. Would say its lungs went, alright."

Sarbien frowned.

"Can we speak a moment?" Tyrnan asked.

He nodded his head to the side of the track and moved his horse away from the rest of the group. Sarbien directed his horse to follow suit.

Once out of earshot of their companions, Tyrnan leaned in towards Sarbien from his saddle. "I know my men and I have been assigned to your group to afford you some form of protection given the current circumstance, however it's not yet been made clear to me the exact nature of your mission. Now, what is nagging at me is this: why would there be a horse lying here dead from exhaustion on the road to Shalima unless someone was trying to get there before us?" Tyrnan didn't even blink, his voice steady and calm.

Sarbien's eyes flashed over Tyrnan's shoulder and settled on the dead horse lying up the track. A carrion crow flapped and hopped on its neck and began pecking at flesh. He blinked back at Tyrnan. "We think that some dark arts are being performed in Shalima. We mean to put an end to this, for it appears that whoever has been practising them has sided with a terrible enemy of Dajda."

Tyrnan's face was a mask. "Those jars that were brought in from around the country, the ones that folk were saying were cursed, is that what this is all about?"

"Aye, seems they have a role in this. We think that someone within the order has betrayed us. Perhaps it was they who exhausted the beast in order to return to sanctuary."

Tyrnan nodded. "Well, at least it's only the one horse." He glanced over Sarbien's shoulder at the five other soldiers and the group of Tuannan. "I just hope whatever is in those mines doesn't outnumber us too cruelly."

A commotion was taking place outside Harruld's study as he gazed over Carte, his focus locked on the harbour-front in the distance, the lead-grey sea blending into the bleakness of the cold horizon. Harruld turned his attention to the voices outside his door. Although muffled, it was not difficult to make out the gist of the dialogue.

"But Lord Harruld insisted he must not be disturbed." A wobble in the voice. Weakening resolve, no doubt.

"Boy," the other voice said, bristling with veiled warning, "I'll hurt you." Clear warning. "A lot." Explicit warning.

"Don't doubt him, lad," another voice spoke, softer this time. More reasoned.

"No, Sergeant." The guard's voice was a strangled squeak. "I must insist—"

There was a loud thump against the study's oak door and a clanking of metal on stone. The study door swung open and an old warrior stepped inside over the guardsman's unconscious body, whose helmet was still rocking around its conical point on the stone floor. A thinner man of equal years to the first stepped into the room. Another young guardsman stood open-mouthed by the door, staring at his formerly conscious colleague.

Harruld grimaced towards the injured guard on the floor outside his study. "Sergeant Subath, did you really have to?"

"Yes, My Lord. I believe I did," the grizzled sergeant said, his eye twitching with irritation. "I warned him."

"He did warn him, My Lord," the thinner man said. "I thought it was a perfectly reasonable request."

"Major Merkham, welcome." Harruld approached from beside the window and clasped hands with the two men. "How come you're here so soon? I only sent word a few days ago. Can't say I was expecting you here for well over a week."

"Lord Abbonan managed to get word to us at Hardalen from Terna. I'm guessing after Captain's Kalfinar and Broden made it to Terna with their reports. Once Commander Lucius heard of assassinations of senior-ranked officers, he locked himself in his chambers and relinquished his command at Hardalen to me." Major Merkham reached inside his long, heavy travel coat and pulled out a small, red leather envelope. "Here's his letter resigning his commission."

"Accepted," Harruld said simply as he tossed the envelope onto the pile of papers on his desk. "Been wanting that for some time. So where is the little crow now?"

"Well, after we received Lord Abbonan's command to withdraw from Hardalen—"

"Excellent," Harruld interrupted. "Glad to see Abbonan and I were thinking along the same lines. Sorry, Major, carry on please."

"My Lord, after we received the command to abandon Hardalen, we readied the garrison. Commander Lucius had locked himself into his chambers and refused to come out. He claimed he was safer in there than on the journey to Terna, or even in the cities themselves."

"So what did you do?" Harruld asked.

Merkham looked across at Subath, whose eye was twitching less as his calm returned.

The rough, old sergeant cleared his throat and spoke, "Well, My Lord, we, um, we left him where he wanted to be left. Far as I'm aware, he's still cowering in his chambers. Reckon he'll be a bit cold and hungry by now, mind you. Might be that'll prompt him to make his way down to Terna."

Harruld blinked open-mouthed, momentarily. "Well, no point crying over Lucius. The man was a hindrance; a bloody pompous little arse. You both being here now is fortunate. I sent orders to Abbonan directing the garrison be stripped and half of the men sent here. How many of you have come to Carte?"

"Just over half of the garrison, My Lord," Merkham answered.

"Good."

"And we've several detachments from Abbonan's ranks, as well as twelve of naval coastal patrollers. Just in case the Solansian's lost fleet turns up."

Harruld smiled for what felt like the first time in weeks. "I'm going to give that man a kiss the next time I see him!" Harruld exclaimed.

"Might be you'll be doing that sooner than you think, My Lord," Subath grumbled as his attention was drawn by the groaning guard on the floor near the study door.

"How so?"

Subath stepped over to the concussed guard. "He's been doing a bit of planning himself," he said as he hauled the groggy man up by the oxters. Subath bent over, picked up the dented helmet, and handed it to the guard. "Warned you, boy," he said with a smile and then closed the study door. "Lord Abbonan's reckoning on there being some kind of attack from Solansia. He thinks that there's little gain in attacking Terna, and, if anything, the hit's going to come from the borderlands in the east, where they can attack quickly. If word comes to Terna quick from you, Lord Abbonan said he'll send the majority of his men and leave a skeleton force in Terna. He even said he'll come himself."

"He did, did he?" Harruld asked, his eyebrows raised high, wrinkling his forehead.

"Aye," Subath grumbled. "But you can read that yourself. He wrote it all down in a letter for you, in case we banged our heads on the voyage and forgot it all." Subath grinned, his wolfish smile managing to look vicious and good-natured at the same time.

"Dajda, Subath," Harruld laughed. "You should've bloody told me."

"Where's the fun in that?" Subath laughed. "Now, can we dispense with the lord's and sir's? No one about to see me take the piss out of you now, eh?" The old warrior reached over and clapped the governor around the shoulder.

"Aye, alright, you old bastard," Harruld laughed, relieved at the fortunate return of his two colleagues, his two friends. "And thanks for looking after my boy at Hardalen. He was looking better."

The spirit soared above the man-things as they ran. The searcher and his companions entered a building for a moment and then left, followed by two more. One was a child of the spirit's master, though it could see the soul was wretched, and fractured husk now beyond the Master's love. It would be destroyed, the spirit would see to that, and the Master would be pleased.

Something odd struck the spirit as it tracked the man-things progress through the alleyways. There was a faint light within one below. Glimpses, blinks of warm light, unseen by the spirit until the man-things left the house. A light of life, unfamiliar to the spirit; a light of love.

More flashes from below. The spirit swooped in, slow and careful, closing the distance, wary not to get too close. Sniffing the air, the spirit got a vague sense there was something different down there running with the man-things. The sense was not strong. The spirit needed to be closer.

Again, distance was closed, but the spirit was cautious not to arouse the senses of the female, the one with the unusual power: the touch of the Liar God. That one was dangerous, the spirit thought as it hovered over them, sniffing the air, tasting at the scent as it rose. Another being was with them, being carried by the female. The light flashed free from whatever obscured it momentarily, showing itself for what it was for but a second.

The spirit shrieked, fleeing skyward, screaming upwards from the creature of light.

"What's that?" Broden asked as the dreadful shriek sounded above them, trailing off into the darkness.

Chentuck made a sign of protection over his chest as the sound died off. Kalfinar looked skyward before his eyes settled back on Evelyne. Her lips moved as she looked in amongst the wrap of blankets at the girl.

"Evelyne," Kalfinar interrupted. "The spirit."

She broke her attention away from the child and faced the group. "Yes. The spirit follows still." She looked down at the small girl in her arms. "I think we have her to thank for frightening it off."

Kalfinar stepped over to the child. He pulled back a fold of blanket and peered into the small girl's face. As usual, she appeared to be in the deepest of peaceful sleeps. "The child frightened it off." Kalfinar asked.

"Yes, her radiance has been awoken."

Broden wiped his brow with the back of his hand. "As long as she can keep scaring it off, I'm happy." He looked at the back of his hand, grimaced, and flung the gathered sweat onto the ground. "Assuming it'll come again," he added.

"It'll come," Kalfinar said in a low growl, his eyes locked on Evelyne's.

"Yes," she half-whispered. "It will come again, if it can. And it will bring others, if it can take them." She held his gaze.

"What is this that follows you? This spirit?" Ohasha asked.

"It is the creature of one who would do us harm. It works against our objective and so it works against yours. We have little time." Kalfinar turned his attention to Evelyne. "What do you feel?" he asked. "Is the Horn getting farther away?"

"The distance grows," she answered. The twitch in her eyes betrayed the strain. "The distance stretches slow and steady. I feel much fear."

"They're leaving the harbour," Broden grunted. "Doubt they've been able to set their sail good and proper yet."

"Come, we must hurry," Rondo urged. The small man was eager to make progress, rather than linger about the alleyways of his home city as the raiders murdered and robbed all around them. "If we're to take the Father of the People's ship, we're going to need a crew."

"Raiders abound at sea. We'll need a crew who are used to dealing with such men. A crew who don't mind the stink of blood on them," Ohasha said as she flashed a hungry smile. "I'm the only one in possession of such a crew."

Kalfinar nodded. "Suppose it's time we paid your crew a visit. Best get moving. We can't let them get too far ahead of us."

They navigated their route through the alleys and streets, hiding in shadows to avoid any passing raiders or sounds of conflict. Soon, they found themselves in front of a small wooden door, about the height of a child. A curious symbol was painted in rude strokes into the top right corner of the door frame.

Ohasha approached and knocked a set routine. The wait dragged on, with Ohasha growing more agitated with every passing moment. "I'll string that husk up, if he doesn't—"

Then a voice spoke in Cannan and a small hatch opened up on the door from where none appeared to exist. A pair of eyes peered out from within.

Ohasha responded in her native tongue, her words rapid and with a clear edge to them.

The sounds of bolts sliding free could be heard outside before a stunted man with small arms and legs stepped out. The man wore a long beard that stretched down towards the belly of his shirt. Kalfinar noted many small smoulder marks on the man's shirt. An absent recognition rang in his head. There was a glaze to the man's eyes and a familiar smell lingering in the air.

Ohasha led them beyond the cramped reception chamber and through dark lit hallway to a staircase. Several large candle tapers sat in metal rings lining the wall, casting an amber glow about them.

"Follow me," Ohasha said as she headed down the stone cut spiral staircase, a glowing torch in hand.

That smell. What is it about this place?

Something struck a chord within Kalfinar. The core of his stomach dropped and his arse felt like it was about to expel itself, such was the cold, hard realisation. A grip of clammy panic ran through his scalp, swelled in his armpits, prickled at his hands, and stung out of his fingertips. Panic.

There you are, old friend. It's been so long, too long apart. Yes, there you are.

Kalfinar's mind reeled as his cold, sweaty palm traced the rough spiralling staircase, following the flickering orange light and the warping, stretching shadows cast by Ohasha's torch.

Down, deeper into the abyss. Down, deeper, down. Back to the smoke.

Kalfinar gritted his teeth. A weight pulled at his bowels. Fear. He strained and squeezed a panicked moan, drowned out by the slapping of boots on stone. Sweat beaded and rolled down his face. Still, he followed the others deeper down.

There you are. Smoke and blood, whores and mud.

Ohasha entered the large chamber where several dozen of her people busily worked. Money and valuables were weighed, orders assigned, and grievances aired. She cleared her throat and a ripple of attention spread throughout the room. "The Mother of the People is dead. Murdered by raiders."

Silence, save for Kalfinar's heavy breathing.

In the flickering light of the braziers and candles, mouths hung open.

Ohasha's massive guard, Agurk, visibly sagged at the news. His broad shoulders dropped a little and a strangled sob escaped from his throat.

"The Daughter of the People has been kidnapped." Ohasha snapped the words, urgency tightening her throat. "We have a ship, the Father of the Peoples, but we need a crew to get her back."

The tears in Agurk's one eye grew large. They burst free from his long lashes and splashed onto the ground before him. His eye narrowed and he dashed away his sadness, a sharp resolve framed his face and his voice broke the stillness between them, "These men must die, every last one of them."

Rondo spoke, "We need enough to man the ship and enough to protect it too."

"And we shall have them," Ohasha said. "Who will join me at sea again and spill our revenge upon the waves?"

Evelyne placed a gentle hand on Kalfinar's shoulder, causing him to flinch. "Kal, the distance is growing. We need to be quick."

He heard her, but the words didn't register. He looked up at Evelyne and into those ice-blue eyes. But all he saw was the worry.

And the pipe.

Broden strode at the head of the large body of armed crew as they marched through the Nabruuk streets. Evidence of the raiders' work was all around. Fires raged at random points and, on several occasions, bodies lay in the streets. They walked up the straight promenade alongside the harbour-front, approaching the Father of the People's private dock. The main host of the raiders had departed, leaving only the injured in Nabruuk. When encountered, the crew dispatched them with ruthless efficiency.

Broden grumbled towards Kalfinar, "Guess they don't have the stomach when the opponent holds a sword, eh?"

No reply. Not even a customary grunt.

Broden looked around. Kalfinar was not in the group, that he could see, at least. He budged past Chentuck, who walked beside Evelyne. "Have any of you seen Kal?"

They looked around at the faces of the Cannan men and women. There were hardened faces, some scarred and brutal, others warped with a hungry vengeance. But none of them Kalfinar.

"Haven't seen him since we left Ohasha's chamber," Chentuck spoke.

"I saw him," Rondo said. "On the stairs, up to the street. He was talking to the doorman."

"Where in the darkness is he?" Broden stared all around him. "You carry on towards the ship. I'll find him."

"I'll come too," Chentuck said.

"No, stay with Evelyne and the child," Broden said before turning and pushing through the flow of bodies, searching for his cousin. As the big man broke through the last rank of bodies, he saw a familiar shape run around the corner of the last street they had come down.

The group had moved onto the dock by the time Kalfinar approached Broden. Kalfinar placed his hands on his knees and heaved at his breath, risking a glance at Broden glowering down at him.

"Where the fuck have you been?" Broden demanded.

Kalfinar sucked a deep breath and straightened up. "Sorry," he said, his palms held up in contrition. "Thought I saw someone following us."

Broden's face did not shift a whisker.

"Thought I'd check it out."

"Couldn't you at least have told us you were going?" His brows knitted in the middle and his forehead wrinkled. "Fuck!" he spat.

"Sorry," Kalfinar apologised. "Guess I didn't think."

"No you didn't." Broden huffed out a heavy breath. "Come on, we'd best catch up."

They ran towards the dock as the few remaining members party made their way inside.

As he ran alongside Kalfinar, Broden glanced across. "So, were we?"

"Were we what?" Kalfinar asked, looking confused.

"Were we being followed?" Broden asked again, the slightest frown cutting his face.

"Um, no. I think it was just my eyes playing tricks on me is all."

"Tricks, aye," Broden grumbled. "Eyes will do that in the dark."

He glanced at Kalfinar as they reached the dock and slowed down. *Are my eyes playing tricks on me, cousin?* "Come on, let's get inside."

They joined the rest of their party in boarding the Father of the People's ship, ready to pursue the Horn as it sped across the Canna Sea.

The spirit soared high above the sea, watching as the ship cut through the oily sheen of the water below. Fear gripped at it as it watched. Certain of its task, the spirit was aware that below, amongst the scurrying flesh on that ship, was a creature of terrible strength, one the Master would see destroyed. The female one held it, the imperfect creature, one of the liar Dajda's children. It had seen the spirit, it knew it was near, and the fear grew in the spirit as it soared above, waiting for an opportunity to strike.

The man-thing's ship cut through the waves of the black sea, bearing down on a small flotilla. The spirit heard shouts and cries of dashing man-things, the pathetic little beasts, as they went about their frantic business; nothing like panic, alarm, fear, and blood to offer the spirit its chance.

The female, the powerful one, would be distracted. She would not be able to prevent the spirit from closing in on the child of the weak Canna god. She would not be able to stop the spirit from taking the little man-thing's soul and lashing out at the searcher, at the female, the traitor's, and the child of Dajda.

Oh, what a gift that would be to the Master. Such a service would see the spirit regain the Master's love and it would, once more, sit at the Master's right-hand side, trusted and enveloped in embrace. What a gift indeed.

The ship rose and plummeted as waves crashed against its prow. The light in the cabin below deck swayed and rolled unpredictably, causing Broden's stomach to roll and churn like the sea. He puffed out his cheeks and rolled his eyes at Evelyne, who smiled as she sat rocking the child in her arms.

"Will she sleep like that all the time?" the big man asked, trying to distract himself from the nausea and cheesy, slippery taste in his mouth.

Evelyne smiled and brushed the small girl's curly hair from her forehead. "She wakens when she wishes. When she is ready."

"Seems like a handy thing that, sleeping through sea travel." He smiled and rubbed his churning stomach.

"Where's Kalfinar?" Evelyne asked.

"He said he was going to get some air. He's not been looking great," Broden answered with a cringe. "Might be feeling a bit sick himself."

"Well, we'd better get him," Evelyne said while closing her eyes shut. "We're getting close. The Horn is near. We need his eyes."

"I'll fetch him." Broden stood up and with a reluctant sigh, stepped out of the cabin and towards the steps that led up.

"Kal!" Broden shouted from the last steps before the deck. "Damn it, Kal," he muttered to himself as he looked down the stairs towards the cabins below and then back to the dimly lit deck, "you know I hate coming up here, you bastard."

The big man shook his head, sucked in a deep breath, and bounded up the last steps and onto the deck. He could see the dim lights of the raider's flotilla in the distance. Ohasha stood at the wheel, whilst some of her crew busied themselves with the rigging, ensuring the ship made the most of the sea winds. The remainder of her crew sharpened their weapon's edges and fixed the flights of arrows and bolts. There was blood coming, of that there was no doubt.

His stomach lurched as another wave broke on the prow. He staggered, but regained his balance as he made his way along the deck, searching for Kalfinar. "Where in the night are you, Kal?"

He made his way past the crew as they darted about the ship, making ready for the coming conflict. Broden stopped several who ran past, only to apologise when the faces turned not to be Kalfinar's.

Broden's stomach stopped churning and began to pulse. It was fear. He made his way towards the ships's aftercastle. There was no light coming from the elaborately designed stained-glass windows at either side of the door. His throat tightened as a memory flashed in his head.

Carte, down by the docks.

Broden swung the door open, revealing little but blackness inside. What small light flooded in from the deck was of no use, barely illuminating a stride's length of floor into the cabin. Broden grumbled and stepped back onto the deck, staggering sideways as the ship lurched from another wave. He stumbled towards one of the few lit lanterns fixed into a bracket near stairs leading to the poop deck.

Taking the light in hand, the big man returned to the aftercastle and moved inside. A plummeting tug of despair wrenched at Broden's guts. "Dajda, no!"

Kalfinar was slumped in a chair, with his legs spread wide. His head was tipped back, towards the ceiling. A jalsinum pipe lay nearby, its contents spilled and smoking on the floorboards underneath his hanging hand.

Broden dashed to his cousin and searched for a pulse with one hand as the other cradled Kalfinar's head, tipping it forward. His eyes were glassy; big, black pupils staring at nothing. He was alive, but deep in the throes of intoxication.

Kalfinar laughed as he splashed about in the sea with his wife and daughter. The sun shimmered on the lapping water while they played, his little daughter shrieking with joy as Kalfinar let her ride his shoulders. What a happy day it had been. One of their best.

Then, out of nowhere, the sky turned grey and cold. The water nipped with chill. His wife looked at him, the corner of her eyes creasing as fear grew on her face. The playful shrieks of joy turned into cries of sorrow. Kalfinar watched as her hands rose to cover her nose and mouth as tears filled her eyes.

There was a metallic mumble of thunder and, again, a word. Kalfinar lifted his daughter from his shoulders and looked into her face. Her features ran like a rain-soaked painting. The obscure sound struck again, muffled, like an underwater cry, and her face was gone.

They were both gone.

"Kal!" Broden shouted his name again and slapped his face. "Kal, for fuck's sake, wake up!"

Kalfinar's red-rimmed and bloodshot eyes blinked and he took a ragged breath, followed by a racking, jagged cough. Spots of blood coughed out of Kalfinar's mouth and over Broden's legs.

"No, Kal," Broden mumbled while Kalfinar stared blankly before fumbling for his jalsinum pipe. "No, Kal." He restrained Kalfinar's searching hand. "You've had enough."

A flash of anger flared in Kalfinar's eyes and Broden felt the muscles of his arm stiffen as he still restrained his hand. Kalfinar's jaws tensed and he bore his teeth, his brows knitting with an addict's anger.

"Kal, no!" Broden's voice was tough, but edged with a pleading ring. "Don't do this. We need you now."

Kalfinar tensed his arm again in a bid to get out of Broden's grip, but the bigger man was much stronger.

"Shhhssh," Broden repeated, trying to sooth Kalfinar's swelling rage. "Shhhssh, Kal, shhhssh."

Kalfinar's jaw relaxed and his arm went weak in Broden's grip. "I was with them," he said in a ragged voice.

"I know. I know you were."

"Should've left me. Why couldn't you leave me?" Kalfinar pleaded.

"We need you here," Broden said as he pulled his cousin close, burying Kalfinar's head into him.

Kalfinar drew his weak arms tight around Broden's neck and shoulders.

A gentle sobbing sound, pathetic and wretched, grew from Broden's chest, breaking into a symphony of sadness, percussion of mucus and rhythm of pain. "I'm sorry, Kal, but we needed you here with us."

"What happened to him?" Evelyne asked as Broden half-dragged Kalfinar into their cabin below decks, the semi-unconscious man stumbling and tripping, kept upright only by Broden's supporting arm around his waist.

"Jalsinum," Broden grunted as he heaved Kalfinar into a cot. "He must've got a hold of some down in the underground. Dajda knows how."

Rondo got up from his seat and went across to Broden. "You said you think he has taken jalsinum?" the little man queried.

"Aye," Broden sniffed. "He's had problems with it in the past."

Kalfinar stirred, his eyes flickering open, revealing mostly white.

Between the aftercastle and the cabin, Kalfinar had lost control of his bladder and wet himself. The dark stain on his trousers announced his shame.

"I'm sorry, my friend." Rondo wrung his hands, his eyes darting between Kalfinar and Broden. "Had I known, I would have kept a closer eye on him, for if there is an addict in the underground, they will surely find a pipe."

Broden shook his head then rubbed his two massive palms over his face, chasing away fatigue and frustration. "Hardly your fault, Rondo," he said. "We need to sober him up." He barked, lashing out and kicking at a harmless chair as it sat unoccupied. "How much time have we got?" He looked at Evelyne.

Her face contorted as she shut her eyes and focused on the Horn, the child asleep still in her arms. "We're close. I can sense the panic." She opened her eyes. "The little one here senses the fear too. She's awake."

Evelyne drew back a fold of the blanket that covered the small child and revealed her face. The child wore an urgent and stern look beyond her years.

"Chentuck," Broden shouted to the Ravenmayne, "get up on deck and make sure Ohasha has readied the crew. We need to make sure they are ready for what is coming."

"We don't have much time, Broden," Evelyne spoke. "We need Kalfinar to steer us to the right ship. We can't possibly face the full flotilla and, without his sense, I can only get us so close."

"Should we just take him up as he is?"

"We'll have to try our best." Evelyne turned and headed up the stairs, carrying the small child with her.

Rondo slid his arm under Kalfinar's shoulder as Broden heaved him up. Kalfinar emitted a series of grunts and muttered a string of babble as his eyes rolled about in their red-rimmed lids.

"Let's get him back up on deck." Broden said.

They struggled to get him up the stairs, thanks to the rocking ship and Kalfinar's haphazard footing. Once they had made it to the deck, they saw they were gaining on the flotilla. Broden ordered what few remaining lights that were lit be snuffed out, causing the ship to fall into darkness as it slid up behind the raiders' ships.

"Kalfinar," Evelyne's voice was gentle, a whisper on the sea breeze, "open your eyes."

"Leave me with them." Kalfinar's voice was hoarse and his eyelids, shiny with grease, flickered, revealing only the whites of his eyes.

"Open your eyes, Kalfinar," she urged again. "Tell us what you see. Where is the Horn?"

Kalfinar's eyes flickered, revealing glimpses of remarkable eyes. *I've seen these eyes before. They belong to someone. Are you special to me?*

The voice that echoed in his ringing ears sounded again, sounding fluffy and far away.

Those eyes. They flashed again before him. *Evelyne!*

Kalfinar opened his eyes fully to see Evelyne and Broden, and that beautiful child, the one with light in her heart.

"What can you see, Kal?" Evelyne's voice. It was her that had been speaking to him. "Look out there. Tell me where she is."

Kalfinar peered into the dark with burning eyes, glancing between the ships in the flotilla that they approached. A faint light glowed from the stern's window. He mumbled some words; could've been anything, for his tongue felt like it had swollen.

"Are you sure?" Evelyne asked.

Kalfinar glanced at her remarkable ice-blue eyes and then blinked over to the ship. "Yes. There she is. The one of light."

The child looked up at Evelyne. A silent message seemed to pass between them, Evelyne nodded. The child reached out from Evelyne's embrace, stretching to place her hand on Kalfinar's cheek.

His head suddenly felt flush, like it had just been cleansed with cold water. The suddenness of the sensation caused him to step backwards, being held aloft by a steadying hand from Broden. The jalsinum fog had been lifted.

Kalfinar blinked his eyes and looked up again to the same sign of light that radiated from the ship ahead in the distance. "I'm sure. Get everyone ready."

Chapter Twenty-Six

KALFINAR RUBBED his burning eyes with the edge of one palm. He stood alongside his companions and Ohasha's boarding party as their ship crept up on the raider's vessel.

"Broden," Kalfinar whispered, his voice croaking. "Forgive me. Not as strong as I thought I was."

The big man smiled, but his eyes looked sad. "Aye, it's done." He placed his hand down on Kalfinar's shoulder and shook it.

Evelyne approached. The child was absent from her arms. "Remember," she said, looking at them both when she spoke, "we'll not have much time on the ship to turn her. In human form, the child is just flesh; unprotected and exposed. She must be awoken before she can be harmed. There's no time for hesitation. No time for fear. What I order you to do, you must do, no matter what. No matter what. Understood?"

Both men nodded. There was no room for doubt.

Evelyne continued, "Ohasha and her boarding party will give us enough protection and cause enough of a distraction for us to get into the aftercastle. Once we're in, Chentuck and Rondo will keep the door sealed from either side. We need her awoken." She looked at Kalfinar. "Are you ready?"

Do I look ready? Eyes red and shot. Face slick with the jalsinum grease. Ready for the gutter. "Aye, I'm ready," Kalfinar said, his voice thick with regret. His self-pitying tone even annoyed himself. *Prick.*

"Good." She held his gaze. "We can't fail, simply can't."

The night air hung heavy with a welcoming mist. The dimmed lights of the raider's ship bobbed like a group of fuzzy amber nimbuses through the moist, briny air. They drew up beside the ship and the voices of the raiders were clear to Kalfinar as he and Ohasha's boarding party tensed by the starboard-side, weapons gripped in fists.

As he spun his hatchet in his left hand and his sword in his right, Kalfinar smelled the stink of the sweating raiders. Broden and Evelyne stood ready on either side of Kalfinar, offering tense, shallow breaths as they waited for the moment.

The old raider leaned against the ship's port-side, his sheathed sword cradled by the cross-piece in his folded arms. He drew a deep breath from his tabac pipe before freeing an arm and sticking his middle finger up to the new lad.

The young prick had a stupid look on his face, nervous over something. He was always nervous over something. Bloody mist, sends all the new ones mad the first nights. Too wet, them lads, like all the new boys. Too damn wet.

Bloody affront havin' him out here babysitting the watch. Should've been below deck drinking up the booty and bartering over the loot from Nabruuk. A bloody affront.

He inspected the proffered middle finger. The bloody splinter went right up between the flesh and his closely nibbled nail end. Hurt like a salted razor. Come to think of it, there wasn't a bloody finger on either hand that didn't hurt. Would be better off just pulling the damn lot o—

The ship lurched and a shuddering, grinding sounded before a bang rang out in the wet darkness of the night. The old raider stumbled onto his knees and a roar cut through the mist outside the port-side of the ship. Roped grappling hooks flung over the side and across the deck, one narrowly missing the old raider's face as it scraped across wood. He fumbled onto his feet and grabbed at his sword.

There was a flash of light followed by a loud whining noise, and then black.

————————

Kalfinar's hatchet smashed the old man in the side of his head, sending him pirouetting to the ground in a spray of blood. He didn't stand a chance. None of the raiders on that side did.

Ohasha's crew leapt onto the port-side of the raider's ship and slaughtered all who stood in their way. The starboard raiders snapped out of their surprised daze and charged across the deck, weapons being drawn and screaming into the night as calls for support echoed across the ship.

————————

"Move!" Broden roared as he faced two raiders running towards them. "Get into the cabin now!"

Kalfinar grabbed Evelyne by the elbow and they charged across the deck towards the aftercastle cabin, flanked by Chentuck.

Broden kicked the swinging arm of the first man as he approached on his left before swivelling and engaging the second man bearing down on his right. The clash of steel stung his hand and up his wrist. He risked a glance to the aftercastle. They were almost there.

The man on his right swung low. Broden parried, kicked out at the man's sword arm, and slashed down two-handed, cleaving through the man's face. He gurgled and coughed out a thin trail of blood, his eyes rolling up into his head before he fell to his knees while fingers searched the savage rent.

The second man had recovered and pressed Broden hard. The man's violent snarl seemed misplaced on his young, freckled face.

Shit, shit, shit.

He had just enough time to parry the first and second blow, but a third jarred his shoulder as it thumped into his blade.

Broden spotted another raider with shaggy hair approaching wielding a mace. The mace flashed out and bit one of Ohasha's men across the side of the face; dropped him like timber. The shaggy one kept coming.

Fuck.

A flash of alarm ran through Broden's spine. He couldn't afford to fight them both at once. If he did, it would be a close thing, sure enough. Freckles pressed on, but he came too close this time, allowing Broden the chance to act. Freckles' momentum carried him past Broden, exposing his back. As the raider stumbled forward, Broden used his own momentum and swung his sword. Steel heaved across the man's back, flattening him to the wooden deck with a squeaking wretch. He wouldn't be getting up.

The shaggy one came on, pausing in front of Broden with a grin. *Big fucker, eh. Right outta the Salt Coast marshes, you are.*

Broden risked a glance. Kalfinar was at the cabin.

Kalfinar's back slammed against the cabin's outer wall. He risked a glance through the window. Intense light and warmth; same as in Enulin, with the last one.

"She's there," he whispered.

"I know," Evelyne mouthed. "I can feel her urging me. We must be quick!"

The shaggy one let out a roar and stepped forward.

Broden raised his sword in both hands, but the man's cry cut off abruptly, becoming a gritty belch, followed by a tearing cough. A sword point had punched through the big raider's chest, making a tent of his leather vest. The raider's wide, shocked eyes searched over his shoulder to a small man: Rondo.

He nodded to Broden, sliding free his sword and shoving the raider over. The man dropped like a sack of shuddering stones.

"Go!" the little Cannan called out as Agurk, Ohasha's massive guard, strolled up beside him. The little man regarded the big Cannan. "We'll keep them off you long enough."

Agurk smiled a bloodthirsty grin at Rondo.

Broden nodded and dashed towards the aftercastle as Kalfinar burst into the cabin. Chentuck entered next, followed by a knife-wielding Evelyne.

Despite being dimly lit, the situation in the cabin was clear: three raiders, one young woman who was probably Daughter of the People, and the most beautiful light Kalfinar had ever seen. Beneath the splendid glow was another young woman. A raider stood behind each women holding knives to their throats. Another raider stood before them. He held two small hatchets, spinning them as a wicked grin split his stubbled face.

"Don't be foolish," the raider spat, his accent marking him a Salt Coast Solansian. The man licked his cracked lips, his tongue darting in and out like some kind of rotten lizard.

"Kalfinar," Evelyne whispered, "the Horn."

"Shut up, fucking bitch!" the raider snapped. "Kill those fu—"

Kalfinar's hatchet snapped through the air, burying deep into the face of the raider. The man went rigid and toppled backwards with his arms flush to his side, hatchets still gripped.

Chentuck leapt into action and engaged the raider holding the knife to the Daughter of the People's throat.

Before the first raider's body hit the ground, Kalfinar covered the distance between him and the guard holding the Horn. He did not break a stride as he carried forward, his sword point level, driving through the raider's eye and lodging into the cabin wall behind. The man's other eye went wide with shock. Screams pierced the air as Kalfinar turned towards the Daughter of the People. The woman kneeled on the floor with her hands bound behind her back, screaming but alive.

Broden charged into the room. All the raiders were dead. There were two girls in the room, one whose screaming was tailing off as he entered. She wore a stunned look on her face as she regarded the Ravenmayne amongst those who saved her life.

"Shut the door!" Evelyne barked towards him. She was kneeling by the other girl, undoing the bindings around the silent girl's arms.

There was a look of supreme calm on the girl's face as Broden shut the door. "Everyone alright?" he asked.

"Aye," Kalfinar whispered, stepping over and pulling his hatchet from the head of the Solansian raider. He wiped the weapon down and slung it from his belt. "You?"

"Fine."

"We need to be quick. Come on," Evelyne snapped as the sounds of battle continued outside. "Hurry."

The spirit observed the blood-spilling from its perch on the ship's main mast. The man-thing's slaughtered each other well, a pastime the pathetic creatures seemed well adapted to. The spirit feasted on the smell and taste of blood in the air, invigorating itself. The chaos would mask the spirit, allowing it to get close enough to take someone, the little Cannan. Close enough to strike out at them all. Now was the time for redemption; time to be enveloped in the Master's favour.

Evelyne moved quick in the poorly lit cabin. Footsteps could be heard outside, followed by the clash of steel, wet cries, and the sound of bodies crumpling onto the deck.

Chentuck held his sword ready by the cabin door, but no one came. Agurk and Rondo held firm on the outer, deck-side of the cabin. More footsteps pounded across the deck towards the aftercastle.

"She's well in the trance still. The cut should be easy." Evelyne handed the blade to Kalfinar.

"What are you doing to Katela?" the Daughter of the People sobbed.

"What we must if she or any of us are to live out the night," Evelyne barked back, her voice edged and certain. "Look away, for your own good."

The Daughter of the People sobbed and turned her head, pulling her knees tightly into her chest. "Don't hurt her. She's my friend." The Daughter of the People's sob was muffled by her buried face.

The spirit saw the little man-thing standing at the rear of the ship beside a giant. The lust for blood grew in the spirit. Now was the time.

Take the small man-thing. Nothing is protecting him. The spirit shot towards him.

Agurk parried before smashing his fist into the raider's face, flattening the nose bone. The raider stumbled backwards. His heel caught on the body of a comrade, betraying him to the deck. Before he hit the floor, Agurk had sliced the raider's belly open. He turned to see Rondo stepping away from the raider he had just cut down. The little Cannan nodded to Agurk. A moment later, Rondo was thrust backwards through the air, crashing against the cabin wall and flopping onto the raider he had just killed.

"No!" Agurk shouted, and hunkered to the ground, half expecting an arrow from some unseen bowman. Nothing came. Agurk crawled towards Rondo and flipped the little man over, there was no arrow or bolt. He slapped him on the face, nothing.

Then Rondo's eyes opened, and something hit Agurk in the neck.

The spirit punched the little man-thing's knife into the one-eyed giant's throat, showering the creature's new body in blood. The look of shock on the big man-thing was wonderful. The spirit shoved the dead weight off and stood, unsteady on the pathetic little man-thing's feet. The spirit stretched out its new neck and fanned its fingers, thin and slick with blood. The spirit pulled the man-thing's knife from the throat of the giant and moved towards the cabin door.

"Something's coming," Kalfinar mumbled to Evelyne while rubbing the amulet around his neck.

"Carry on!" Evelyne snapped as Kalfinar's head turned towards the door.

"No, there is something—"

The door swung open to reveal Rondo covered in blood.

"Just Rondo," Chentuck said, lowering his sword and heaving out a relieved breath.

"No!" Kalfinar roared.

Rondo thumped the knife deep into Chentuck's stomach and withdrew the blade.

Chentuck sagged and vomited dark blood as he fell to his knees.

"Kal, no!" Evelyne shouted. "We must finish."

She gripped at him, but Kalfinar shrugged her off and placed down the knife. He pulled out his sword as he stood.

Chentuck lay motionless on the floor, a pool of dark blood seeping across the deck on the cabin.

"Kalfinar, no!" Evelyne screamed.

"So there you are, demon. Come back to claim me, have you?"

"The Master will feed off you all." It was not Rondo's voice when he spoke, but a fractured cacophony of voices, metallic and vile, sounding all at once.

Kalfinar's heart thundered and he leapt forward. The spirit's knife flashed across Kalfinar's chest, just missing his mail shirt. Kalfinar pressed his attack and forced the spirit backwards by his blows.

Broden picked up the knife, half-deafened by the screams from the Daughter of the People.

"Do it!" Evelyne shouted over the noise, holding down the arms of the girl.

The knife cut easily into her flesh.

The spirit rallied with a series of ferocious kicks and slashes before trapping Kalfinar's sword arm with a tight grip, preventing him from swinging. Kalfinar's other hand moved towards the axe slung through his belt, but the spirit caught the limb and held firm.

The spirit slammed its head into Kalfinar's, causing him to see flashes of light. Kalfinar dropped to his knees. The strength returned to his arms and he tensed before stabbing his sword upward, punching clean through Rondo up to the cross-guard.

Despite the wound, the spirit still struck. Its hand flashed to Kalfinar's throat and tore away the amulet around his neck, before collapsing to the floor.

Kalfinar's world went dark for a moment and then flashed with fire and terror, dread and pain.

Broden risked a glance and saw Kalfinar lying on the floor as convulsions gripped his body. The back of Kalfinar's head slammed against the deck in a rapid tattoo along with his feet, spit flying from his mouth and blood spreading in tendrils down his face from his nose.

"Concentrate!" Evelyne snapped.

Broden pulled the incision open, exposing the girl's beating heart. The hammering on the floor stopped. Broden looked back to where his cousin lay. Kalfinar had ceased thrashing, and stood unsteadily. His arms shook and blood dripped from his chin while a grin split his blood-speckled face.

"That's not Kal." Evelyne whispered.

The spirit stared ahead at the vile creature before it, somewhere between man-thing and child of the liar, Dajda. It would never see that process through, for it was about to die.

Evelyne whispered an incantation and placed her middle and forefinger onto the girl's beating heart as Kalfinar, possessed by the spirit, bore down on them.

"Kal, don't make me," Broden shouted as he stood. He crashed a fist into the side of Kalfinar's head, sending him reeling to the floor. A flash of light momentarily dazzled Broden. As his eyes adjusted, he thought he saw the girl floating a foot off the ground as a beam of bright light shined upwards from her chest. Then he saw a blinding pain at the side of his head.

The spirit's foot smashed the big man-thing in the side of the face and sent him slumping over. The female had turned the Liar God's child and woke her. The spirit felt panic. It was too late.

The spirit felt it. There was only one chance now: harvest the man-thing's soul. The spirit flashed a hand to the hatchet in the belt and grabbed it, pulling the blade up towards the throat of the searcher's body. At least this one would die. At least the Master would be pleased and embrace—

The Horn of Dajda opened her mouth and sang. Shrill notes caused the spirit to drop the hatchet as it sliced a shallow cut into the searcher's neck. It fell to his knees as the song redoubled with another voice. The girl, the Horn of Dajda, sang out with her sister. Together, the voice rose, and grew stronger. There was nothing in the moment but their song.

The spirit fought and struggled. The pain was immense. Too much. It was being dragged, torn from the one it possessed, the searcher. It was being ripped from within, burned and scorched by the horrifying song of the liar's children. The spirit's grip loosened.

Evelyne risked a glimpse around. Broden had come to and held his hands over his ears as Kalfinar toppled onto the deck, his face to the cabin ceiling. His body arched, belly high and shoulders low, and then dropped before arching again and slamming back down, over and over. The song rose, richer and sharper. Kalfinar's body arched one last time and, with a shuddering jolt, the spirit screamed from him, wailing as its spectral claws clung on. Its hold on Kalfinar failed it and it was locked firmly in the air above them. Exposed for all its horror, vile eyes burning hatred towards them, its claws snapping and slashing as its shimmering form quivered with rage.

As the Horn of Dajda sang, a shrill chorus between the two ships, Evelyne approached the spirit, causing it to slink back as far as it could. The spirit slashed out, but the song was too great, and the attack harmlessly rebounded off the walls of the spirit's invisible prison.

Evelyne stood before the spirit. It looked smaller now, frightened. She tilted her head to the side, appraising the creature before her mouth stiffened and her eyes set firm. Her hand flashed out and stabbed the spirit's head with her middle and forefinger. Its wretched body burst into a bright white flame. The thing let out gut-wrenching wails that trailed off as the cabin grew uncomfortably hot. In a pop and a puff of smoke, the spirit was gone.

"We've got to hurry," Evelyne said as Broden got to his feet. "Come on and help me with the others. We need to get them back to the ship."

"Chentuck." Evelyne approached the stricken Ravenmayne where he lay face down in a pool of blood. She placed one hand on his shoulder, the other on his hip and rolled him onto his back.

He was dead.

Sorrow gripped Evelyne and she dabbed away the brimming tears. She moved the few short steps to attend to Kalfinar. The sound of fighting had not picked up again after the song of the Horn.

Broden looked up from Rondo's dead face to Evelyne, "What was that noise?"

She continued to tend Kalfinar as he slid back into consciousness. "That was their song."

"Didn't sound much like I thought it would," Broden said.

Evelyne brushed the hair from Kalfinar's brow. "The Horn of Dajda are not like the Anulii. They are not warriors, but they can defend themselves. That song is how they do so."

Broden nodded. "Reckon it can get us out of this mess?"

Evelyne smiled. "I think so. Listen."

The only noise was the hyperventilating Daughter of the People.

"See," Evelyne said, "there's little fighting out there. It will start again, once their senses come back. We must be quick."

As she spoke, Kalfinar's eyes flickered open. The blood vessels in the whites of both eyes had ruptured, sending bloody tear tracks down the side of his head.

"Welcome back," she whispered.

Those eyes.

Kalfinar was grateful for the sight of them. He was grateful for the hair that tickled his face and for her soft hands on his skin. Most of all, he was grateful for freedom from the spirit's grip. He saw it all. Saw hell. He tasted the power of the spirit's master. He tasted dread.

"Thank you," Kalfinar croaked.

He tried to prop himself onto his elbows, but his whole body felt like he'd just been trampled. He sucked in an agonising breath. His lungs sent stabs of pain along his chest and into his stomach. He shuddered with discomfort and propped himself up before rising unsteadily to his feet.

Kalfinar looked fully in the face of the beautiful light-being. The young girl radiated the same calm and serenity as the little girl on the ship. He glanced around the cabin, observing the scene within. "What happened?"

"The demon that sought you," Evelyne spoke, "it sought to take advantage of the chaos. It took Rondo first and then it took you." She reached out and placed the amulet in his hand. "Put that on, just in case. Once the spirit took you, it tried to kill the girl before we could wake her, but it was too late. Once we had awoken her, it stood no chance against the two of them. Their song tore it from you and held it while I destroyed it."

"It's gone?" Kalfinar asked. "Forever?"

"From what I understand of the nature of such spirits, it's gone, but it's safer to keep the amulet on for now until we can be sure."

Broden interrupted as the sound of fighting resumed outside the cabin. "We need to hurry. Let's get ready." He grabbed his sword. "Evelyne," Broden asked as she raised the Daughter of the People to her feet, "can they sing again?"

She nodded once. "You'll all have to cover your ears if you can, understood?"

Kalfinar stood unsteadily, sucked a deep breath into his aching chest, and placed his hand on the cabin door. He glanced back to see the Daughter of the People grab an oil torch from its wall-bracket. With a face of stiff resolve, the young woman tossed the oil lamp into the corner of the cabin, causing it to burst into flame. Caught between shock and approval, Kalfinar nodded, signalling for the song to begin.

The cry was shrill, redoubling as a voice rose from the other ship. When the cabin door swung open, men, women, raiders, and volunteers fell to their knees while clutching their ears. Not too many of Ohasha's were still alive.

They quickly covered the deck, leaping over bodies until they got to the port side of the raider's ship. A body caught Kalfinar's eye as he approached the rail. It was slumped against the main mast, the feathers of a crossbow bolt protruding from the chest. Dark hair hung lank over the face. Around the left leg was a metallic brace. Ohasha had given her life in service, as vowed.

Kalfinar hauled the Daughter of the People onto her father's ship, the two being still bound together. One by one, Ohasha's volunteers crossed over. The ship's crew were suffering from the piercing song of the Horn of Dajda. Some were on their knees, palms squeezed tight over their ears, whilst others staggered about, offering whatever help they could.

Kalfinar looked back to the raider's ship. The flames in the aftercastle grew larger, cracking the glass windows and licking out like the tongue of some hungry demon. He looked across at the deck of the raider's ship. No more of Ohasha's boarding party were moving.

"We've got to get away," Kalfinar roared, the effort stabbing pain into his back and shoulders. "The other ships in the flotilla will come around soon."

Broden and Evelyne nodded.

Kalfinar removed one hand from the side of his head and pulled his axe from his belt. Running down the starboard-side of the ship, he cut free the ropes.

Flames from the aftercastle spread across the cabin front onto the poop deck. The hungry fire crept forward, igniting bodies as it consumed more of the vessel. The ships slowly drifted apart.

Kalfinar raised his hand and the dreadful song ended. The shrill cry rang in their ears as mist enveloped the raider's ship. Within a moment, the only sign it had been there at all was the growing nimbus. It flared and spread as hungry flames consumed the ship.

"The rest of the flotilla will have noticed the flames by now. We can out run most ships, but we need to get moving. Where are you being pulled?" Kalfinar asked Evelyne.

She closed her eyes for a moment and then opened them. "We must sail across the Yellow Sea for Carte. With all haste."

Chapter Twenty-Seven

"SO WHAT OF THIS SICKNESS THEN?" Subath asked Olmat through a mouthful bread.

Olmat looked up from the book he was reading by the fire in Governor Harruld's study. "How do you mean?" he asked.

"Well," the sergeant said, tearing off another mouthful and rolling it around the inside of his cheek, "I was just wondering what I need to look out for." Subath swallowed a mouthful of wine and wiped his mouth as his grin split. "Because, you know, I want to know if my old pecker's going to be dropping off."

"If your prick drops off it'll be your own fault," Major Merkham said from the other side of the study where he reviewed troop allocations with Harruld. "With all the terrible things you've done to it in the past, I'm surprised it hasn't dropped off of its own accord."

Subath laughed and slapped his fist on the table in applause.

Harruld looked up and smiled thinly. "Best run through the symptoms for him, Olmat," Harruld said. "We can't have one of our most experienced men distracted by looking at his prick the whole time."

"Well, first thing, Sergeant, I can assure you from what I understand of this type of infection, there is not much chance of your," Olmat nodded towards Subath's lap, "falling off. Although, from what I hear, you haven't had much need for it of late."

The shock of Olmat's joke appeared to strike them dumb, each man casting a glance between the other, before bursting into laughter.

Olmat afforded himself a little smile before he carried on. "Realistically, gentlemen, this is one of a particularly nasty family of pathogens. It's probably spread by contact and, if in the vicinity of bursting boils, it will be airborne for a period. Normally such pathogens are quick-acting, however, the extent of the exposure can mean a longer or shorter incubation period in those infected. The guardsmen who entered the chamber after the release would have been struck with a heavy concentration and, as a consequence, would have died in short order. From my knowledge, they would have suffered extremely exaggerated symptoms. I suspect the majority of the cases will have been contained within the lower reaches of the High Command and, within the next few days, if anyone is going to die, they will. As for those of us up here, well we need to look for weakness and pain in the chest, as the infection starts there from what I can see. I believe such pathogens then attack the skin, forming itchy and red streaks in the flesh. This is the beginning of the boil stage. Weakening of the chest with heavy coughing will also be present. If my assessment is correct, this will be followed by internal haemorrhaging caused by organ degradation, external haemorrhaging, and then, ultimately, death."

"Sounds delightful. Think I'd rather my prick dropped off." Subath dropped the stick of bread and swallowed the last of his wine. "I'll have to make sure and try to give this sickness a wide berth if it ever comes my way."

"Not so sure even you would be able to scare this off, Subath," Harruld grumbled.

"Indeed," Olmat said. "That is what I can deduce as it stands at the moment. I've experienced several similar conditions in the past, however this is somewhat tainted with dark energy, so there may be yet more for us to learn. Be vigilant and if anyone feels unwell, regardless of your symptoms, let me know."

Olmat closed the book he had been reading and placed it beside him, before, with some effort, getting to his feet. His knees creaked as he straightened and the old familiar pains and aches rose out of their slumber, radiating through his limbs as he moved towards the door. "Goodnight, my friends," he said as he went. "I'll see you in the morning."

The others bid him goodnight as he left Harruld's study, closing the door behind him. Olmat shuffled past the guardsmen, noting the helmet's bent nose-guard and bruises on the young man's face while carrying on towards his chambers. Pains and aches, step after step. Familiar and unfamiliar, step after step, and pains in the chest. *Hurry, Kalfinar. The pillars fall. My time is coming soon.*

Harruld returned to his discussion with Merkham as the door closed behind Olmat. Allocation of officers was proving to be more difficult than at first thought. Too many untested men in command, too many hasty commissions, too few veterans able and hungry to lead.

"The cheek of Olmat, eh?" Subath scratched noisily at his stomach under his mail shirt. "To think the ladies are not crawling over each other for old Subath!"

Harruld and Merkham looked up at the dirty grin on the scarred man's face.

"Wish we had more of you!" Merkham said.

"Exactly what the ladies say!" Subath laughed, slapping Merkham's back, almost sending him flopping over the table. "Mind you, with the itching I'm getting, I'd say it may well be the whoring that'll be the death of me." A look of resigned disappointment cast over Subath's face before he shook it off and leaned his scarred hands onto the table. "Now then, show me where I can put myself to use."

Harruld looked to Merkham, who nodded and grinned before looking back at Subath.

"No!" Subath said, shaking his head as he stepped back from the table.

"Yes!"

"No, no, no."

"Yes, yes, yes!" Harruld smiled.

"No, you can't! I refuse it."

Merkham adopted a stern look. "You can't refuse it. Not if it comes as a direct order of the chief marshal of the High Command. Isn't that correct, sir?"

"Why, I believe it is, Major Merkham."

Subath's shoulders sagged and his face squirmed as Harruld's gaze settled on him.

Harruld walked over to Subath and placed a hand on his shoulder. "Sergeant, there have been few officers who've served with as much distinction as you have. Even fewer have ever commanded such respect as you do."

Subath's eyes rimmed with moisture. "No."

"You should have been commissioned to general by now, but for your bloody-mindedness. A bloody-mindedness that I, amongst others, have tolerated for so long only out of our deepest respect. Unfortunately for you, our current circumstances force me to make this decision. So, as of this moment, you are being promoted to general, acting as commander of the defence of the city of Carte."

Subath's eyes squirmed shut and a pair of tears slid between the wrinkles and scars of his face. "I spent my whole life in this army." Subath's voice cracked as he spoke. "I never had a mother. More'n likely she was an army whore. Dunno which caste of man my father was. I guess it doesn't really matter, does it? Anyway, my point is, sirs, I had no life, no family growing up. Not until I came to service, anyhow. I felt at home with the men. I felt I had family. Felt I had fathers, and was a father in turn. Those men were, they are, my children." Subath looked up and smiled. "I dare say a few of them actually are my children. Anyway, what I'm getting at is I never really felt like I could leave them and command from such distance. I'm too good with my men, too good with a sword in my hand. No disrespect meant, sirs, but I'm no soft-handed soldier."

"Subath," Harruld spoke, "everyone will have a sword in their hand. There'll be no danger of any of us avoiding that action. Accept this order, I implore you. Not as chief of the High Command, I implore you as your friend. Here you have the chance to stand alongside those of us who remain, as a father to the Free Provinces, to the whole Cullanain, and defend Carte."

Subath rubbed his hands over his head and down over his face. He looked long at their backs and palms. They were scarred on the back, nicked, rough and lumpy. His palms were notched and calloused. He looked at Harruld who held his hands up in front of him, turning them front and back: rough and scarred, notched and calloused.

"Not so different from yours, old friend."

"Aye, not so different after all, sir."

"So you'll accept?" Merkham asked, inspecting his own, soft palms as he spoke.

Subath held Harruld's gaze before responding. "Aye. I accept."

"Good," Merkham replied.

"One question though, sir." Subath looked between the two other men. "How come Governor Harruld is not commanding the defence of Carte?"

Harruld pulled out a chair and sat, exhaling a long and heavy sigh. "I'll play my part, old friend." His face seemed to turn grey, care-worn, and weary. "It seems time and tide wait for no man, regardless of rank or circumstance."

"What do you mean?" Subath asked, his eyes distracted by Merkham pouring a glass of water and handing it to Harruld.

"Old friend," Harruld said, nodding his silent thanks to Merkham for the water, "I'm afraid I'm dying."

Grunnxe swept into the pavilion heaving with breath and wiping blood from his knuckles with a rag. He threw the rag into the face of one of his officers standing at attention, causing him to flinch.

"Control yourself, man, or you'll be next." Grunnxe spat at the officer's feet and moved onto the dais where his heavy throne sat, slumping into the seat.

The Priestess, standing in the shadows behind Grunnxe's throne, stepped forward and leant over the king's shoulder. She whispered into his ear.

Grunnxe nodded and waved a dismissive hand. The Priestess slunk back to the shadows. The old king's face frowned and his lips pursed tightly together. A tension thickened in the air between the assembled officers; the king's building rage seemed to unsettle his commanders. Finally, his fury subsided and the colour drained from his face.

"Now, can I assume that as we plan to launch our offensive tomorrow, that there are no further fuck ups when it comes to getting your ragged-ass battalions into order?"

There was silence from the officers.

Grunnxe's colour started to rise again, though his voice remained calm. "Please consider that if no one answers me, I will choose someone to make an example out of, just as I did with Altyel out there. Go ahead. Go and look if you want to see what crucifixion does for a man."

Grunnxe had barely finished speaking when every officer in the pavilion answered, a cacophony of voices assuring the king of the order of their troops.

"Tell me again!" Grunnxe shouted and again a chorus of voices shouted their response. Grunnxe smiled, a hungry, violent lust in his eyes. "Again!"

The scent of damp and long-since rotted matter curled around Sarbien as he made his way deeper into the dark of Shalima mines. The constant sound of unseen droplets seemed like tapping nails counting time. Although he could not see them in the dark, the fumbling steps of the soldiers and the occasional oath uttered under their breath spoke volumes. The soldier's eyes could not match Sarbien's gifted sight in such dark places.

Captain Tyrnan reached out from behind and tugged at the back of Sarbien's coat, causing him to stop and half-turn.

"The men are nervous," Tyrnan whispered, his lips close by Sarbien's ear. "Do you know what you're looking for down here?"

"I know enough," Sarbien replied, his eyes capturing Tyrnan's hard features. "We move onwards." Sarbien turned and began stepping forward, before stopping and turning back. He leaned in close to the captain's ear. "Tell your men that if they have run so dry on courage, that they are welcome to make their way back out of the mines. Just remind them however, that it is a labyrinth down here. Should they get lost, they may never again see the light of day." Sarbien turned and stepped off, deeper into the mine.

Anthony shambled forward. His blistered and weeping hands slipped and slapped across rock walls as he made his way deeper into the dark belly of Shalima. His kind master's words coaxed him onwards and guided his every step.

"Yes, Master. I shall be with them soon." The words slurped in his mouth, spraying spittle as he spoke.

His teeth had been spat out or swallowed and his lips were cracked and split. He lurched forward further, then stopped, craning his rotting head to the side, listening in the stale blackness.

"Yes, yes!" he shouted. "I hear them, Master. Take me at last into your embrace."

Anthony dragged himself forward, fumbling around a damp, low-ceilinged corner. He saw light up ahead. A faint orange glow and the slightest movement of rank air. It smelled of blood.

The soldiers crept in the darkness, much closer behind Sarbien than before. Sarbien could sense their anxiety rising. He did not begrudge the soldiers their nerves, for he himself had spent several days trapped in underground caves in his youthful, exploring days. He felt fear then and had learnt the value of respecting the darkness. He allowed himself an invisible smirk as he moved deeper, the ball of thin silk twine unravelling as he went.

"What was that?" Captain Tyrnan voiced from behind.

Sarbien stopped moving and stood still. "I heard nothing," he replied.

"No, there was—"

An echo. Shouting in the blackness.

Sarbien turned to the soldiers, their hands driven by fear to rest upon their weapons.

"Heard that alright," Sarbien whispered. "Stay calm. Noise travels far in the body of the mines. There's no telling how far that sound has travelled."

Sarbien looked at their faces. Nervous to a one, except for the Tyrnan.

His hard features remained fixed on Sarbien's, before turning to his men and whispering, "I need every one of you to remember why you are here. For our families, our homes, for our people. Fear not the dark of the mines, but fear Grunnxe instead and use that fear to steel yourselves."

Sarbien gripped Tyrnan's shoulder in the dark, nodding his gratitude. "Come on, we must carry on. Let's see who was kind enough to make all of that noise."

Anthony's dazzled eyes stung and wept as the orange glow grew stronger. He staggered towards the light while making out blurred and shadowy forms a short distance below. They chanted together, a sound that comforted him. The master told him it was good, he had done well, and would soon be rewarded.

"I am with you, Master. Your child, always. Into your arms, I commit myself."

Anthony lurched his way down the rocky slope towards the floor of a wide inner-chamber of the mines. As his eyes adjusted to the light, he saw before him two dozen priests robed in a mix of black and white rough-hewn habits like his own. They stood around an altar, streaked with the blackened stain of old blood and the not-so-blackened streaks of fresh blood. The whole chamber reeked of gore and sulphur. To Anthony, however, it smelt of the freshest scent. A fragrance so wonderful it threatened to intoxicate and send him to rapture.

"Master, take me home," he shouted, causing the priests to spin and face him.

One priest stepped forward. A thin, nasal voice escaped from the shadows cast by the habit's hood, "Who are you, monster? Speak!" The priest drew a dagger from within the arm of his habit and held it before him.

Anthony began to giggle, spit flecking from his burst lips.

"Answer me!" the priest demanded, his voice cracking with rage.

"The master said he will reward me."

The priest cast back his hood, revealing a thin, sharp face, wrinkled with care and age. His eyes turned hard and he spoke, "What do you know of the master?"

"Anything I wish for, I shall be given." Anthony began to giggle once more.

The priest dropped the dagger as fear contorted his face. His mouth gaped and his eyes bulged with dread.

Anthony giggled on, his wretched face warping in dark arousal as the priest's throat was crushed by the unseen force. "Into your embrace I send myself, Master."

Chapter Twenty-Eight

THASKIL'S MIND raced as his horse hammered down the road from Apula's main gate towards the encampment. He knew Sergeant Rushnall was correct in that it would mean a flogging from Bergnon for disregarding his order to remain in Apula. *The fucker can flog me if he wants, but I'm damned if I sit here any longer.*

Thoughts and images had gnawed at Thaskil as he ran the militia through their drills and inspections. *Where was Arrlun? Why had he run? Did he even leave of his own accord?*

The questions repeated over and over. Each thought was coupled with the image of Bergnon's bleeding head and altered demeanour. Something was being hidden. Thaskil could feel it tugging at him. Tormenting him. He meant to find out, flogging or not.

He slowed his pace as he approached the encampment, being careful not to draw too much attention. Dismounting, he walked his horse to the picket and tied its reins tight. Glancing over his shoulders, Thaskil pulled his hood over his head and trudged through the churned up red earth towards the tent he shared with Arrlun.

Where are you, friend? Show me where you've gone.

Thaskil trudged through the billets until he reached his tent. He untied the flap and slipped inside. Thaskil felt under the camp-bed for Arrlun's possessions. There was nothing. He lifted the light-framed bed. There was nothing underneath, not even the leather pouches. *Who's been in here?*

It pained Thaskil to think it, but his gut told him it had not been Arrlun. He placed the bed back into place and sat. He rested his head in his hands, rubbing his weary face and feeling the dryness of his eyes. *Damned dust, it gets everywhere—*

The sharp whinny of a horse sounded not far from the tent. The sound repeated, coupled with shouts of alarm and curses from men. Thaskil snapped to his feet and strode out of the tent, his head turning from side to side to see where the commotion had come from. He saw nothing. The horse whinnied again and this time Thaskil could pinpoint it. He ran between the tents until he found the source of the noise: a riderless grey mare with a star shape branded on its flank.

Thaskil stopped breathing. *Arrlun's horse.*

He ran as fast as he could towards the beast. It charged up on its hind legs as the soldiers around failed to get it under control. As he approached the horse, his eyes flashed about the gathered men. Thaskil could not see Arrlun amongst them.

"Whoa there, whoa," he spoke gently as he approached the anxious horse, his palms turned down towards the ground.

The mare heaved a breath and hooved at the ground, its head bending down as Thaskil calmed it with his gentle words.

"Whoa there, girl." He reached out and grabbed the bridle with one hand, and stroked its cheek with the other. As he soothed the beast, he looked along its neck and side. It was still saddled, but there was no sign of a rider. No sign of Arrlun. Thaskil stroked the horse's cheek once more and ducked under its head, moving towards the other side. He looked down its flank. *Blood.* There were streaks and smears of blood down the horse's side, but no wounds upon the horse itself. Thaskil's heart raced and fury burned his face. *Someone was laid out across you, weren't they?*

"Take this horse and corral it alone," Thaskil ordered the soldier nearest to him. "Make sure the saddle and the bloodstains stay as they are. Understood?"

"Yes, sir," the man replied, taking the reins from Thaskil.

"You," Thaskil shouted at a young private who was passing with messages.

The young man stopped and pointed to his chest.

"Yes, you!" Thaskil snapped. "Get over here."

The private hurried over to Thaskil and saluted.

"Never mind with that," Thaskil barked. "Tell me, where is Major Bergnon?"

The young private looked side to side, open-mouthed. "I think he was last seen riding into Apula a few hours ago."

Apula, why the hell is he in Apula? "You think, or you know?" Thaskil asked, stepping nearer the private.

The private flinched a little. "I know, sir," he stammered. "One of the farriers said he saw him just after lunch."

"Good," Thaskil grunted, his eyes following Arrlun's mare with the blood-streaked side as it was led towards the corral. "I want you to communicate a message to the rest of the officers."

"Yes, sir."

Thaskil grabbed a fistful of the private's chainmail shirt, pulling his face right into his own. "Make sure this is verbal only and, on your life, make sure no one but the officers learns of this. Do you understand?"

"I understand, sir."

"Good. I wouldn't want to have to kill you," Thaskil said, his voice barely a whisper. "I want you to tell the remaining officers that Major Bergnon is to be arrested on sight."

The young private swallowed hard as his eyes widened.

"Now listen carefully to what I am about to tell you. Tell the rest of the officers the charges against Major Bergnon are treason and murder."

Bergnon's breath blew hard as he crashed into the armoury wall. Dried plaster streamed in a dusty drift over his face and hair as he slumped to the floor.

Brostoff walked the few steps between them and crouched down to face-level. "I take it by now you and I are getting clear on who's given the orders around here, eh?" Brostoff growled.

Eck and his companions watched like hungry dogs as Brostoff hawked a lump of phlegm from his throat and spat into Bergnon's face.

Bergnon's fury grew within. It took all his will not to reach for his sword. *The time I kill you will come soon, you fucking prick.* The image of Natalya flashed constantly in his mind. She was the reason he was here. The reason he tolerated such humiliation. She was the reason he betrayed his own country. And the reason he murdered his friend. *Kill me. You'd be showing me mercy. Please.*

"Aye," Bergnon mumbled as he wiped the stinking spit off his face with the back of his hand. "You're the boss."

"Aye, I am the fucking boss. Now don't you go and forget it, eh?" Brostoff sprung up from his hunkers, extended his huge hand to Bergnon, and hauled him to his feet. "Now, tomorrow, once the signals are sent back and forth, then we blow this damn wall apart, aye?"

Eck and his men grunted their approval.

"Brostoff," Bergnon chanced reminding his newly appointed senior, "who's going to foul the well?"

The big man's eyebrow furrowed and, for a moment, it looked as though he would strike again. "Eck, you get on the fouling of the well. Do it tonight and take the traitor with you."

Bergnon's mouth gaped. "But I can't be seen to—"

Brostoff put one hand on his sword and slid it an inch from the scabbard.

Bergnon imagined Natalya's face and was silenced.

"You'll fucking well do as I tell you, hear?' Brostoff snarled, his scabbing muzzle drawn up to reveal stained teeth.

"The well, boss," Bergnon conceded. "Got it."

"Aye, just make sure you do or I'll be fouling the well with your stinking leaky bucket of a carcass."

Sweet mercy, I wish you would.

"Sun will be setting soon," Brostoff added, looking up to where the guardsmen's bodies were hidden. "You'd best be getting a move on. Take one of them guards up there and give him a swim."

Thaskil's horse galloped up the escarpment and stopped at the main gate of Apula beside the guardsmen standing to attention.

"Have you seen Major Bergnon?" Thaskil asked.

"I've only started my watch, sir," the guardsman said. "But the corporal up above the portcullis has been on since midday. He may know."

Thaskil thanked the guard and swung down from his horse, handing the guard the reins whilst he bounded upstairs in search of the corporal. He reached the top of the stairs and moved within the walls and past the wooden wheel of the portcullis towards the office of the chief of watch. He opened the door and found the corporal smoking a pipe with his feet up, peering out of the arrow slit. The corporal stumbled and half-fell, smouldering tabac spilling out onto the floor as he saluted Thaskil.

"Have you seen Major Bergnon this afternoon?" Thaskil asked.

The corporal looked confused, perhaps surprised not to be reprimanded by the young officer.

"Must I repeat myself, Corporal?"

"No, sir. I saw the major not long after lunch. He didn't say where he was headed. I just assumed he was off to see you with that new batch of militiamen you brought in the other night."

Thaskil's mind snapped to the militiamen. Bergnon had acted strange, sending a portion of the militiamen off to make deliveries. Thaskil hadn't noticed at the time, but some of the men had never returned.

Thaskil turned on his heel and began to leave the small room, before he turned back. "Corporal." His tone was ice cold. "If I catch you half-witted when you're on watch one more time, I'll have you flogged and then put on the front line to face whatever may come. Do I make myself clear?"

The corporal gulped and nodded. "Clear, sir. It won't happen again, honest. Sorry, sir."

"Aye, I know it won't." Thaskil stormed off and collected his horse. There was only one place he was heading to next.

Bergnon heaved the bagged-up corpse of the guardsman over his shoulder as Eck stood by the door picking dried dirt from under a chipped fingernail.

"Aye, just stand there," Bergnon said snidely as he steadied himself with the weight of the body. "I don't need any help."

"Fuck you," Eck spat on the floor and ate whatever dirt he retrieved from his rank finger.

"A real charm, you are."

Eck just leered toothlessly.

"Could you at least get the bloody door?"

Eck peeled himself from the wall and opened the door, dragging his heels as he trudged outside toward the horses.

Bergnon heaved the body outside, his eyes scanning the street and windows to make sure no one was watching. He could not afford to be recognised, not now with things so close. In a few short steps, he closed the distance between the guardhouse and the horses, and shoved the bagged body across the saddle.

"Right," Bergnon said as he watched Brostoff shut the door behind them, "let's get this done fast and quiet."

"Fuck you."

The sun had set as Thaskil made his way through the streets of his hometown, his thoughts dominated with Arrlun and what end he had met. Could Bergnon have really murdered Arrlun? Doubt and fear made his mind lurch, his guts spasm, and his stomach roil. Damn it, he felt like he was going to shit himself.

What if I've got it wrong? It's Bergnon, for Dajda's sake. Doubt, fear, hurt, anger. *No, it all ties together too tight.*

Grief mingled with anger. Aching, crushing sorrow blended with hate and blinding revulsion. He picture Bergnon's face yesterday in the rain. The blood from a wound probably inflicted by Arrlun as he fought for his life. Traitor's blood staining the collar of a murderer. His resolve stiffened and he jabbed his heels into his horse's flanks. The shod hooves of the horse clattered through the streets. The guardhouse was not far. His guts churned.

"It's slipping off," Bergnon hissed as he led the horse through the streets towards the central well of Apula. "Make sure he's bound tight. We don't want to cause a bloody scene here."

Eck grumbled as he moved to fix the lashings holding the corpse in place.

The night was clear and the moon cast a steely-blue light over everything. Not the best conditions for going unnoticed, but it was better to be at it now, Bergnon mused. Their movements would be blurred amongst the other traders making their way home at the end of

the day. Despite this, the light from the windows of the townsfolk illuminated enough to make Bergnon uncomfortable. He drew his hood
tighter over his face, drawing a scoff of derision from Eck behind him,
his broad, greasy face boldly on display.

"Afraid yer friends will see you with the likes of me, eh,
Major-man?"

The man's crackling laughter caused Bergnon's skin to prickle, but
he ignored the taunt. *Not far to go. Mind on the job.* Bergnon thought
again of his love, for whom all of this descent into a wretched nature
was for. *Mind on the job.*

"Hey, Major-man," Eck called out, his ragged voice causing a
couple traders to look up as they passed. "Hey, Major-man," Eck
persisted, "that slut girlfriend of yers didn't ignore me half as much as
you." He sniggered a filthy laugh as he got Bergnon's attention. "The
bitch was quite fond of me after—"

Bergnon turned and smashed his fist hard into Eck's face, crumpling him to the cobbles of the street. "Dajda damn me!" Bergnon
hissed a curse as his actions caused the passers-by to stop. Gasps of
shock caused him to wince. He pulled his hood tighter about his face.
So much for mind on the job. Stupid move.

Eck groaned on the ground. "What you do that for?" He spat blood
and felt about in his ruin of a mouth, pulling out a loose tooth, one of
his last. "Was only playing with you."

Bergnon grimaced as more people gathered. He grabbed Eck by the
front of his coat and hauled him to his feet, pulling his bleeding face in
close. "If you ever speak of her again, I swear I will stick you full of
holes and put you in the fucking well."

"Aye, yer brave now, I'll grant you that, but just mind how you go
with Brostoff. He's not half as forgiving as I am." Eck wiped a long
smear of dark blood from his nose and mouth with the back of his
hand. "Now get yer fucking hands off me." He shoved himself away
from Bergnon and looked at the gawkers. "Damnit," Eck muttered,
warping his face into a sneering smile. "Just a little disagreement with
my brother here."

Bergnon gathered up the reins and led the horse on. The central
well wasn't far now.

"Come on," he grumbled back to Eck. "We need to get a move on."
As Eck made up the distance between them, Bergnon turned and whispered over his shoulder, "We'll need to do another loop. I don't want

anyone following us. Especially not if they go and speak to the city guard. Keep your trap shut from now on."

"Fuck you."

Thaskil stood in the shadows of an alleyway across from the armoury. He could see the distortion of light as people moved about within. The horses and cart tied up outside were the same as those the militiamen Bergnon had appointed to make the delivery used. There would be too many of them in there for him to tackle alone in a straight fight, but a concern had grown within him as he sat in the darkness and deliberated his next move.

What if none of the officers believe me? What if they are involved too? Suddenly a great deal of fear welled up from within. *Have we been betrayed? Am I about to die?*

He waited, afraid, alone, and thought of Arrlun. His anger grew again, flooding over him and washing away his fear. He gripped his sword hilt and drew the weapon from its scabbard. *Steel always promises revenge. Keep the fear at bay and give me strength.* He dashed across the street and crouched against the cool stone wall beneath the building's window. He craned his neck to glimpse into the armoury. Six men sat around the table, playing cards and laughing. Thaskil recognised some of the militiamen. The others wore uniforms of the city guard. *Men have died for those uniforms.*

He crouched under the window and tried to listen to their conversation, but their voices were muffled and he could not accurately make out their words. Frustrated, he crept alongside the wall towards door and made his way up the wooden steps, being careful not to alert the killers inside with creaking floorboards. He leant his ear against the door and waited. Sooner or later, someone must give away Bergnon. His guts twisted and gurgled, a noise like thunder in the dark. He swallowed a panicked breath, frozen with fear that someone may have heard. He edged off the steps and slipped into a dark spot underneath them. *Like a snake hiding in the dirt.*

"Not now, someone's coming," Bergnon hissed as Eck started to unfasten the rope holding the corpse on the horse. Bergnon looked up to see a drunk stumbling through the central square of Apula and waited, his pulse thundering until finally the drunk had passed out of sight. "Now, quickly."

Eck undid the fastening, hauled the body off the horse, and slumped it onto the wall of the well.

Bergnon drew a knife and slashed open the hessian bag. The corpse stared back at him with dried, dead eyes. Bergnon paused, holding the corpse's gaze.

"Come on, we don't have time for this! And the fucker stinks," Eck snapped. He unsheathed his knife and punched it into the guts of the dead man, releasing foul gas as he tore across the belly. He shoved the body into the well and looked down for several long seconds, before the deep echo of a tinny splash rose up.

Polluted with your treachery. Bergnon shook away his torment. "It's done." He was about to move off when he caught movement in the corner of his eye. He turned, his mouth very dry and his breath shallow.

"If you make as much as one more move, with Dajda as my witness, I'll have you stuck full of arrows and there'll be three bodies in that well."

———

Thaskil hunkered himself deep in the shadows underneath the wooden staircase of the guardhouse. He was safe from the eyes of what few folk were passing by, yet still within earshot of the conversation within. It had been almost an hour and the militiamen had not mentioned Bergnon once.

Come on, you fuckers. Just say his name. Dajda! He struggled to make space and stretched out his leg, denying the cramp in his hip any glory. He stretched out the other leg and tried to get the blood flowing. The sound of footsteps moving towards the door made him freeze.

"What in the damned darkness is taking them so long?" a gruff voice said just before the door creaked open.

Light sliced through the darkness in a sharp line over his eyes. *Don't look down, you bastard.* Thaskil's sword inched halfway out of the scabbard. There was no more room. *Would serve me right to be stuck like a hog in a pen, fool.*

The faceless voice above stepped onto the steps, blocking the light from the guardhouse and casting Thaskil into darkness. "That bloody major and his scheming. He'll get us all killed," the voice grumbled, half under his breath.

Thaskil's heart sank. *It's true. Damn you, Bergnon. Damn you forever into the hells.*

"Get in here and close that door, idiot," a commanding voice called out from within.

"Ach, I've gotta go for a piss anyhow," the gruff voice from the stairs replied. "Back in a moment."

"Well at least close the fucking door. It's freezing out there," the voice from inside called.

The door closed, leaving Thaskil in darkness.

The militiaman stepped into the street holding a small oil lamp, and moved around to the side of the armoury. The man placed his lamp on a stack of wood before unbuttoning his trousers.

Thaskil crept out from under the stairs and began to circle the militiaman, keeping to the shadows. *Let's find out the truth, all of it.*

He edged closer as the man started to relieve himself, piss noisily splashing against the junction between the building's plaster and city wall. *Going to spill the beans, scum.*

Thaskil closed the distance. His sword caught the moonlight with a little wink before catching the man's neck. The man stumbled with a gurgle, knocking over his oil lamp, spreading oil and flame.

Damn it. In the heat of the moment, the desire to ask questions lost out to brutal revenge. Thaskil's heart thundered. He now had to see this out. Had to finish it. *Five to one, great odds, fool!* He tried to stamp out the flames, but it was no use. *Don't have long.*

He looked around in the dark for something, anything, to help, and grabbed the militiaman's knife. There was a length of muddy rope coiled alongside some barrels and loose planks. Thaskil grabbed it and stepped towards the stairs leading to the armoury door. He tied off both ends in front of the door, a couple of inches above the planks and moved around the side of the building near the barrels and stacked planks, barely casting a glance at the dead man whose blood stained the gable wall like some nightmarish art.

Thaskil crept back towards the stairs and crouched down beside them, careful to stay in the shadows, but avoiding having to hide in the cramped space underneath. He steeled himself, thought once more of

Arrlun and the betrayal of Bergnon, and let fly a scream. He heard the chairs within grind backwards on the wooden floor.

Footsteps charged to the door. The first man out struck the rope and went flying clear off the steps, landing in a heap in the road. The second man stepped over the rope and looked down at it, not seeing Thaskil rise and slash his sword across his ankle tendons. The man fell to the ground, half in the building and blocking the exit of the third man.

As Thaskil ran around towards the steps, he stabbed the man in the road.

The third man leapt over his screaming comrade and onto the street, engaging Thaskil. "Get your arses out here!" the man roared to the two men remaining in the armoury.

Steel clanged, temporarily glinting cool in the blue hue of the moonlight before raging hot in the fire's red glow. The flames spread from the pile of planks and barrels and onto the beams of the armoury.

Voices screamed as Thaskil slashed an overhead blow. Someone was crying for help. Thaskil hammered his sword strokes down on the militiaman, kicking and spraying spit through gritted teeth. The man could not match Thaskil's fury as he battered him backwards.

The two other militiamen had swords drawn and spread out in a wide circle around him.

"Give it up, boy," the big man he had been fighting said.

Thaskil realised he was laughing, then feigned an overhead strike. The big man raised his sword to parry the blow, but at the last moment, Thaskil's sword altered direction and bit into the man's wrist, severing his sword-hand. Thaskil kicked the man's midriff, sending him onto his arse screaming.

The two other militiamen charged.

Thaskil spun to meet them, releasing the knife in a throw that caught one of the men in the cheek and sent him stumbling face-first towards the ground. Thaskil met the second's blows with a series of quick parries. He replied with three close blows, turning the man around and causing him to step backwards towards the armoury. Thaskil pressed on with two high blows, sending the man backwards up the armoury steps until he eventually tripped over the screaming form of his comrade with cut ankles. The militiamen lay atop one another in a heap. Thaskil's sword thumped into the man's chest. The wounded man beneath began to squeal like a pig as the sword passed from the chest of one man and into the stomach of the other.

Thaskil's face was a screwed up mask of hate as he twisted his blade, causing a whoosh of air to flow from the militiaman underneath the other. He withdrew his sword and stepped back towards the one-handed man on the street.

The man tried to stand, but Thaskil approached and slammed his sword pommel into the man's temple, sending him to the ground. Thaskil looked around at the destruction surrounding him. *Six men. Revenge is a stronger course of medicine than fear, I suppose.*

The fire he started was burning wild now, having spread to the armoury. The flickering tongues of flames lapped hungrily about the building. The fire's light danced on the street. He knelt down and bound the arms and feet of the unconscious militiaman using the man's own belts. When he stood, the city guard approached.

"What's going on here, Lieutenant?" one of the guards asked.

"These men are involved in a plot against the Free Provinces," Thaskil replied. "We must take this one away for questioning. Bring him to the brig and lock him up on his own." Thaskil's eyes took on a hard look, holding that of the guardsman. "Make sure no one gets to him apart from me, understood?"

"Clearly, sir—"

A huge explosion of fire and stone ripped around them, and the night was blotted out in blackness.

The scout rode hard towards the king's pavilion, having been let through the perimeter by his bodyguards. His horse's mouth frothed as it breathed hard. The scout's own breath rattled from his flared nostrils and open mouth. The scout risked a glance to the crucified body of Baron Altyel and wondered if soon he too would find himself feeding the crows, such was the mad king's wrath. He swallowed hard and reined in, leaping off his horse in front of Grunnxe's pavilion.

The scout made his way past the king's personal guard and approached the main body of the pavilion, where the old king sat in council with his generals. The ever-present shadow of the Priestess hovered behind his throne. As usual, the sight of the Priestess sent a shiver down the scout's spine, finishing as his bowels twisted.

"What is it?" Grunnxe growled.

The scout gulped at his breath; the desperate efforts of a drowning man. The generals looked nervously towards him.

"The wall, Your Highness," the scout mumbled. "The wall at Apula. It's been blown."

"What?" Grunnxe roared, rising to his feet. "It's too early!"

The king's face turned red in fury and he made to move towards the scout. The Priestess reached out a gloved hand and held the shoulder of the mad king while whispering something in his ear.

The fury drained away and Grunnxe looked up at the scout. "Ready the forces, we march on Apula within the hour."

Chapter Twenty-Nine

THE IMAGE of the knife plunging into Chentuck washed over Kalfinar's mind again and again. He shoved the wool blanket back and swung his feet down onto the wooden floor of the cabin he shared with Broden.

"Can't sleep?" Broden asked.

"No. You?"

"Nah."

"I think I'll get some air. Guess you're staying put?"

"You know, I just might. The grain of the wood in the ceiling here is quite captivating." Broden smirked.

Kalfinar stepped out onto the deck and past the night crew, making his way towards a quiet part of the ship. He stopped short of the steps to the aftercastle and leaned against the railing to watch the black water slide past the ship and turn to froth in its wake. The image of Chentuck's lifeless body flashed in his mind. "Damn it!" Kalfinar snapped and thumped the railing.

He turned away from the inky water and walked towards Evelyne's cabin. He paused for a moment and sucked in a deep breath through his nostrils. He knocked on the door and opened. Evelyne looked up from a chair, wiping away tears while beckoned Kalfinar in.

He stepped in and closed the door. "Where are the girls?"

"They're sleeping in the cabin next door."

"You should get some sleep too."

"We all could do with some rest." Evelyne said.

"Evelyne," Kalfinar stepped closer to where she sat.

She looked up at him, the glisten of tears obvious once more on the rims of her eyes.

"I want to apologise for my part in—"

Evelyne stood from her seat. "No. This is not your doing." Her voice had an edge to it and her face was set firm. Two angry tears broke from her eyes and fell to the floor from her pale cheeks. "Kal," Evelyne stepped closer and took his hand in hers. "Chentuck was killed by the spirit. That was in no part your doing." Her voice had softened and a gentle smile dawned on her face.

"But the jalsinum." Kalfinar looked down at the floor, shame welling within.

"Was flushed from you by the child. It was the spirit that killed him."

Kalfinar looked at Evelyne's hand as it held his. Her skin was soft and warm. How she rubbed the top of his scarred and nicked hand with her thumb reminded him of how his wife used to when she held his hands. "He was a good man. He deserved better from me. I was wrong about him at the start of all this." He looked back to Evelyne. She held his eyes with an intensity he was not used to. His stomach fluttered and the sense of shame returned. He forced himself to smile. "You know," he said as he reached out with his other hand and held hers in his, "when we sat together on the ship and I held the girl as she slept, it was the happiest I had felt in years."

Evelyne smiled.

"It felt like all of this fear and pain, it was stripped away and all we were left with was that moment in that room. It changed something in me."

"It changed something in me too," she replied.

Kalfinar held the gaze of her ice-blue eyes and felt her grip tighten. His heart began to race. He glanced at her lips as they parted and then back to her eyes. She had seen him. He moved his face closer to hers and felt her nervous breath hot on his face. "I feel like—"

She kissed him.

His hands broke from hers and wrapped around her waist as they kissed. His heart thundered while their lips worked together.

"Kalfinar!" came an urgent shout from the deck.

They broke from their kiss and stared at the door of the cabin as they held each other.

"I'm sorry," Kalfinar said as he broke away from Evelyne. He moved towards the door and opened it to see Broden standing on the deck. "What is it?"

"The Daughter of the People, she's going to throw herself into the sea. Come quick."

Kalfinar followed Broden as he bounded up the steps towards the rear of the poop deck. Evelyne followed behind.

"Don't come any closer!" the Daughter of the People shouted at them and the few gathered crew as they arrived onto the poop deck. She stood with her back to the railing, looking at the faces of those standing before her.

"Why are you doing this?" Kalfinar asked, taking one step closer.

"Don't," she said in a cold tone. "Don't come any closer."

Kalfinar raised his palms to her and stayed where he was.

"I'd heard of you before we met," she said, looking at Kalfinar. "I heard that you are a good man."

A drunk and smoke-fuelled brawler. And a shitty excuse for a man. "Tell me," Kalfinar asked. "How is it you came to know of me?"

"We have a mutual friend, Captain. He spoke much of your qualities. Qualities I have born witness to this very day. You and your companions, you are all very brave."

"My lady, with respect, what does that have to do with why you are here?"

"Everything. Your friend, Bergnon, once served as the Free Provinces emissary to Canna. From time to time, he would visit."

Kalfinar nodded. "He often spoke of his love of your country and your people."

She shuddered and began to cry, as though her tears had been held back for an age. Kalfinar stepped towards her.

"No! Stay back." With defiance, she wiped her tears away with the back of her hand. "Don't try and stop me. Just let me say what I must."

"I'm sorry."

"I am the reason you are betrayed. This is my fault."

"What do you know of our betrayal?" Kalfinar's tone hardened.

"The raiders came for me. To force my love."

"Who is your love?" Kalfinar's voice was low and hard. *Don't say his name, girl. Don't let it be him.*

"I'm sorry. Bergnon and I were married. It was in secret. They used me to get to him, and I've brought death to my people. My Mother. I'm sorry for everything."

"No!" Evelyne roared as she sprinted towards the railing. She was too late.

The Daughter of the People heaved herself backwards and into the darkness of the night sea.

"Take another deep breath for me," Olmat said as he placed his hands on Harruld's chest. "That's fine. You can put your shirt back on."

"What's the verdict?" Harruld asked as he pulled his shirt over his head, popping his hands through the arms and out the cuffs.

Olmat hid his concern as he washed his hands with his back to the governor. He dried them off and turned to his long-time friend. "You know as I do. The progression is steady."

Harruld mouth squirmed into a wry smile. "Well, a case of when, rather than if."

"When, rather than if," Olmat repeated. "The same for us both."

Harruld stood up sharply, heaved in a deep breath, and buttoned the front of his jerkin. "No point in worrying about the inevitable, is there?"

"No." Olmat's rheumy blue eyes stared at the floor. "I suppose not." He looked up from the ground and saw that Harruld stood before him.

"What is it, Olmat?"

The old physician offered a meek smile. He felt his head wobble on his thin neck as he looked up. "I'm a little embarrassed to say so, but as it comes closer I'm afraid to die. I don't want to go, but then I look at you and how stoic you are as you face it." His eyes dropped to the floor again. "I just wish I had your courage."

Harruld reached out and squeezed Olmat's bony shoulders. "You've given every one of us who knows you your strength and courage. You've sacrificed everything for us and shown more fortitude than anyone I have ever known in doing so. Fear is natural, Olmat. It is being human, it—"

A knock on the door to Harruld's study interrupted them.

"Come in," Harruld shouted.

"My Lord," the guardsman with the dented helmet came in puffing. "I've been ordered by General Subath to inform you that Lord Abbonan and his fleet have arrived. The lord is making his way here and will be with you before long.

"Excellent. Best you just send him straight in. I don't want you denting the other side of your helmet."

Lord Abbonan burst into the room without even a pause or a knock, followed by General Subath and another officer whose face was obscured by a bloody rag held over his nose.

Abbonan grinned and spread his arms. "Harruld, my old boy, how in the hells are you?"

Harruld laughed as he came around his desk and embraced the larger man. "Still alive, just about." They broke their embrace and clasped hands. "By Dajda, it is good to see you, Abbonan. Take a seat." Harruld ushered him towards a seat at the long table. "Subath, sit, please. And who is this?" Harruld asked of the officer with the bloody rag.

The officer removed the rag from his nose and saluted the Governor of Carte. Commander Lucius appeared to be sporting a freshly broken nose. "My Lord," the Commander lisped.

Harruld strode towards the commander and, without stopping, smashed his fist into his broken nose. Lucius squawked, dropped to his knees, and fell over. A stream of fresh blood, mixed with black, clotted blood bubbled onto the floor.

"Take him to the infirmary," Harruld ordered the guardsman. "When he comes to, see that he gets treatment for that."

"Must say," Abbonan said, "I'm glad you didn't welcome me that way."

Harruld turned back to his table and picked up a handkerchief to wipe the blood from his ring. "Subath, I presume it was you who broke that nose in the first place?"

"Aye," Subath rasped. "Been wanting to do that for years. Figured I'd take advantage of my grand rank. Felt quite nice."

"Aye, it did," Harruld said as he sat into the high-backed chair at the head of the table. "But we're short of officers, fine or otherwise. We can forget his resignation. Let that be the last wailing he gets."

"My Lord," Subath agreed, sticking his lip out in an act of mock petulance.

"So, I hear we're to expect a spot of trouble?" Abbonan said.

Harruld grunted.

"Well," Abbonan continued, "I've brought an additional twelve warships to patrol the bay, just in case any of the Solansian fleet shows up. It's not much, but it strengthens the Carte fleet."

Harruld scratched the figures down as Abbonan spoke.

"I'm sorry to say, however, I was only able to bring five thousand men. We can't leave Terna totally exposed. I wish I could've brought more."

"Nonsense, you've done more than enough," Harruld said. "We're awaiting troops from Enulin and Gerloup. In the meantime, with the swords you've brought, and the fleet of our northern boys, we are much stronger. And with Lord Abbonan, the Great Sea Wolf, at the fleet's helm, we can rest easy in the face of raiders."

"You flatter me," Abbonan laughed. "It's been a long time since I led a battle at sea. The Great Sea Wolf is more of a Parlour Wolf these days!"

"I've heard that said," Harruld laughed, "but I'm glad to see you've come out of retirement for one last fight. Now, let's get your men barracked and on orders. What's the current status?"

"So far, the lads are holed up on the ships," Abbonan replied. "We can start filtering them into the city and allocating them space at the walls, gatehouses, and towers, if that helps?"

"No," Harruld replied, scratching down figures as he spoke. "You take your men and barrack them in the High Command. Subath will lead the men at the outer walls. I want men who know the city at the front."

"Aye, sound enough," Abbonan replied, casting a wink at Subath. "And of my ships?"

"Be ready," Harruld said grimly, looking up from his work. "The raiders may not be long in coming. We can't let them take the harbour and unload their men. They'll set a torch to everything."

"We'll be ready. We'll have them sunk before they make it into the bay."

Sarbien and two of the Tuannan shuffled back low towards Captain Tyrnan and his soldiers.

Being careful to minimize noise, Sarbien whispered, "There's something happening down there. Looks like some kind of ceremony. I've seen this kind before."

"Can we see?" Tyrnan asked.

Sarbien whispered, "Just bear it in mind, once you see it, it cannot be unseen." Sarbien watched as the soldiers moved into position to see the actions below them. They did not watch for long. The soldiers stepped back to their positions and hunkered down, being careful their footfalls did not make noise. Even in the faint light that flooded up from the cavern below, Sarbien saw their faces were pale and drawn.

Captain Tyrnan glanced up at Sarbien with sorry eyes. "Some things cannot be unseen," he whispered.

Sarbien watched as one of the Tuannan turned away from the sickening sight of the ceremony in the cavern below.

"Let him be," Sarbien said to a Tuannan named Lughna, who had moved to help her friend. "Not all can take such a sight for long."

Sarbien looked back into the cavern from the shadows of the rocks above. The large space was lit by hundreds of candles placed on ledges and in cavities amongst the rough walls. In the centre stood a large altar, its blood-stained plinth and sides etched with deep-cut runes and primitive imagery depicting creatures of tooth and claw.

Surrounding the altar stood two dozen holy people, clothed in a mix of black and white rough-hewn habits. They acted under the commands of one ragged-looking individual standing at the altar. He leaned over a devastated body.

The ragged man gesticulated with wild movements and danced around the altar. His flesh was covered in black boils and hung off the bone in places. By his image, this man seemed undead.

Sarbien scratched notes into a small book.

"Something's happening," Lughna said, causing Sarbien to look up from his notes.

Forming a large circle around the altar, the ragged man grabbed one of the crowd and shoved him into the side of the altar. The holy man turned around and wailed as the ragged man walked towards him and slashed out his throat with a flick of his wrist. Gurgling, the holy man bled out at the foot of the altar. The ragged man turned around to face the others and spoke in a foreign tongue, one all too familiar to Sarbien.

"Those are the words of the Ravenmayne," he muttered to the Tuannan by his side. The voices from the cavern began to chant over and over and colour drained from Sarbien's face.

"Are you alright?" Lughna asked. "You look unwell."

"I'm fine, child. A little frightened, that's all."

"I'm frightened too," she said.

"There's no shame in fear, child." Sarbien smiled to reassure the young holy woman.

"What are they saying?" she asked.

"What they are practicing down below is the magic of the dead. Necromancy."

The runes around the altar took on a faint glow as the chanting grew louder and more resonant in the great cavern.

"You see that light," Sarbien whispered. "It's the same as that which radiated from the urns when they were brought back to Carte. This is the source."

"But what of the necromancy?" Lughna asked. "What place has the magic of the dead with the urns?"

Sarbien ignored the question and scribbled some more notes as he listened to the words of the ceremony. He stopped for a moment and looked down at the action on the cavern floor. The runes grew brighter and brighter before Sarbien returned to his report. The scratching of his pen soon halted and he looked back towards the ceremony.

"What is it?" Lughna asked.

"That name," Sarbien shuddered. "We've been looking towards Bhalur the whole time." He looked around at his party. "These prayers are not being offered to Bhalur. They are being offered to Balzath. An underling. A demigod of Bhalur's." *The Usurper.* Sarbien's hand shook, scratching marks into the parchment. "All this time, we thought we had Bhalur under control. We thought there was little energy in him or his kind. Only what we granted through the balancing ceremonies. If Balzath has been receiving worship of the Ravenmayne in Bhalur's absence all of this time, then we may very well be faced with a more powerful foe than we expected." His eyes turned from the Tuannan back to the cavern.

The holy man whose throat had been ripped out began to twitch, his feet first and then his fingers. The ragged man hunkered down in front of the corpse, lifting up a twitching arm and letting it flop to the ground. The ragged man stood and turned to face the others, laughing while raising his face towards the cavern ceiling with his eyes shut tight. The body shuddered and writhed on the bloody sand before flashing open a pair of milky white eyes.

Sarbien stared long at the cavern. "They mean to raise the dead with their necromancy. Those who have been touched by the plague will have spirits channelled into them. They will take the souls of the living, and Balzath will grow in power."

"What must we do?" Lughna asked.

Sarbien was silent, his mouth agape.

"What is it?" Lughna asked. "Sarbien?"

She shook his shoulder, but he stood transfixed. Tears broke from his eyes and rolled down his face.

Standing on the cavern floor was the ragged holy man, arms stretched wide and head tilted back. His eyes were wide open and amongst the rank and rotten flesh of his face shone two bright, ice-blue eyes.

Sarbien shook himself from his inner anguish and scratched down the rest of his report. He closed the book and handed it to Lughna. "I have to try and stop this. You take this and go with the captain. Deliver it to Carte with much haste. They must be warned."

"But I want to stay here with you. It's my service to Dajda," the young woman insisted.

"Go now. There is only going to be death here. You serve Dajda all the more with this task."

Lughna nodded and wiped a tear with the back of her hand.

Sarbien grabbed the arm of Captain Tyrnan and gripped it hard. "Take this silk and follow it to the surface. If it kills every single horse you have, get that message back to Carte.

The captain nodded and turned before leading Lughna up the stony path and into the black cave.

Sarbien turned and faced the abomination in the cavern below. The being who was once his son.

The air around Thaskil hummed and muffled voices sounded with a tinny resonance. Blurred sparks drifted in his vision. He stumbled and fell as a stabbing pain in his side betrayed some injury.

Hands gripped underneath his arms and hauled him to his feet before slamming him against a wall. With weak arms, he fumbled for his sword, half-expecting a rush of steel into his guts whilst his head cleared, but nothing came. Unable to hold, Thaskil's knees buckled and he slid against the wall until he was sitting on the cold ground.

Shadows silhouetted against a blazing background moved all around him while voices called out in panic and alarm. A dark form dropped down in front of him, reaching out and shaking his shoulder.

"Lieutenant," the metallic voice rang out. "Lieutenant, can you hear me?"

"Aye," Thaskil croaked, his throat dry and ragged. His foggy vision cleared and he saw the armoury had been completely consumed by flame and collapsed in on itself, taking with it a section of the city wall of nearly forty feet wide. The flames had begun to spread to neighbouring buildings. City guards and townspeople threw water as quickly as they could come by it.

"What happened here?" the guardsman asked.

Thaskil looked for the big militiaman he had clonked over the head and bound. He wasn't there.

"The prisoner," Thaskil blurted.

He scanned up and down the street. Between the throngs of people rushing back and forth with water buckets, he saw the militiaman hopping up the street and into the darkness.

"There!" Thaskil shouted, his sore throat ripping out the word. With some discomfort, he hauled himself to his feet and chased after the guardsman who had already taken off in pursuit of the prisoner.

Thaskil's side burned as he ran up the street; a broken rib, no doubt. The guardsman had caught up with the militiaman and had him kneeling on the ground, still bound and his head sticky with dark blood. Nevertheless, he appeared a foul and fearsome sort.

"Well, well, well." Thaskil tutted while grasping his side, "looks like we've caught ourselves a big fish tonight. So what shall we call you, big fish? You got a name?"

The militiaman snorted a great lump of bloody mucus and made to gob it at Thaskil. The guardsman's fist slammed into the prisoner's face as he curled his lips to spit, sending the stringy gobbet to the ground.

"Have some respect for the lieutenant," the guardsman growled.

"I know your officers," the man grunted. "Not much there to respect, if you ask me."

"Believe me, big fish, we'll get around to asking you plenty about how you feel of alliance officers." Thaskil stared hard at the militiaman as he spoke, "I overheard a little conversation you and your friends had before I interrupted."

The man's eyes narrowed. "Aye, you did well, lad. Sneaky like. But I tell you, all that guile and all that luck won't hold back what's coming for you. Nothing will. You're all dead." The man nodded to the stump at the end of his arm. The belt tied about it had staunched the bleeding. "This'll go black and fester. Blood's going to go bad. May as well run an edge to my throat, eh?"

"Not likely. You'll tell all before the pain that's coming to you stops, believe me."

"Oh I don't doubt there's pain coming: Grunnxe and all his hordes and monsters. You've gone and blown the wall, lad. That's the signal. Pain's already on its way."

Thaskil's focussed on the hole in the wall. His finger drummed a rapid beat on the cross-guard of his sword. His throat tightened with fear.

The man chuckled a dirty laugh. "Your finger's tapping time to the twitches of your arse, lad. Frightened?"

"Take him and lock him away. No one gets in to see him but me. Put a team of four on his cell. Understood?"

"Aye, Lieutenant. It's done," the guardsman replied. "Come on, you pig. On your feet."

Thaskil rushed atop the battlement and stared into the night. The full moon's cold light stretched over the Field of Storms where the winter poppies had been replaced by wheat, still clear to see as it swayed in the breeze. All around him, he saw nothing; no sign of an approaching army.

He glanced back at the fires as city guards and townsfolk battled them. He looked back out towards the Field of Storms. Rubble was strewn in front of the breach. There were large enough chunks to be hauled back into some form of defensive bulwark. *Still, what hope have we of holding onto the city when the wall is breached?*

He made his way down from the wall and approached a sergeant of the city guard. "It's Sergeant Omree, isn't it?"

The sergeant nodded, saluting Thaskil.

"I want you to get a platoon of troops out in front of that blasted section and dig a trench half a man deep. Dig it wider than the section of wall that's down and then get whatever wood that can be gathered and line the pit with it. Pour in as much naphtha as it takes to cover the wood. Make sure there's enough to burn for a good while. Get some heavy horse and teamsters, and get those larger pieces of masonry hauled back towards the line of the wall." Thaskil looked over the shoulder of the sergeant and beyond the gap in the wall. "Scatter a good few bits of rock between the wall and the trench. I don't want any advance to be easy."

"We have caltrops, sir," the sergeant said. "We can scatter them across the distance too?"

Thaskil grinned. "That's perfect. Put as many down as you can find. Now, once the boulders are hauled back, build them as high as you can, and create a pinch point. If anything's going to come at us tonight, they'll come at us here. Let's not make it easy for them. I want a kill-zone right where that wall used to stand," he said, pointing to the gap. "When they come at us, those that make it past the trench and the rough ground can't come more than a few at a time. We'll use their numbers against them."

"Aye, sir."

"One more thing. I want word sent to the battalion camped down by the old trenches. Have them told that they are to relocate to within the city, along with all horses and supplies. It must be done tonight. You can use as many as you need to finalise the defences here."

"I'll see it done, sir." The sergeant saluted and turned on his heel.

As Thaskil walked off, he heard the Sergeant Omree issuing commands with determined authority. "Now," Thaskil muttered under his breath, "let's see what this big fish has to say for himself." He stalked off holding his side and hauled himself into his saddle. *The trap is closing on you, Major.*

Grunnxe scratched at his beard and leered toward the faint light in the distance. He leaned back in his saddle and smiled as Apula's flames flickered.

"Looks a nice big hole, eh!" he roared, slapping the Priestess across the back. Her hooded head turned towards him, and Grunnxe shrunk back.

The Priestess's voice had a metallic coldness and a lethal emphasis on each word. "Old man, you do not get to touch me."

Grunnxe winced as each word struck with increasing tightness about his chest.

"You don't talk to the king like that!" one of the commanders shouted from the side.

"Shut your mouth," Grunnxe roared, all his fear finding a vent, "or I'll drive my sword through it!"

The commander shrunk away at the rebuke.

"All of you dogs listen!" Grunnxe's voice took on the usual steel, now that his fear had been bled away. He pointed toward the Priestess. "This is the voice of our god! Respect the voice! Respect it not and you will pay!" Grunnxe looked back at the Priestess and accepted a subtle nod. "Come aside with me a moment, if you will," Grunnxe whispered to the Priestess.

They rode a small way off into the darkness, stopping by heavy bushes of gorse, lit cold blue in the night.

"You're content that it's not too early?" Grunnxe asked the Priestess.

The faceless hood nodded. "I am content, King. The city will fall and fall fast. With your soldiers, and my servants, you will have superior numbers. Strike now."

"Your servants? You mean the Ravemayne?" Grunnxe asked, puzzled by the words of the Priestess.

"The Ravenmayne are my children, as are the servants—" The Priestess's head recoiled hard as a wave of light smashed against it. She swayed in the saddle for a moment before straightening, rubbing the smoking side of her hood. "My words are a lie. The Master's rebuke is quite correct. The Ravenmayne and the servants are the children of the Master God, Balzath. I, too, serve at his will."

Grunnxe's eyes flashed around, wild with fear. "What was that?" he half-mumbled.

The Priestess continued rubbing the side of her hood. "That was the Master God. I displeased him; forgetting my station."

Grunnxe swallowed hard and tried to stop fidgeting, keeping his attention focused on the Priestess.

"The Master God sends us his servant now. I hear them."

"I hear nothing," Grunnxe said, bemused.

"You sense little. The spirits of man are too weak. They come now," the Priestess hissed, her statement trailing off into nothingness.

Her words were followed by a wail that grew louder and screamed across the night wind like the hot breath of a desert fire. The noise rose to a deafening whine, a tearing screech. It caused man and Raven-mayne alike to place hands over ears to protect against the blood-chilling noise.

"Children of Balzath, I grant you form and flesh. I grant you claw and tooth." The Priestess stood up in her saddle, arms spread wide. "Come into this realm and feast on man. Bring their sweet souls back to our Master God and bring us dominion!" She muttered words, causing the Ravenmayne amongst the horde to make symbols over their faces.

The Priestess released a flash of light from her mouth and breathed life into the spirits wheeling and wailing all around. In an instant, clawing at the ground before the horde of Solansian warriors and Ravenmayne, stood a battalion of creatures, shimmering skinned, and bowlegged.

They stood taller than a man by two feet and had long arms knotted with muscle. Their shining black claws dug at the earth as they leered at the terrified army with ragged teeth. Saliva of sorts exuded from their mouths and fizzed as it touched the waxy blades of grass.

The soldiers gasped in horror, unsure whether to stay or to run. Grunnxe was transfixed. His focus only shifted when the Priestess spoke.

"The Master God, Balzath, means to take victory quickly and so he grants you his servants. Now, on to Apula and bring him souls!"

Chapter Thirty

"GIVE HIM ANOTHER ONE," Thaskil ordered. The militiaman's head snapped back and then rolled forward. He drooled a string of bloody spit from with burst lips. "Now then, you going to speak?" Thaskil asked.

"Fuck you."

No, fuck you, actually. "I can see this isn't going anywhere fast."

Thaskil shook his head and left the cell, closing the barred door with a metallic whine and crunch. He stood outside the cell collecting his thoughts when the sound of a struggle came from the entrance to the dungeon of the High Command.

Thaskil walked along the stone hallway, lit by lamps and the cold light that spilled in from the small barred windows of the cells. He stopped dead in his tracks, his mouth hanging open. Standing in front of him, bloodied and in chains, was Bergnon and another man.

Bergnon struggled and thrashed before being slammed against the wall by the escorting guardsmen. He looked at the guardsmen with rage in his eyes before straightening up, aggressive and ready. His bloodshot eyes flashed towards Thaskil. A look of sorrow fell over him and Bergnon sagged against the wall.

One of the guardsmen spoke, "We found the major dropping the body of one of our guards into the central well with this mercenary scum."

"Well, well, well." Thaskil walked towards his commanding officer, whom he thought both mentor and friend. His guts churned as he walked, the urge for vengeance flared through his body like a fire. *Not this time. No, this time you speak and you tell me everything.*

"Thaskil, I'm—"

Thaskil drove his fist into Bergnon's stomach, causing his breath to explode from his lungs and driving him to his knees.

"No, you don't speak. Let me tell you how this works. I take you and your friend here and I throw you in the cell with that other big bastard friend of yours. Then all three of you sing like a chorus."

Bergnon gasped for breath, his mouth gaping like a landed fish.

Thaskil hunkered next to Bergnon's ear. "But before anything, you tell me here and now what you did to Arrlun."

Bergnon's trembling head turned to Thaskil, but he was unable to hold his stare. "He's dead."

No! Thaskil's heart thundered and his fingertips tingled as the shock hit. He felt tears welling in his eyes, but he clenched his jaw tight and stood. Thaskil grabbed a fistful of Bergnon's hair as he went and dragged him scrambling to his feet.

"How did you do it?" Thaskil growled.

Bergnon's head leaned against the stone wall. He rolled it sideways and looked at Thaskil. "He wasn't meant to follow me. Wasn't meant to happen. I swear it."

"Your word isn't worth a shit to me. Did you do it?"

Bergnon swallowed hard and leant his head back against the wall. "May as well have done, but no, it wasn't my sword."

"Bastard. You killed him all the same."

Bergnon nodded, blinking free two tears that streaked down his dirty and bloodied face.

"And what of your ear? Was that him?"

"Aye. I was trying to comfort him and he bit me."

"Comfort him!" Thaskil barked an ironic laugh. "How very compassionate of you. Where's his body?"

"He's gone," Bergnon sighed. "It was taken off beyond the Field of Storms."

"Well, you'll be lucky if I even grant you that courtesy by the time I'm done with you." Thaskil grabbed a handful of Bergnon's shirt and hauled him forward, almost tripping him as his ankle chains restricted his movement. "Time for you lads to start spilling words."

The guardsmen grabbed the other prisoner and followed Thaskil as he led Bergnon towards the cell that held the big militiaman. As they entered the cell, the prisoner within smiled a bloody smile.

"Hello, Major. Eck. Fancy seeing you here."

"Brostoff," Eck muttered, "not worked out too well for us, what?"

"Guess not, but I reckon it may work out a bit worse for our sorry major friend." Brostoff leered at Bergnon before looking at Thaskil. "Well then, what'll you give us to talk, eh?"

Bergnon glared at Brostoff.

"What do you want?" Thaskil asked, feeling the power shift to him. *Looking nervous, Major.*

"Turn me and Eck here free." Brostoff slithered a fat tongue over his rotten teeth. "We'll be off and away before you know it. No harm, no foul. Save for you taking my hand, that is."

Thaskil made a show of considering it for a moment. *Set you lose? Why unleash a rabid dog only for him to turn around and bite the hand that unbound him?* "Done. Speak and you'll go free this night. I may even have a surgeon look at your wound and make it right. But then you'll leave the Free Provinces and never come back. Never. Do you hear me?"

"Aye, I hear you, laddie." Brostoff grinned while casting a glance at Bergnon.

"Shut your mouth!" Bergnon shouted. "Don't listen. He'll only tell you lies!"

Thaskil slammed a knee into Bergnon's guts, sending him gagging to the straw-lined floor of the cell.

"No, it is you, Major, that must shut your mouth. Brostoff, that's your name?"

The big man nodded.

"Carry on, please."

"Your man there, the major, you see, he has a Missus Major. A nice little piece of arse from across the Yellow Sea in Canna."

Thaskil looked at Bergnon, who kneeled on the floor with his forehead leant on the ground, breathing hard. *The look of a broken man. No more than you deserve.*

"You see," Brostoff continued, "Missus Major is no less than the Daughter of the People."

Thaskil's eyes widened and the guardsmen nearby gasped. All eyes turned to Bergnon, who peered up from the cell floor.

Brostoff continued, "Word is they married each other in secret. Didn't want anyone to know, but old Grunnxe has his spies and tattle-tales. Someone squealed and the old man had his way in. You threaten any man in such a way his prick's concerned and you have what some call leverage. Seems the major sold out his people to keep his little slice of arse safe and well. He gave us everything: your commanders, officers, where they slept, what they ate for supper, and how often they shit. He gave us Apula and even killed himself some of his own men in the wake of his rotten betrayal." Brostoff hawked up a gob of spit and spat it down at Bergnon's head. "The traitor gave the old man every-thing. Grunnxe is coming. He's coming tonight and, when he takes Apula, he's coming for Carte. He wants the whole of the Cullanain and the major here has given it to him, steaming right and rich on a golden platter."

Thaskil's face betrayed no emotion as Brostoff reeled off Bergnon's crimes. "Fetch me a dozen carrier pigeons. Carte must know what's coming."

"At once, sir." One of the guardsmen saluted and ran off.

Brostoff flapped his meaty tongue over his blackened teeth, leering a foul smile at Thaskil. "Well, young sir, we kept our end of the bargain. Gonna set us free now, eh?"

Thaskil turned his back and walked out of the cell.

"Hey, you said you would—"

Thaskil ignored the protests and called back as he walked off, "Guards, kill those two." He disappeared off around the corner. *No one keeps their word in this world. What good is mine to a pair of murderers?*

"Wait," Brostoff and Eck cried. "You promis—"

―――――――

The ragged being that had once been Sarbien's son, Anthony, danced and twirled an insane jig as the holy men and woman around the altar chanted their sonorous prayer. The runes glowed brighter as their prayer went on.

"How long will we watch this? The others left hours ago and all they are doing is praying," one of the remaining Tuannan asked Sarbien.

He turned from the spectacle, his eyes rimmed red. "The moment is not right," Sarbien said, his voice thick with emotion as he thought of his son. "Would you have us run down and fight their magic with nothing? We have no energy, remember. Dajda sleeps."

"We have some bows and three soldiers. I can shoot. You can shoot. We can do something. You said as you sent Lughna away that we must stop them. Have you changed your mind?"

"Child, there are too many."

"What about the one leading them? The monster down there, we can kill him—"

Sarbien swivelled and grabbed the Tuannan's habit. His angry whisper sent spit onto the other man's face, "No one kills him, do you hear me? He's not to be touched by anyone. Anyone except me." Sarbien relaxed his grip, the anger melting away from his face. "I'm sorry, lad. It's just that, well, look at the creature's eyes below."

The Tuannan peered over the rocks and waited until the creature stopped twirling and dancing before getting a good look.

"You see his eyes?" Sarbien asked.

The Tuannan nodded and turned back to Sarbien. "I think I understand."

"Aye, I'd say you do. There are few others I know of with eyes that colour, save my own seed. He went missing the night that Capriath was killed down by the urns. I dare say my son was his uncle's killer."

"He is your son no longer."

The chanting ceased and the cavern was plunged into an eerie silence. Even the shallow breathing of those remaining near the roof risked betraying their presence. Sarbien and the Tuannan, along with three other soldiers, peered over the edge of the rocks and saw the altar's runes glow white with heat.

The creature that was once Brother Anthony stood atop of the altar and muttered silent words before tossing his head back and roaring in the guttural tongue of the Ravenmayne. Without warning, the runes blasted a beam of light in one direction.

Sarbien's head sank down and he whispered from his chest, "I fear that energy is directed to Carte."

"But that would mean—"

"Yes," Sarbien said, "death will haunt the streets of Carte. I'll go down. Perhaps there is still a shred of my son left within him. If I fall, shoot him, and as many of the others as you can. The fewer that chant, the harder it will be to sustain the urns from this distance. If we can stop the power of the urns, perhaps what horror unfolds in Carte can be halted. Get ready."

Sarbien stood, his joints stiff from so long in the cold, damp cave. He wound his way down to the floor, being careful to obscure himself behind rocks as he went.

He stopped behind the final edge of rock, breathing deep, his heart racing. Footsteps of soldiers following sounded from behind. He turned and offered them a weak smile, anything to give them strength. It pained Sarbien, yet it gave him heart to see such duty despite fear etched across their faces.

"If I fall, take as many as you can."

The three soldiers nodded, chests rising up and down from nervous breaths, eyes wide.

"In Dajda's name." Sarbien said, and walked out into the open.

The creature that had once been Brother Anthony, Sarbien's own flesh and blood, turned from atop the glowing altar. His bright, ice-blue eyes stared straight at the approaching man.

"My son, come back to me!" Sarbien implored as Anthony grinned. "It is I, your father. Come back into my embrace, child."

The creature tilted its head sideways like an inquisitive beast.

"Come away from the darkness, my son, my Anthony. Come away from the darkness and back to almighty Dajda's love." Sarbien kept moving towards the altar, tears welling in his eyes at the sight of his son covered in blackened boils. Sarbien was almost overwhelmed by the stench of rot as skin blistered and fell from Anthony's oozing body.

The creature righted its head and bore his teeth. "Dajda has no love for me!" shouted the creature, leaping down from the altar. "I am a child of the Master God. Balzath is his name and in his name I hold more power than Dajda could ever grant."

"Then forget Dajda. I am your father, Anthony. Come back into my embrace." Sarbien stood with his arms open.

The creature swayed where he stood and muttered silent words, as though in secret dialogue with someone or something. "Yes," the creature grunted and stepped into Sarbien's embrace.

"My son," Sarbien said, holding back his desire to vomit. "Come back to me now."

"Yes, Master, it will be done," the creature muttered as he squeezed Sarbien hard, raising him off his feet, crushing the life from him.

Arrow's screamed free from bows. Fighting men roared as the creature that was once Anthony squeezed harder.

Sarbien felt blinding pain as his body shattered.

Snap, snap, snap.

Chapter Thirty-One

BRODEN HAD BEEN on edge the whole night and next morning since learning of Bergnon's treachery. The thought of Bergnon betraying his own people, causing the deaths of so many, and plotting the murder of friends cut the big man deep. The sight of the Daughter of the People falling into the blackness compounded his mood.

The atmosphere below deck, where he sat alone with Kalfinar, was dark and heavy. Few words had been spoken since the fervent discussion of the night before, such was the shock and weight of the betrayal. If their fears were correct, Apula would be handed to Grunnxe and with it, the east of the Free Provinces.

"I don't know about you," Broden said quietly, breaking the tense silence, "but I keep hearing you read those words of that account from the Teporan Mane fella. Seems a lot of this is making sense to me now." He looked up at Kalfinar, who was rubbing at his wounded shoulder.

Kalfinar's forehead was beaded with sweat and his eyes had dark circles under them. He sat staring into nothingness, a glazed look across his face.

"Kal?" Broden asked, reaching out and shaking him by the shoulder to stir him from his thoughts. *Come on man, snap out of it.*

"What?" Kalfinar jolted, his eyes snapping back into focus.

"Kal, you look awful. You need to get some rest."

"Nonsense, we'll be in Carte soon. There's no time for rest."

Broden looked at Kalfinar's hands and noted his fingers were pale and cold. Tremors ran from the tips of his fingers and up his arms.

I've seen you like this before, cousin. I remember the look of you as you started the slide. I'll not let you go back, not this time. There'll be no docks for you. Broden stood up, grabbed Kalfinar by the front of his long-coat, and hauled him to his feet. He was shocked by Kalfinar's lack of resistance as he stood, although he avoided Broden's gaze.

"What has got into you, man?" Broden shouted.

Kalfinar said nothing.

"Listen to me, we need you to get your head right! We need you to stop dwelling on what happened back in Canna. Forget the fucking jalsinum. It didn't matter in the end and it had nothing to do with Chentuck, Rondo, or the Daughter of the People. Damn you, Kal! Neither of us could have stopped any of this happening. You'd better stop thinking about the smoke, stop thinking you're to blame, and stop pissing well wallowing in self fucking pity!"

Kalfinar looked up at him. "I'm ashamed to admit—"

Broden slapped Kalfinar backhanded across the face, causing him to stumble backwards and plop onto the seat with a thump. Kalfinar's eyes watered and he looked up with a shocked expression.

"Sorry, Kal," Broden mumbled. "Felt the message had to sink in."

Kalfinar rubbed the reddening side of his face and smiled as a short chuckle resonated from his throat. "Sometimes I forget how big your bloody hands are."

"Aye," he replied. "They're good for knocking sense into people."

"I was going to say I'm ashamed to admit I wasn't thinking about Chentuck or the Daughter of the People. I was thinking of Evelyne."

"Oh?"

"We kissed."

"You did what?" The big man clapped his hands together and laughed. "Best bloody news I've heard in weeks."

A coy smile ran across Kalfinar's lips.

"I was wondering how long it would take you to realise what was staring in your face."

"You knew."

Broden nodded.

"It didn't feel wrong." Kalfinar's smile waned, replaced with the beginnings of that forlorn look Broden was so familiar with.

"Don't go there, Kal, or I'll give you another." He raised the back of his broad hand in mock threat.

"You got it," Kalfinar said, rising from his chair and sidestepping the big man.

"It's a good thing, Kal. Nurture it. Don't push it away. Especially not in times like these."

Kalfinar nodded and made for the door of the cabin. "Come on, let's see how close we are to Carte."

"Ah," Broden grumbled. "You know I'm not going up there." He rubbed the back of his neck and smiled with a little embarrassment. "You know me and ships."

"We've dropped anchor." Kalfinar said as he entered the cabin below deck. He heard footsteps charging down the stairs.

"You have to see this," a crewman shouted.

"What is it?" Kalfinar asked.

"Warships in the bay," the Cannan man replied. "Looks like they're expecting visitors."

"Aye, unfriendly ones, I'll wager," grumbled Broden as he stood and stretched his arms wide, popping his shoulders.

"Shit!" Kalfinar held his hands to his head as he swore. "The ship, it's not of alliance design and we've no flag to fly. Could be trouble."

"Nights be damned!" Broden exclaimed. "We better hope the harbourmaster can get to us in time."

"Gentlemen," the crewman interrupted, "excuse me, but the ship, it is the Father of the People's. There will be flags of the royal seal we can fly. They ought to be in the captain's cabin."

"Can you see if there is one and hoist it?" Kalfinar asked.

The crewman nodded and left the cabin.

"We'd better take a look," Kalfinar said as he started out of the cabin.

"S'ppose I better get it over with," Broden muttered. He followed Kalfinar up the stairs to the deck. The sun hung low and hazy in the sky, casting a cold yellow light. Their breath plumed in the chill air.

"That's the Terna fleet as well," Kalfinar said as he leant onto the rail. "Abbonan must be here."

Three dozen ships sat in the bay, a floating army barring the way into Carte. A small sailboat cut free of the armada and made its way towards them, where they sat bobbing on the tide.

"I have it!" the crewman shouted from across the deck. "I have the seal."

"Quick, get it hoisted," Kalfinar called back as Evelyne approached from the aftercastle.

"Trouble?" she asked.

"I doubt it's too bad," Kalfinar replied.

Broden turned and greeted Evelyne with a broad smile.

"Cut it out," Kalfinar hissed at him.

Evelyne eyed Broden with suspicion as she stepped up towards the rail. "The Terna fleet is here."

"Aye." Kalfinar felt soft skin on his fingers. He looked down to see Evelyne's touch. Kalfinar looked up at her subtle smile.

The crewman rushed over. "Seal's up. That should get their attention."

"Thank you." He looked at Evelyne. "We need to get word to the High Command and get you searching for the third Horn. Do you sense it is near?"

"It is in the city, yes."

"Good." Kalfinar turned and walked off towards the starboard of the ship where the small sailing vessel had pulled up. He cleared the way of Cannan sailors and leaned over the rail, seeing a harbourmaster surrounded by city guard. "Ahoy," Kalfinar called, causing the harbourmaster to startle and look up.

"Ahoy there," the master called back. "I'll be with you in a moment. First of all, name and purpose?"

"Certainly. I'm Captain Kalfinar of the Free Provinces High Command. We are bringing urgent word to my father, Governor Harruld, Chief in Command. My reports are of utmost importance to the defence of the Free Provinces and must not be delayed further. Shall I continue?"

The city guard aboard the small ship whispered and stared up at Kalfinar, who was easily recognised by them. Some of the men smiled and nodded towards him, whilst a few others wore scowls and whispered amongst each other.

The harbourmaster had one foot and his hands on the rope ladder and stopped. Recognition was etched across his face and he looked somewhat embarrassed. "Well, actually, I suppose that will just about do it, Captain. But forgive me, I need to inspect the ship. Standard protocol in times like this."

"I understand."

"We won't be long. Once were done, just follow us into the port."

"My thanks. I'm indebted to you."

They descended from the gangplank. It seemed chaotic by the docks, more so than usual. Kalfinar's eyes scanned the surrounding masses of people, charging back and forth. City guardsmen were everywhere. He spied the streets and alleys of the docks beyond the throngs, and felt the familiar twist in his guts and tightening of his chest. His fingers began to tremble and sweat formed on his brow, in spite of the chill air. *Smoke and blood, whores and mud. Here you are, laddie. Back to the docks. Back where you always find yourself.*

"Kal," Broden's voice half-shook him from his thoughts. "Kal!" Broden stepped up and shook Kalfinar by the shoulder. He leaned in close and whispered through his teeth, "Get your head straight. Now is not the time to lose yourself. We need you, damn it."

"Aye," Kalfinar replied, wiping his brow with the back of his hand and swallowing hard. His throat was dry. "Sorry. Let's get moving."

The streets were busy, although not with trade or the general hum of city life. The military presence was strong. Armed men and no few women were almost everywhere. Kalfinar recognised the streets by the docks as they passed through on their way to the High Command, but they were different. There was none of the colourful music of the city; no beggars, drunks, or whores. Trouble was in the air. The city reeked with tension.

Kalfinar dropped back to where Evelyne rode. Her face was fixed without emotion.

"Do you feel it is closer?" he asked, his eyes darting all around, watching the feverish activity.

"We're getting closer. We need to be deeper into the city. I'll feel more as we go."

"When we get to the command, we'll get our reports in and leave straight away."

She nodded.

As Kalfinar rode back towards Broden at the front of the group, he glimpsed down a side street and gasped.

"The bodies?" Broden asked.

"Aye, the bodies."

"The sickness, it must have made it out of the High Command."

"To what extent, I wonder?" Kalfinar looked back at the building and cursed to himself. "It's the bloody undertakers." He shook his head in frustration. "There's no sense in that at all. They can't bury corpses in times of disease. Should burn them."

Broden looked across at his cousin's sudden harshness.

Kalfinar stared at the building before scoffing and turning back. He rubbed his eyes as they rode on. Kalfinar's head pounded and he was sweating. *You want it. Back to the smoke. Slip away. Go on and slip away.*

"Kal," Broden whispered, "you alright?"

Kalfinar looked up. "You know, I think I might just need another slap."

As they approached the drawbridge at the front of the military High Command, a dozen troops ran urgently across their path, causing Kalfinar and his party to turn in their saddles.

"Wonder what's going on," Broden said.

"Who knows?" Kalfinar said with a tired voice. "Some madness or another. Come on, we've little time to linger."

They crossed the drawbridge and entered the High Command without trouble. Kalfinar and Broden ascended into the main building to report to Governor Harruld. Evelyne followed along with the Horn of Dajda, the two girls walking hand in hand as they went.

They opened the door to Harruld's study and saw him gathered with Olmat, Subath, Abbonan and Merkham. Another familiar face sat towards the far end of the table. Lucius peered up at Kalfinar from between two blackened eyes. Maps and papers were spread out wide around them, making the table was no less chaotic than the streets of Carte they had just ridden through.

"Kal, thank Dajda." Harruld rose from his seat and walked around the table to embrace him. "I'm so very glad to see you. To see you all."

He smiled to them each, stopping at the two strange girls. "You are most welcome."

The Horn of Dajda smiled back, their eyes glittering. Harruld paused a moment, captivated by them.

"Father," Kalfinar said, drawing Harruld's attention. "We learned from the Cannan Daughter of the People that Major Bergnon is the one who betrayed us."

Harruld sighed wearily. "I know. We received word from Thaskil in Apula yesterday," the governor said. "Bergnon has been taken prisoner."

Kalfinar nodded.

"And the Daughter of the People? Where is she?" Harruld asked.

"I'm sorry," Evelyne said, "but she threw herself into the Yellow Sea after she confessed to us. There's nothing anyone could have done."

"Damn it." Harruld stalked back to his chair and slumped into it. "Cannan's aren't going to like that. The theocrats in their Council will want to press us for her loss."

"We'll have to deal with their reaction another time. There's more," Kalfinar added. "Solansia has raided Canna and destroyed the grain shipments and the Cannan merchant fleet. They killed the Mother of the People."

"Hells be damned. Is there no end to the bad news?"

"Is Apula safe?" Broden asked Harruld.

The governor looked back towards the men gathered around the table. He sighed. "It seems Grunnxe will seek to take Apula. Thaskil's requested reinforcements."

"Are you sending them?" Kalfinar asked.

"We'll send what we can, but we have to be mindful of an assault on Carte also."

"Thaskil and Arrlun aren't equipped to lead the battalions alone. They need help," Broden said.

"Arrlun is dead. It seems he had suspicions of Bergnon's betrayal, so he murdered him."

Kalfinar balled his fists and his jaw flexed in silent rage.

"I'm going to kill him," Broden growled.

"There's a long queue for that job," Subath rasped.

Olmat spoke from the end of the table, his voice sounding thin and weak, "Let this anger pass on for now. We must speak of the Horn. You have two, but you now seek the third, the Key."

"Yes, we found two, Uncle," Evelyne spoke. "There's still one more."

"You feel it close, don't you?" Olmat asked.

"Yes, it's very close." Evelyne smiled. "I feel it is only but a short time before the Horn's voice is set free and the Key is found."

Kalfinar looked between the two of them, perplexed by their unusual exchange. "Sorry, forgive me if I've missed something here, but what are you talking about?"

"Olmat." Evelyne nodded at the old physician. "He holds the Key, the chief voice of the choir."

The old man smiled, his head wobbling on his weak neck.

Kalfinar glanced back and forth between them.

"The urge is strong, but I can feel it telling me we must wait on you, Uncle."

"I will not be long, child. My body is weakening. Soon the Horn will sound and they will come."

Chapter Thirty-Two

"HOW'RE THE PREPARATIONS GOING?" Thaskil asked the sergeant he had instructed to enhance the defences of the weakened city wall.

Sergeant Omree wiped his hands clean with a rag, or as clean as they could be.

Thaskil still smelled the thick aroma of smouldering wood. The din in the night air paid testament to the hard work of the city guard and citizens of Apula, intent on keeping their home safe in the face of the coming conflict. Despite the tension, the industry and toil appeared to have bred togetherness. It was visible as they worked, establishing the bulwark of rubble in the breach.

Omree had stripped off his tabard and chainmail. Sweat pooled under his throat and armpits, despite the chill of the night. The sergeant heaved a deep breath and raised his grimy arm in salute.

"Going well, sir," Omree responded, turning and pointing towards the dark beyond the breach. "The heavy horses have hauled most of the large stones back to the breach and we're almost done shifting the rubble into the plain between here and the trench. Once we're done there, the wood and naphtha will go in."

"Good. You're making good time."

"Fear is the finest of motivators. We'll get the caltrops laid once the trench has been filled." The sergeant leaned in closer to Thaskil. "Just one thing, sir."

Thaskil noted the man stank, no doubt the legacy of his hard work over the last few hours. He was sure he smelt no better himself. "Go on." Thaskil mirrored the sergeant's actions.

"It's the trench. We don't have the men, nor the time to create anything too wide or deep." He wrung his hands. "It's really not going to be any more than a shallow trench, but I think if we fill it up, it'll burn long and high. All being well, if we get the chance, we can always improve it later."

Thaskil smiled at the sergeant and clapped him across the shoulder. "The trench will be fine. As long as we can slow them down and, you know, prevent a full-on assault, we should be in a stronger position to hold out."

"Aye, well I think we could be." The sergeant rubbed the back of his sweat and soot-streaked neck. "I was thinking as well, sir, if I may?"

"Speak freely," Thaskil prompted.

"Well, I was thinking, why don't we embed stakes into the outer edge of the rubble bulwark? We could make it as unwelcome an experience coming up as possible."

Thaskil pictured it.

"If we fill it full of stakes, we could slow them down further," Omree continued. "We can get the wood turners working on them right away."

"Bloody good idea, Sergeant. Get to it."

"Aye, sir," the sergeant replied with a salute before running over to a subordinate, relaying his orders.

Thaskil stood and watched as the denizens of his home city busied themselves supporting the defences against an army of unknown size and, from what Thaskil had seen, unknown powers. Their commitment and endeavour in the face of danger moved him. He thought of Arrlun, killed by a friend. He thought of Bergnon's betrayal and felt anger flare in his gut. Last, he thought of his home, its people, and its place at the frontier of the Free Provinces. If their sovereignty were to survive at all, Apula must stand.

Thaskil looked around and saw only citizens and soldiers; not an officer amongst them. If Apula were to stand, it would have to stand with Thaskil at the helm.

The Field of Storms stretched out in front of the Solansian horde. The order had gone out to narrow the ranks. The less wheat trampled underfoot, the better, for the army would need to be fed over the winter.

Grunnxe smiled as he watched grain swaying in the cold night breeze. He had gambled on the Apulan people bowing to the greater needs of Free Province and sowing crop amongst the fertile lands. *When I take this city, I will change their coat of arms from a poppy to the grain head, in honour of my victory.*

The awful grunting of the beasts of Balzath pulled Grunnxe from his thoughts.

The creatures stalked at the front of the army, causing the Solansians and Ravenmaynes to watch with unease. Their limbs and backs appeared hard, like scaled reptiles, and their colours shimmered and changed in the moonlight.

Grunnxe grinned as they progressed. An army of Solansia, enhanced by the creatures of their new master god. What fortune he had. The city was in sight, crippled and with a knife to its back. It would not take long to force the city on to its knees, so why wait? Why hold on in Apula for the rest of the winter months before taking Carte? It would be best to make for Carte with haste and crush the Free Provinces at its beating heart. Then Grunnxe could finally take his place back as the king of all the Cullanain. He smiled to himself.

"Something pleases thee?"

Grunnxe snapped his attention around towards the monotone Priestess beside him. A shiver crept down his back when he looked into the shadow of the hood. He hesitated a moment, but then felt a rush of blood; an injection of courage. "I was just thinking that perhaps we would be wise to move on the Carte once Apula looks to be in our hands. There is nothing to gain by allowing Carte time to prepare and recover from all the damage wrought on the Free Provinces. The Master God wants dominion. Well, this way he can have it all. We can take them all and Solansia can have its rightful place in the world again."

The Priestess laughed, an empty tinny noise.

Grunnxe felt anger flush from his belly and up his throat. "What?"

"And you shall be king of all." The Priestess laughed again before falling silent.

Grunnxe fidgeted and looked about during the prolonged silence.

"Your thirst for blood pleases the Master. He told me himself."

"Huh," Grunnxe mused. He was still not convinced about this silent link the Priestess had with the Master God.

"But I think you greedy and feel you foolish to rush—" The Priestess was hit again with a flash to the head.

Grunnxe looked in shock and his hands began to tremble.

The Priestess raised her head and spoke, her voice weaker and contrite, "I forget my place and spoke out of turn. The Master has told me we must set the city of Apula to the sword. If victory is within our sights, then the Master will see that an army is placed before Carte, but we must guarantee the destruction of Carte, and the death of every Tuannan, and all that remains of the High Command."

Grunnxe smiled. The Priestess in conflict with the Master God; it could only be good for him. King of all and chief next to the Master God, Balzath.

An intense heat spread from Grunnxe's feet, rising up his legs and around his middle. The heat spread down his fingers and up his arms before swamping up over his neck and into his head. The sensation intoxicated him and he felt comfort. Then came a vicious flash and intense, hateful flames. Something snapped and clawed in his mind. There was fury and pain. So much pain. More than he could endure. And then light.

A low voice growled in Grunnxe's head, at first striking terror into his heart, but then he felt ease. *"My child, hear thy Father's voice."*

I hear you, Father.

"Thou art to sit at my side, foremost amongst my children. Carte must fall. See this done and Bhalur shall be in thrall to thee."

Grunnxe realised it was the once-god Bhalur, deposed, weakened, and now forced to serve one whom was once his subordinate. Grunnxe thought of being free of the yoke of the Priestess and serving Balzath by destroying Carte. He smiled.

It will be an honour, believe me.

Thaskil leaned against the cold stone of the dungeon corridor, peering into the darkness of Bergnon's cell. From the flickering orange glow of the few lamps along the wall, he could just make out the form of Bergnon, knees pulled up to his chest with head and arms resting motionless. Thaskil looked at the piece of parchment in his hand, deliberating whether Bergnon deserved to be told the news of his wife. His stomach reeled with anger, fear, anxiety; it didn't matter.

"I can hear you breathing," Bergnon croaked without moving his head.

Thaskil approached the bars of the cell, dropping himself into a chair with a sigh.

"How're the defences looking?" Bergnon asked, raising his head to reveal angry purple bruises along one side of his face. His nose had been broken.

Thaskil snorted and looked away, shaking his head in disgust. "How're they looking?" he shouted. "You blew a fucking hole in them. The walls had never been breached before and you blew a fucking hole in them!"

"Forgive me, but it wasn't me who set the fire that caused the explosion."

Thaskil's face twisted in hate. *You may as well have, just as you may as well have killed Arrlun, and every man, every woman, and every child that will die, be widowed, or orphaned as a result of what has been done and what is still to come.*

"I'm sorry." Bergnon shook his head and settled it back against his knees.

"Sorry for what." Thaskil leaned forward, his face almost pressing on the bars, "Sorry for selling us out? Sorry for Arrlun? Sorry for the quick tongue that will soon be sticking fat out of your head?"

Bergnon looked up, his bloated face drawing not a hint of sympathy from Thaskil. "I'm sorry for everything, lad. Whether you believe it or not, I would give it all back. I would sacrifice myself, if only she were safe. I'm sorry for it all." He buried his head into his knees and sobbed.

Thaskil looked at the parchment in his hand and back at Bergnon.

The beaten major raised his head again. A long, thin string of snot stretched from his arm to his nose before breaking. "You would be doing me a kindness, lad, if you were to kill me now. This world is just full of blackness and, without her, there will never be light again." Bergnon stood. The coldness of the dungeon and his beatings caused him to stiffen. He walked towards the bars, close enough for Thaskil to smell the stale stink of blood and sweat, and stood half a sword's length from Thaskil.

All I need to do is drive my hilt home and you're done. The urge to run the traitor through was strong, but Thaskil resisted. There would no doubt be enough blood to come and he wasn't quite sure if he wanted Bergnon's on his hands, despite it all.

They stared for a long moment, holding each other's gaze, unflinching.

That man despairs. Thaskil stood and placed his hand on the pommel of his sword.

Bergnon pressed his chest against the bars, his eyes widening, despite the swelling.

"I'm not going to kill you today." Thaskil handed the piece of parchment to Bergnon. "Here, you may want to read this. Came from Carte by pigeon tonight."

Thaskil pulled back the chair and headed into the flickering amber light of the corridor. *Those words will hurt him more than anything I can do to him. Death would be a mercy he doesn't deserve.*

Bergnon unrolled the small piece of parchment and strained his eyes in the flickering light as Thaskil's footsteps echoed down the corridor.

He read the tight script and looked up, holding the parchment in trembling fingers and tears brimming in his eyes.

"Thaskil, come back!" he shouted. His voice shook with emotion and wild sorrow contorted his face. "Thaskil, come back. She's gone. I have nothing. Nothing more. Let me help. I can help you. I can stop this. Please!"

There was nothing save for his own heaving panting. He looked back at the words with tear-filled eyes and sunk to his knees, laughing and weeping, edging towards madness and hell.

"Are we ready?" Thaskil asked, looking from the battlement over the makeshift defences by the breached section of Apula's wall.

"Aye, sir," Sergeant Omree replied, exhausted from relentless activity preparing their defences. "With the right type of man on the walls, hard men, and no few good bows up here, we could hold out a while."

"Good." Thaskil smiled, clapping Omree on his shoulder. "Go and get some rest. You've worked hard."

"Thank you, sir, but if it's alright with you, I'll just as soon as stay here with you. There's a fight coming and I mean to be here when it arrives."

Thaskil smiled and looked behind the man to the massed troops, city guard, militia, bakers, stonemasons, husbands, and wives. They looked back, some with fear in their eyes and others with pride. Stubborn resistance flared in his guts.

"Men and women of Apula," he cried out, his voice carrying far over the crowds, "free people of the Free Provinces, we are threatened with the dawn of a dark day. We are threatened by one who would seek to change our way of life, to steal away our freedom, and put us all back into the yoke of slavery. What were we, the people of Apula, in the days before the Solansian grip was broken? What where we?" he challenged those below to answer, his eyes imploring.

They were silent, but their eyes cried with pride.

A lone voice cried from distance and echoed against the walls, "Our ancestors bled in the mines, they toiled in their fields, and they died for the Solansian's salt!"

Thaskil looked towards the High Command keep. The voice came from the basement. From the dungeon.

"Aye," an old citizen picked up the rally cry, "we were slaves for them and they want to put us back in bondage."

The crowd began to shout and cheer. Thaskil felt his guts untwist, straighten out and strengthen, like the crowd's resolve.

He raised his voice as he spoke, "Aye, Grunnxe wants to make us all slaves again and take back the old lands, but we will not yield! The city walls have been breached, but they're but made of stone and mortar. We, the people, together, are stronger than any stone."

The people cheered.

"Together, we are stronger than any steel," Thaskil continued.

They punched the air and waved what weapons or tools they held.

"We are stronger than any invader. Stand with me and let us fight for Apula, for the Free Provinces, and for freedom!"

The cheer rang up loud, causing the skin on Thaskil's body to tingle and twitch, his hair stood as goose-pimples raised. *Aye, we can hold out a while. A short while.*

"Good timing, Lieutenant." Omree nudged his side, causing Thaskil to turn around. "Look!"

The sergeant pointed across the Field of Storms. In the shimmer of the distance stretched a long black shadow.

Thaskil stared long and hard at the dark mass, as it shifted and spread. "That can only be an army," he whispered to Sergeant Omree.

"Aye," the sergeant replied, "and a fucking big one at that."

"Aye," Thaskil replied, his guts twisted.

Chapter Thirty-Three

KALFINAR'S FOOTSTEPS echoed up the hallway of the High Command into the wing where he had shared an apartment with his wife. He stopped and turned back, shaking his head. *Don't go back. There's nothing there but pain.*

Despite his fear, he turned and stalked back in the direction he had been walking. He stopped in front of an ordinary wooden door. Their door.

Kalfinar placed his hand on the wrought-iron handle, cold and familiar in his hand, and depressed it. *I'm coming home, my love.* As the door opened, something told him to stop.

There was someone inside.

He listened and heard someone weeping. *This is my place!* Anger flared and he stormed in. *Who would dare—*

Evelyne sat hunched on the floor, behind the heavy oak table set against the wall, the only furniture in the room. She wept into arms crossed over her knees. Her long brown hair fell in waves, hiding her sorrow.

"Evelyne, what're you doing in here?" Kalfinar asked, hunkering down in front of her, placing a hand on her shoulder.

She lifted her head. Her cheeks were shiny wet from crying. She wiped her eyes of tears. "My father's dead."

"You don't know that."

"I feel it. He's gone."

Kalfinar's eyes dropped to the floor and he clenched his jaw. "I'm sorry." He just about managed to fumble out the words.

"I didn't know where else to go," she said, her voice but a whisper. "I heard you here one night."

Kalfinar looked up at her.

"It seemed like the right place to come. I can tell this place has seen many tears."

Kalfinar looked at her red-rimmed eyes, so full of hurt. "Aye." His voice was soft, gentler than he had managed for a long time. "This is a fine place for the crying." He smiled and squeezed her shoulder. "But it was a fine room for laughter, too."

"There's been no sign of Anthony." She blinked free two more tears that fell onto her sleeves. "No one's seen or heard from him since before the urns were opened. He's in terrible darkness. I can sense it." She buried her head into her arms as a wave of sorrow washed over her again.

Her hurt stung Kalfinar and he found he forgot his own pain. He placed his arms under her shoulders and stood up, pulling her to her feet, and held her tight in an embrace.

Evelyne lifted her head from his chest, eyes pleading.

He looked at her face, but he could not lie to her.

"Kal." Evelyne placed a hand on his cheek.

It was warm and welcome. *But this is wrong. Not here.* Kalfinar broke away from their embrace, taking two steps backwards. "I can't."

She wiped away the bead of a tear on her cheek. She stepped towards him, an earnest look on her face. Kalfinar's heart quickened as she closed the space between them. With head bowed, she tangled the fingers of her right hand about his. Her left hand cupped the small of his back.

What little pressure she applied seemed to carry the force of a storm, crashing open some door within him he had long since thought locked. He met her lips in a tempest of hot breath. Their hands fumbled together, a collision of awkward travellers. Hers to his face; his to her back.

The hot urgency of their kiss grew and a small moan sounded. Hers, or his, or both of theirs. Her hands slid from his face, her fingertips gliding over the cotton of his shirt and settling on top of his belt. She pulled away and looked into his eyes.

Kalfinar's wife's face flashed in his mind and he squeezed his eyes shut. *There will always be us, my love. But this can't be wrong.* When he opened his eyes, Evelyne was there, those ice-blue eyes bright and beautiful. Her smile was gentle, reassuring.

Kalfinar kissed her again as she worked at his belt. His heart thundered in his chest and the sound of his blood rushed about his ears like the angry sea on the shore.

His trembling fingers fumbled with the buttons of her shirt. One, two, and the curve of her breasts disappeared into the vest beneath. *How long has it been?* He unbuttoned the last and kissed at her neck. Her skin smelled of lavender oil.

Evelyne opened his belt and broke away from him. "Take off your trousers." She hopped on one foot as she pulled off the boot from her right foot, almost losing balance and stumbling over.

Kalfinar made to grab her, lest she fall to the floor, but she righted herself. They laughed as she tossed the boot into the corner of the room and kicked off the left.

Kalfinar pulled off his own boots as she unbuttoned and slid off her trousers. She stepped up and pushed him against the edge of the table. He sat against the surface as she unbuttoned his trousers, kissing him against the scarred edge of his jaw. He flipped their positions, placing her on the surface of the table.

She smiled and pulled him in close.

Kalfinar smelled her hair and kissed the top of her head. They had remained in an embrace for several silent minutes since they made love.

"It's strange how our hearts work," Evelyne whispered as her head lay on his chest.

"How do you mean?" he asked.

"I was sure, as Tuannan, I'd never feel such closeness to anyone but Dajda."

Kalfinar leaned back and, with gentle strength, moved her head from his chest. He looked at those beautiful eyes as they searched his face. "You feel closeness to me?"

"I've always felt a closeness to you. I can't explain it. When you came to my father's house, I recognised in you something that had always been out of reach to me."

Kalfinar smiled at her and kissed her smooth forehead. "I fought myself to think nothing of you." For a brief moment, he feared he had injured her with his words, but then she smiled. "But I couldn't pretend like I didn't care. As much as I may have tried."

"Well, I'm glad you stopped trying." She rested her head back onto his chest. "Where do we go from here?"

"We fight."

"We fight?"

"Aye. We fight for tonight, tomorrow, and the next day."

"Do you feel you have the strength?"

He raised her head to face him once more. "You've given me your strength."

"Are you sure you'll be fine?" Kalfinar asked as he and Evelyne walked up the stairs towards Harruld's study.

"Thank you. I feel better," Evelyne said with a smile, her eyes still betraying the grief that coiled within.

"If you need to, we can go. We don't need to."

"No. Something has happened, we need to know, and we must react."

Kalfinar nodded to her and opened the door to his father's study.

Evelyne entered and Kalfinar followed behind her.

"Evelyne, Kalfinar." Harruld stood up from his seat. "I'm glad you're here."

Kalfinar looked at the captain standing behind Harruld's desk. The dark circles under the man's eyes and the expression of fear spoke a hundred words; none happy.

"What news, Father?"

"Sit down, both of you."

They sat and Kalfinar placed his hand over Evelyne's.

"This is Captain Tyrnan," Harruld said.

The captain nodded in greeting to the two of them.

"I sent him and a platoon with Sarbien to Shalima mines. They went to find the source of the energy sustaining the urns."

"I know," Evelyne said. Her voice wavered as she spoke. "I have felt what you are to tell me." Her chin began to crinkle and shake. "My father is gone, isn't he?"

"I fear so, child," Harruld said. "I'm sorry, but there's more."

"Anthony," she said. She bowed her head and sniffed as tears fell from her eyes.

Kalfinar squeezed her hand. She took a deep breath, composed herself, and nodded for Harruld to continue.

"Sarbien's report told us that Anthony's spirit has been possessed by the enemy.

Evelyne emitted a small moan. "My brother."

Harruld continued, "The enemy we face is not as first feared. What is being sustained in Shalima is not Bhalur."

"What do you mean? What is it?" Kalfinar asked.

"One of Bhalur's own, one of the demigods. Balzath is the name of the beast. It appears to have taken Bhalur's place as the recipient of worship from the Ravenmayne. All this time, we thought we had control of the power, but Balzath has grown strong while we sat around, smug in our success."

"What does this mean?" Evelyne asked, a new resolve etched on her face as she wiped away her tears.

"It means, child, that what we face is stronger than we first feared. Your father passed on a report to Captain Tyrnan to take with him to us."

Evelyne straightened in her seat, resolute.

"The report tells us that Balzath is sending forth another attack through these urns that will raise those who have died from the plague and set them loose on our streets."

"Dajda!" Kalfinar exclaimed. "The bodies must be burnt before they rise."

"I fear we may be too late," Captain Tyrnan said, breaking his silence from where he stood at ease by Harruld's desk. "When I rode into the city, there was disruption on the streets. Folk were being attacked by others. I saw the city guard skewer a man who'd killed another. The kept on fighting, even on the end of two spears." Tyrnan's brows knit together tight as he spoke. "The thing's eyes were white. I've seen that before, in Shalima. The Priest of this Balzath, your brother, I'm sorry to say, my lady, raised one of these white-eyed things from death in Shalima. It then set about some prayer. Sarbien reports it may have been a means to send the curse into the city. I fear he was right, and the dead now walk our streets with demons inside them."

Chapter Thirty-Four

"LIEUTENANT THASKIL. I was just looking for you, sir," the private called out as Thaskil entered the dungeon in the basement of the High Command.

"What is it?" Thaskil asked, looking the young man up and down. *You can't be any older than me. We could've played together in the street as children.*

"Sergeant Omree has all the troops and supplies within the walls, sir. He's allocated archers to the walls, veteran bowmen also. We've pulled together another four hundred militia and veterans to add to the sixteen hundred already in the city. He awaits your orders for distributing."

"Two thousand defenders," Thaskil grunted. *That's not enough.*

Thaskil stared past the private towards the wall.

"Sir," the private said, "have you any orders for the sergeant regarding distribution of the troops?"

"What?" Thaskil lurched out of his musing. "Yes, of course." He stumbled over his words, trying to remember his lessons in defensive siege work. "A fifth each, to the other three walls, half of which in reserve and ready to respond to the breach. The other two-fifths to the breach and the surrounding quarter."

"Aye, sir. Consider it done." The private saluted and ran off.

Thaskil stood still for a moment and breathed in deep. No doubt

Bergnon had heard the exchange. He mopped the sweat from his brow and straightened the leather jerkin on top of his chainmail, not that it really mattered. He walked around the wide stone corridor, past the flickering oil lamps and empty cells and stopped before Bergnon's cell.

He was sat hunched against the wall, the setting sun over the Field of Storms stretching rays in through the barred window and across his bruised face. "So, have you come to finish me?"

"Don't honestly know if I've the mercy in me," Thaskil responded, not even looking at Bergnon, instead pulling the chair out and dumping his weary body into it.

"Pity that."

"Why?" Thaskil asked, sinking his face into his hands, his elbows perched on his dirty trousers. "I mean, I know why you did it, but how, how did it come to this? There were other choices you could've made, surely?"

"Aye, lad." Bergnon looked towards the small barred window.

Thaskil regarded the dust motes as they danced along the stream of light, the breeze drawing the detritus through the bars to freedom. Bergnon spoke, drawing Thaskil's attention.

"Probably had a multitude of ways, I guess. Just didn't seem at the time like I had anything. And now here I am. A ruin, a traitor, a murderer. And she's dead." Bergnon looked back, holding Thaskil's gaze for a moment.

"All for nothing, then," Thaskil said.

The moment hung heavy between them, their eyes exchanging accusations, questions, and fears.

Bergnon broke and stared away. "Not for nothing; for her. She was worth much more. Love is madness." He turned his head back, tears falling from his swollen and bruised eyes. "I love her. Dajda, I love her so badly. I'd do anything for her, but do I wish I acted differently? Do I wish I stopped certain things? Aye, of course I do."

Thaskil gazed at the stone of the floor, nodding his head. "I don't doubt it. I know you didn't want Arrlun to die."

"No, lad, of course I didn't."

"But he died all the same and you were to blame." Thaskil looked up, eyes hard again, belly burning with fresh anger.

"I can't deny that, nor would I, but I regret it. Not that it matters much now."

"No, it doesn't, I suppose," Thaskil said, his eyes flicking up to the barred window as the strobe of sun slid away. "No, it matters little. We're all probably going to die here tonight."

"But we can die with honour," Bergnon said as he stood from his crouched position, moving closer to the bars. His bloodied and bruised fingers wrapped around the rust-splotched bars of the cell.

Thaskil coughed a laugh. "I can maybe die with honour, if I don't piss myself with fear. But you, you'll die with nothing but shame."

Bergnon's face didn't shift at the barb. He gripped the bars and held Thaskil's gaze. "I can help stop this, this that I caused. Let me help. Let me recover some honour. Let me have the chance to find some redemption." His eyes pleaded. "I can help you."

Thaskil stood and stepped up to the bars, their faces almost touching. He tried to deny it, but a little bit of him felt like running to Bergnon. He felt like there was protection in him. "You've no honour. You've no word. The second I let you out of that cell, you'd flee and be gone. A traitor has no right to redemption." Thaskil felt his blood rising. He turned around and lashed out at the seat with his heel, sending it crashing and splintering into the wall at the side of the cell. "No! No redemption for you. Fuck you." He turned and stormed away.

The sound of alert rang clear and the defenders of Apula roared.

Harruld and Kalfinar watched from the window as the ragged man battered the trader back, causing him to fall over his market cart, sending sorry-looking winter vegetables spilling onto the cobbles. The attacker sallied forth, followed by several more wild-looking individuals, scrambling onto the stricken man and clawing at him as he held weak arms aloft in meagre protection. The stricken man thrashed and screamed with little effect, and in the blood and the frenzy of it all, the man died alone, and without help.

Kalfinar regarded his father. His face was grey, a symptom not of the scene he just witnessed from his vantage point in the military High Command, but of something else altogether.

They turned from the window and back to Broden, who sat in the study alongside the dozing Olmat.

"This is a hell on earth." The governor sagged into his seat.

"Subath has teams of men dispatched to rid the streets of these creatures," Broden said.

"He needs to be careful. They grow in number," Olmat's weak voice sounded, causing them to turn to him.

"I thought you were sleeping, old friend," Kalfinar said, walking over and placing a gentle hand on Olmat's liver-spotted hand.

The pace at which Olmat had deteriorated shocked Kalfinar. But that shock paled to the surprise that this man, the simple physician who taught him how to call birds, the man that brought him into the world and schooled him, was the one being in the world who could end the horror now. Dark thoughts rose in Kalfinar, thoughts he damned himself for thinking. *No, he can only die a natural death.*

"What of the people?" Kalfinar asked. "We can't abandon them to whatever fate is out there." He pointed towards the window, looking his companions in the eyes. "We must send out more platoons and make sure the people can find succour. If none is to be had, we must bring them back here. At least we could guarantee their safety."

"At what cost?" Harruld asked, his expression belying the burden in issuing such words. "We know there's a plague at work. We've isolated it in the High Command. If we bring in the people, we could be inviting death to sit by our very table."

Kalfinar's face twisted in anger. "How can we sit and condemn our own people to death?"

"You're a soldier and a leader of soldiers. This is a decision of war," Harruld snapped in response. "That's not to say it's a decision taken lightly, nor is it a decision that rests easy on my shoulders or, indeed, yours."

Kalfinar spread his hands on the wall above the window, staring into the city with his back to his father.

"These are the decisions of a leader, son, and you'd best learn to see their place in the world. I've committed men to their death and it pains me every moment. The citizens in the streets, the men bricked into the command, they're all weighing heavy on me."

Kalfinar looked back at Harruld. The drawn expression on his face was evidence enough of the man's pain. *How can it be that we must make such choices? How can we abandon all humanity? Abandon our flesh and blood to devils and become devils ourselves.*

Broden stared at the floor and broke the silence muttering, "It's said they can hear the screams of the men in the lower reaches of the High Command."

"Dajda take them into her embrace," Harruld responded. His eyes screamed regret, circled by dark rings laden with the stress of one who commits men to their end. "There was one down there, his name was Gillen Habston. He stood chest out, chin high, accepting fate for the better-ment of his own people. For the protection of his country. That was a hero. I keep seeing his face." Harruld stared out the window beside Kalfinar as the sun set. Another scream sounded, a woman's, and then stillness.

"They grow in numbers," Olmat mumbled.

"We must do something," Broden echoed Kalfinar's earlier sentiments.

Kalfinar looked up. "Aye!" He turned and stared at his father. "Let's take more men out and sweep the city. We can get rid of these demons."

Harruld shook his head. "No, it's too dangerous. You're needed here."

"Damn it!" Kalfinar snapped. "Let us go. We must go."

As if on cue, another scream wafted through the window, causing Harruld's face to twist in a grimace.

"Uncle," Broden implored, "let us take more squads. We can protect the people."

Harruld stared out the window and then back at the faces of those around him. He exhaled, his chest wheezing as he began to scribble down an order. "Broden, command four further platoons of guards and sweep the city."

Broden nodded. "Thank you, Uncle."

Harruld continued, "Subath already commands the defences on the outer walls. He'll be sending out roving patrols. You may be able to link up with them. Do what you can for those you can help."

Kalfinar walked the few steps to Broden and placed a hand on his shoulder. "Let's get ready."

"No," Harruld said. "Kalfinar, you must stay."

"What?" Kalfinar barked. "You have to let me go!"

"I don't have to let you go and I won't. That's an order," Harruld responded, his voice calm as he folded his order and handed it to Broden.

"You can't keep me cooped up in here while Broden is out there risking his skin. You've to stop protecting me, Father." *You think I'll go and lose myself in some dark hole by the docks. Smoke and blood, whores and mud.*

"I'm not protecting you," Harruld replied, leaning back in his chair. "I'm doing what's necessary. You're needed here with the rest of the command. Truth be told, I don't want to send Broden out there, but you've demanded I do something and I'm responding to that. This is not a negotiation. It's an order and it's final." Harruld looked at Broden. "Well, what are you waiting for?"

Broden's mouth gaped before he snapped it shut. He saluted Harruld and offered a silent shrug of apology to Kalfinar. The door clicked as Broden pulled it shut behind him.

"Is that understood?" Harruld asked Kalfinar as he stared hard at him. Another scream drifted into the room, causing Kalfinar to squirm, his anger bristling.

"Aye," he grunted through gritted teeth. "Understood, sir." He snapped to a rigid attention at another scream. "Do yourself a favour, Father, and shut your window."

"Go for the heads! It'll drop them quicker," Broden roared as the creature crashed to the ground, its glassy white eyes staring empty at the darkening sky from its ruined head. *Blood red sky, how very apt.* "Dajda, almighty!" he exclaimed as another creature lurched towards him, the mouth hanging open but the white eyes hard. Broden swung his sword up with both hands, splitting the creature's jaw up to its forehead, causing it to stiffen and drop. *That'll do for you.*

Broden glanced around him as the small body of soldiers fought through the dwindling crowd of creatures. The platoon was made up of boys, young guardsmen in their first conflict, but their battle cries raged in the night even so. The platoon cleaved their way through the creatures, felling them much quicker now that they knew to target the heads.

"Make sure they're staying down," Broden ordered.

"What are these things?" a guardsman asked, chest heaving after cutting down another.

Broden sheathed his sword and huffed out a breath, looking at the dead creatures around him. "They were your kinfolk and neighbours," he said with regret. "Dead of an unnatural plague and brought to life again with dark spirits."

"The dead should stay dead, sir. That's the way the world is meant to be."

"This is black work, lads." Broden shook his head. "The blackest of work."

The young soldiers' faces were ashen as Broden moved away and stepped over the bodies collected around them, checking the creatures for movements or signs of whatever kind of life resided within them.

"Come on," Broden said. "We've work to do if we want to clear the streets of these demons." *Best make sure we've all eyes as we go. Dajda knows how many more of these things are out there.*

Broden wiped his sword clean on the painter's smock worn by one of the creatures. A pale-eyed head lay a full ten feet away, nestled against the lifeless feet of another of its kind.

The platoon rushed to control a fire that spread from an oil lamp smashed in the entranceway of a shop as a creatures leapt out from the shadows. The flames grew tall and licked their way beyond the door-frame and onto the porch, spreading a bright glow in the waning light of dusk.

"Leave it!" Broden hissed. "We don't know how many more will be drawn to it as we work. We must keep out of sight."

The platoon backed away and followed Broden into a building across the street, making sure it was empty as they crept through.

"Clear in here," a guardsman whispered.

"Keep your eyes keen." Broden breathed against the cloudy window pane, waiting to see if any more of the creatures would be drawn to the flames. *What manner of magic can bring the dead back to the living. Dajda, give us strength enough to protect the souls of your children.* Broden dropped his head and stared at the floor, his feet enveloped in the dark of the night. *What's the point, you're not even listening.*

"Here they come," a voice rumbled low at the back of Broden's neck, causing him to look up.

The flickering glow of the flames spread a warm light up the street. The flames grew in violence, tongues tearing through the roof of the shop across the road. Three of the creatures ran into view, sniffing at the air, mouths agape and legs squatted. Their arms jutted out from their bodies and their fingers were spread and curled like talons. Their necks stretched forward as their bodies leaned over, craning their white-eyed heads side to side, sniffing at the air.

Broden stared at them with horror until his attention was drawn upwards. There was a flash at a window in the upper-level of the shop next to that which was being consumed by fire. A small girl stared down at the creatures, panic etched across her face.

"Dajda!" Broden hissed. "Look! There's a child across the way."

"Aye, I see her," one of the guards replied.

"Let's rush them, get the child, and get moving," another rasped. "There'll be somewhere along the way we can place her where she'll be safe."

Broden looked back at the window where the child had been, but there was no one there anymore. He felt a sharp shock run through him and before he knew it, he had burst through the door and was running across the street. The rest of the platoon followed behind.

The three creatures snapped around at the men storming across the street and leapt towards them. Broden dropped his shoulder and crashed through, sending them tumbling. He kicked his way into the door of the building where he'd seen the child. The ground floor was empty, save for the bowls of fabric and cutting tables. He bounded up the stairs, holding his breath as he ascended into the first floor. Smoke was accumulating as the fire spread into the building.

"Girl!" he shouted, spluttering as the smoke clawed at this throat. He put the leather of his greave up to cover his mouth and nose, for what little good it did him. "Girl!" he called again.

Before him, a small child appeared, coughing through the thickening smoke. She held a knitting needle in both her hands before her in a weak form of defence. When she saw Broden through her smoke-stung eyes, she dropped the needle and collapsed in a heap. Broden sheathed his sword and grabbed her into his arms before half-stumbling down the stairs and back into the street. The platoon had made short work of the creatures after Broden had sent them sprawling to the ground.

"Come on," Broden said, his voice ragged from the smoke. "Let's keep moving. We need to get her somewhere safe."

"The cathedral," a guardsman said. "It's ten minutes from here. Should be safe."

"Let's move out."

Thaskil leapt up onto the battlements to the side of Sergeant Omree. Those who stood to fight cheered around them as the Solansian forces advanced into view, their ranks spreading out wide before them in the Field of Storms.

"That's a lot of men." Thaskil grimaced and rubbed at his stomach as he looked across at the ranks of Solansian raiders.

Sergeant Omree nodded beside him before shouting an order to the remaining troops pouring the last of the pitch into the trench, "We'll give them a few surprises along the way."

Thaskil smiled and slapped the man on the back of his shoulder. "Good man." He looked back to see a rider on a white horse come galloping free of the advancing army.

The rider pounded a thin line through the wheat that now grew on the Field of Storms.

Thaskil straightened his jerkin and turned to Omree. "I suppose these will be the terms of our surrender."

The sergeant sneered and spat over the battlement. "Old Grunnxe obviously hasn't studied his history too well. Apula's never fallen in the time of the Free Provinces. Why would a little pin prick in our wall change that?"

Thaskil smiled, his guts settling in the moment. "Do you know something, Sergeant?" He stared out as the rider advanced. "I think I'm going to enjoy fighting beside you. You know what I'd like to do with that rider?"

"Aye, sir." Sergeant Omree waved his arm down and the front rank of archers let fly a volley of arrows.

The rider pulled on his reins, causing his horse to rear up, before spinning around and galloping back towards the Solansian army. The arrows fizzed off into silence and darkness. Moments later, a cry sounded in the distance beyond the walls.

"You know, sir," Omree added. "I think I'm going to like fighting beside you too."

"That's good." Thaskil turned, pulling his sword from its scabbard and his small one-handed battle-axe from his belt loop. "Because I've a feeling there is going to be quite a bit of that going on soon."

Omree laughed. It grew in strength and vigour, as the blood rose in his veins. He turned to face the gathered troops and citizens below, and those on the battlements. He raised his arms and let free a war cry, and the city roared loud with him.

The first ranks of Grunnxe's army broke free, a rush of blades running across the plain of the Field of Storms.

Grunnxe watched as the first ranks of men ran across the Field of Storms towards the breach in the walls of Apula. He squeezed at his arousal and laughed. He wouldn't be waiting much longer. The old king sneered at the back of the Priestess's head as the Master God spoke to him, instructing him to crush Apula in haste, make his way on to Carte, and break the will of people beneath them.

"Break this city of man, break it quickly and bring me Carte soaked in blood."

"Whatever you ask of me, Lord, I shall deliver to thee." Grunnxe sneered as the Priestess turned around in her saddle to face him.

"He speaks to you?" The Priestess hissed.

"Tell the worm." The voice was strong and stirred Grunnxe's belly.

"Yes, My Lord," Grunnxe said aloud. "The Master God, Balzath, wishes you to know you are no longer favoured, Priestess."

The Priestess snapped back her hand, the long black cuff falling back to reveal a gloved hand and the greyed flesh of an arm. The arm shot forward, but no energy, no force, flew from it.

"The Master God, Balzath, wishes you to know that he grants you no power until you take your place in service to Grunnxe."

"I am Bhalur. I was once God on high!" the Priestess screeched.

The voice laughed within Grunnxe's mind.

The Priestess threw back her hood and ripped off the black cloth covering her face, revealing red burning eyes and pallid, grey flesh. Her long, thin strands of white hair shook as she shouted, "The Master God, as he calls himself, is no more than a betrayer, a usurper, and he will betray you in the same fashion he betrayed me—"

The Priestess's voice cut off sharply and she was cast off her horse and into the earth by an unseen force. Her head snapped back and forth as if slapped by some invisible adversary.

"The Master God, Balzath, wishes you to know that words of such violation will not be tolerated."

The Priestess looked up from her prone position, dark blood

trailing from her nose and mouth. She wiped the fluids with the back of her hand and looked at it curiously.

"It is blood," Grunnxe laughed. "That's right, once great Bhalur. You bleed and if you know what's good for you, you'll learn your place in this world quickly or I and the almighty Master God will see you bleed a lot more."

The Priestess shakily stood and walked towards her horse, red burning eyes cast to the ground as she went. She hauled herself into the saddle and looked at Grunnxe.

"Have you remembered your manners, she who now bleeds?" The old king stared hard as he drew several inches of his sword from the scabbard.

"My place is with you, Great King, and in service to my almighty, the Master God, Balzath." The Priestess head was bowed in supplication.

The power of the voice flowing in Grunnxe's mind was intoxicating. The Master God had chosen to speak to him now. Grunnxe, King of Solansia, and rightful Father of the People of the Cullanain was now the right hand of almighty Balzath. Balzath wanted Carte and Grunnxe would give it to him.

"Commander," Grunnxe roared, his voice ragged and hard, "commit the full Ravenmayne forces to the wall and follow the first rank in."

"No!" the Priestess interrupted. "They are my children!"

Another invisible blow struck her face. A trail of dark blood splattered across Grunnxe's breastplate. The blow left the Priestess sagging and wheezing over the horn of her saddle.

"No, they belong to Balzath," Grunnxe rebuked the Priestess. "The Ravenmayne worship Balzath above all. The Master God sees fit to use them. If they die, they die. They'll be replaced four hundred fold before this week is through"

The commander had turned around on his horse and was looking at them open mouthed. "But, Your Highness, that's a full four thousand troops. Are you sure?" The man looked nervous as he questioned the invigorated king.

Grunnxe's face set like ragged stone. "Do I look like I need to be questioned by the fucking likes of you or that fallen spirit over there?" He withdrew his sword and pointed it toward the shaking commander.

"It's done, Your Highness." The commander cleared his throat and roared the order.

The flag waved the Ravenmayne horde off, four thousand forgotten people. Four thousand with thirst for vengeance in their hearts. Grunnxe felt a swelling press once more on the inside of his trousers.

"Apula will fall. Onwards to Carte."

Chapter Thirty-Five

"IT'S RIDICULOUS! I should be out there with him," Kalfinar snapped as he stared out of the window of Harruld's study.

He and Evelyne were alone, having answered the governor's summons, only to find him absent from his study.

"Calm down," Evelyne said, stepping up behind Kalfinar as he stared out the window. Her arms wound around him, squeezing his chest as she rested her head against his back.

Kalfinar tangled his fingers about hers.

"Broden will be fine."

"I'm not achieving anything stalking these corridors. I should be out there, where I matter."

"You matter right here, right now."

He turned, breaking free from her embrace, and rested his hands on her hips. Her eyes sparkled with the flickering light of the stand of candles behind him. He kissed her.

"Apologies, I had business—"

They broke from their kiss as Harruld walked into the room, stopping as he saw them.

"I'm—ahem, I'm sorry," Harruld blurted. "I didn't know you'd be... well."

"No need to apologise," Evelyne said, stepping away from Kalfinar and pulling free a chair from Harruld's table before sitting down with a casual smile.

Kalfinar replicated her actions, sitting down next to her. Both stifled slight laughter.

"Well excuse the interruption in any case." Harruld carried on into the room, followed by Abbonan and Merkham.

Kalfinar caught Abbonan's eye as he pulled free a chair opposite him. The Governor of Terna flashed a quick look to Evelyne, then back to Kalfinar, and winked.

Kalfinar turned away from the grinning Abbonan and looked to his father. "What news?"

"Troops have been allocated and reserves drawn up. Reinforcements have been ordered from Enulin and Gerloup, but they'll take time. Maybe too much time. We've too few officers and even fewer who've true battle experience. As for the city, we've had several squads back to the High Command from patrols."

"Broden?" Kalfinar asked.

Harruld shook his head. "The word back is grim. The dead have been taken by spirits and try to kill any they come across. Evelyne, can you explain what's happening?"

"They're harvesting," Evelyne said, her eyes closed.

"What does that mean?" Merkham asked, his thin face etched with confusion. The grey bags under his eyes had grown.

"The demons within the dead harvest the souls of those they kill and feed them to Balzath. It is how the demigods would have fed under Bhalur's will, but for Balzath to feed on such scale will only serve to give him greater strength."

"Dajda!" Abbonan exclaimed. "Does Balzath mean to slaughter us all?"

"No," Evelyne replied, opening her brilliant eyes. "It would not sustain him to pursue such a course. To take souls in such abundance would make him very powerful, but strength wanes. If there is no one to worship, there's no more strength to be had, and so Balzath would diminish. To endure, he'll seek to put all under the yoke."

"So what am I doing still sat here? I should be out there keeping our people safe!" Kalfinar said, his earlier frustration rising again.

Evelyne placed a hand on Kalfinar's thigh and squeezed.

"We defend," Harruld said, "and we lead. Specifically, you lead."

"What?"

"He said, 'Specifically, you lead,'" Abbonan said, his humour replaced with solemnity.

"Me? But you lead." Kalfinar looked at Harruld.

"Aye, for now, but I'm sick."

"What? What's wrong?" Kalfinar asked, his stomach knotting.

Harruld's face shifted into a humourless smile. "My blood's bad. Has been a while. I'm weakening and soon I'll go the way we all do in the end."

Kalfinar stared at him for a long moment, searching for words, but he found there was nothing he could say.

"Kalfinar," Merkham's words captured Kalfinar's attention, "even if your father wasn't ill, he couldn't continue to hold dual rank as governor and chief marshal. Our constitution forbids it beyond a period of transition. The remaining senior members of the High Command voted that you would be the next chief marshal of the High Command."

"This is madness. I'm a fucking addict!"

"You were washed clean of that on the ship," Evelyne said. "The child, remember?"

"But I—"

"But nothing!" Harruld barked, slamming his fist on to the table. "You need to stop this now! The command has voted. You're to assume your position with immediate effect and, for Dajda's sake, stop being committed to your past failings! They're past and they're gone. You're to take rank this night! Defend this city, this nation, and Dajda, above all. We're finished here. Merkham, run through the oaths with him." Harruld stood from his chair and made for the door.

Kalfinar watched him go, his cheeks stinging like he had been slapped.

Harruld opened the door and stopped. He turned back to the table and looked at Evelyne and Kalfinar, then smiled. "You look fine together." He walked out.

Kalfinar looked across at Evelyne. She smiled.

"Excuse me," Merkham coughed. "Don't mean to spoil your moment, but I need you to swear your oath of office, Chief Marshall."

"What do you see?" Broden hissed over the shoulder of the guard as they hid in the darkness of the alleyway.

"There's nothing there," the guard replied, keeping his eyes on the square in front of the cathedral.

Broden glanced down at the small girl who clung to the leather jerkin and chainmail. She stared up at him, red-rimmed eyes peering out of a soot-stained face. She hadn't uttered a word since she had been rescued.

Broden offered a meagre smile. *More likely to scare the poor kid with a face like this.*

"What do you want to do?" the guardsman in the front asked, glancing back over his shoulder.

Broden noted the anxiety on the faces of the remainder of the platoon. "Here." He handed the girl over to a guardsman further back in the shadows. He crept to the entrance of the alleyway and peeked into the cathedral square. The huge open square was lit with a flickering glow as oil lamps reflected off rain-soaked cobbles. "We make our move. Quick and quiet. Let's get into the cathedral with as little fuss as possible."

The platoon nodded in agreement, the men drawing their weapons careful and slow so as not to make any unwarranted noise.

Broden took the girl from the guard and cradled her to his chest with one massive arm, his sword ready in the other. He looked down at her. She had shut her eyes and small tears ran free, leaving smoke-stained trails down her dirty cheeks. Her breath was rapid and shallow. *You're terrified, child. So am I. So am I.*

"Sir?" one of the guardsmen whispered, drawing Broden from his thoughts.

"What?" Broden glanced up to see expectant faces on his men; eager and frightened. He composed himself in the moment. "Move out to the right. Stick to the edges of the square. It's just two sides to cover and we're there. Be mindful of gaps between buildings in case any of these ghouls are hiding. Aim for the side entrance. It's less visible, more likely to be open, and easier defended if not. Move low and move quick. Keep your eyes keen."

The men nodded and darted out of the alleyway, turning right and sticking to the edge of the square.

Broden's feet pounded the cobbles, hard and fast. His eyes scanned the square and the gaps between buildings. His sword arm was ready and his left was pinned to his chest, holding the little girl in place. Over the sound of his breathing, his footsteps, and those of his men behind him, Broden could hear the child sobbing. He stepped away from the building edges as he approached an alleyway, mindful not to pass it within grabbing distance. He slipped past, sword arm raised ready. *Keep going, keep going. Almost there, keep—*

The sound of a man's scream ripped through the still air.

Broden turned to see one of the platoon spinning into the square away from the mouth of the alleyway he had just passed. One of the creatures clung onto his back like a mountain lion tackling a deer.

The guardsman spun and flailed, trying to get the creature off with little effect.

Broden and the rest of the platoon leapt to his aid, with those closer hauling at the creature. As Broden reached them, the guardsman had been torn free, and the creature sent reeling to the glistening cobbles. Four of the platoon surrounded the creature as it hunched, ready to pounce, white eyes darting between them.

"Look at his apron," one of the guardsmen muttered. "He used to be a tanner."

Broden glanced at the heavy leather apron. "Well, he's not a tanner anymore," Broden snapped. "Kill it."

The guardsmen fell upon the former tanner and despatched it. The injured guardsman was resting on his hunkers, a cloth pressed firmly against his neck.

"Are you hurt?" Broden asked, stepping over.

"It bit me. See." The man removed the rag from his neck and dark blood welled out of the ragged wound.

"Dajda!" Broden exclaimed. "That's deep. You'll need that stitched. Can you walk?"

"Aye."

Broden nodded. "Come on." He called to the rest of the platoon, "We need to get moving. Help him up and let's go."

Helping the injured guardsmen, the group moved through the square to the cathedral, eyes darting side to side to make sure no more of the creatures were drawn to the commotion.

Broden clearly heard the sobs of the child now. "It will be fine, child. We're almost there."

They slipped alongside the massive cathedral and away from the open space of the square. The reach of the lamp light diminished the further they got from the square and Broden felt his pulse quicken. He hushed the child and indicated the same to the injured guardsman. With slow, deliberate steps, they felt their way along the wall, nerves shredded and breath quick.

Broden saw the faint glint of metal ahead and his pulse settled. They had reached the smaller side door, the caretaker's entrance. He reached out and turned the handle, being cautious not to make too much noise. The metal groaned a little in the dark, but it may as well have been a mill wheel grinding. Then it stopped. It was locked.

"Fuck!" Broden hissed, his pulse quickened.

"What do we do now?" one of the platoon whispered.

Broden stood in silence, musing over his options, none of which he fancied. "This is probably the largest and easiest to defend building we could find in the city short of the High Command. If we're to hold up for a while and try to get some of the people to safety, this is the best option. I say we either try to pick the lock or we try to break the door down."

Broden could only see shadows and smudges of his men's faces. Their silence gave him little comfort as to his choice.

"If we pick it, we stand out here for longer. If we break it down, we make more noise and have to repair it fast. What do you think?" Broden stood for a moment, the sound of breathing being his only companion. "Right then, I guess I'll break it down."

Broden turned to face the door and made himself ready to slam a heavy boot against it when the sound of metal turning in the lock caused him to pull back.

The door opened a sliver and an arrowhead poked out from the blackness within.

"Let me warn you, breaking down this door would be very bad for your wellbeing," a faceless voice crept out from behind the door. "Put away your swords and declare yourself. And don't try anything rash. My arrows are not the only sharp things behind this door."

"I'm Captain Broden of the High Command and this is my platoon. We've been dispatched on orders of Governor Harruld to clear the city of these creatures and take the people to safe keeping. We've an injured man and a child here in need of succour. Our man needs stitching. He's losing a lot of blood. Please, can you help?"

"Show me your orders," the voice called out after a moment.

"Place them in the crack at the bottom of the door and no funny business or the inevitable will happen with those sharp things I told you about."

"Understood," Broden replied. "I need to reach into my jerkin. Is that fine?"

"Fine. Go slow."

Broden removed the order signed by Harruld. He took a couple of steps towards the door and knelt down, his left arm tight around the little girl and his right extending the folded piece of paper into the crack in the door. The arrow tracked him all the way. He stepped back and stood up straight as the piece of paper was whipped into the blackness behind the door. A spark of light flashed from within and Broden heard some mumbling inside. A moment later, the door creaked open and Broden saw several bows and spears levelled at him and his men.

"In you come, but remember, any funny business and we'll have you. Understood?"

"Aye, we understand," Broden replied. "Thank you." He led the way into the cathedral, the small child still sobbing into his chest.

***

"How is he?" Kalfinar asked Evelyne as she opened the door to Olmat's chamber.

"Soon," she said, stepping aside and letting him in.

The room was smaller than Harruld's study by half. The stone walls were bare, the only decoration being an intricate stained-glass window depicting a blazing star. Olmat lay on a narrow bed, clothed in a deep blue, ankle-length gown. The two girls, the Horn of the Anulii, sat beside the old man. The younger girl smoothed Olmat's thin white hair with the palm of her small hand whilst the older hummed a soft, slow melody.

"How are you?" Kalfinar whispered to Evelyne.

"Fine. You?" she asked with a gentle smile.

"Little time to feel anything. I'm glad to be here with you."

"Do you want to speak to him?" she asked, leading him towards where Olmat lay. "Uncle," Evelyne whispered.

The smallest of the girls stood up from Olmat's side and hugged Kalfinar around his knees.

"Whoa!" Kalfinar laughed. "What a fine welcome." He cupped the back of the small girl's curly head as she tipped her face back and smiled at him. His heart swelled with a sense of joy at the sight of her. *Are you my angel?*

"Kalfinar," Olmat's thin, reedy voice sounded. "Come close, lad. My eyes are failing me."

Olmat was fading, that much was plain.

"How're you, old friend?" Kalfinar asked, his hand resting on Olmat's bony shoulder as he sat down in the chair beside him. *What a curse of fate, you that I love so dearly; who I now wish death upon.*

Olmat's rheumy blue eyes had lost their vitality and clouded. He managed to force his dry and cracked lips into a weak smile. "I'm on my way, it seems. The last of three. My brothers are dead, that is why I slip now so quick from this world."

Kalfinar leaned in closer to Olmat. "You three, you were the three pillars that Teporan Mane wrote must fall to call forth the Anulii. First there was Capriath, then Sarbien, and now, finally, you."

Olmat nodded, his head seeming so little and his neck so thin. "It appears we three were entwined to this fate from the start. It was our role to live in service of and die for the name of Dajda. After we pass, I'm sure three more will come to be. Three more to keep watch. They too will serve Dajda as we have done, and diminish also when their time comes."

Kalfinar clasped Olmat's trembling hands and regarded him with a sorrowful smile. *Not long until you rest, dear friend.*

"When you make it through this," Olmat's voice grew in strength as he spoke. "Don't fan the flames of your pain and burn all your life away. Don't waste it for nothing. You know they wouldn't want that for you."

"I know," Kalfinar said.

"No, you don't!" Olmat croaked with urgency. "If you love only in death, in a memory, it can breed despair in a soul. You must find love in the living. It will bring you peace."

Evelyne hunkered down beside Olmat and Kalfinar, and placed a hand on each of theirs.

Kalfinar looked at her and smiled. "I think I understand now."

"Bowmen!" Thaskil cried out, his words being relayed down the battlements. "Next volleys on my command. First volley, set to flame and into the trench. Let's cut them in half. Second volley, bring it in and take down those on the inside of the trench."

Sergeant Omree stood by Thaskil's side and watched as raiders sprinted forward, wailing war cries. They appeared as masses of shadows swarming forwards to the breach. Some tripped and ran into the large blocks of masonry blown from the wall, whilst other stepped on caltrops, falling to the ground with screams of agony. The positioning of the obstacles and the fallen comrades caused the pace of the advancing raiders to lessen.

"It's working. They're slowing," Omree said.

"Light the arrows!" Thaskil called as shadows of men swarmed over the open ground. *So many.* He waited and watched as the line of flame spread to either side of him. *Dajda, let this work.* "Fire!" he screamed, sweeping his raised hand down to his side as the order echoed down the battlement.

The line of fire leapt and climbed high in the air, gliding a trail of light in the dark and arching downwards like the fall of an axe. Some appeared to strike the ground, spluttering out, while others found their mark in flesh, the flame's journey carrying on before spluttering out. Some of the arrows found their way into the trench. Flame burst into an explosion of violent life, engulfing the trench, blasting heat and light against the walls of Apula and flashing fire and death onto any nearby. Some unfortunate raiders who had fallen in the trench ran across the ground towards the walls like comets, trailing liquid fire before their terrifying screaming subsided. A wild cheer sounded from the battlements.

Omree turned and clapped Thaskil on the shoulder. "It worked."

"Aye," Thaskil agreed, "seems to have done. It's just the small matter of the masses now tearing across the plain that we have to deal with."

"You've got your tactics sound. They won't know what's hit them." Omree grinned and moved from the battlement to the masonry bulwark filling the breach.

Thaskil stood and took one last look as the raiders ran towards Apula. *That's all well and good with this volley of raiders, but what do we do when the flames die down?* "Archers," he called before descending from the battlement, "at my command, fire into the kill zone. Fire!"

The explosion of light caused Grunnxe's horse to rear, almost sending him crashing onto the ground. The horse settled and Grunnxe stared in disbelief as flames spread wide and tall in front of the breached walls of Apula, splitting the advancing troops.

"*Break the city's back. I want Carte,*" the voice of the Master God urged Grunnxe, causing his bowels to twitch and his head to pound.

"What in the sweet, suffering fuck was that? Commanders, follow your men in. Make sure this city falls. No more tricks from them. Nothing else can be tolerated. Break this city in the name of the Master God, Balzath! Break it now!"

His commanders made to protest, mouths working at words not yet issued.

Grunnxe scoffed at their concerns. "We've no time for playing such games. The mouse can nip and run all it cares, but the cat shall have its way."

"*Take Carte and grind it into dust. Within that city, there is a source of power than must be mine. Take Carte and bring me the heart of Dajda. My servants infest the dead and claim souls from Dajda. They make it ready.*"

The heart of Dajda? Grunnxe questioned.

"*There is one there who carries the Liar God in her heart. Take her and we shall hold dominion over all.*"

Grunnxe sensed urgency from the Master God pressing against his temples. *Carte is far, Master.*

"*I shall take thee in the palm of my hand and carry thee so. Go to the Valeswater.*"

As you will it, Master.

"But, Your Highness," one of the commanders closest to him whispered, "the defenders are putting up stiff resistance. We'd be best to ensure the city falls before we split our forces."

Grunnxe clenched his teeth and leaned in close to the commander. "We have no time to dilly dally with Apula. It will fall. Just make sure it does. I will leave two further battalions here. The rest travel with me to Carte."

The commander swallowed his fear and saluted.

Grunnxe leaned in close. "And one more thing. But for the fact no one could hear your dissent, I would've torn your throat out and bathed in your blood. Remember my mercy well next time you think to question your king and the voice of your master, Balzath."

The commander flinched in his saddle as an unseen force struck him.

Grunnxe grinned and patted the commander's thigh. "That's just the warning. The real punishment would hurt a great deal more and it would last a long time."

Grunnxe spun in his horse, holding the attention of his remaining commanders. "Men, we march to the Valeswater. The Master God, shall spirit us to Carte, where we will crush the Free Provinces and take back the Cullanain in the name of Solansia and Balzath." Grunnxe dug his heels into his horse's flanks and caused it to rise up on its rear legs and paw at the air with its front hooves.

The Priestess watched, now nothing more than a servant; the once-great Bhalur now whipped at the call of those who once served her so.

The little girl clung to Broden, though she had stopped sobbing. Exhausted, the young child had fallen asleep as he carried her up the stairs. Broden looked around in amazement while he and his platoon reached the large room within the cupola at the top of the cathedral.

Weeks before, he had sat in this room surrounded by Tuannan chanting prayers of protection to Dajda. They were full of conviction; full of power. He looked now at pale and frightened faces as they entered the double doors. The holy men and women, the magic casters, the Tuannan, and a small number of worshippers, sat huddled in pockets across the large floor. There was no air of conviction, prayer, nor hope.

"This man needs help. He's hurt," Broden's voice boomed through the room. "Who among you can help?"

There was silence amongst the gathered few, some heads even dipping down, cradled hopelessly in their arms.

Broden's face flushed and he huffed, turning to his platoon. "I'll do it myself."

"I can help," a young woman called out behind Broden and he turned, observing the Tuannan stepping her way between those seated on the floor.

"Thank you," Broden mumbled, bowing his head in respect to the young holy woman. "I'm Captain Broden of the High Command. One of my platoon is hurt. He's bleeding badly."

"My name's Althia," the young woman said as she passed him and approached the injured guardsman. She hunkered down to the injured man and removed the makeshift dressing applied to the wound. "Take him to one of the quarters. I can treat him easier there. Follow me." Althia passed through the double doors of the cupola, followed by Broden and the others.

"What happened to him?" Althia asked Broden as she pulled tight the final stitch on the guardsman's neck.

"One of those things bit him," Broden whispered as he tucked the small, sleeping girl into one of the cots beside the injured guardsman. He brushed a long, red curl away from the sleeping child's face with a thick finger and smiled. *Same colour of hair as me.*

Althia tied off the stitch and bit the thread. "We were at prayer when they first came," she almost whispered, looking down at her blood-stained fingers. "We could hear the screams from outside the cathedral. When we went to look, we saw people turning on each other. One of my fellow Tuannan went to intervene and was killed before us. He was torn to pieces by them. We panicked and shut the doors. All that were inside have remained so."

Broden sighed and leaned back from sitting on the end of the bed, his back resting against the stone wall. "Fear has stopped you opening your doors to others, save for when you thought the door would be broken down."

Althia sniffed and nodded her head. "Fear does strange things to a person," she replied, looking up to Broden, shame in her eyes. "When tested, many of us will see the true colour of our character." She looked back at the injured man. "Many of us who thought our souls strong and good have seen a harsh truth."

"You can always do more." Broden peered out the window to see fat snowflakes flutter past, some sticking to the window pane. He looked back at Althia. "I mean, you could open your doors and receive the people. Give them succour where they can't find it for themselves."

Her face was wrung with concern. "But those creatures?"

"We have platoons of men clearing the city of them. We can rescue the people where they're trapped and bring them here."

"The others," Althia whispered, looking at the door. "They'll not support you. Their fear's too great."

"Are your people out there not worth the saving?" Broden shot his words angrily, causing the child to stir. He winced in a silent apology and rubbed the small girl's back, hushing her. He looked back to see Althia smile. "What?" he whispered.

"She looks like you."

Broden blushed and tried to fix a firm look on his face at the same time.

"You know it is alright to be strong and caring at the same time."

Broden held Althia's gaze. "Precisely my point."

"These numbers can't be right." Kalfinar stood up from the ledger and rubbed his face. His eyes felt gritty and he needed to wash. He walked over to the window in Harruld's study and peered out at the night. Fires had sprung up in several places throughout Carte. *If you're out there, Broden, keep safe.*

He turned to face the gathered officers not yet posted throughout the city. "Have all of the garrisons and reserves come in from Ilsinuer?" Kalfinar asked, stepping back to the ledger. His finger traced the numbers presented by Merkham. "It just doesn't seem right." He looked at Merkham and his father.

"It isn't right," Merkham replied without preamble. Dark circles rounded his eyes, causing him to look even more gaunt than usual. His mane of grey hair hung over his forehead with an almost oppressive-looking bulk. "Even if we left a skeleton force at each of the outlying garrisons, we should still have four thousand additional troops. Be it weather or a more sinister foe, something must be holding them up."

"Damn it," Harruld snapped, causing his resting hounds to startle and look up at him as if chastened. "Our forces are diminished and on half-rations. Dajda lies deaf and sleeping, and our people are hiding from terror in our own city walls. Whatever else is to strike at us, it may as well do it now." He looked out the window and choked on a rough laugh devoid of humour.

"What is it?" Kalfinar asked, his brows furrowing.

"It's snowing," Harruld grumbled.

Chapter Thirty-Six

"KEEP FIRING!" Thaskil stood atop the crest of the bulwark that filled the breach. He roared to the bowmen on the battlements to either side of him. His throat was raw from shouting. He tasted blood, whether from his constant roaring of orders or from air so full of death, he wasn't sure. "Keep those arrows coming!" *The fewer swords we have to face in the breach, the better.*

He looked into the plain full of approaching raiders. The fire in the trench still burned bright and no more of the Solansian's were coming from beyond the flames. The trench had done its job and split the army, for now at least. *How long do we have before the flames die away?*

The raiders on the plain charged forward, an advancing tide of menace backlit by a wall of fire. Some were betrayed to the ground by scattered caltrops and some from the rain of flaming arrows descending from the night sky. Their high-pitched screams carried forward on the shimmering, fire-warmed air. Theirs numbers had diminished, that much was clear, but they were still outnumbered.

Still so many. Thaskil felt his guts spasm as the Solansian forces bore down on him and the ranks by his sides. *Breathe, just keep breathing.* Thaskil glanced to his left.

Sergeant Omree stood by him snarling, sword in one hand and battle-hammer in the other. Thaskil turned his head and looked at the defenders. Some bore faces of anger, and eyes filled with a fight and courage that was absent in him. Other faces did not look so brave. The majority of faces showed little but terror. Fearful eyes caught his look and flashed away, perhaps filled with shame. *I share your shame, but I'll not let it consume me.*

"Men!" Thaskil roared at the top of his voice. "I am afraid!" Eyes were drawn to him. "I'm shitting myself with the fear of it! But I will not let fear become me and neither should you. Our fear is our motivation. It is our fuel."

Eyes grew hard with fresh-born resilience.

"Fuel your fire with fear and beat these fuckers back to the salt marshes they came from! Let's send them skulking home as we have always done!"

The roar from the defenders felt like it would lift Thaskil from his feet.

This is a rank that won't break. Thaskil turned and shouted down at the defenders on the city-side of the breach. Sergeant Rushnall stood at the front of the ranks, a vicious-looking, short-handled axe in one hand and a buckler on the other arm. "At my signal, Sergeant, come join the party."

Sergeant Rushnall grinned. "Leave me something to play with, lad!"

Thaskil turned back and watched as the flood of armed troops hammered their way across the flat ground. His heart hammered faster than he thought possible. The tightness of his throat felt like he was being strangled. He was sure he had pissed himself, or at least was going to as soon as the blood came. He stilled his thoughts and looked at the plain. *No winter poppies. A crop of corpses is all. Here they come.*

He felt like crying. He felt like laughing. Thaskil could smell them now. He could see individuals with glowing eyes approaching the bulwark. *Ravenmaynes.* He drew a long and steady breath through his nose. Opening his mouth, he snarled like a beast, and roared as loud as his ragged voice could manage. "Come on, you bastards!"

The ranks roared with him, atop the masonry bulwark filling the breach in the walls.

The first of the Solansian forces scrambled up the steep bulwark. Some stumbled amongst the uneven path and other fell as arrows, spearheads, and sharpened stakes punctured their flesh. But it was little impediment and the raiders scaled the piled masonry at speed.

Here they come. Thaskil spun his battle-hatchet in his left hand and tightened the grip on his sword. *Nearly.* "Ready!" he roared, the cry echoed behind him in the ranks of the defenders. *Nearly.*

The Solansians charged up the bulwark like a black tide rising to claim the sand for the sea; inevitable.

Nothing is inevitable. "Fight!" Thaskil screamed aloud and burst forward, leading the ranks of defenders into the rushing menace.

The first raider Thaskil dropped took a sideways slash of his sword in the face, taking half the black mask and the lower jaw on its way. The body crashed and was instantly replaced with another. Thaskil caught a sword thrust with his hatchet, pulling down and dragging the sword out of the way. He stabbed his sword point into the man's mask, causing him to squeak.

The backswing of another defender nearly caught Thaskil in the face as he engaged the next raider. He ducked backwards, bumping into one of his companions and setting the man off-balance. Thaskil righted himself and blocked the enemy's sword stroke. He kicked out at the man, an unmasked Solansian, and plunged his sword into the man's chest. As he withdrew, a fist smashed into the side of his head, causing him to stumble into the dying Solansian.

Thaskil dragged himself to his feet. Black spots in his vision obscured his sight, but he saw enough to know the raider that had punched him was following up with a killing blow, except the enemy dropped to their knees with an arrow in the throat.

Thaskil's vision cleared as a huge raider cut down one of his city-folk in a bloody spray. The big bastard was fully seven feet tall. He lifted free his mask, showing the leering face of a Ravenmayne, teeth pointed and eyes blazing.

"Come on, fucker!" Thaskil roared, closing the distance between them. He raised his sword in an overhand blow; a feint.

The Ravenmayne met the sword stroke and leapt out of the way of Thaskil's hatchet blow. Another Ravenmayne came at Thaskil from the left, but was cut down from a blow to the back before he engaged. Thaskil pressed on the big one, thrusting twice, causing the giant Ravenmayne to concede ground. The Ravenmayne stumbled and fell backwards onto the masonry. A stake point burst through the Raven-mayne's chest, gore-covered.

Keep going! Thaskil picked his next fight and stepped in, avoiding sprays of blood and flailing metal.

Thaskil slashed, thrust, and kicked at any raiders who came his way. Hot blood splashed against his hands and face. Still, his grip held firm and he battled on. Parry, thrust, kick, slash. Thaskil screamed Dajda-knows-what in the face of the raiders as he slashed and thrust. The sound of crossbows loosening bolts sent a shiver down his spine. It was like the song of blood angels to him. The more dropped by the bolts, the better for all.

Thaskil pushed a body off his sword and roared another order, "Rushnall, fold in!"

The ranks of defenders on the bulwark swelled and the press of men started to form a knot around the congested raiders, making them so tightly choked that the raiders were unable to swing their weapons fully and, if they could, they slashed and stabbed at their own with backstrokes. The defenders pushed forwards, their ranks closing on the raiders like a noose looping the neck. The defenders met and tightened their hold, slashing the raiders down.

Thaskil risked a glance behind him towards the plain; no further Solansian forces were charging them. His heart sprung and his pulse quickened. A flush of blood hammered from his ears all the way to his fingertips. *May just do this!*

"Let's finish them!" he roared aloud and leapt back into the fray, smashing aside a Solansian sword with his own and slapping the blade of his battle hatchet into the gap between face-guard and shoulder, showering himself in blood. He kicked the gasping raider out of his way and plunged his sword into the side of another before bringing his hatchet back down with a soppy crunch into a black-clad collarbone.

All around him, raiders fell as disarray and panic spread. Bodies piled up as the defenders' ranks tightened.

No space to fight; no fight to offer. Thaskil kept swinging his weapons, sending more and more raiders to the ground while homing in on the centre of the rank.

Other defenders following behind dispatched any wounded as they squeezed the enemy further.

This is inevitable. Thaskil stepped back from the rank, another man taking his place and engaging the trapped raiders. He turned from the screaming, howling, ringing circle of men and looked around the bulwark.

Bodies lay everywhere and a waterfall of blood and wasted life cascaded over the masonry of the breach. His head swam in the moment. He bent over, resting his blood-soaked hands on his blood-soaked trousers, and wretched up the contents of his stomach.

Yet more for the waterfall of waste.

Grunnxe reined in beside the slow rush of the Valeswater, and turned to face the gathering forces behind him. *We're here, Master.*

There was silence in his head. The Master God did not speak.

The Priestess slid up beside Grunnxe's horse, her head bowed and shoulders slumped.

"Feeling a little chastened, are we?" Grunnxe mocked the Priestess.

The sound of bubbling water drew Grunnxe's attention away from the Priestess. He turned to the Valeswater and saw it roil. It splashed onto the bank as jets of water sprung up several feet and then fell back to the churning mass below.

"What's happening?" Grunnxe mumbled, not asking the question of anyone.

"You've much to learn of the Master's way, Great King."

The Priestess's words slapped at Grunnxe. "Shut your mouth." He knew his rebuke was childish, but he didn't care.

He turned back to the Valeswater to see jets of liquid grow taller and more frequent before freezing in mid-air. The water shimmered and then spread wide. Tall stands of water grew and merged into one, standing as a hundred-foot-wide wall. The wall of water flickered and grew dark in colour before it resolved into a scene. Grunnxe's mouth fell open as a city appeared in the distance of the wall of water.

Carte.

The creature stopped thrashing as Broden smashed its head against the cobbles one last time. The snow on the ground made a dirty brown paste with the dead blood of the monster.

Broden stood, breathing hard, and took the few steps required before gathering up his sword. The fight around him was tailing off. The dozen creatures that had taken them by surprise, sprinting through a fog of snow, had been dispatched. The eight citizens they had gathered on their latest sortie from the cathedral had knotted together and embraced each other with fear as the platoon fought away the terror.

"Everyone fine?" Broden hissed in the dim light of the morning, struggling to see the furthest of his platoon through a thick fall of snow. The response came back one by one; all fine. "Let's keep moving. We're not far from the cathedral. You'll be safe there." Broden set off running, quick and quiet.

His men flanked the group of civilians and hurried them along.

Broden squinted through the snow, desperate to see the cathedral up ahead. *The groups of those things are getting bigger. Can't keep fighting them like this.* He finally saw the imposing shape of the cathedral. He stopped and turned to his group.

He leaned in and whispered to them, "We have to make it across the square. Remember, whatever happens, keep running. Aim for the side door. Tell them you're with Captain Broden's party. Understood?"

The group nodded and grunted, too frightened to speak.

"Say it. Say it back to me," Broden snapped.

The mumble fell from their frozen mouths, "Captain Broden's party."

"Good. Let's go." Broden turned and, as a single body, the group sprinted into the square towards the cathedral through a white haze.

They ran low and hard, eyes almost shut to avoid the flakes of snow, but open enough to see where they were going.

Broden heard a cry from behind as one of the group slipped in the snow on the cobbles. A commotion followed which he could only assume was guardsmen tripping over the prone civilian. "Keep running!" Broden hissed as the group made it across the square and down the side of the cathedral. "Get to the door!" he ordered one of the platoon before turning back towards the square. Just through the haze of snow, he saw a city guardsman running towards him. "Come on, keep coming!" he cried out as he closed the gap, the guardsman coming closer, becoming clear.

The man had blood trailing from his mouth and his eyes were white.

Fear ran through Broden. *Not one of mine.*

He ducked, just avoiding the swing of the creature's claws. Broden spun and brought his sword crashing down, but missed the mark. The creature turned and crouched, white eyes blinking, fresh blood and flesh still clear around its mouth.

Whoever fell stayed down. Broden circled the creature, waiting for an opportunity. He stole a glance over its shoulder and saw two more forms approaching through the snow. *You're in trouble now.* He swung, causing the creature to leap to one side. He swung again and missed once more.

The others grew closer.

Not long. Have to be quick. He feigned a blow and followed with a kick, sending the creature reeling to the snowy ground. Broden pounced and drove his sword home under the chin of the prone monster. It stiffened as he slammed the sword into its skull.

Fuck! A pair of rough hands grabbed him from behind and hauled him up. Broden moved to strike at his unseen assailant, but was slapped across the face before he had half a chance.

"Don't be stupid, laddie," said a familiar, ragged voice. "Come on, keep on running. The other lads will deal with them."

"Subath!" Broden spluttered. "I've never happier to get a slap in the face from you!"

"Aye," the old warrior growled as they approached the cathedral's side entrance. "Never been happier to dish one out either." Subath roared at the door and shoved Broden in once it was opened, following in behind. "Keep the door ready. The others will be back in a moment," Subath ordered those on the door. "Come on, you. Up the stairs." Subath gave Broden a slap on the back and began making his way up into the cathedral. "We've to have a little talk."

As they reached the top of the stairs leading to the cupola, Althia walked by carrying a bowl of warm water and some cloths. Broden stopped in his tracks.

"Althia," Broden called out, causing her to turn.

"Captain Broden." She smiled at him. "I'm just tending to some of the injured you brought in earlier."

"How's everyone faring?"

"We've plenty of help. We're managing just fine. It's surprising how much food there is in the cathedral stores."

"Hardly," Subath grumbled under his breath. "The church takes what it desires, from my experience of it."

Broden ignored the comment. "How's my man?"

"Last I looked, he was asleep, as was the little girl you brought in." Althia smiled and shrugged her shoulders. "I'm afraid I have people to tend, Captain."

"Of course, of course."

As Althia made her way off, Subath called after her, "Is there somewhere private I could talk with the captain?"

Althia smiled. "Of course. There's a free room next to where the injured guardsman and the girl sleep. You may use that."

They made their way into the room. Subath clicked the door shut and turned gravely to Broden.

"What wrong?" Broden asked, plonking himself down on the bed with a sigh.

"The outer wall's been abandoned." Subath's face cut a sorry sight.

"What? What's happened?"

"This happened!" Subath raised his hands, pointing out the window and towards the cupola. "The walls were overrun. Those creatures came from all around. The troops on the walls have either died fighting them, locked themselves in the towers and gatehouses, or are making their way back to the inners walls of the High Command, as I've ordered. I've tried to send word, but the damned pigeons can't fly in snow this fierce. I would send a runner but..." The old fighter shrugged his shoulders and nodded towards the window. "Well, you know."

"Dajda!" Broden made a blessing on himself and stood, staring out the window as snow flurried down.

"No one's listening, Broden. We're in this alone still."

"There's time still—"

A scream punctured through from the adjacent room, cutting Broden off.

He and Subath sprang out the door and burst into the next room, swords free from their scabbards. Before them they saw the injured guardsman standing with one foot out of his bed, hunched, fingers like talons, and white-eyed.

He growled at the two soldiers and shot a glance back to the small girl who had squirmed towards the back of the bed. She held her covers before her face in a hopeless act of defence. The creature looked towards Broden and Subath, who stood with mouths agape at the beast. It swung a clawed hand at the air between them and snapped its teeth.

"Not that one. She's under my protection," Broden muttered before leaping at the creature, his cry thundering around the cupola.

Broden slashed at the creature. His first blow cut off a swiping hand, spurting blood across the wall. Subath's sword slammed into the creature's shoulder blade, dropping it to one knee. Broden's second swing cut free the head. The disembodied head fell onto the bed and settled, white eyes staring at the ceiling.

The child continued to wail as the creature's body was kicked over by Subath onto the floor between the beds.

Broden turned to Subath, a dawning on his face. "They grow in number."

"And what?" Subath replied.

"You said you were overrun, then the guardsmen who had me in the square, and now him." Broden nodded to the guardsman's corpse on the floor. "They're growing in number, because every time they kill or injure one of us, they are increasing their forces."

Subath's lips moved in silence.

"What is it?" Broden asked.

"I'm trying to work out how many people are in this city."

Broden's face dropped. "Dajda!"

Subath's lips stopped moving and he looked up. "We have to get back inside the High Command. We're nothing but meat out here."

Chapter Thirty-Seven

KALFINAR SCRIBBLED a signature and blotted the order. He handed it to the young soldier. The lad's hand tremored.

"What age are you, boy?" Kalfinar asked the young man.

"Fifteen, Your Highness."

"Not a 'Highness', boy. Just 'sir' will do."

"Yes, sir."

"Go on, get going."

"Sir." The youth saluted and hurried off.

"Are we so stretched that we're taking lads off the street and putting them in a uniform?" Kalfinar asked Merkham and the gathered officers.

"Aye," Merkham replied, raising his head from where he scribbled on the large map of the city. "We're that stretched."

As Merkham finished speaking, another messenger burst into the room, causing heads to turn.

"Chief Marshall, sir." The messenger saluted. "Lord Harruld's physician has sent for you. He says it's a matter of some urgency."

Kalfinar started running before the messenger had finished. He bounded the short hallway, boots slapping flagstones, and burst into his father's private chambers.

"Father!" Kalfinar stopped in his tracks with Evelyne coming into the study just behind him. "What's happening?" Kalfinar asked as he approached his father.

Harruld was lying along his chair by the fire with a thin, glass tube venting blood from his arm. He had a wet cloth over his eyes while a physician listened to his heart through an ear-piece.

"He can't hear you, boy," a thin croak came from the chair in which Olmat sat. "He's being bled."

"Kalfinar?" Harruld's voice sounded. "Is that you? Take this bloody cloth away from me," Harruld snapped at the attending physician, who removed the wet cloth.

Kalfinar approached his father. "What's he doing to you?"

"Treating a sick and weary man. I'm old. I've fought and stressed through my entire life. My blood's tired. The physician's getting rid of some of the old stuff. He seems to think my old body can make some fresh blood." Harruld laughed a weak sound and then grimaced as the physician removed the tube draining blood from his arm. "But what I can't make can be found in other ways."

"Take a seat and roll up your sleeve, Chief Marshall," the physician said to Kalfinar.

"What?" Kalfinar reacted slowly to his new title.

"Your father needs some of your blood."

"I'll not need much." Harruld grinned and pulled himself upright. "I've felt more invigorated for a few days after each purge, but it has ceased to have as much of an effect. The physician seems to thinks the blood of a vigorous kinsman could help."

"Seems like I'm your man." Kalfinar placed a hand on Harruld's shoulder and sat down beside him.

"Here, let me help," Evelyne said to the physician as she unfurled the tubing and affixed the barbed siphon on the end.

"Place the other end into the bottle. There's one in the bag over there." The physician pointed to the large, leather bag on the side table by the window.

Harruld watched her for a moment as she walked to the other side of the room. He turned back to Kalfinar. "Are you happy?" he whispered.

Kalfinar looked at the back of Evelyne as she reached into the bag. "I am, even with our world falling around us." A crash of glass sounded and Kalfinar sprang to his feet. "Evelyne!"

She stood staring out of the window.

"What's wrong?" Kalfinar asked, stepping up beside her.

"Demons come," she said.

"Do you mean the creatures?" Kalfinar asked. "The ones attacking the city? They're spirits of Balzath, aren't they?"

"No, worse than that comes," Evelyne said. "I had a sense that something was coming."

As Evelyne finished speaking, footsteps pounded up the stairs nearby. They turned to face the door and Merkham came into the room, followed by one of Subath's subordinates.

"What news?" Harruld asked, his voice trembling.

Merkham answered, "The outer walls, My Lord. We've been forced to abandon them and retreat. The creatures are too many."

The chin of the young officer next to Merkham wobbled.

"Lad, speak up," Kalfinar ordered.

"Sir," the young man responded, "about three hundred of us have made it back behind the High Command walls. A skeleton force is holed up in the towers and gatehouses and Subath is lost in the city. His group hasn't made it back. We've lost unknown numbers to the creatures. They swell in numbers with every one they take." The officer broke down as he finished.

"Hells," Kalfinar muttered. "Lad, head back to your platoon. Orders will be issued. For now, just get some rest and something to eat."

The officer composed himself, saluted, and then left the room.

Merkham stood in silence, looking out the window. "When did it stop snowing?"

They each looked out the window. The rising sun was shining, breaking between heavy, dark clouds.

"Didn't even notice," Kalfinar mused

"About ten minutes," offered the physician attending Harruld. "The snow broke not long before Captain Kalfinar and the lady attended."

As the physician stopped speaking, more footsteps sounded from the stairs.

"More bad news." Kalfinar faced the door.

A sergeant from the signals tower came puffing and red-faced into the room.

"Chief Marshall, sir." The man gasped for breath and offered a tiny roll of paper towards Kalfinar.

"Thank you. At ease," Kalfinar said, unfurling the paper. His eyes scanned the message. "It's from Abbonan. Solansian ships have been spotted. They sneaked in on the fog. Abbonan has taken charge of the fleet and moves to engage them."

"With the outer walls weakened, we'll need to get everyone back to the High Command. We need to send out troops to help them."

Harruld rubbed his eyes. "Dajda damn it, Kal!" he snapped. "Have you not heard what Merkham just said? Only three hundred made it back."

"What about Broden? Subath? All of the troops out there? The people? Are we abandoning them to the mercy of monsters?"

"We pray for them," Harruld mumbled.

"No one is listening." Kalfinar spat his words, his heart racing.

He walked to the window, staring over the walls of the High Command and into the city. The sun was breaking crimson through the clouds, washing the city in a red as the snow reflected the light of the sun. *Blood sun. Painting a city in blood. How very apt. Where are you, cousin? Where are you?*

Broden peered out the window at the square, now lit in a blaze of scarlet and pinks by the rising sun.

"How's it looking?" Subath asked.

"Square's clear," Broden said, his eyes scanning for any signs of the creatures. "Are the people ready?"

"Aye, shit scared, but they're ready."

"Good. Have they taken weapons?"

"Of sorts. The caretakers and the holy ones weren't so happy about the congregation ripping up their benches and taking their candlesticks, but when I told them that they'd be the only thing between them and being eaten, it sort of did the trick." Subath croaked a laugh. "It's amazing the fine silver candlesticks that come out of the vestry in moments like that."

Broden smirked and clapped Subath on the shoulder as he walked past and into the main body of the cathedral. He looked at the frightened people gathered. There stood at least two hundred souls rescued from the city, frightened holy people, and Tuannan, all powerless whilst Dajda slept.

"You ready?" he called out.

Some mumbles and nods were all he received.

"That'll have to do," he grumbled to himself. "Remember to keep running. The High Command's only a mile from here. If we run fast and smooth—no stops—we can be there in a little over ten minutes. Fast and smooth." He scanned the eyes of those around him. The atmosphere prickled with fear. He stopped at Althia and offered her a reassuring nod. "Are you ready?" he called out once more.

Althia smiled, nodded, and then glanced down at the small girl who clung tight to her.

Broden walked over, leaned in close, and whispered to Althia, "Come with me to the front. Stick tight and don't stop."

She nodded, wiping away a tear with one hand. Broden turned and approached Subath with Althia and the child not far behind him. Subath had his hand on the lock to the front doors of the cathedral.

As Broden approached, he unsheathed his sword. "Let's go."

Thaskil wiped his sword and hatchet on the shirt of the raider he had just killed, serving only to dirty his blade further. He looked around the bulwark. There was not a scrap of fabric he saw that was not coated in blood.

"Even the sun rises in blood this morning," Sergeant Omree said as he came up beside Thaskil. They stared out across the Field of Storms, watching as the fire in the pit flickered, its tongues of flame dancing smaller now in the red morning light. "Why aren't they committing everything? It's been two days of probing and each time we repel them."

"I don't know. They're toying with us, I fear. Maybe they're just grinding us down. The real attack could come when we're at our weakest."

Omree looked back down the bulwark as defenders and citizens alike aided the wounded, taking them to makeshift infirmaries in nearby halls while replacing injured troops with armed men, women, and anyone else able to swing a blade and set free an arrow. "Things will get pretty desperate soon."

"Aye," Thaskil grumbled, wiping away a drop of blood that had gathered on his eyebrow.

"Reinforcements may still come. There is time," Omree said with a knowing grin.

"They'll never get here in time." *Time.* Thaskil laughed. *It is only a matter of time.* "We need to hold on. Dig in. They'll eventually come. Tell the men reinforcements will come. We just need to hold on until they do." *Time's run out. We'll need a miracle.* Thaskil turned and clapped Omree on the shoulder. "If you need me, I'll be in the dungeons."

Thaskil didn't bother to wash himself or change clothes, but he did take time to properly clean his weapons. He sheathed his sword and slid his battle-hatchet into his belt before entering the dungeon, slamming the heavy wooden door shut behind him. He took two deep breaths. *Keep yourself together, man. Keep a hold on your nerve, for Dajda's sake.*

Having composed himself, Thaskil walked around the corner of the dungeon hall, along the straw lined floors, and past the empty cells until he stopped in front of Bergnon's.

The sorry major was sunk on the floor, head buried in his arms, resting on his knees.

"Wake up," Thaskil croaked, his voice flat and exhausted as he slumped into the chair before the bars.

Bergnon raised his head, his face swollen and filthy with caked blood. "No sleep for me." His voice was hoarse.

"You know," Thaskil said, pouring a cup of water and sliding it through the bars towards Bergnon, "I could hear you shouting to me. Despite it all, I could hear you. Amazing that, isn't it."

"Aye, laddie, it is," Bergnon grumbled, nodding gratefully for the water. "I saw the traps worked. That first assault, they just got sucked right in."

"I'm amazed I listened to you about that—" Thaskil broke and began to weep, the flood of emotion pouring out of him. "And it worked." He lurched from the emotion. "This is not for me. This duty is not for me. I know nothing of tactics. Nothing of leading men."

"That's not true—"

"Damn you," Thaskil spluttered through mucus and tears. "Look at me. My very soul is soaked in blood now. It'll never wash off. I'll never wash clean."

Bergnon rose to his feet and clung to the bars. His sorrowful face pressed out between the metal, tears welling in his puffy red eyes.

Thaskil shuddered through the sobs as he breathed rapid, shallow breaths. He had never felt more sick in his life. "I may have swung the blade, but you've killed them all. You've killed me." He shuddered from the rapid breaths and sobs. "This duty is not for me."

"I'm so sorry, lad. I truly am." Bergnon too broke. "You led them better than almost anyone I've seen. You can do this. Let me help you again."

Thaskil looked up from his hands.

"I'm at fault for this all, laddie. Every death is my doing, every sword stoke from my arm. Let me use it truly. Let me help right some of this wrong I've wrought. Let me find some redemption, please."

Thaskil fought the urge to spring to his feet and open the cell door. He couldn't deny he wanted for someone to take charge and free him of his burden. "No amount of blood can return you to the light, Bergnon. You've made sure of that and the knowledge of that is your curse." The imagined image of Arrlun murdered flashed in Thaskil's mind. "You saw to it that Arrlun died. You had friends and comrades murdered by assassins while they slept and you've cursed the souls of millions by siding with the darkness. All for one person and she's dead. She's fucking dead. It was for nothing." Thaskil wiped his tears away angrily, defiant against the fear lurching in his guts.

Bergnon slid down the bars of his cell and slumped against them, his forehead leaning against the rust-spotted metal. His blank eyes stared at the blood and filth-spattered boots Thaskil wore. "You've not been in love before, have you, lad?"

"No, not least in ways to draw on madness."

"Then you've never been in love." Bergnon looked up and held Thaskil's gaze. "When it comes to you, Thaskil, when love finally finds you, think of me. Perhaps in that moment, you'll see some way to forgive me in part for what I've done."

Thaskil stood up and wiped away the last of his tears, smearing dirt on his cheek. "You've taken away any chance I've ever had, Major, for I'll no doubt be dead by the time the sun sets tonight." Thaskil walked off, stopping after a few paces and turning. "So you know, I'm not keeping you caged out of mercy to spare your life. I want you to be rescued by your people and to live out what days you have remembering what you've done." Thaskil disappeared around the corner of the dungeon hall before opening and slamming the door shut.

"Thaskil!" Bergnon roared, his voice trailing off in a ragged croak at the end. "Thaskil! Let me fight! Let me fight with you. I can help, please. Please! Dajda, forgive me for what I've done..." Bergnon's roars trailed off into words warped by sobs.

Thaskil leant against the wall outside the dungeon, listening to the sobs and spluttered words. His mind reeled. *Am I doing what's right for the people out there? Are anger and vengeance more important than sense and trust?*

He smashed his clenched fist into the wall and tore open the door. Pounding down the hallway, he caused Bergnon to leap up from his misery. Barely pausing a moment, Thaskil removed the key from his pocket and unlocked the cell door, shoving it open with a heavy metallic grind. He stood there, face to face with Bergnon. The silence between them was thick.

"Need I say it?" Thaskil said. *What are you doing? Are you mad?*

"I don't deserve your trust, but believe me, I will give my final breath to you, or you may take it yourself."

"If it comes to it, I will," Thaskil said before walking away, "Come with me. We've a city to defend."

Chapter Thirty-Eight

"READY THE BALLISTAE!" Abbonan roared from the ship's aftercastle through a horn, amplifying his voice to the engineers on deck.

He heard his orders being repeated from the ships alongside. No doubt, down to the last of his armada, the orders were being relayed. The ship was approaching the first of the raider vessels as they cut through choppy waves into the bay. The sailors on board scurried to and fro to prime the ballistae, readying to loose the bolt towards the waterline of the enemy ship.

"Ready the onagers!" Abbonan roared.

Sailors ran to prepare the onagers. The first volley would be of heavy stone balls, hollowed and filled with embers taken from braziers. The second volley would be made up of the plugged vats of pitch. Abbonan watched as the fleet of raider ships approached further. His ships outnumbered the raiders, but their vessels were smaller and more manoeuvrable. All he needed was to begin in a blaze of violence and glory and the rest would tuck tail and run, he hoped.

"Here they come," Abbonan muttered as the raiders bore down. "Dajda be with us."

He heard roars and cries from the enemy and saw men waving weapons. No doubt, they would try to lash the boats together and board the ships, fighting hand to hand. Abbonan had issued his orders and the marine infantry were ready to repel any attempts, but in the squeeze of ships, it was sometimes inevitable. He drew his sword and steadied himself. The stink of unwashed men wafted over him as the wind changed; a repellent scent of those whom he aimed to repel. Fitting, he thought.

"Engage!" Abbonan shouted as the ships came within several lengths of each other.

The crash of ballistae rung clear in the air. The roar of raiders redoubled. Abbonan observed some bolts find their mark, punching deep into the waterline of raider ships and causing sea water to rush in, whilst some slid off the bow and into the waves without harm. Others hit their targets, but bristled out of the front of the ship like the spikes of a beast.

"Reload!" Abbonan roared, his orders again echoed down the line of ships.

The raiders began sending arrows as their boats approached the defenders' ships.

"Hot stones!" Abbonan roared.

Pairs of sailors wielding heavy metal tongs carefully moved stones filled with red-hot embers into the nests of the onagers. Abbonan heard cries from the neighbouring ship, causing him to turn. One of the hot stones had been dropped and rolled down the deck of the ship, smashing sailors before coming to rest by rope, bursting it into flames and casting embers.

"Douse that!" Abbonan roared through his horn. "Douse it now!" He turned back to his own ship and roared his command, "Engage!"

The onagers released their stones with a distinctive thump, sending stones flying towards the raider ships followed by a volley of pitch into the same mark. Raider ships burst into flame, accompanied by the frantic cries from the raiders themselves.

Abbonan afforded a glance to the neighbouring ship as his sailors battled to put out their own fires.

Several of the raider ships pulled back, falling lower in the sea as they took on more water, whilst others struggled to contain flames spreading up ropes and sails, consuming masts and deck alike.

"Ready to engage!" Abbonan roared through his horn as the ships pulled up alongside and began casting ropes. "Come on, you bastards!" Abbonan ran down the steps from the aftercastle, his sword unsheathed and his battle cry loud.

"Keep running, we're almost there!" Broden cried out to the group with him as they pounded through the snowy streets of Carte.

The ragged breath of all those who ran behind him rasped loud in his ears. The little girl clung tight to his chest, with Althia running just behind him. The screams from the rear were increasing with frequency. He saw the walls of the High Command ahead, and the urge to keep powering on redoubled within.

"Almost there!" roared Subath by his side.

A blood-curdling scream sounded, sending a shiver down Broden's neck.

"Eyes forward!" Broden barked. "There's nothing you can do for those that fall." He could hear the sobs of the little girl beginning and his jaw set. *I'll not let them take you, not like this.* His feet pounded harder, his legs a blur as he crashed towards the High Command.

A cry came out from the rear of the group, "There's so many! Hurry!"

"What in the dark hells is that?" Kalfinar asked as he peered out Harruld's window at a knot of bodies charging up the street towards the gates of the High Command.

"What's wrong?" Harruld asked, alarmed.

"Pass me your eyeglass," Kalfinar said, reaching out for the magnifying piece. He grabbed it from Harruld and placed it to his eye, honing in on the charging people. "Broden and Subath!" Kalfinar yelled. "They have civilians with them. Open the gates!"

"Issue the order!" Harruld barked to the attendant guard. "Get it there quick." He stood and approached his son by the window. "What're they—"

"The creatures!" Kalfinar shouted, handing the eyeglass to his father and charging out of the room.

"Wait, Kal!" Harruld shouted as Evelyne leapt to her feet from where she knelt with Olmat. "Where are you going?"

The governor peered at the street using the eyeglass. Towards the end of the long street, a horde of white-eyed creatures bore down on Broden and Subath's party as they sprinted towards the High Command gates. Harruld looked up from the street, his eyes scanning the city. Random pockets of flames still burned, sending pillars of smoke skyward. Beyond the city, to the bay, he saw ships clashing and burning.

"Dajda has abandoned us."

———

"Everyone onto the drawbridge!" Broden roared with all his might.

"They're getting closer!"

"There are so many!"

"Dajda."

"Help us!"

They were baring down on the High Command, but the gates weren't opening.

Broden waved as he ran. "Open up! Let us in!" He cried loud and clear, but it was no use. *Don't be stupid. They won't open the gate unless there's a direct order from Harruld. He won't have seen you. You'll have to make a stand.*

He glanced at Althia and the child. Both were crying now, though Althia strode on, getting closer to the gate all the while.

"I have to leave you now," Broden said. "Once you make it to the gate, stay at the back on the drawbridge, but try to stay out of the press and scramble, you hear?"

"Yes," she said amidst gasping breaths.

"Good. The gates will open. In the meantime, we'll hold them off as best we can. The drawbridge gives us a pinch point. They can't come all at once." He smiled and gave her shoulder a squeeze. "Have hope and I'll see you inside."

"Be careful!" Althia cried as Broden broke away.

Subath followed, edging down the outside of the knot of people and taking the remaining troops with them to the rear.

Dajda, help us. As Broden caught sight of their pursuers, his heart felt like it had frozen to ice in his chest. The group of creatures closed quickly. *So many.* Broden glanced at Subath. Uncertainty etched across his face also.

"Men, fall back! Let the people get onto the drawbridge!" Broden shouted. He looked at the remaining elements of their platoons. *Less than twenty-four men against hundreds.*

"Here they come! Get ready," Subath roared beside Broden.

The troops backed up to create a wall of swords and spears between the people and the creatures. Broden heard some of the men muttering prayers; some blubbering. He didn't blame them.

Arrows shot into the creatures from the walls. Those that found their mark mostly met bodies, but some hit heads and dropped creatures. Broden felt some relief at the support from the walls, but the numbers were still too great. The creatures closed the distance.

"Ready!"

"Open the gate! Open the fucking gate!" Kalfinar screamed with all of his might, his voice rising to a comical pitch as he pounded across the courtyard towards the main gate of the High Command. *Hold tight. Just hold them back a little longer.*

The screams and the hammering on the huge gate brought intense panic to the air. Bows fired from the gatehouses above.

"On the orders of the chief marshal," Kalfinar roared, "open the fucking gate now!"

The metallic grind of the gate-wheel turning and chains rolling came to his ears like a bird's song in spring.

"Come help me," Kalfinar ordered the gathering soldiers, a mass of which now stood behind him as the gate peeked open. Desperate fingertips poked through. *Hurry, damn it. Come on.*

The doors of the gate spread further and a flood of terrified people spewed in, some collapsing over each other in a rush to escape the mob of claws and teeth on the other side.

I'm coming, Broden. Hold on. "Help them!" Kalfinar roared as he ran forward. "With me!" He squeezed past the onrushing people, fighting hard not to be swept with. "Let me through!"

He used his strength to pull people past him and make his way onto the drawbridge. Before him, through the remaining civilians, he saw the frantic defence of the troops. Kalfinar felt the surge of blood and he charged forward, troops following behind.

He burst into the fray. His sword chopped and stabbed, dismembering limbs and hacking once, twice, three times before finally dropping creatures. The first sight of the wild, white-eyed creatures chilled him and he suddenly felt very conscious of the amulet around his neck. *Spirits in them.*

"Kal! Aim for their heads!"

Kalfinar recognised the voice. "Broden, fall back. We've you covered. Get back!" He stabbed and kicked, but the press of creatures seemed relentless, with more seeming to join the fight all the time. The force of amassed creatures appeared almost capable of pushing them back through the gates. "Fall back!"

"Come on! Get clear, for fuck's sake!" Broden shouted from the rear of the drawbridge.

The exhausted troops broke away, dragging the rest back with them, swords slashing as they went. Kalfinar heard the snap of the bows before arrows to the head sent creatures tumbling. He kicked and shoved, hurling many of the monsters into the moat where they floundered without hope of re-joining the fight.

"Get clear!" Broden shouted to Kalfinar and the remaining troops on the last length of drawbridge.

Kalfinar and the final few troops stabbed at the pulsating mob of creatures with spears and swords, holding them off.

"Break away, men!" Kalfinar shouted.

The troops broke and dashed in past the open gate.

"Shut the gates!" Subath cried. "Spears ready!"

As the last of the men scrambled across the drawbridge and past the gate, the horde of creatures clambered over bodies of monster and man. Broden and Subath had joined the knot of men beside Kalfinar, thrusting spears as the gate slowly shut. Bows twanged above them as the monsters clawed, trying to get past the forest of spears in front of them.

"Hold them off!" Subath roared in a ragged voice as the gates narrowed further. "Hold them o—"

Subath's order was cut short as he was yanked to the slushy ground, one the creatures having crawled under the spear points and hauling the old warrior off his feet.

"Not like this, you bastard!" Subath roared as he saw the monster clawing up towards him. He shook free a boot and crashed his heel into its snarling white-eyed face. "Shut the fucking gate!" he roared again, still smashing his heel into the pulpy face of the creature.

The gate narrowed almost shut now. Subath scrambled to his feet and grabbed his spear, thrusting it into the skull of the creature just as the doors of the gate thumped together.

"You all there?" Broden asked as the old battler wiped the snow off his arse.

"Aye, I'm fine, laddie. Sure I've fought off worse in a whore house?"

Broden clasped Subath's wrist and smiled. "Made it."

"Aye, better late than never, Chief Marshall." He grinned his ragged smile at Kalfinar and slapped him on his shoulder.

Broden turned his head and grinned wide at his cousin. "Chief Marshall, eh?"

Kalfinar shook his head. "Don't you two start. Were there many of them out there?"

"More than I'd care to imagine," Broden said as he cleaned his sword with a handful of snow. "They spread amongst the people they take. What of Olmat?"

"He's fading. Won't be long," Kalfinar said, clasping wrists in greeting.

"Sorry to say it had better not. Carte's nearly on her arse."

"Aye." Kalfinar looked Broden and Subath, "Abbonan's engaged raider's ships in the bay."

"And we've lost the outer city," Subath said with a weary sigh. "We were overrun."

Kalfinar rubbed at the back of his neck and sighed. "Aye, we're very nearly on our arse."

Chapter Thirty-Nine

"EVERYONE WHO'S ABLE, get out there on the plain and gather up whatever arrows and bolts can be salvaged," Thaskil called from on top of the battlements. "Never mind your sensitivities. Take them from the flesh as readily as you would the ground. Bring them back and separate them out. We'll need every last one you can retrieve."

He turned back to Bergnon, who stood behind him beside Sergeants Omree and Rushnall, both of whom eyed the traitor with suspicion.

"When do you think they'll come again?" Thaskil asked Bergnon.

"Night, I'd guess," Bergnon mused, looking out across the plain. The large black cloud of smoke still billowed from the trench as it burned its final fuel. "They're hiding their strength behind that wall of smoke."

"Maybe a good thing," Thaskil muttered. "Seeing an army that size of would steal the heart of a man."

"Aye, it may do, but it also hides their movement, their unit numbers, and their strength. I'd rather be frightened than blind," Bergnon added. He walked to the edge of the battlement and watched as citizens and soldiers alike scrambled to collect as many arrows and bolts as they could, many being ripped from bodies of dead raiders. "You know we have to get rid of the bodies. This place will become unholy with the stink before long, and then comes disease."

Thaskil joined him, looking at the sea of corpses covering the bulwark and littering the plain.

"A field of corpses," Thaskil muttered.

"What?"

"Nothing. What'll we do with them?" Thaskil quickly changed the subject.

"We burn them," Bergnon mused. "In front of the breach. It'll slow their approach."

"What about the rest of the walls?" Thaskil asked. "Won't they attack from any other side?"

"Why would they?" Bergnon asked, bemused. "Didn't I teach you anything? It is the path of least resistance, lad. Why work at a wall without a great big fucking hole in it if you don't need to. And they have the numbers to spend."

Omree interrupted, "Why should we listen to him? It's because of this snake we've got a breach at all."

Thaskil waved his hand in acknowledgment. "I know," he sighed. "I know."

"I'm dead anyway, Sergeant, regardless of what happens," Bergnon said, a humourless grin crossing his battered face. "I can at least do the right thing before I die." He held the gaze of the younger man for a moment. "I'm not stupid enough to ask you to trust me, but against your better judgement, you may just have to."

Omree threw up his hands in mock surrender and turned away, exasperated and exhausted.

"They'll come to the breach again. Now we need to make sure we have some surprises for them when they do."

"Like what?" Thaskil asked. "We're down to our last of everything."

"Not everything. In the basements of the High Command, in a cool house in the north wing, there should be mining powder. If we use that powder in concentrate, it can devastate."

The flames of the trench began to sputter out as the sun was setting. Thaskil returned from washing himself and donned a fresh uniform, fittingly that of an Apulan city guard. He stooped and looked at himself in the glass of a shop window as he made his way back to the breach. It felt odd to be in the red surcoat he grew up seeing, rather than the deep green of the Free Provinces Pathfinders.

An old soldier came running from across the street. "Lieutenant Thaskil, Sergeant Omree wants you on the wall right away, sir."

Thaskil broke into a sprint and bounded his way towards the breach and up the steps to the battlement, two at a time. He arrived in the soft rays of the evening sun to see Omree and Bergnon staring across the plain.

"What is it?" Thaskil asked.

"Look," Omree said, pointing ahead. "Behind the smoke and the haze. It's the Solansian forces."

"I can't. I can't see any…"

Thaskil's words trailed off as he stared beyond the grimy smoke of the smouldering trench. The massive army he had expected was not there. The body of troops was still substantial, but Apula had held back more in the past.

"Where've they all gone?" Thaskil asked no one in particular.

"Carte," Bergnon offered. "That's the only place they can go. They want to end this quick. Grunnxe must have thought he had Apula sewn up and decided he wanted to taste the sweeter fruit."

"We must send word." Thaskil rummaged a small piece of waxed paper from his pouch and scratched a message onto it for the command in Carte. "Omree, take this and replicate it. Send out a half-dozen Carte birds. They need to know Grunnxe's coming."

───────

"Subath! Broden!" Harruld stood, arms wide, and a smile wider still as they entered his chamber. "Some good news at last."

Evelyne stood up from beside where Olmat slept. She rushed over and gave Kalfinar a hug and a kiss.

"This is new!" Broden said, his eyebrow arching.

"Aye, well," Kalfinar fumbled for words as Evelyne's fingers found his.

"Don't need to explain yourself to me," Broden said, raising his palms. "And in any case, I'm happy for you both. At least some joy can be found in this hell."

"Thank you, Broden," Evelyne said.

"A dispatch has come in from Apula," Harruld diverted the subject, sitting down in his seat as all eyes turned to him, expectant. "Apula holds."

A whoop came from Broden and Subath.

Kalfinar deflated. He hadn't realised he'd held his breath in the moment.

"Thaskil and the ranks have held Grunnxe's forces off so far, but it seems grave news follows good." Harruld's face was weary and grey.

"What is it?" Kalfinar urged.

"It appears that despite being instrumental in an act of defence, the trench of pitch they burned at Apula obscured the fact that much of Grunnxe's army departed. It's feared that they make their way to Carte."

"But that'll take them weeks," Broden said.

"They'd be quicker by boat, if they go by the Valeswater," Kalfinar added.

"Sooner," a weak voice came from behind, causing them to turn around. Olmat was awake and turned his head. "Grunnxe is spirited by the darkness. He'll soon be at our door."

The old king's heart thundered in his chest as he looked upon the city of Carte. He turned towards the Priestess and growled, "This is what we've come for! This city will bring back the Cullanain to the Solansians and re-establish our Solansian Empire. We will yolk the people and they will serve the great Master God, Balzath."

The Priestess shuddered, her grey, pallid skin barely visible under her heavy hood.

"Is there something you want to say, oh once-powerful Bhalur?" Grunnxe made a mocking bow at the former god, laughing and wiggling his tongue.

"Nothing, Your Highness," the Priestess replied, the hatred in her voice scarcely contained.

"Wonderful," Grunnxe replied, "because I don't think our great god would care much for you addressing his new herald with such contempt, would he now?"

The Priestess paused. "No, he certainly would not."

Grunnxe fixed his stare under the hood of the Priestess. He could not see her face, but he imagined it was twisted in rage and, inwardly, was grateful to have the protection of the Master God. "Good, now let's get everyone dismounted and into formations. I want to present in front of our new city in time for the full light of morning to make us shimmer." Grunnxe smiled at his nodding commanders. "Let's allow them the glorious sight of the sun reflecting off our forces before we rip them asunder, eh?"

A great cheer rang into the air from the gathered commanders and officers.

Grunnxe allowed himself a smile, but his eyes were locked on the Priestess, who stood without motion or voice, likely staring at Grunnxe with hate-filled eyes from under her hood.

Abbonan beat back the stinking raider with experienced thrusts and parries. The conceding raider tripped backwards, providing the opening Abbonan needed. He slid his blade into the man's chest, finishing him with a quick twist of the wrist before pulling the sword free and evoking a weak spurt of blood. Abbonan wiped his forehead with his coat sleeve and looked about.

The raiders had been largely repelled from another boarding, but in the distraction, several of their larger ships had broken free and were closing on the docks.

"They'll be laden with men!" Abbonan roared out. "Onagers, prepare for long range fire. We need to stop those ships docking."

"Sir, we'll need to get closer. They're almost out of range."

"Damn it!" Abbonan snapped and ran towards the wheel, finding his helmsman struggling with an arrow in his gut. "Malvern!"

"It's not so bad, My Lord," the helmsman groaned, lifting his palm to reveal a bright red stain across his belly. "It's not in deep."

"Dajda, nevertheless man, get below decks to the physician. I'll take the wheel."

"Aye, My Lord." The helmsman released his sticky grip and laboured towards the stairs.

"Right, lads," Abbonan roared as the last of the raiders was cut down and their ship set to flame. "Let's get off after these bastards!"

The roar went up loud and the sailors set about their stations, readying the ship to sail after the advancing raiders.

"This was all just a bloody tactic to get the fucking raiders on shore." Abbonan was muttering to himself, not really heeding the noise. "You're a fool Abbonan, a damned—"

He saw a flash of light to his left and felt his head wobble. He dropped to his knees and heard muffled voices calling out to him. He tried to stand and take the wheel before falling back onto one knee.

"Bloody inconvenience," he muttered, wet and bubbly. Flecks of blood landed on the wood of the wheel, the details of which he now noticed in intense minutia. The grain of the wood. Its anomalies and warps within its fibre. A small fly stuck in the varnish of it. "Bloody inconvenience."

Placing his hand to his throat, Abbonan felt the feathers at the end of the arrow shaft pressed neat to his neck and, with his other hand's trembling fingers, felt the majority of the arrow's body. He took his hands away and held them to his face, shining wet with bright, red life.

"Bloody inconvenience." Abbonan's knee gave way and he collapsed onto his back, staring up as the morning sun stained the sky whilst his draining life stained the deck.

"Hal," the guardsman called over his shoulder to his comrade. "You better take a look at this." He motioned beyond the arrow slit.

"What is it?" Hal replied, keeping his eyes fixed on the ground below his arrow slit on the other side of the outer wall. "I'm kind of busy here with those bloody creatures. They're still trying to climb the walls up to us. Suppose it makes it nice and easy for me to ping them in the head. They just keep looking up and I keep firing." He laughed as he released another arrow, finding its mark in the head of the creature below. The thing crashed to the ground and was soon obscured by the advance of another.

"No, Hal, I don't mean the creatures. I think you're going to want to see this."

"Fine," Hal snapped, turning from his work and stomping over. "Move over and give us a look." Hal's mouth sagged open as he peered out the arrow slit to see the huge army advancing on them, billowing a massive plume of dust in their wake. "Dajda have mercy."

"I think we'll have to send a pigeon to the High Command."

"Aye, I think so."

"He's slipping away. I can feel it getting closer." Evelyne brushed Olmat's thin hair as he slept in Harruld's private chambers.

"It pains me so to wish death upon him." Kalfinar stood behind Evelyne, buckling vambraces over his mail sleeves.

"It's his role in this. There's no ill in your wish. It's what's required."

"Doesn't stop it feeling wrong. Damn it!" he snapped, fumbling with the buckle.

"Let me." Evelyne stood from where she sat with Olmat and turned Kalfinar's forearm over, taking the buckle and pulling it tight.

He looked at her as she busied herself sliding leather through buckle. *What eyes you have.*

"What're you going to do?" she asked as she finished buckling the leather of the other vambrace.

"We've to fight for the city. There're too many of our people out there. If we abandon them now, they're at the mercy of those monsters. Before long, Grunnxe will come too. With no one manning the walls, he'll just flood right into the city and we'll all be damned then. We can't afford to just sit here behind these walls. The longer we wait for Olmat to die, the more of our people are slaughtered and enslaved by Balzath. No, we've got to fight."

She nodded at his words, but her eyes were full of sorrow. *Don't foul your eyes with tears.* "We're mounting an assault of the city. We're pushing back to take the outer walls."

Evelyne raised her hands and took Kalfinar's wrists in them. She pulled Kalfinar close, her ice-blue eyes brimming with tears. "When you go out there, be careful and come back to us here."

"Aye," Kalfinar mumbled, pulling her into an embrace. "We'd better get back to the others," he said, breaking away before leading Evelyne into the hallway.

As they entered Harruld's study, a clerk ran up the stairs and entered behind them.

"Chief Marshall," the man said.

"Speak."

"The Solansians." The man's whole body began to shudder.

"What news, man?" Kalfinar snapped.

"The news is grave, sir." The young man stumbled over his words, his voice thick with emotion. "The Solansians, they're before the east gate of the city." The clerk's chin wobbled and his lips trembled as he spoke. "We're lost. The city's lost."

"We are not lost!" Harruld's chair screeched back and he stood with fury, slamming his fist into the table, causing water cups to jump and spill. His voice boomed around the room, blasting the frightened clerk in the face and even taking Kalfinar by surprise. "The city is not lost and will not be lost. This is Carte, the seat of the Free Provinces. We will fight to the last breath and we will reject them one and all! Have some courage, damn you! Have some faith! We need only hold strong until Dajda can wake and bring forth the Anulii. We need only stay strong for a short while and we shall prevail! Nothing is lost. Nothing!" Harruld's chest heaved in and out as he regained his breath.

The clerk stood statue-still, chastened, and appearing ashamed.

"Fetch me my armour," Harruld snapped, causing Kalfinar, Broden, and the others gathered to look at him in shock.

"Plate or leather, My Lord?" The clerk asked.

"Leather." Harruld replied grimly. "Too weak for the damn plate."

At once, My Lord." The clerk scurried over to the large press at the far end of the study and began lifting out the governor's armour.

"Father, you cannot—"

"Kal, Chief Marshall or not, don't presume to tell me when I can and cannot fight for my people. We need every sword we can swing this night." Harruld walked over to his window and lifted his eyeglass, scanning the city.

Kalfinar walked up behind and clasped his shoulder.

"Then fight with me, Father," he whispered.

Harruld turned to him and smiled. "Aye." He stepped away, placing his eyepiece against Kalfinar's chest. "By the way, you'd best take a look at the bay," Harruld added, stretching his arms above his head as the clerk approached and placed a quilted undershirt over his head. "It looks like the raiders have broken through. They've taken the docks."

"We've ships still in the bay," Kalfinar said, scanning the water in the distance with the eyepiece. "It looks like there's a ship about to offload marine guards. With a bit of luck, the units dispatched to the dock quarter can repel them."

"I'm leading a support battalion down to the docks," Merkham interjected. "We'll ride down any of the creatures we find and cut our way through them. Once we get to the walls, we'll be able to lay down some more fire on them. Hopefully the marines can do the rest."

"Good," Harruld said, straining as the clerk dropped his chainmail over his head, links jingling as they fell around hips. "Subath, you and I will lead towards the east gate. Kal and Broden, you're with us. Let's give old Grunnxe a bit of a sting, eh?"

"Are the rams finished?" Grunnxe stormed towards the work party as they hurried to finish the battering rams. "And the ladders, are they ready? I'd like to get in and take this city before noon." Grunnxe stood before the frightened soldiers a fuming monster of lust, ravenous for the taste of blood.

The Master God urged him forward all the time. *"You must hurry, you must strike now while they lie undefended, unprotected. Attack them!"*

"Your Highness, we should be finished in the next half hour," one soldier spoke up, shrinking to a shadow of a man as he uttered the words under the intense glare of the old king.

"I heard that half an hour ago." Grunnxe's voice was calm, but his hand went to his sword, resting on the pommel.

The soldier who spoke up squirmed as his fellow workers stepped away from him.

Grunnxe stepped up to the man, snarling in his face, "If that ram is not charging towards those unprotected gates in the next ten minutes with you at the front, I will personally rip out your heart with my bare hands and shove it up your fucking arse!" As he spoke, Grunnxe's voice rose from calm to a spit-flinging shriek of pure fury.

The soldiers redoubled their efforts with the spokesman working feverishly, urging the others on. Grunnxe grinned at the improved effort and turned around. The Priestess was staring.

"What are you looking at, you fucking sexless ghost of a god?" He stormed up to the Priestess. "Take that fucking hood down so I can see your face when I speak to you." Grunnxe charged down on the Priestess and ripped the hood back, revealing the grey and sickly flesh, sunken red eyes and a lumpy bald head crowned with wisps of thin white hair.

"The Priestess is your servant to command, and will obey, or she will be obliterated."

The Priestess stared back at Grunnxe with pure hate in her eyes. "As my king commands it."

"Good," Grunnxe grumbled as he walked off and faced the gates of Carte, "because I'd hate to have to cut your head off, just as I would with those cockless bastards I call soldiers." He turned and stared hard at the Priestess. "I'd truly hate to."

"It will come to that before the end."

The Master God's words filled Grunnxe with pleasure. He was soon to reclaim his people's empire and he would drink his vengeance with the blood of his enemies. He stared back at the gates of Carte. There were few guards visible on the battlements. It appeared all of his plans had come together; the city lay broken, the Free Provinces in ruins.

He tipped back his head, outstretched his arms, and released a huge roar into the dusky light of early night. "Harruld, come and meet me as a man! Bring your little boy with you! Solansia has come to claim you. It has come to claim you all in the name of the Master God, Balzath!"

"Patience, child," the voice spoke to Grunnxe. *"Thy vengeance can wait. I send my servants for a greater prize."*

Chapter Forty

KALFINAR STOOD atop the lowest level of the High Command battlements. Before him were the gathered ranks of the Free Provinces command, all eyes fixed on him as he stood alongside the remaining senior staff and his father, the governor of Carte. He scanned across the massive courtyard, looking at the massed warriors.

"Men and women of the Free Provinces," Kalfinar's voice boomed across the courtyard. "We are gathered here this night faced with a great foe before us. We stand at the edge of a great darkness." Kalfinar's heart thundered in his chest as he spoke. He scanned the ranks and saw every spectrum of human emotion. "We face enemies within our walls and enemies beyond. What we do not face are enemies within our hearts. My brothers and sisters, children of the Free Provinces, take courage in those who stand by you. Take strength from their arm, take strength from mine, and together we can hold back the tide. Together, we shall fall onto this plain of darkness and repel the enemy. We reject Grunnxe and his ways. We reject this evil he brings before us, and we reject the fear he would see diminish our bold hearts!" Kalfinar stared across the silent ranks, pride flaring within his heart. "We need only hold them off a while and Dajda will wake, calling forth a flood of power so pure it will wash clean this evil. Together, we will steel our hearts and stem this dark tide. For our people out there, for our brothers and sisters, when we break out of these doors, no matter what we face, spirit or man, have no fear. Ride out with me, brothers and sisters, in the name of Carte, in the name of the Free Provinces, and in the name of Dajda!"

The roar erupted like an explosion, rising high into the night sky, filling their hearts with a power and urge so strong that many shook with it.

Kalfinar turned around to his gathered commanders, Harruld, Broden, Subath, and Merkham. "Well, what do you think?" he asked them.

Subath winked. "Well, if that doesn't get them hard, then I don't know what will."

Broden broke into laughter, followed by the others.

"Gentlemen," Harruld interrupted in a sombre tone, "let's go to war."

The drawbridge slammed down with an almighty crash and the doors of the gate swung open. Merkham's units to charged out of the High Command and into the city. The foremost horse-borne officers led the way with infantry sprinting behind them, ready to pick off any of the creatures bowled over by the charging horses.

The stream of soldiers pouring out of the High Command was continuous; rank after rank, hundreds and thousands.

Kalfinar rode out with Harruld, Subath, and Broden by his side, their horses clearing the drawbridge and thundering through the snowy, cobbled streets. Their horses' breath smoked from their noses in the cold air. They hammered down the streets, passing by blazing fires as buildings burned, the air choked with smoke. They charged for the east gate of the outer walls of Carte to face the gathered forces and meet them in battle.

"If any of the creatures come at us, mow them down. Steer the hooves to their heads!" Broden roared.

They crashed through the streets, those mounted acting as the vanguard and smashing creatures that sprinted howling from side streets and alleys, being sent clattering to the ground before being dispatched by the onrushing troops.

Kalfinar steered his horse into the pair of creatures that screamed down the street towards them, smashing them to the ground where they were ground beneath by the following horses.

Hal screamed orders down the line of the battlement, "Keep them off the walls!"

The troops below them charged with rams to the gate whilst others approaching carried huge ladders to mount the battlements. The archers released their arrows, felling as many as they could, but the numbers were immense. There were floods of black-clad men, screaming wild battle cries that made the blood chill in the veins.

"Pitch!" Hal screamed to troops heating the fire liquid in large cauldrons. "Have it ready. They're coming!"

The rams flowed across the ground before the gates like giant ballistae missiles. The men steering them were protected from the rain of arrows by shields and wet hides interlinked above their heads. They thundered into the face of the doors on the east gate of the outer walls of Carte, but the gates were strong and the blow caused little harm.

"Pitch!" Hal roared and the pitch rained down over the ram.

Men dropped screaming as boiling oil clung and burned them.

"Fire!"

Arrows of flame shot from the gatehouse, sticking into the hides and shields above. Flames burst to life and spread onto the clothes of any so unfortunate as to be soaked or splashed by the pitch. The ram dropped and lay wreathed in flames.

The ladders were lifted towards the walls, their slow and steady advance hampered only when archers found their marks and dropped lifting raiders. Soldiers stood by the walls, primed and ready, some terrified, tears welling and fingers shaking. Sword arms flexed and encouraging words were whispered, but the ladders kept coming.

The first of the ladders crashed against the top of the battlements. Defenders sprang into action, forked spears being used to push the ladders backwards or shoved to the side, clattering off stone as they tumbled to the ground. Arrows whizzed and whipped past defenders as they tried to clear the ladders, but there were too many and too few defenders.

One by one, Solansian troops flowed over the walls and onto the battlements, engaging the outnumbered defenders.

Kalfinar's horse pounded down the final mile of the city towards the outer walls. The creatures came at them steadily, but the horses saw they posed little threat when approached head-on, being cast aside to be dispatched or ground into the snow and cobbles by the steel-shod hooves of the cavalry behind. The soldiers on foot fared the worst, succumbing to bites or being separated from the protection of their troop mates.

"Quicker! They're on the battlements!" Kalfinar shouted as the top of the battlement above the eastern gate came into view. "Come on, come on!" He whipped at his horse, thrashing it to go faster. *Olmat, I'm sorry old friend, but you must die. You must die. Die, damn it.* It broke his heart to wish it, but if they were to stand any chance at all, the old man had to die soon.

"What in the cold night is that?" Hal asked as a legion of iridescent beings approached the walls. "That's not normal..."

As they approached closer to the wall, the fire of the battering rams illuminated them further and Hal saw their true form. He hadn't noticed, such was his terror, he had pissed himself. He also didn't notice, such was the intense fear that gripped him, the sword point that punched through his chest.

The guardsman's body slid off the raider's sword and flopped onto its back. The raider smirked when he noticed that the dead man had pissed himself. He stepped up towards the gate wheel and began turning.

"No!" Kalfinar screamed as he saw the gate of Carte split open. A strange light, a mix of fire and shimmering colours, appeared from behind the opening doors.

The mounted party pulled up their horses and leapt from their saddles at the wall of the battlement beside the eastern gate. Kalfinar bounded up the steps towards the gatehouse, clearing them two steps at a time. He glanced up ahead and saw a raider leap down from the battlement onto the steps, sword drawn and ready to engage him. Kalfinar dropped his shoulder and ducked the blow, returning with a heavy side slash, opening the man from hip to belly, and sending him crashing onto the ground several metres below.

Broden, Harruld, Subath, and dozens more flooded up the battlements after him.

"Behind you, Kal!" Harruld cried out, warning him of another attacker approaching from the second tier of the battlements.

The raider leapt down to engage, landing behind Kalfinar, but falling straight into Harruld's sword thrust. The raider fell backwards and grabbed Harruld's surcoat, hauling the governor to the stairs he had just ascended.

Harruld shoved the dying man over the side of the steps, but lost his balance and crashed his knee against the corner of stone, causing a backlog of defenders trying to follow their chief marshal.

Kalfinar reached the top of the battlement and found dozens of Solansian raiders dispatching the final guardsmen.

"On your own," one of the raiders growled, approaching Kalfinar with menace.

"Kal!" Broden roared from behind. "Hold on!"

Kalfinar scanned the eyes of the raiders around him and pulled free his battle-hatchet. *Got to get to the gatehouse.*

The raiders snapped into attack, two coming at Kalfinar at once, one jabbing a spear and the other coming in close with a crashing blow from his heavy axe. Kalfinar dodged the spear thrust and bent under the axe, spinning around and slamming his hatchet head into the back of the axeman's knee. He folded to the ground, knees crashing onto stonework as he squealed.

The spearman thrust again. Kalfinar dodged, but not so much to avoid it. The spearhead jabbed into his surcoat, tearing a hole and ripping free several rings of his chainmail.

Kalfinar grabbed the shaft, hauled the spearman towards him with one hand, and slammed his sword into the man's neck with the other. The spearman gurgled and fell over onto the writhing axeman.

More raiders ran to engage him. Kalfinar stabbed at the injured axeman, twisting and freeing his blade before turning and running from the pursuing raiders on the battlement.

Gatehouse. Got to shut the gate.

Harruld and Broden mounted the battlement and engaged the raiders with quick sharp blows, dispatching the men as Subath and further defenders flooded onto the top tier of the battlements.

"Gatehouse!" cried Harruld and he charged forward with Broden, crashing into the wheel room.

Kalfinar was close to being overwhelmed by five raiders protecting the man opening the gate. Kalfinar was being battered back into a corner of the room, furthest away from Broden and Harruld as they entered. It left the man at the wheel exposed.

Broden closed the distance between them, lopping the man's head free before even one of the raiders could turn. He didn't break a stride as he re-joined Harruld in slashing at the surprised raiders in a furious flurry of blows, cutting them down to nothing.

"Shut the gate!" Kalfinar roared as screams of terrified men and horses sounded from below the gatehouse.

More defenders back peddled into the wheel room, pressed by raiders attempting to take the small room.

"Help me!" Broden cried as he used all of his strength to turn the gate wheel, resistance coming from the press of raiders below.

Harruld and Kalfinar joined him and strained at the wheel. The three men, veins bulging in their heads, forced the wheel around with all of their might, slamming the gate shut with a crunch.

Harruld risked a quick glance out an arrow slit. A legion of beasts milled outside the gatehouse, screaming and roaring. Some clambered up ladders with clumsy limbs while others attempted to climb the stonework of the walls, talons finding purchase between blocks.

Harruld's blood chilled at the sight and sound of them. He glanced beyond the milling masses, and beheld the sight of the Solansian forces, thousands strong. At the front sat one man apart from the others, a ragged scar down through one eye. A scar that Harruld had made. Grunnxe, the old king reborn.

"He's here," Harruld grumbled. "He lives."

"Well he won't live for fucking long if he comes near me," shouted Kalfinar. "Come on!" He roared as he left the gatehouse to the care of others, bursting out of the stone building and back onto the battlements to engage raiders.

Broden and Harruld ran out, battle cries loud as they cut into the masses of raiders clambering over the walls.

Harruld kicked out as the black-clad man clambered over the battlement, sending him screaming to the ground with a thud. He slashed at the attackers as they spilled over the battlements.

Kalfinar kicked one raider off the battlement and slashed at the back of another. The man yelped and collapsed. The next face to appear at the top of a ladder received Kalfinar's sword point before he moved on to the next raider.

The big man held two axes and spun them in some act of bravado before Kalfinar blocked the blow from the left hand and then, with a rapid stroke, severed the right hand. The shock left the raider immobilised. His head soon went the way of the hand.

Broden blocked the sword with his own blade and kicked the man's balls. He grabbed the gap between the raider's cuirass and neck and slammed the cross-guard of his sword into the man's face, once, twice, three times. Blood bubbled out of the man's nose and lips.

Broden tossed him from the battlement and slashed at an onrushing raider, cleaving him open across the belly. The man whooped and fell onto his knees, stalling the advance of a comrade who soon fell in similar fashion.

Subath couldn't help but laugh. The raider had made a long, wet fart as he collapsed, his chest opened from a sweeping blow.

"Right, which one of you salt-mining fuckers is next?" He strode to where Broden was punching the life out of a raider.

A Solansian head popped into view to Subath's right. With a casual flick of the sword, he sent the man's head flying in a slow, elegant arc.

"Can't be having that," Subath grumbled and hauled the ladder off to the side, sending it and those climbing crashing to the ground. "Next?" He strode forward to the next raider, laughing at the memory of the fart.

Kalfinar stepped past the dying Solansian and risked a quick glance over the battlement. He ducked his head back in, avoiding the arrow that whistled past where his head had been. A huge number of Solansian forces massed on the other side. Alongside them thrashed the shimmering creatures of Balzath, using their strength to try and beat open the gate.

"Kal!" Broden's voice rang out amidst the din of fighting and dying.

Kalfinar sought out his cousin amongst the chaos, spotting him on the lowest tier of the battlements. The fighting was harder down there with defenders pressed by creatures that had made their way into the city before the gates were shut.

Broden engaged another raider, batting away the weak attack and using the momentum of the enemy to turn himself, bringing his blade down in a backhanded stroke that took the legs from under the man. He jabbed his sword point down and gesticulated towards Kalfinar. "Your father!"

Kalfinar broke into a run, his eyes scanning for his father within the melee on the two lower tiers and the open space before the gate. There was no clear sight in the confusion of bodies.

The huge monsters shimmered in colour as they swung heavy limbs between knots of bodies, killing defender and raider without prejudice.

Kalfinar sprinted along the top tier of the battlement, his boots slapping down with hard claps. He dodged fellow defenders as they shoved ladders away or stabbed out at raiders clambering above the walls. He leapt over a raider sprawled before the steps, eyes wide and black, mouth hanging open in the silent protest of the dead. Kalfinar leapt down the stone stairs, almost losing his balance as he bounded them, his eyes searching the battling masses.

A raider stepped backwards into his path as he reached the bottom of the steps. The two collided and Kalfinar sent him crashing face-first into the battlement wall. The raider jabbed an elbow backwards,

catching Kalfinar in the corner of his eye and bursting skin. Blood
seeped from the wound and blinded his right eye. The raider shoved
backwards, sending Kalfinar arse-first onto the lower steps.

Kalfinar saw the raider turn and leap at him with a short sword
drawn. He grabbed the man's wrist and shoved the sword point away
from his face. Kalfinar slammed his forehead into the face of the
raider, busting his nose. The man grunted and blood bubbled from the
wound. He head-butted the raider again, and again. The raider's
resolve weakened and Kalfinar shoved him onto his back before
jabbing his sword into his throat.

Kalfinar stood and wiped the blood from his face while scanning
the fight below. The monsters were causing mayhem, sending men
flying up into the air and crashing into knots of fighters. He spotted
Harruld by steps of the first tier. He broke into a run as he noticed
one of the Desverukan slaughtering its way in the direction of his
father.

Kalfinar dodged a sword and dropped his shoulder into the back of
the raider that stood before him, sending the man flying off the second
tier. He slashed a wide backhanded blow at the next raider, taking the
man's sword arm from him. Kalfinar didn't look back to see his
companions finish the man, but he heard a squeak as a sword likely
took him in the belly.

He was approaching the steps down to the first tier when he saw
the beast clear a path to Harruld. "Father, behind you!" Kalfinar roared
a warning.

The raider dropped to his knees before Harruld as the governor's
sword slid from him. He turned in the direction of Kalfinar's shout and
then back behind him.

The creature fixed hungry red eyes on Harruld and broke into an
apelike run, obsidian claws scraping on the stone of the battlements.

Kalfinar saw a pair of raiders running up the steps to the second tier
towards him. He ran beyond the steps to the area above where Harruld
readied to meet the attack.

As the beast pulled back a huge arm, ready to swing its talons at
Harruld, Kalfinar leapt from the second tier of the battlement and
slashed his sword down onto the beasts arm, slicing the clawed hand
clean from the limb and spraying the battlement with thick, black
blood.

Harruld swung his sword to protect himself from a swipe of the beast's other arm, catching the talons with an awful metallic screech against his blade's edge.

Kalfinar leapt to support his father, but another raider jumped between them and onto the battlement. He met the raider's attack with a distant, mechanical efficiency, his focus on his father as he engaged the iridescent monster.

Harruld parried the thrusts of the beast's clawed fist, but its power was intense and it battered him back against the stonework of the battlement wall. Kalfinar heard straining from Harruld as the older man struggled against the unnatural strength of his foe, slipping to one knee.

Kalfinar parried the sword of the raider. Panic flared in his gut and tightness coiled about his throat. He parried a wild blow from the raider and saw an opening. Kalfinar swung his hatchet into the man's collarbone, sending him reeling to the ground with a shriek. Free of the raider, he burst forward to engage the beast as it hammered blows onto his father's sword. Kalfinar screamed as he bore down on it.

Harruld moved his sword to meet another blow from the beast, but as Kalfinar was only a few more steps away, he saw the beast's clawed hand change direction at the last opportunity, avoiding Harruld's block.

"No!" Kalfinar roared as the claws ripped into his father's chain-mail, and sending an eruption of blood out of his mouth and nose.

The beast picked Harruld up and smashed him against the battlements before Kalfinar could fall on it with his sword and hatchet. The creature released his grip on Harruld and tried to engage Kalfinar, but he was too quick, his sword slicing deep into the beast's side before he ducked under a blow and leapt behind it, slamming his hatchet into its back.

The demon reached behind with its one clawed fist, looking over its shoulder at the wounded spot as Kalfinar ran around its front stabbing his sword through the beast's throat. He twisted the wound open and withdrew his sword with a gout of black, steaming blood before embedding his axe between its demonic eyes. Eyes he had seen before in his dreams.

The monster shivered and then collapsed onto the ground.

The ring of metal and the cries of pain, rage, and desperation were all around. The air stank of blood. Despite it all, Kalfinar heard nothing. He knelt by Harruld as he lay, head propped up against the battlement with the dead monster lying beside him. He had several ragged tears through his armour and mail shirt. Dark, thick blood oozed from the large rents where the beast's talons had ripped through him. A large, purple bruise had formed around the split at the corner of his forehead and his skin paled quickly.

"Father." Kalfinar held his hand in his, squeezing it. His father's hand was loose.

"Kal," Harruld coughed out flecks of blood as he weakly spoke. "It doesn't hurt."

"Father, hold on. We can get help."

Harruld coughed again, frothy blood bubbling from his wounds and mouth. "No help." He smiled before coughing spots of blood onto his beard. His front teeth were smashed and stained red. "A good death, I think."

"Aye," Kalfinar whispered.

"Better than wasting in a chair."

Kalfinar squeezed Harruld's hand as his eyes fluttered shut. "Father?"

Harruld's eyes opened and he focussed. "No more grief. It will consume you. Fight for the living—" Harruld's voice cut off as his pupils dilated. His ragged breath rattled and wheezed to nothing as his chest ceased to rise.

Stunned, Kalfinar brushed the side of his father's face and closed his eyes. He stood up, his hands gripping his weapons tight as he turned, fury brimming inside. Broden and Subath approached, blood dripping from their weapons as the two men gasped for breath.

"Damn it!" Subath roared, slashing his sword into the corpse of the demon before him.

"Kal," Broden said in a low voice.

Kalfinar stared about as groups of defenders were ripped apart in short order. "This is our city." He pointed his sword towards the ranks of men being overrun by monsters below. "Let's take the fight to them." Kalfinar trembled with rage as he stalked across the battlement, his heart thundering.

Chapter Forty-One

"HERE THEY COME." Bergnon said, his eyes fixed on the remaining Solansian forces charging towards the breach.

The half-light of dawn glinted off the sparkling sea of armour and blades that bore down on the defenders, a last stand of soldier and citizen alike. Bergnon stood atop of the bulwark with Thaskil and Omree by his side and a small knot of fifty men waiting behind them on the street, lightly armed and without cuirass or mail. No further defenders of Apula were present within two city blocks of where they stood, save for the two archers standing above them on the battlements to either side of the breach. The hammer of heavy footfalls and the cry of warriors set their hair standing on end; their skin prickling.

Thaskil stared ahead as the forces bore down, negotiating their way around the burned-out pit. "Do you still feel like doing the right thing?" he asked Bergnon, who stood beside him, unflinching.

Bergnon didn't utter a sound. He kept his eyes fixed on the buckler as he tightened it on his forearm before drawing his sword.

Thaskil nodded and withdrew his battle-hatchet. "Is it time yet?" he asked Bergnon.

"Aye, it's about time, lad." Bergnon turned and began walking down the bulwark, followed by Thaskil and Omree. They approached the knot of soldiers at the bottom of the bulwark, Bergnon meeting them first. "Remember, let them see you. Let them get close enough to smell you and then run. Run like the beasts of the hells are on your heels."

Thaskil looked at the faces of the nervous young men. *May as well be.*

"You were chosen for your speed," Bergnon continued. "Make it count this morning. Make it count." He clapped the nearest soldier on the shoulder and set off, breaking into a run.

"We'll see you in the square, brother." Thaskil shook several hands of city men as he walked past them. "Run swift and sound."

Thaskil and Omree set off following Bergnon as he advanced up the dimly lit boulevard. He ran past heavy iron urns placed alongside the streets, thin lines of black powder linking them. Piled on top of and around the urns were fist-sized lumps of masonry, metals, and whatever caltrops could be recovered from around the breach.

"Hope this plan of yours works," Thaskil said mid-breath as he caught up and ran alongside Bergnon. The sound of the advancing raiders still sounded clear in the night air behind them.

"We'll soon find out, I suppose," Bergnon replied.

Thaskil peered down the unlit side streets where he knew hidden archers waited. "It has to work," he mumbled to himself, his words lacking conviction.

They pounded through the streets, eventually emerging into the large market square to meet a gathered mass of defenders standing in broad ranks, weapons held tight in their grips and chins set firm in the face of death. Thaskil scanned the buildings around the massive square lit in an amber glow by the many oil lamps and braziers burning around them. Groups of archers held the rooftops and balconies surrounding the square, their blood-stained arrows ready to kill once more.

"Ready!" roared Thaskil as they crossed the square, his cry answered by the grim determination before him in a wall of defiance.

His skin tingled as they raised their weapons, beat their fists against their hearts, and their swords against their shields. He released a ragged war cry, joined by Omree to his side, and amplified by a roar from Bergnon.

The ferocity of the major's cry caught Thaskil by surprise. *What is love if it drives you to madness?*

The archer on top of the battlements fled across the walls as his flamed arrows crashed into the lines of high-piled, oil-soaked bodies. The raiders turned in surprise, tripping each other as flames spread like wildfire along their ranks, splitting the forces on the outer edges of the advance and causing them to backtrack. A massive explosion sounded from one of the piles of bodies.

The screams of raiders sounded and the archer saw scores of dead and injured in front of the walls of Apula. Another explosion sounded as the flames spread further. Drums of fire-powder and stones hidden amongst the outer edges of the piles of corpses erupted in random order, tearing through attackers without prejudice.

The spreading flames funnelled the raiders who had avoided the blasts towards the breach and, as they climbed the bulwark, their cries grew louder, shrieking with an intense and ravenous bloodlust. They scrambled up the masonry, their eyes lit with fiery fury, ready to cut their way into the heart of the city.

The group of defenders appeared to shake with nerves as raiders burst over the bulwark. The soldiers, selected for their speed, turned upon seeing the flood of raiders and ran for all they were worth.

The archer waited in the dark of the side street. He heard the roar advancing from the area of the breach. It wouldn't be long.

The first of the defenders ran past the opening to the side street, followed by another, and then more. The full body of Apulan troops made their way past the archer's street, followed a short time later by a flood of clattering, shrieking raiders; a sea of black-clad death. His heart hammered and felt like it was beating all the way out of this throat.

He knew the count. *Let them come. Count it down and let them come.* More and more of the raiders flashed past his street, a constant flow of merciless sharp edges and spikes. *Let them come. Keep to the count.*

Runners crashed into the square, appearing to be expelled from the city streets by the building pressure of raiders. The cries of coming violence flooded towards where Thaskil stood. His knees trembled. *Dajda, I hope no one can see my fear.*

"Ready yourselves!" Thaskil roared. "Hope this works," he mumbled to Bergnon once more, but the traitor said nothing. Thaskil stole a quick glance and saw mania in his former mentor's face. *A lust for redemption or a lust for death?*

The runners were halfway across the square when the swarm of raiders burst from the entrance of the square, fanning outward, their screams rising at the sight of the gathered defenders and coming fight.

Thaskil let fly a roar, echoed all around him by his companions. *Better make whatever time I've left count.*

The archer finished his count and swallowed a deep, shuddering breath. His hands trembled as he notched the arrow and fumbled with the lid of his hot coal brazier. It held one small, glowing ember.

With a practiced care, he touched his oil-soaked arrowhead to the coal and released his breath as the flame burst into life. With a measured effort, he pulled the arrow fletching back to his cheek and took aim as the flood of raiders continued past his street entrance.

He released the arrow. The flame arched in the night sky whilst the archer repeated the action with another arrow, being careful to ensure he hit his mark at least once and, finally, the arrow dropped from its climb, heading towards the ground.

The raider's heart thundered in his chest as he was carried along on a sea of fury. His companions around him were whipped into a frenzy, hungering for fight. He wanted no fight; he had never fought in his life.

He looked at the half-blunt and notched blade in his hand. *What use is this, especially in the hands of a farmer?* All he wanted was to be home, working his small plots, and being with his wife and children. *Be hard for them, on their own at this time of* year–

A flash to his right caught his eye as he ran. He glanced across and saw a streak of light, a flamed arrow falling from the sky towards him. His blood turned to ice before the arrow landed in front of him in a pile of rubble and spluttered out. Another flaming arrow appeared in the sky.

"Hey, Manix," the raider asked the man next to him, "what're all those mounds with the black lines between them?"

Fire sparked and spread from the mounds of masonry.

"What the—"

The mounds exploded. Blasts from the left and right, in front and behind. Death flew all around, fire and edge.

The first explosion ripped through the roars and battle cries, sending a bright orange flash into the night sky behind the raiders as they advanced towards the square. One explosion was followed by another and another, until the dawn sky was full of flame and deafening thunder.

Thaskil was caught by surprise as Bergnon exploded through the raiders, a possession taking him to levels of ferocity he had never before seen. *Can a man find redemption at the end of a blade?*

"The Free Provinces!" Thaskil roared, leaping into the fray, his battle-hatchet meeting the first blade and diverting it at the same time as his sword punched through a raider's ribs. His hand was hot and wet from blood. *No, there's only sorrow and sin at the end of a blade.*

Bergnon crashed into the raiders, his buckler smashing into the face of the first man he met. His sword swept to the side, meeting flesh and bone. He swung the blade, every breath fuelling rage and hate as if sin could be washed away in blood. *Nothing washes clean in blood.*

A sword appeared from the side, sweeping just past his face. Bergnon stepped backwards and saw the Ravenmayne advance. A shoulder barged into him from behind, sending him reeling towards the advancing enemy.

Bergnon raised his buckler in time to divert the sword stroke, but the force of the blow carried through, sending a flare of pain into his arm. He corrected his stumble and sprung up with the buckler, smashing the Ravenmayne under the chin and tearing free his mask. A stream of blood flowed from his mouth and a dazed look appeared on the Ravenmayne's face as Bergnon's sword took him under the armpit and up into his body. A spurt of dark blood gouted from his mouth when Bergnon pulled free his sword.

A frightened boy stepped into his way, not even twenty years by the look of him. His battle cry trembled from fear. He caught Bergnon's sword stroke with the edge of his own blade, but he was weak and his sword arm folded back. Bergnon's sword bit into the boy's skull and he stumbled over in an awkward fall.

Bergnon stepped over the dying lad and drove his sword through the back of a raider who was pressing one of the defenders. He moved to the next target and was engaged to the left.

He raised his buckler and deflected the blow with a grimace. Fuelled by fury, Bergnon carved a wide, red line through the chest of the raider. He stepped on to find the next kill. *I'll be with you soon, my love.*

Thaskil slammed his forehead into the raider's nose, smashing bone and dropping him. He jabbed his sword into the man's chest and withdrew, stepping on to engage the next.

The Solansian had just slid his sword out of the body of an Apulan soldier. He turned as the man dropped to the blood-stained cobbles of the square and faced Thaskil.

Despite the din of the battle, Thaskil heard the raider call, "Come 'ere, pup!" The man's large beard flexed as he shouted over the sounds of violence and agony.

Thaskil closed the short distance and caught the man's overhead blow between his hatchet and sword. The raider slammed a big boot into Thaskil's stomach, beating the wind out of him and almost dropping him to his knees.

"You'll have to do better than that," the raider grunted, stepping in and swinging a sword towards Thaskil's face.

He leaned back, away from the raider's blade, and brought his sword up in a counter-swipe, through the man's beard and nicking his chin. A line of blood ran through the wiry hair and dripped onto the stones of the square.

"Not bad," the bearded man said before pressing Thaskil with a series of blows, forcing him to concede what little ground there was for him to fight in.

Thaskil bumped into fighting bodies, each jostling for enough room to strike out or avoid an enemy's blade. He didn't see the thrust. A jerky, stiff feeling spread in Thaskil's left side. As he made to repel the bearded Solansia, he felt the pain flare. He glanced down to see a sword point being pulled from his side just above his hip. A Ravenmayne was on the other end of the sword.

The bearded raider pressed his attack, his sword jabbing forward.

The moment seemed slow to Thaskil, as if he was dreaming. The pain in his side burned as he lifted his weapons in defence. His arms were heavy and the weapons felt like blocks of stone. To his left, he met the Ravenmayne's sword with his hatchet, hooking it between haft and blade and driving it down. His sword followed and punched through the Ravenmayne's throat. With a wet wretch, Thaskil freed his sword and ducked out of the range of the bearded raider's driven stroke. The wound in his side bit again and Thaskil almost toppled over. He felt tired.

The Solansian roared and, with two hands, made to swing his sword down in a massive blow. The stroke never fell on Thaskil. With eyes wide, the big raider looked to his right.

Bergnon was baring his teeth as he pulled free his sword from under the man's armpit.

"Bergnon!" Thaskil wheezed.

The bearded raider looked at the man on the end of the sword with a quizzical appraisal. "That's not fair," the man said.

"Life's not fucking fair." Bergnon pulled free his sword and hacked into the man's neck, dropping him to the bloody cobbles.

"Thanks," Thaskil said over the din of battle.

"You hurt, lad?"

"Aye. My side." Thaskil hauled himself upright. He looked at the wound. Bright red blood slicked his left thigh as it seeped from the wound above his hip.

"Let me see." Bergnon took a quick look at the injury. "Doesn't look too bad. You feel able?"

"Aye, think I've still got my humours about me. How's it panning out?"

"We're hurting them, no doubt about it. We need to press, though; make it count. Can you fight on?"

"Aye," Thaskil said with a hungry grin. "I'll go until I drop."

"That makes two of us then."

Chapter Forty-Two

KALFINAR'S FURY could not be quenched. Solansian raiders fell like wheat as he harvested his wrath.

Broden and Subath scythed through the enemy alike. Fires burned around them as Solansians tossed torches within buildings and kicked over braziers. Furious fighting raged across the battlements as raiders scaled ladders and fought to break through the resistance at the gatehouse. It was a battle that the raiders were winning as defenders were ground down and pushed back.

Won't be long. Kalfinar stole a glance at the gatehouse. *The end comes close.*

"Kal!" Broden cried to his left as one of the massive, clawed monsters bore down on him.

The big man dispatched the raider before him and tried to join Kalfinar as he met the beast, his hatchet slamming back its swung fist. Broden set about taking the creatures legs away. Kalfinar ducked under another massive swipe of its claws and thumped his sword up under where he supposed its ribs would be, tearing a hole in whatever manner of flesh the monster possessed and setting free rank blood from within.

It swung a clawed fist behind as Broden slashed at its massive knees, just missing tearing his head from his shoulders. The monster collapsed onto the ground where Broden darted around, meeting Kalfinar in the middle. They fell upon the beast, its fanged maw gaping and snapping as sticky saliva was blackened with foul blood. They dispatched the creature and turned to engage another swarm of raiders descending from the battlements.

Subath cut his way through to them, leaving a pair of Solansian fighters glassy eyed in the dirt. "Too many," he roared as several more of the beasts slashed and tore defenders in their way, draining life onto the mud around them.

Kalfinar was assaulted by the sounds of battle. The stink of smoke and blood tore at his throat. "We have to fight for the living!" he roared back as he fought on, engaging a massive Solansian swinging a double-headed axe.

His sword thrusts hammered the raider backwards. Kalfinar's second weapon, his hatchet, gave him the advantage of versatile strokes to slice and stab out the man's life. He brought down an over-head sword blow and, at the same time, brought up his hatchet from below; one of the weapons would find its mark.

Before he could deliver, Kalfinar was knocked off balance by the falling body of another defender. His rear foot slipped on mud, churned up from blood, snow, and filth. Sliding to the ground, his rear foot under his body, Kalfinar was exposed. The giant raider leapt forward, his evil axe slamming downward.

Kalfinar swung his sword up to block the blow. *No use. It'll cut right through.*

A blurred shape smashed into the raider as someone leapt off the tier above. The two bodies rolled and thrashed amidst the grime. The raider rolled on top and punched the form below before stiffening, yelping, and falling over onto his side. The man below shoved off the legs of the dead raider and stood up, a bloody hunting knife held in his hand.

Kalfinar looked closer at the defender who had saved his life.

The man wiped his knife and approached Kalfinar. "This is yours. You left it at Hardalen."

Kalfinar laughed. It was all he could do as he stood up and received the knife from Lucius. "Thank you."

"It's your knife," the commander said.

"Not for the knife," Kalfinar nodded to the corpse four feet in front. "For that."

Lucius shrugged his shoulders and stepped past Kalfinar. "It's nothing. You'd have done the same for me."

Kalfinar grunted another laugh and returned to the fight.

"What's so funny?" Subath asked, having finished off the last of a knot of raiders.

"Lucius just saved my life."

"Come on, laddie. Wits about you, aye? You get a knock on the head?"

"No, he did." Kalfinar laughed again.

"Well I'll be fucked!" Subath barked. "You hear that, Broden?"

Broden kicked the body off his sword with a grunt and turned towards them. "Aye, and I think Kal's dreaming of miracles. Kal, while you're playing make believe, maybe you could make believe we have a hope here!"

Kalfinar looked about him. "Not so good, is it?"

Defenders were engaged all around as raiders swarmed and monsters tore through knots of the Free Provinces' forces.

"Aye, not so good, laddie." Subath's grin had gone. Instead, he looked old and tired. "Not so good at all."

"The gates!" Broden roared. "They're opening."

"The gatehouse is lost…" Subath said, his voice trailing off.

"Aye," Kalfinar mumbled as more defenders grouped together with them.

Raiders continued to spill onto the battlements, and from behind the opening gates came the flash of shimmering colour and the war cries of the monsters and men.

"And so it comes," Kalfinar said, his brow wet with sweat and blood, his arms tired and heavy from battle. He thought of Evelyne. *I'm sorry I didn't get to tell you what happiness you have brought me. I'm sorry I didn't get to say goodbye to you, love.*

"Aye, so it does," Broden said.

Kalfinar glanced around as the press of bodies grew tighter, forcing the three of them back-to-back, facing a death of body and a death of spirit. All was to be lost.

"We tried."

"Aye, we tried."

"One last push, lads," Subath said, his voice providing some small comfort; the instructor and the cadets, two generations of defiance at the end.

"Aye, one last push." Kalfinar nodded.

"For the Free Provinces," Subath roared, his cry bringing cheers from the defenders.

"For the people," roared Broden, raising louder cheers still.

"For Dajda," roared Kalfinar, taking himself by surprise.

"For Dajda!" an almighty cry sounded around him from the battling defenders and it chilled Kalfinar within.

The gates of Carte swung open and in flowed a swarm of monsters and men, tooth and sword, claw and flame. The defenders roared aloud and pressed to engage, but the mass of enemy used their force of numbers and drove forward, pushing the defenders back. Man engaged man whilst the spirits of Balzath withdrew from the fight and raced off into the city towards the High Command.

Kalfinar watched as they battled against the rush of raiders. "Where the fuck are they going?"

Evelyne stood by the window in Harruld's study listening to the sounds of battle raging throughout the city. Fires burned everywhere, buildings and entire streets ablaze, ships burned in the bay, and the sounds of fear and pain all around. The smell of smoke clung to the cold air. A flood of iridescent forms could be seen hurtling towards the High Command, followed by the roar of thousands of warriors.

She knew what they were the instant she saw them. *Have you fallen, my love? Am I truly all alone now? I'm sorry I didn't get to tell you what happiness you have brought me or to say goodbye to you, love.* Snow began to fall again and she bowed her head in sorrow. She turned from the window and back towards Olmat.

The old man lay, his rheumy eyes beholding the two Children of Light that knelt nearby holding his weak hands. "My dearest Evelyne," Olmat croaked. His voice was weak to the point of a dry whisper.

Evelyne raced across the room towards him. "Uncle," Evelyne gasped, her knees crashing to the stone floor. "I feel a grave danger approaches. Are you almost ready?"

The old man's eyelids closed over. "Almost, child."

Screams sounded from the gate of the High Command below. Evelyne sprang to the window. Looking below, she saw one of the shimmering Desverukan on top of the battlement, sweeping defenders from its path. It sniffed at the air, and then flashed its eyes towards her, holding her gaze for a moment. A cry of alarm sounded in her head. *They come for me.*

The demon broke into a stride, heading for the main castle of the High Command. Towards her.

Evelyne unsheathed the blade that was up her sleeve. "There's no more time," she shouted towards Olmat. "A Desverukan comes for the heart of Dajda." She stood beside him and cleared the fabric away from Olmat's chest. "We have to do this now!"

"The Key cannot be forced," Olmat said with a feeble voice. "It will not work."

"There's no more time!" she urged.

Screams could be heard in the body of the High Command keep.

Evelyne held the knife over Olmat's chest, hovering inches from the wispy white hairs that curled above his heart. "Uncle, I pray you pass."

Tears formed in her eyes as she heard the clattering racket and heavy breathing of the demon as it made its way towards the chamber. The guard outside roared, perhaps in a vain act of bravery, but the courage withered and was soon replaced with a mangled scream of agony.

The two Children of Light stood up and, with calm grace, approached the door and began to hum a beautiful sound.

"Olmat!" Evelyne urged.

The old man wheezed, his breath slowed and rattled, but his chest rose again.

The door splintered as the Desverukan battered against it.

Olmat exhaled, and breathed again.

The door smashed open and a vision of horror stepped in. Shining black talons clacked on the stone floor and blood dripped from fangs and horns. Red eyes stared at the Children of Light and then to Evelyne.

The Horn of Dajda opened their mouths and sang a discordant song, ear-piercing and shrill, at the monster. It stepped forward and swept them aside, sending them crashing into the wall.

Olmat exhaled, and breathed again.

"You'll not take Dajda!" Evelyne screamed at the demon.

She turned the knife towards her heart. Before she could strike, she was bowled over by an unseen force. The knife fell from her hand and her vision blurred and disappeared.

Evelyne awoke and found she was being carried over the shoulder of a demon, being spirited away at pace amongst the host of Desverukan. Olmat and the Children of Light lay unconscious over the shoulders of three creatures in front of her, their limbs bobbing as they raced through the ravaged streets of Carte with the eastern gate coming into view. Battle still raged.

Evelyne's throat issued no sound as she tried to scream. Her limbs felt lifeless and her body held no strength. Within her mind, she heard a tormented wail. *Dajda fears.*

Kalfinar hammered back the throng of raiders that pressed against him and the rest of his desperate companions. The knot of defenders grew smaller as beast and man alike cut through them. The grace of the falling snow contrasted the chaos of the battle. Kalfinar had lost his hatchet some time ago and battered against the raiders with two-handed chops of his sword. There was no grace in his tired, furious strokes.

The smoke stung at his eyes and the taste of blood was everywhere. *Smoke and blood. Smoke and blood.*

For every one they cut down, another raider stood in place of the fallen.

"We can't hold on for much longer!" Broden shouted as he batted away a sword and ran through its owner.

"Too many!" Subath roared. "Too many!" He ducked and swept the leg from a Solansian, leaving the man chasing his wayward limb as his life-blood welled into the slush and dirt of the ground.

The booming note of a trumpet sounded from beyond the walls, and the fighting stopped.

Kalfinar pressed the raider before him, but the man stepped back, turned, and ran away. Kalfinar and the defenders watched as the forces of Grunnxe retreated and flowed out of the eastern gate of Carte like sand through an hourglass.

"What in the hells is going on?" Broden growled, his sword held ready.

"Something's coming," Kalfinar said, pointing towards the faint light that grew from the main boulevard into the city. "The light. Demons!"

"Dajda, get ready!" Broden shouted to the remaining defenders.

Kalfinar dashed towards the corpse of a fallen Solansian and picked up the man's battle hatchet. As he re-joined Broden and Subath, the demons roared into view, streaming towards the eastern gate in a flood of spectral colour. There was something amongst them.

Kalfinar strained his eyes against the flurry of snow and the murky light of the dawn. The monsters carried something. They carried someone.

Evelyne! No! "No!" Kalfinar roared and ran towards the mass of demons as they streamed out the gate. He sprinted towards the rear of the pack, watching the limp form of Evelyne disappear into the distance beyond the gate and towards the ranks of Grunnxe's army.

Chapter Forty-Three

BERGNON WIPED clean his sword with a rag torn from the clothes of a dead raider. Thaskil approached him. He had a hand resting on his injured side and grimaced as he walked.

"You fine, lad?" Bergnon asked.

"Aye, fine. Just hurts a little," Thaskil said, his eyes scanning the square before them. It was littered with bodies of Solansian raiders and Free Province defenders alike. "That's the last of them scattered."

"Good," Bergnon grumbled. "You commanded brilliantly." He looked up at Thaskil as he sheathed his sword. Reaching to his side, Bergnon unbuckled his sword belt, wrapped the leather around the scabbard, and offered it to Thaskil. "I offer myself back to your custody."

Thaskil looked at him for a long moment before accepting the sword from his former mentor. He nodded towards him before removing a pair of shackles from the pouch by his side. "I hate you with all of my heart for what you've done to our people. To our friends. To Arrlun. I hate you for it."

Bergnon nodded.

"You've committed such treachery, such sin, that it would seem that my blade should wet itself with your blood now. But, even still, it wouldn't wash away your corruption."

"Blood washing away blood," Bergnon almost whispered. "It

leaves nothing but blood still. There's no forgiveness for me. No redemption, even now."

"No, there'll never be redemption for your kind. Yet you fought with more fire and heart than I could muster in myself. You gave us hope and granted us a chance." Thaskil outstretched his hand, offering it to Bergnon.

The major stared at it with a look of disbelief and then shame squirmed on his face. He clasped Thaskil's hand and squeezed it.

"I hate you, but for this effort of yours, you have my gratitude," Thaskil said.

"I don't deserve it, lad." Bergnon released Thaskil's hand. "I just wish I could see her one last time. Then you can throw me in a pit where I belong, or hang me from a tree, whatever's deemed fit for me. But I know I'll never see her again."

"I don't know about love, but from what I've seen, maybe that's the cruellest punishment." Thaskil reached out and took Bergnon's wrist. He placed a shackle upon one. "In any case, you may well get the pit or the tree. If I know anything of the High Command's ways, I think they'll string you."

"Aye," Bergnon said, "that's my reckoning too." He offered up his other wrist to be shackled. "For my part in this hurt, I am sorry."

"You know," Thaskil said. "I happen to believe you are." He thought for a moment. "Show me your palm."

Bergnon turned the unshackled hand around, revealing the grime and blister-lined palm.

Thaskil took hold of Bergnon's wrist and pulled the hand closer. He withdrew his knife, catching Bergnon's nervous look and holding it for a moment. He drew the blade deep across the palm of the offered hand.

Bergnon winced as the blade travelled and blood welled up from the wound.

"Leave the city and get yourself out of the Free Provinces." Thaskil wiped the blade and sheathed it.

Bergnon looked at him, confusion spreading on his face as he held his wounded hand. "I don't understand."

"Mistake this not for a mercy," Thaskil growled. "Every time you look at that scar, I want you to remember everything you caused. Every death you are behind. Every family you've ruined. Remember them all and then remember her. And hurt."

Bergnon made to speak, but closed his mouth and held Thaskil's stare.

"Go. Now." Thaskil turned and walked towards the High Command, not casting a backward glance at the traitor.

Kalfinar ran out into ground beyond the gate. Before him was scattered the burning wreckage of buildings, war machines, and men. He stopped and stared at the mass of Grunnxe's army as the Desverukan were swallowed up into the black body of the host.

Broden stopped beside him, followed by Subath. The sounds of hundreds of defenders could be heard approaching from the gate.

"What's going on?" Subath asked. "They had us on our backs."

"Kal?" Broden asked.

I'll not stop searching for you. If I have to tear the Cullanain apart and beyond. I'll not stop searching for you.

"Kal!" Broden shouted.

Kalfinar turned and looked at his cousin. Blood-spatter and filth covered his face, but the concern was clear in his eyes.

"We've failed. The Anulii are not coming." Kalfinar looked back at the horde as a figure on horseback trotted towards them.

"What?" Broden asked.

"The sleeping saviours, they do not come. The demons have taken her, and so, they've taken Dajda too. Look." Kalfinar pointed towards the horseman.

"I know that man like I know me ol' mam's tit," growled Subath.

"Grunnxe," Kalfinar hissed.

The old king turned his horse to the side and revealed the prostrate form of Evelyne over the back of his horse. "Your world is finished!" Grunnxe called out, his voice aided with an unnatural volume. "Your Liar God and her proxy belong to Balzath now."

A huge shimmering and swirling rent was torn in the horizon behind the horde, bathing all in a silvery light.

Kalfinar shielded his eyes from the light and broke into a run, his teeth gritted and fury burning in his throat.

Grunnxe's army moved towards the silvery light as it grew. The obscured silhouette of the horde blinked into the brightness and then disappeared as the tear vanished, leaving only horizon behind.

Kalfinar stopped, his breath heaving. "I won't stop searching for you."

The End

Mailing List

Sign up via my **Website:** dominickmurray.com

There will be no relentless spamming!

Too Cold to Bleed Book 2 of the *Red Season Series* will be available in 2018!

Reviews

I hope you enjoyed reading *Red Season Rising*. Reviews make a massive difference to authors, whether they be on the purchasing site, Goodreads, or in any other media. I would be hugely grateful if you could take the time to leave a review.

A great and wise writer once said to me, "Don't make the mistake of reading your reviews." I'm not sure quite how easy that is going to be!

For every review *Red Season Rising* receives, I will run 10 kilometres, and fend off the writer's belly! Mind you, for every bad review, I'll console myself with a donut...

Acknowledgments

"Thank you" seems so small and insignificant a pairing of words when I consider the huge sense of gratitude I feel for all those who have helped, listened, endured and encouraged me over the last few years.

Polly, for your endless support, patience, and love, I am eternally thankful. You keep me anchored in the real world, with you, where I belong.

My Parents, for raising me in a home of warmth, love, and legends.

My siblings, for sharing a wonderful childhood, and for your friendship today.

For my friends, present, and absent, thank you for all the laughter and memories.

McB, JP, AR, and the Edinburgh Genre Writers Group – my thanks for your reviews and encouragement.

About the Author

D.M. Murray was born and raised in Ireland in a home full of love, laughter, animal hair, and chaos. He lives in Scotland with his wife and majestic labradoodle, Hudson. When not hunched over his laptop, being stared at intently by Hudson, D.M. is to be found on long walks with his wife, or enjoying the wilderness of Scotland. Or bodging some DIY. Or working in the Renewable Energy industry.

D.M. Murray can be found on:

Website: dominickmurray.com
Email: dominickmurraywords@hotmail.com
Twitter: twitter.com/DominickMurray6

Further Thanks

Editing by TJ Redig
Cover Artwork by John Anthony Di Giovanni, JAD Illustrated
(www.jadillustrated.com)
Design by Shawn King, STK Kreations
(www.stkkreations.weebly.com)
Map art work by Marie Claire Murray Design and Illustrations Ltd

A big 'thank you' to TJ, John, Shawn, and Marie Claire for their
excellent work!

RED SEASON RISING

D.M. MURRAY

THE RED SEASON
I

Printed in Great Britain
by Amazon